# Close to the Sun

by

## Donald Michael Platt

# Close to the Sun

by

## Donald Michael Platt

**www.PenmorePress.com**

Dedicated to:


Colonel Raymond F. Toliver, 1914–2006, USAAC, USAAF, USAF, Fighter Ace Historian, Eagle inducted at Maxwell Field 1988; the author who suggested I write this novel, and without whose input and permissions *Close to the Sun* would not exist.

# Acknowledgements

To Michael James, for becoming first a friend, then my publisher, and for his energy and enthusiasm regarding *Close to the Sun*.

To Christine Horner, Media and Web Designer for her thoughtfulness in creating an outstanding cover; Susan Wenger, Social Marketing Manager for her excellent marketing; Chris Wozney, Copy Editor, for her careful and thorough eagle eye proofing; and Midori Snyder, Consulting Editor.

To William and Amanda Chohfi, who always read my final drafts, for their erudite suggestions and input and for being among my strongest and most enthusiastic partisans.

To Sandy and Dr. Claudia Samuels, another of my strongest partisans, who have shown by their actions that *Close to the Sun* should be published and filmed.

To author, educator, screen and TV actor Seamon Glass, who over the decades has done much to endorse my writing, especially *Close to the Sun*, through his actions.

To my military readers: Patrick Assayag, Colonel USAFR, Arthur Tulak, Colonel U.S. Army, Ethan Samuels Lt, U.S. Navy, for their positive prepublication reviews.

To the following bloggers for their favorable advance reviews: Erin Al-Mehairi from *Oh, For the Hook of a Book* (http://hookofabook.wordpress.com); Diana Silva at *Book*

*Nerd* (http://booknerdloleotodo.blogspot.com/). Frishawn Rasheed at *WTF Are You Reading?* (http://www.wtfareyoureading.com/); Margaret Cook at *Just One More Chapter* (http://www.justonemorechapter.com/); Ashley at *Closed the Cover* (http://www.closedthecover.com/); and Madi Preda, http://www.*authorspromotion*.wordpress.com/

To the aces of several nations and other flyers who generously answered my questions for their input.

To Bodo the Cat, constant companion on my desk and part-time editor throughout all drafts of *Close to the Sun*.

# Reviews

This novel introduces readers to three young men, each sharing one dream: to be the best and to rule the skies as only pilots can as an Ace! Donald Michael Platt writes characters who, while striving for perfection in their careers, are flawed in their personal lives. Close to the Sun is a masterfully penned tale of war, ambition, love, loss, and fighter ACES!

*Lieutenant Ethan Samuels, USN, former Squadron Aviation Intelligence Officer for Strikefighter Squadron Two-Two:*

A must-read, Close to the Sun, by renowned author, Donald Michael Platt, is an unconventional look into the psyche of those brash United States Army Air Corps, dogfighters and their counterparts in the dreaded Luftwaffe. Donald Michael Platt's work has the unique ability to put the bombastic, brash, endearing, flawed, and honorable nature of American and German aviators on display. His juxtaposition of the personalities and histories of the American protagonists with those of the German antagonists humanizes the war from the rarely visited perspective of the elite class of old school ace pilots. Just as striking is Donald Michael Platt's unique contrast of the regal, audacious, and somewhat pristine aerial combat, with the horrific reality of the World War II battlefield.

*Diana Silva at Book Nerd:*

(http://booknerdloleotodo.blogspot.com/).

I highly recommend Close to the Sun for anyone who enjoys learning about WWII, fighter pilots, or is just looking for a cast of great characters. I commend Donald Michael Platt for giving a voice to such a trying time in U.S. history. I loved learning about Hank Milroy, Karl, Fürst von Pfalz-

Teuffelreich, and Seth Braham. I thought that the author was really able to capture their uniqueness and their combined passion for flying as pilots during such an intense time in history. I have to confess that my favorite was Catherine "Winty" McCabe. I loved that the author included her in this story. Women were definitely not considered when it came to become pilots, but Winty really pushed the limits and played by her own rules. Princess Maria-Xenia, Elfriede "Elfie" Wohlmann and Mimi Kay all added a female voice and experience during this time period. The author really developed each of these characters and their individual stories became part of one big story.


*Arthur N. Tulak, Colonel U.S. ARMY:*

I really enjoyed Close to the Sun. I was impressed with the level of detail and thought about the extensive research Donald Michael Platt must have done to write this. Any military officer reading this novel, aviator or no, will inevitably recall his own days as a cadet or officer candidate and his buddies who strived alongside in the journey to becoming a commissioned officer. The characters in novel will likely call to mind and even resemble some of their fellow cadets. The horror and carnage of war are also accurately captured from the aviator's point of view, and later from the ground soldier's perspective.

The author demonstrates keen insight into the minds of officers at war, and accurately captures the struggle of doing one's best at his assigned task, even while he might personally question the overall campaign, the strategic or theater level decisions being made above him, and the seeming futility of the conflict. Officer Veterans from any of America's modern foreign wars and conflicts will find themselves back in theater, in Afghanistan or wherever they served, remembering these difficult questions.

*Margaret Cook at Just One More Chapter*

*(http://www.justonemorechapter.com/).*

I found *Close to the Sun* to be an entertaining read, was well written, with well-developed characters who have both depth and emotion. A unique plot, told from the point of view of pilots prior to and during World War II. It is a well-researched and engrossing book.


*Erin Al-Mehairi from Oh, For the Hook of a Book*

*(http://hookofabook.wordpress.com).*

I couldn't stop reading Donald Michael Platt's Close to the Sun, an amazing story told from the perspective of male fighter pilots at the onset and during WWII. He makes one remember that the lives, desires, and pursuits of these men had almost nothing to do with the plan of their governments and as well that they really weren't all that different from each other in many regards. The details in this novel were spectacular, creating imagery and depth in the scenes and characters, as well as the dialogue being so nostalgic and well-written. The romantic nuances of his storytelling felt incredibly authentic with the tug and pull of the men being called to serve and the women whom they loved who had their own high hopes, dreams, or work. I loved how he portrayed this women the most—strongly and fiercely independent. Donald Michael Platt did a marvelous job showcasing his male characters love of flight above all things, as when they soared in the clouds like eagles and all other cares ceased to exist. He has written a lasting legacy to many pilots on all fronts that served during this time.

As an Air Force brat myself, with fond memories of the flight line as a child, I truly feel Donald Michael Platt captured the essence of the obsession of flying and made you feel the euphoria and drive of those pursuing this dream. I highly recommend this book to anyone who has a penchant for WWII historical and/or aviation novels, yet would like to read a fresh and original story.


Ashley Le Mar at Closed the Cover

(http://www.closedthecover.com/).

Donald Michael Platt's ability to capture both the magic of flight and the grim reality of war creates a mesmerizing literary world. CLOSE TO THE SUN is both compelling and horrifying—a true must-read for fans of wartime fiction. It is a powerful book that enables readers to experience the thrill of flight as a fighter pilot and horrors of war from the comfort of their reading chair. An exceptional read, entirely engrossing and intoxicating. Fast-paced and riveting I couldn't get enough of Hank, Karl and Seth's exploits! CLOSE TO THE SUN is a thrilling novel that leads readers through idyllic dreams of heroism and the grim reality of war. Donald Michael Platt provides readers with a unique coming-of-age story as three adventure-seeking boys discover far more than how to be an aerial combat pilot. CLOSE TO THE SUN is an amazing tale of adventure, heroism, war and the drive within us all that keeps us going when things look bleak.

He clasps the crag with crooked hands;
Close to the sun in lonely lands,
Ringed with the azure world he stands.

The wrinkled sea beneath him crawls;
He watches from the mountain walls,
And like a thunderbolt he falls.
*—Alfred Lord Tennyson, " The Eagle"*

# To the Reader

*Close to the Sun* is a novel about fighter aces, who as boys idealized the Knights of the Skies from World War I and matured during the grim reality of World War II.

Imagine riding on a moving platform thousands of feet above Earth shooting at a moving platform that is firing back at you, with dozens more moving platforms, friends and foe around you, engaging in the same battle. That is a typical Second World War aerial fighter plane combat scenario.

The concept of acedom began during World War I, known first as The Great War until 1939 when another great war broke out in Europe and Asia. A fighter pilot became an ace after shooting down five planes during air-to-air combat with second party visual confirmation. Ground targets did not count. The Red Baron, Manfred von Richthofen, was The Great War's top ace with 80 Luftsiegen, air victories. Other German, French, and British pilots scored well into the 50s, 60s, and 70s. Eddie Rickenbacker, America's ace of aces, achieved 26 victories in a mere two months of aerial combat before the war ended.

The discrepancy between U.S. and Luftwaffe aerial victories widened during World War II, which by then required gun camera film proof or second party visual confirmation. With its vast supply of manpower, the United States usually took its fighter pilots out of combat after fifty missions, but some did fly a hundred or more.

America's leading aces in the ETO, European Theater of War, Francis "Gabby" Gabreski with 28 victories and Bob Johnson with 27, flew fewer than fifty missions each. About five-percent of all U.S. fighter pilots achieved acedom during WWII.

Luftwaffe fighter pilots flew hundreds and some more than a thousand missions, many between extended hospital stays. Eric Hartmann, the top ace of all wars, had 352 Luftsiegen in over 1400 sorties, Gerd Barkhorn 301, Gunther Rall 275, and many others scored in the 200s and 100s.

All principal and most secondary male and female characters who appear in *Close to the Sun* are fictional. The 375th Fighter Group and its 135th, 136th, and 137th Fighter Squadrons are fictional composites of historical units that flew in the ETO during WWII. The 375th's bases near Thetford, England, and Ath in Belgium are fictional; the towns are not.

Schloss Teuffelreich in the Pfalzland also is fictional.

All Luftwaffe units are historical.

The City refers to San Francisco.

Author's Notes and a list of fictional characters as they appear can be found at the end of *Close to the Sun*.

# German Glossary

Luftwaffe—Air Force

Luftsieg—air-to-air victory

Abschuss—Shoot down — an air victory

Sortie—combat mission

Rotte—two plane element

Schwarm—four plane flight

Schwarmführer/Rottenführer—Schwarm/Rotte Leader

Staffel—Squadron

Staffelkapitän—Squadron Leader

Kaczmarek—Wingman

Gruppe—Group made up of several Staffeln

Geschwader—Luftwaffe Wing made up of several wings

Leutnant—Lieutenant

Hauptmann—Captain

Oberst—Colonel

Feldwebel—Sergeant.

Fürst—term used to address a titular head/Prinz of a principality, Prince in English

Graf—count

Indianern—Luftwaffe slang for the feared P-51 Mustang

"They are the knighthood of this war, without fear
and without reproach; and they recall the legendary
days of chivalry, not merely by their daring exploits
but by the nobility of their spirit."
— *David Lloyd-George,*
*Speech in House of Commons, October 29, 1917*

# PART ONE

## Nestlings, Juveniles, and Fledglings
## 1928-1940

By the rings around his eyeballs
You can tell the bombardier;
You can tell the bomber pilot
By the spread around his rear;
You can tell the navigator
By his sexton, maps, and such;
You can tell the fighter pilot,
But you can't tell him much.

U.S. Army Air Corps drinking song
(to the tune: *Ramblin' Wreck from Georgia Tech*)

# Chapter 1
## Three Nestlings, 1928

Ten-year-old Hank Milroy recognized the small head, streamlined body, and long tapering wings of a Peregrine falcon circling in the bright blue Wyoming sky above the Bridger Mountains. More beautiful than any aircraft, the predator glided above the earth in a search for prey. And not alone. A second falcon skimmed over the tops of brush and shrub and flushed a plump mountain quail from the undergrowth.

At its sighting of the quarry, the first Peregrine banked from on high. Wings taut, she burst out and down from the sun. The falcon's speed increased with the length of the dive to impact. The stunned pheasant dropped to the ground, and the Peregrine swooped down, talons ready to deliver the coup de grace.

From his vantage point at the edge of a bluff, Hank had an unobstructed view of the Peregrine's search and kill and how the falcon used the sun to surprise its prey. The quail lacked speed, armor, and intelligence. Bombers were easy targets like that pheasant, without a prayer of a chance against a skillful predator ace. No way would he ever be a bomber pilot, observer, or navigator.

Hank envied the sleek Peregrines—hawks, kites, and eagles too. Like those raptors, he also had been born to fly, and by golly he would fly fighters the same as all the legendary aces of the Great War he'd read about and admired: Rickenbacker, Von Richthofen, Immelmann, von Boelcke, Fonck, Collishaw, and Mannock.

Hank mounted and rode his quarter horse to the family ranch outside Cody, named for the legendary Buffalo Bill. He went to his bedroom where he'd covered the walls with overlapping photos and drawings of aces from the Great War and their pursuit planes. A formidable model air force hung from the ceiling beams: Spads, Fokkers, Sopwith Camels, Se-5s, Bristol F-2Bs, all from The Great War; and the recently developed Curtiss A-3 Falcon.

A photo of the Curtiss JN-4 atop Hank's desk was a reminder of a great thrill last year at an air show. He'd paid seventy-five cents for a ten-minute flight in the "Jenny" and for the first time experienced the sensation of being airborne, free as the birds soaring high over the Milroy ranch. That day Hank knew he'd be a pilot, a pursuit pilot.

He focused on separate photos of American and German aces from the Great War. In each one a trio stood arms linked in front of their planes.

*Who will I link arms with as a fellow ace one day?*

*Who will be my opponents high above the clouds and close to the sun?*

***

Friedrich, Fürst zu Pfalz von Teuffelreich, poured a glass of Moselle from the family vineyards and stood beside a life-size portrait on the far wall in which he posed in Luftwaffe uniform with the Pour le Merité, better known as the Blue Max, hanging from his neck. In the background, Prince

Friedrich's Fokker DR I triplane soared toward the clouds above a flaming Sopwith Camel.

Ten-year-old Karl Sebastian Otto Rudolf sat on a sofa beside older brother Wilhelm in the great room of the family's Berlin mansion waiting to hear more. How chivalrous his father had been. How typical of their caste, which was why von Boelcke, von Richthofen, and the entire pursuit arm of the Luftwaffe were renowned throughout Germany as Knights of the Skies.

Karl wished he'd been old enough to fly in the war. He was certain his turn would come after Germany rearmed and reversed the terms of the hated Diktat, harsh terms of surrender forced upon the Fatherland by the enemy at Versailles, when the alternative had been starvation under a severe blockade. After the envious French and English stripped Germany of all planes and Zeppelins in 1919, the Weimar Republic rebuilt in secret the Luftwaffe and sent its pilots to the Soviet Union for training.

Prince Friedrich continued, "When I got an opponent in my sights and fired my guns, I never saw the aircraft, only the opponent, and I often tipped my wings to salute a gallant foe. My last opportunity for a Luftsieg occurred early in the morning on the eleventh day of November. A tenacious Amerikaner ran out of ammo, and I broke off the combat. I flew alongside the fellow, looked my opponent in the eye, and saluted. He was a courageous foe, an ace too, with six Iron Crosses on the Spad's fuselage. To murder an unarmed man is unthinkable. Remember that, my sons. And so, at war's end I had forty-nine Luftsiegen."

Karl maneuvered a model of a Fokker DR I into an attack against an imaginary foe. "Papa, in the next war I shall be an ace like you."

"Then always remember Hauptmann Oswald Boelcke's instructions for fighter pilots from the war, which will still be valid in the next. I shall recite them for you.

1. Try to secure advantages before attacking. If possible, keep the sun behind you.

2. Always carry through an attack you have started.

3. Fire only at close range, and only when your opponent is properly in your sights.

4. Always keep your eye on your opponent, and never let yourself be deceived by ruses.

5. In any form of attack, it is essential to assail your opponent from behind.

6. If your opponent dives on you, fly to meet him.

7. When over enemy lines, never forget your line of retreat.

8. For the Staffel: Attack on principle in groups of four or six. When the fight breaks up into a series of single combats, take care that several do not go after one opponent."

Karl promised to memorize and follow the great ace's advice.

***

Eight year old Seth Braham slipped away from his friends and their chaperone, Coach Andy DeLuca. He disappeared in a forest of Great War and new military planes parked on the grass at Chrissy Airfield at the north end of the Presidio adjacent to the Golden Gate. He was on an excursion with the Columbia Park Boys' Club celebrating the tenth anniversary of Armistice Day when the war ended at the eleventh hour of the eleventh day of the eleventh month.

Several pilots had performed mock combat and daring aerobatics, and when Seth heard the engines of a Handley-Page bomber revving nearby, he looked toward his buddies and Coach DeLuca. They hadn't missed him so far. Now or never. He strapped himself in one of the empty bomb racks and awaited the bomber's take-off roll.

"What the hell? Come on down from there, you little brat." An Army Air Corps lieutenant unstrapped Seth and pulled him to the ground. The officer stared at the Columbia Park Boys' Club logo on Seth's sweater. "I should have known. "One of Andy's kids."

He gripped Seth's arm, and they double-timed to DeLuca, an eight-victory ace, standing by the Spad XIII he had flown in the same squadron with the great Eddie Rickenbacker. "I caught this little daredevil trying to hitch a ride in the bomb rack of that Handley-Page over there."

"He did? Thanks, Leo, I didn't see him sneak away. Why did you do it, Seth?" DeLuca looked at the other boys. "Was it on a dare?"

"No, Coach. I wanted to fly and saw the bomb rack was empty."

The lieutenant smiled at Seth's boldness. "He could have gotten killed or caught pneumonia from the cold up there."

DeLuca tousled Seth's curly hair. "We're going to need gutsy kids like him in the next war. Seth, this is Lieutenant Leo Kilrain. He shot down eleven Huns in the Great War."

Seth shook the officer's hand. "Gee, sir, it's sure swell to meet an ace like you."

"The boy has a firm handshake."

"One of my toughest too. Leo, why don't you take Seth for a ride in that trainer over there? Here, I'll give him my scarf, goggles, and jacket so he doesn't freeze."

Kilrain walked Seth to the two-seater biplane. He secured the boy's goggles, zipped the oversize jacket, and lifted him into the trainee's seat. "Be sure you tighten the straps. Good. Now you should know this is the Consolidated PT-1, which we call the Trusty. It has a 180 hp Hispano-Suiza engine and about a 78 mph cruising speed. It can reach over 13, 000 feet of altitude, but we'll go no higher than 7,000."

Seth thrilled to the whine of the propeller when it turned and the accompanying hum of the engine. He waved at DeLuca and his envious friends during the taxi along the grassy airfield. After the plane lifted, Seth saw against the bluffs of the uplands the Presidio's bachelor officers' quarters and a row of small homes for married officers, hangars for seaplanes and land planes at the field's southern edge, and farther east an administration building, barracks for enlisted men, flagstaff, and guardhouse.

After Kilrain banked and turned the Trusty, he heard gollys, gees, and goshes coming from Seth at the boy's first aerial view of San Francisco and the Bay Area. The day was so clear Seth could see the Farallon Islands twenty miles offshore. Below, Alcatraz resembled a stationary battleship supported by a flotilla of sailboats tacking in the breeze and merchants ships. Ferries carrying passengers and their autos to and from Sausalito and Oakland chugged over the white capped choppy dark green water of the bay.

During Kilrain's aerial combat maneuvers and aerobatics, Seth imagined flying combat against the Hun. Upon landing, he shook Kilrain's hand.

"Thank you, sir. Golly, that was swell."

DeLuca brought a camera and asked one of the ground crew to take photos. He placed Seth in the middle, and they linked arms. "Still want to fly, kid?"

"Yes, sir, you bet, Coach. But next time I'd like to be at the controls."

Kilrain patted Seth's shoulder. "Spoken like a real pursuiter."

# Chapter 2
## Hank

"Yessirree, Milroy, it may be hot now, but it gets colder than a witch's you-know-what in the winter. And when it rains, it pours so heavily the base is known as Randolph-by-the-sea."

Hank rode inside a bus filled with flying cadets who were to be part of Class 39B at the United States Army Air Corps' West Point of the Air at Randolph Field, twenty miles north of steaming San Antonio. After two days of relentless testing of hearing, reflexes, and eyesight at Fort Logan, he was one of twelve regional candidates to pass the physical for a year of training. At the end of next June, 1939, one year from today, he'd have silver wings and be commissioned as a second lieutenant in the Army Air Corps making over two hundred bucks a month just for flying, way more than a family of four needed to live on nowadays, and it was the starting salary.

Hank regretted he'd selected a window seat. It imprisoned him. Worse than the intense heat and humidity, Wayne Miller, the clod next to him in the aisle seat, would not shut up. He hoped the Air Corps didn't assign roommates alphabetically. Miller was too close to Milroy.

When the bus left the main highway and turned onto a concrete road leading to a large complex of buildings, Wayne Miller nudged Hank. "Did you know there are three hundred and seventy-one buildings constructed in the center four hundred acres of the base? All told, including the two flying fields, Randolph comprises twenty-three hundred acres. See that tall octagonal tower with the yellow and blue Spanish mosaic tiles on the roof? It's the base administration building. It's a hundred and seventy feet high and contains the administration offices as well as a post office, photo section, signal office, and a theater seating eleven hundred and fifty. Gee, this is going to be a peach of a year for us."

The nincompoop was in for a rude awakening. Everyone at Fort Logan had told Hank the cadets led a Spartan life at Randolph. Hank ignored Miller's chatter and concentrated on the four parkways radiating from the tower to the four points of the compass. Single-lane streets bisected the parkways like spokes on a wheel. One and two story houses lining the streets had a modified Spanish motif with red tile roofs.

The bus proceeded toward a cluster of three-story barracks behind the housing area, turned into a circular drive, and stopped behind other transports. On the manicured grass in front of the smallest building, a sign greeted them: FLYING CADETS REPORT HERE. Upperclassmen in blue uniforms swarmed everywhere, and a trio double-timed toward the bus.

"Jeez, Milroy, they sure look like they're glad to see us."

Hank was not so optimistic. Like big barn cats stalking rodents, the upperclassmen sprang from every nook and cranny to harass the new cadets. Others organized small groups of earlier arrivals into squads; wearing blue slash forage caps, the underclassmen stood at attention in their civilian clothes.

Miller leaned across Hank and stuck his head out the window. "Hey, you guys, is this where we report to learn to fly?"

An iron-assed, redheaded upperclassman's beady blue eyes memorized Miller before he stepped into the bus and froze everyone to silence with an icy glare. "My name is Bob Chilton. The upperclassmen waiting outside for you are Milt Ashley and Joe Grant. Follow their instructions after you get off the bus and put your baggage over there by that sign on the grass. Then they will direct you to the administration desk where you will sign in and receive your first item of military dress, what we call the forage cap. After that, come back and form a double line by your baggage. Okay, move."

Outside the bus, when the new cadets placed their suitcases on the grass, a supercharged Harley-Davidson sped into the circular drive, and its rider wheel-walked the motorcycle to a dusty stop. The biker dismounted and whipped off his Great War pilot's helmet and goggles to reveal a movie-handsome face beneath curly blond hair that needed no combing. Hank figured the intruder to be around five-eleven and a well-built one-eighty-five.

The biker approached Chilton with a confident smile. "Say, y'all, I'm a new cadet. Where the hell do I report?"

The upperclassman regarded the newcomer as fresh meat for the grinder. "Mister, what is your name?"

"Braxton Hale Mobley."

"Braxton Hale Mobley, *sir*. Mister, it is always 'sir' when speaking to an upperclassman."

"Yes, suh."

"Stand tall, Mister Mobley. That means stand at At-ten-shun. Taller."

"You too," Ashley bellowed at Hank and the cadets. "Ten-shun!"

Hank recognized the name Mobley. He'd heard and read plenty about the hotshot triple-threat tailback, whom many thought would run, pass, and kick Texas Christian University to a national championship, Cotton Bowl glory, and pick up that new prestigious trophy along the way, the Heisman. Why had so gifted an athlete dropped out of school? Was Mobley also consumed by a greater desire to fly?

Chilton appeared satisfied with Mobley's exaggerated posture. "Now then, Mister, park your motorcycle right where it is and follow me. We'll see that it'll be placed safely in the motor pool."

"Right."

"Mister Mobley, *whenever* you address an upper-classman you will address him as *sir*. Understand?"

"Yes, suh." Mobley parked the bike and snapped into exaggerated attention. "Mission accomplished, suh."

After Chilton focused on Mobley for a polar ten seconds, he ordered the new arrivals to follow Cadets Ashley and Grant to the veranda-porch of the building where each in turn signed the register book and received a go-to-hell forage cap. Milt Ashley, a baby-faced farm boy with an incongruous steelworker's physique, showed them how to wear their slash caps.

"Pull it down over your right eye so it's one finger width above the right eyebrow. Now, move it to the right so the right side is one finger's width above the right ear." He adjusted Miller's cap. "If we ever see you wearing it any other way, you'll be in manure up to your eyeballs."

Ashley marched the new cadets to their baggage on the grass by the welcome sign and lined them alphabetically into squads of eight. He ordered the squads to stand tall at attention and walked around the men, grimacing as if he smelled rotten fish. "From now on, you will be known as Misters. Okay, Misters, put your eyes straight. Do not let them waver for any reason whatsoever. And when we address you personally, you will answer, Yes, sir. Understand?"

"Yes, sir!" they shouted as one.

Hank evaluated his potential ranking among the cadets. At five-nine and a solid hundred and fifty-five pounds, no one was in better shape, not even the taller Mobley. He'd already put Miller in a niche as a fool and unlikely to last. Mobley was the man to beat for the number one spot in 39B. Even if Mobley had never flown before, the Texan should perform well in a cockpit. Hank had never seen anyone ride a motorbike like that.

Hank conceded one minor battle to Mobley. The temperature was over ninety degrees with high humidity. The new cadets in civvies and the upperclassmen in their uniforms were sweating, some of the former wilting, but not Mobley, who looked as if he had stepped out of an igloo. The Texan was so starchy-creased and well groomed the upperclassmen appeared disheveled by comparison. Hank vowed to do everything possible to avoid standing inspection next to Mobley.

Chilton, Ashley, and Grant next ran the cadets to the Quartermaster, where they stored their bags and received cadet slate-blue uniforms, a three inch wide pair of gold wings for a visor cap and a two inch high silver propeller to be worn on the lower right sleeve. Shirts and trousers were to have sharp creases, ties perfectly knotted and tucked between the second and third buttons below the neck. Belts and shoes had to be "spit shined" and belt buckles polished to the level of a glaring sun. Chilton reminded the cadets they were in the Army Air Corps, with emphasis on Army, when the cadets were issued rifles for marching and close order drill.

***

The upperclassmen assigned the 39B cadets to their quarters by height. Those over five-eleven went to A Company Barracks and would be known as High Pockets. Relegated to B Company Barracks with Hank, Miller, and the other cadets decreed to be five-eleven and under, Mobley protested, to no avail, that the football programs had listed him at six feet.

Cadet Captain Chilton of B Company told the underclassmen they would be referred to as Blowers because they were supposed to be so small they had to talk rather than fight their way out of trouble. When Chilton assigned rooms for the Blowers in B Barracks by alphabet, Hank faced a double-whammy. For the next four months, he would be rooming with Miller and Mobley. Hirsute, stocky "black" Irish Patrick Monahan from San Diego was the fourth man in the room.

The roommates flipped coins for bunks, but before they could store their civilian gear in the trunks at the foot of their beds, Ashley entered with four cadets assigned to an adjacent room. "At ease, Misters. As your Squad Leader, I will now brief you on the routines of cadet life you'll be facing during the next four months of A Stage, if you don't wash-out sooner."

Miller's brow had more furrows than a hundred acre farm. "What's wash-out mean, sir?"

Hank, Brax, and Monahan exchanged pained looks and forged an instant bond while Ashley explained, "Wash-out is total elimination from our program. It can be caused by any number of reasons. Poor academics, inability to bear up under hazing, failure to solo, or collecting too many gigs, as we usually call the demerits."

Miller's nose twitched, rabbit-like. "Sir, I don't understand the point of all the hazing."

"I'll get to that in a moment, Mister. Our intense hazing of new cadets lasts the full four months of A Stage. It is patterned after the programs at West Point and Annapolis. During the first four to six weeks, you will be subjected to extreme physical and mental pressures to determine if you can bear up under the strain. Brains, guts, and athletic ability are necessary for flying, but emotional stability is no less important. If you're the kind of guy who cracks under pressure, we don't want you flying with us. You could endanger your plane, your life, and the lives of the men around you. That's why we have a demerit system."

"What exactly is a demerit, sir?"

Hank winced, and Ashley faced Miller with a nasty grin. "Demerits are issued by us upperclassmen for infractions, such as failure to make your bed correctly, wearing the wrong uniform, smirking, or disobeying an upperclassman, and for having a dirty rifle. If you receive more than five gigs in a week, you earn an hour for each demerit, which you work off by parading on the ramp with your rifle on Saturday and Sunday, mopping floors, cleaning latrines or grease traps in the kitchen. You also buy the Big Casino in demerits if you date a blacklisted girl. If you date one of those, you get six-and-twenty. That means six gigs and twenty hours on the ramp. The jackpot. And when you reach a hundred gigs, you're washed-out."

Ashley paused and looked each cadet in the eye. "Now then, those of you who were in college fraternities will understand what we mean when we call the first four to six weeks Hell Month. And I assume you're wondering about weekends and women. Well, during Hell Month, you will not be allowed off base. Therefore, no women. Our normal sixteen-hour day ought to leave your cocks permanently limp. The only erection you can look forward to is your morning piss hard-on."

"Shee-yit, a full month? Ever since I popped my cherry, I ain't gone two days without getting laid."

"Mr. Mobley, speak only when you're spoken to." Ashley went to Hank's bed. "Now, I will show you how to make your cots, what is expected of you by way of house cleaning, and how to hang and fold your clothes. You will be subject to room and personal inspection any time of the day or night for the next month."

After making Hank's bed, Ashley pointed out its tautness and symmetry of line. He flipped a quarter onto the blanket, and it bounced a good three feet. Then he pulled apart the blanket and sheets. "No freebies, Mr. Milroy. Now, when you are not marching in formation, you must run at double-time when you are in the cadet area. In answer to your most burning question, you will not start flying until the third week. One more thing. There are one hundred and eighty cadets in 39B. By the end of A Stage, four months from now, about half of you will have survived."

Hank did not have time to ponder that ominous statistic. He faced another hour of orientation in housekeeping, personal hygiene, and plenty of hazing from other upperclassmen who came into the room to harass and evaluate the new cadets. They introduced Hank and his roommates to various hazing routines, from calisthenics to memorizing bits of dialogue.

"Mr. Monahan. How is the cow?"

"Sir, she walks, she talks, and she's full of chalk. The lacteal fluid produced by the female of the bovine species is nutritional to the 'nth degree."

"What time is it, Mr. Mobley?"

"Suh, my poor chronometer is in such disarray with the great sidereal movement I cannot tell you the exact time. However, I would hazard a guess that it is twenty-seven minutes, 45 seconds, and one tick after twenty-hundred hours. Suh."

"Mister Miller, what are you?"

"I am a worm, sir."

"And what is a worm, Mister Miller?"

"A worm, sir, is so low, sir, he has to look up, sir, to see bottom, sir."

"Mr. Milroy, bail out."

At rigid attention, Hank struck his left breast with his right fist, as if to grab an imaginary parachute ripcord, and at the same time he bent the knees to lower his body about eight inches. He had to maintain that position until ordered back to attention. Not this time.

Squad leader Ashley barked out more commands. "Down a button." Hank bent his knees to lower his body another four inches. "Up a button." Hank raised himself four inches. He'd been told the exercise was devised to improve the cadets' reflexes and perhaps one day save their lives.

After the last cadet officer departed, Hank's combative juices surged. He remade his bed and put on his new uniforms and shoes. "There's no way they're going to prevent me from making it through."

Brax made a bed tighter than Ashley had shown them. "I can take anything these Yankees dish out. They took it from their upperclassmen, and they survived."

Miller needed Monahan's help with both sheets and blanket. "Why do they call us Dodos?"

Hank practiced setting his go-to-hell cap at the desired angle. "Dodo birds can't fly, so Dodos we are until we solo."

***

Upperclassmen double-timed the new cadets to their first meal at Randolph. In the mess hall, framed insignia of the various Air Corps groups and squadrons hung high along the walls above the porticoes leading to giant wings at one end. A huge map of the United States displaying all the Army's air fields had been painted on a wall at the other end. Hank looked forward to taking off and landing on each one of them.

The new cadets sat on command, eyes straight ahead without wavering. Once seated, upperclassmen next ordered the men to lower their eyes and stare at the cadet wings on the porcelain plates.

Next, the upperclassmen introduced the cadets to the "square meal" to be eaten in unison to a silent cadence. Each man looked at a point straight ahead, placed food on his fork and raised it to eye level. He then moved the fork on a straight line into his mouth. After chewing and swallowing, he returned the fork to the plate with the same movements in reverse and continued eating in the exaggerated square. Ashley told the new cadets the exercise was intended to improve their peripheral vision, a most important factor to develop situational awareness when flying.

Miller became the focus of hazing at their first square meal because he moved his eyes. The upperclassmen assigned the misfit to be table-gunner, responsible for keeping his messmates supplied with food, milk, water, and condiments. When an item was in short supply at the table, Miller raised his right arm. Servers hurried to the table to learn what he wanted. The first time Miller gunned, he looked at the server. For that transgression, Ashley gigged him.

***

That night after lights-out, Hank wanted to talk about flying, but Brax reminisced about his many sexual conquests. Hank believed Brax. He had never seen a human suffer so much from lack of sexual outlet.

Monahan contributed tales about the rowdy escapades of frat buddies, like the night at eight sharp they all went searching for the ugliest girl each could find and bring back to a dance. Miller confessed he was a virgin. A high school track coach told him sex would reduce his speed. Hank continued to be amazed that their less than mentally swift roommate had more than once run a 9.7 hundred yard dash.

After Brax related another graphic tale of amatory conquest, Monahan said, "One day, I expect to read you've been shot by a jealous husband."

"I surely hope so, good buddy, and you can guess exactly when. Just make sure they write on my tombstone, Here Lies Braxton Hale Mobley, Shot on the Rise."

"You'd better pray there's no such thing as reincarnation. I hate to think what you'll be the next time around."

"Pat, if I had my 'druthers, you know what I'd like to come back as?"

Miller bit first. "What?"

"A cake of soap in a sorority shower."

Hank and Monahan tossed their pillows at Brax.

Brax, Miller, and Monahan fell asleep. Hank lay awake, still pumped from the day's excitement. Brax thrashed in bed and moaned the name Wilma Lee until he reached out and fell to the floor.

Hank figured Brax's Wilma Lee had to be a real looker. Then he thought of the girls he'd left behind, but no one special. Although he never went to a cathouse, where he might catch one of Cupid's diseases and ruin any chances for a career in the Air Corps, he'd pranged more than a fair share of girls. Of course, he'd always used a rubber. Getting a girl pregnant would have finished his flying career before it began. Geez, Chilton was wrong. Hank had more than a mere piss hard-on when he remembered the girls he'd pranged.

# Chapter 3
## Winty

"A" Stage kept Hank busy every minute from 0545 reveille until 2230 taps. He learned close-order drill, the same as infantry enlistees in boot camp, between rigorous academic courses: Theory of Flight, Aerodynamics, Airplane and Engine Maintenance, Aerial Navigation, Air Commerce Regulations, Ground Gunnery, Meteorology, Hygiene, Military Courtesy, Military Law, Map Reading, and Radio and Communications. Using radio communications and Morse Code, each cadet was required to send a minimum of twelve words per minute and receive twenty words per minute.

The weaker cadets began to wash out, many for academic reasons, others because they could not take the hazing. A classmate had his bed ripped apart one time too many and decked the cadet officer who harassed him. Miller astounded both instructors and classmates in 39B when he survived the first weeks, and Hank revised his original estimate. Miller might be slow-witted and clueless, but he asked questions and never forgot answers. Miller was incapable of original thought, however, and needed specific direction. If an instructor, higher-up, or anyone else in authority did not require something, he never thought to learn about it. Hank concluded that if the human race had been made up of Wayne Millers, no one would have invented the wheel. Still, Hank, Brax, and Monahan took advantage of his unique skill: no one ironed a sharper crease, and Miller was eager to please his roommates.

Hank found hazing to be most annoying when he was studying. This evening, he had to deal with four intruders. A booming voice commanded the roommates to stand at attention, and the upperclassmen began a thorough inspection. They said the room was not fit to live in and ordered the underclassmen to scrub, clean, and polish it, then stand inspection for neatness of their bodies, closets, and beds. Hank made and remade the sheets and blanket until coins bounced high off them to the satisfaction of the upperclassmen.

***

In the middle of the third week, the cadets received their goggles, which they had to wear as a stigma of Dodoism to and from the flight line until they soloed. On average, it took seven hours of instruction, and those who failed to solo after twenty hours washed-out.

The upperclassmen ran the cadets double-time for half a mile to the flight line and divided them alphabetically into five flights of thirty to thirty-five men, A through E. Each flight went to a different hangar. The roommates ended up in C Flight, which had a different officer-instructor per every six students. Hank was assigned to Captain Leo Kilrain, a tough bantam rooster from New York, who seemed to be a composite of the Warner Brothers Air Corps of Cagney, O'Brien, and the rest of the studio's Irish mafia.

Kilrain surveyed the Dodos with a hard expression, as if deciding which cadet he could beat in a fight and concluding he could take them all. "You'd better get some things straight. Your flying instruction begins in a few moments. Some of you will start to think you're pretty good when you solo by the seventh hour. Well, you'll have difficulty convincing me that ten hours of dual instruction will qualify you as safe enough to handle a bird alone. I'll be going up with each of you at least every other day. I do not consider early soloing to be evidence of great pilot prowess. Some of you will be quick to learn, but after that, you may pick up very little. In my experience, slow learners at this stage often make the best learners in the long run. The last to solo in A Stage are often the first to solo in B. Are there any questions?"

Hank had none. Would Miller say something to irritate their short-fused instructor? Not today; the Dodo stood mute with an idiotic, beatific expression.

After the first day of preflight instruction, Hank read their flying schedule that gave the cadets four flights a week. If he could solo after six to eight hours of dual instruction, the end of Dodoism would be less than two weeks away.

Soloing at the Air Corps school was the turning point of the entire curriculum. Everything would begin at that moment: self-esteem, selection to Pursuit, and a military career. Hank never considered the alternative: washing-out and leaving Randolph Field in disgrace.

The primary training aircraft were open-cockpit, two-seater primary trainer biplanes: PT-3, PT-11, and the PT-13. Because Hank had soloed in a Waco and an Alexander Eaglerock back in Wyoming, he found the PT-13 easy to handle and maneuver. It flew like the civilian planes, but military procedures were different and prevented Hank from soloing on his first flight.

As always, up in the clear blue sky he experienced a unique euphoria, a sense of liberation from earthbound matters. He never felt the cold and wind in the open cockpit. Petty regulations and hazing receded into dim memory.

During the seventh hour of flight training, Hank practiced stall and spin recoveries until Kilrain shouted over the Gosport intercom for him to shoot some landings at Cade Field. After a second successful touch down, the instructor ordered Hank to park the PT-13 on the makeshift flight line. He told Hank to stay in the cockpit and dismounted.

"Okay, Mr. Milroy, take her up by yourself, shoot three more take-offs and landings, and then come back to the line."

Hank's heartbeat accelerated. "You're letting me solo already, sir?"

"Hell, Mr. Milroy, with you at the controls, it's safer for me here on the ground."

Hank checked the controls and taxied to the edge of the runway. Up to now, he'd oozed confidence. This was different. His future was at stake.

Hank received the green-light signal from Ground Control and gunned the motor. After a thousand foot run, he lifted the PT-13 into the air and climbed straight ahead to five hundred feet altitude before leveling off. Hank turned ninety-degrees to the right and climbed to one thousand feet. He made another ninety-degree right turn and entered the downward leg of the pattern. After Hank completed three good circles and bumps, he taxied back to the flight line.

Kilrain climbed into the front cockpit. "Well done, Mr. Milroy. You fly better without an instructor aboard. Now let's see if you can get us home safely."

Hank knew that soling for the first time in a military plane was a special moment, never to be repeated. Back on the ground at Randolph, he saw Brax preparing for a flight. They waved a greeting to each other, and Hank held off informing the Texan he'd soloed. Let Brax discover it when he marched back from the flight line tonight without his goggles.

Hank and Brax saw each other as the man to beat, but they shared a mutual respect. Yet the Texan left Hank's curiosity unanswered in two areas. Brax would not explain why he dropped out of TCU and gave up a promising future as a star football player; and he never spoke of Wilma Lee, whose name he cried out every night.

At the end of the day, before all cadets lined up in front of their hangars, neither Hank nor Brax had their goggles. Gloryosky Sandy! He and the Texan were the only two in 39B who soloed.

Hank and Brax erased their smiles when two upperclassmen approached. Neither wanted a demerit. Because they'd soloed, they'd be At ease! during meals from now on, which would allow them to look around the mess hall at will, while their less fortunate classmates continued to eat square meals.

***

Their fifth weekend at Randolph, all cadets, except those restricted to the base for too many demerits, were given passes from noon Saturday until 2230 hours Sunday. Hank had soloed ahead of Brax, and he now added another leg up on the Texan. Cadet Captain Chilton never forgot Brax's brash arrival and created a gaggle of excuses to gig the Texan, mostly for insolent smirking. Brax was further humiliated to be sharing extra duty over the weekend with

Miller. Monahan also received extra duty. Hank didn't think Pat deserved so many gigs, but the dark and hairy bluebeard needed to shave at least twice a day to satisfy the upperclassmen.

A classmate invited Hank to a party and promised that the local belles thought the flying cadets to be the most eligible of young men. After the first dance, Hank attracted more girls than anyone else. He didn't think he was handsome enough to warrant all the attention, although his older sister had said he'd appeal to women everywhere he went because of his rugged features, well-conditioned physique, Wyoming cowboy charm, and exceptional dancing abilities.

Hank punished the parquets with them all and found the girls merging into a great blur despite his perfect vision. Several advertised they were available for whatever he wanted to do, including one he thought to be the prettiest, a voluptuous, welcoming blonde.

Nancy McCabe, the daughter of a wealthy rancher, wore no girdle or corset, and he could feel every square inch of her warm fleshy curves when they danced cheek-to-cheek. The blonde's boldness worried Hank; she might be a blacklisted girl.

During a break when Nancy went over to the Victrola to select some favorite recordings, Hank became aware of a girl staring at him. She stood by a window ignored by the other cadets. She had short-cropped sun-bleached hair like aviatrix Amelia Earhart and a fresh scratch across a freckled forehead. The tomboy probably had scabbed knees, but Hank couldn't see if he was right because her long brown linen dress, probably a hand-me-down, fell almost to the tops of white cotton socks and saddle shoes.

Hank wanted to know why he had become the object of the girl's unblinking gaze and walked to her. "Hi, I'm Hank Milroy."

She had a firm handshake. "Katharine Winters McCabe."

*Yikes, Nancy's sister.*

"But everyone calls me Winty."

Up close, the blonde was prettier than he'd first supposed. Even teeth, clean skin, and small nose. When the girl matured, she might become a real beauty. He liked Winty's husky voice, so incongruous for someone around five feet tall.

"Just how old are you, Winty?"

"I turned sixteen last week."

*Double yikes. Jailbait. A million gigs and washout.*

"Aren't you too young for these parties?"

"It's my first time. I came here with my sister, Nancy. She's the blonde who's trying to catch your eye, the one who thinks she looks like Frances Farmer. What do you think? Nancy is awfully pretty. She adores flyers. But you already know that."

The music started again. The cadets and girls paired off to dance. Nancy tugged at Hank's sleeve.

"You promised me another dance."

Hank didn't move. This strange little girl seemed more interesting than her sexy sister. Why? He had kid sisters at home and didn't need another.

"Did you hear me, Hank?"

"Sure, maybe the next song."

Nancy glared at Hank and Winty before she accepted another partner.

"What are you doing here, Winty? Do you like fliers too?"

"Yes, but I like flying better."

"You've been up in a plane?"

"Sure, plenty of times. I've soloed too."

Because Winty exuded a high-charged can-do attitude, Hank believed her. "Tell me. Where can a guy get some air time around here?"

Winty smiled. She had dimples too. "That sounds funny coming from a flying cadet. But I know a place."

"Where?"

"Why are you so interested? Are you having trouble soloing at Randolph?"

"I was the first in my class to solo. I also did it a couple of years ago in a Waco and an Alexander Eaglerock."

"Really? Will you take me up if I show you where you can get a plane?"

"I'll do anything to fly. We aren't going to have to steal one, are we?"

Winty grabbed Hank's arm. "My uncle owns a fleet of planes and rents them out. If we hurry, we can still catch Uncle Roy at the airfield."

***

Husky Roy McCabe wiped grease from his face, chewed on an unlit cigar, and pretended to ignore Winty, who wheedled, cajoled, demanded, and begged her uncle to let Hank take her up for a flight. Hank doubted anyone could have resisted Winty's sales pressure, and Roy McCabe finally gave the okay.

Winty climbed into the rear cockpit of a clean Waco, and Hank took the front seat. He turned over the engine and checked the controls. He waggled the control stick back and forth, then side to side.

Winty shouted over the roar of the engine, "Take it easy."

Hank gestured he understood. The stick in the rear cockpit worked too.

Soon they were airborne, and Hank became one with the Waco. He forgot about Winty sitting in the rear cockpit until they were over uninhabited countryside. Hank waved to the girl that he wanted to make a loop-the-loop and a slow roll. Winty responded with a thumbs-up.

After Hank performed some acrobatics, Winty jiggled the stick and pointed at herself when he turned around. Sunuvagun, she wanted to take the controls. The kid must have logged plenty of hours in the air whenever she could charm her uncle or flight-hungry cadets.

Hank gave Winty control of the Waco. She executed a slow roll with no dish-out at the end and other flawless maneuvers, better than those he'd made. Hank took charge of the Waco for the landing. Winty didn't need any help to climb out of the rear cockpit.

"That was a great slow roll, Winty. How did you learn to fly so well?"

She waited until he purchased a pair of Cokes from a machine outside the dispatch office. "My dad and Uncle Roy don't have any sons. You've seen my sister, Nancy. That's why they treat me like the number one tomboy in the world. It's fine with me. They taught me to fly. Even if they hadn't, I'd have found a way to fly. It's in my blood. Flying's my life. I envy you, Hank. You're a man. I'd like to be a flying cadet too and fly a pursuiter."

*A girl pursuiter pilot? Impossible.*

"Do your boyfriends fly?"

"I'm not interested in boys, not the locals, anyway."

Hank couldn't resist teasing her. "Is that why you went to the party, to hunt for a cadet husband?"

Winty almost spat a mouthful of cola. "Hank, I'm sixteen. I've still got to finish high school and go to college."

"Well, a pretty little girl like you will have had plenty of lovers by the time you're married."

"No lovers, Hank. I'm not like Nancy or those other girls you met at the party. My first lover will be my husband. And if I ever do marry, he'll have to be a flyer too."

An awkward silence followed, and Hank worried he had gone too far teasing her. Roy McCabe came out of the adjacent hangar and handed Winty a pair of coveralls. "Okay, kiddo, time for you to crew my Waco. Hank, you can take the old bird up any time if you pay for the gas. This one was on me. And Winty."

He shook hands with McCabe and turned to thank Winty again. Her mood had changed one hundred and eighty degrees.

"Well, what are you waiting for, Hank? Why don't you go back to the party? My sister, Nancy, she'll be glad to see you again. And she can have you too."

Winty ran from Hank and disappeared into the dark recesses of the hangar. He looked at Roy, who gestured as if he wanted no part of whatever had gone on between them. That was the problem. Nothing had gone on between them.

*** 

Between flying, studying, and hazing, Hank thought of Nancy McCabe for sex and Winty for flying. Maybe he could have his cake and eat it too. He looked forward to mending fences with the voluptuous blonde at the next party, but failed to take into account Brax's charm.

Winty did not appear, and Nancy forgot about Hank the moment she saw handsome dashing Brax arrive on the Harley. Nancy suggested he participate in a bike race scheduled the next day after church. Hank and Monahan agreed to crew Brax.

Early Sunday morning Nancy drove a truck to Randolph. Brax signed for his Harley at the Motor Pool, secured the bike on the bed, and got into the driver's side beside Nancy, who gave him her keys. Hank and Monahan climbed onto the bed, and Brax sped for two hours northwest towardsRock Springs renowned for its goat and angora ranches.

After they reached the site of a classic three-loop open challenge on a plateau covered with Mesquite, Hank and Monahan helped Brax lift the Harley from the back of the truck, and Nancy joined a covey of girls drinking beer and whooping it up.

Hank saw Winty standing beside another Harley near one of the trucks. She looked adorable in coveralls, T-shirt, and Stetson, and he waved at the tomboy. She did not respond.

Nancy returned, kissed Brax, and gave him a beer. Again, she wore no girdle or bra under a tight-fitting blue and yellow print dress. "Y'all set to go, Handsome?"

Brax swilled the brew, kissed Nancy, and revved the engine. "What do y'all think?"

Nancy flashed a wicked smile at Hank. "And you?"

"Me?"

"Why don't you race too? Or ain't you got no guts like Brax has?"

Brax slapped Hank's back. "How 'bout it, boy?"

"I'm not your boy."

"Lighten up, good buddy."

Hank had competed on motorcycles many times, in cars too, and won most of the races. "Sure, but I don't have a bike." He glanced at the local boys, who had already mounted their metal steeds. "I don't think they're going to lend me one of theirs."

Nancy jerked a thumb toward Winty. "My sister is always challenging the big boys, but no one wants a little girl to mess things up. They never let her race. Betcha' she'll loan you her bike."

Hank understood their motives. Nancy hoped to see him humiliated for ignoring her in favor of Winty. Brax wanted to prove he was the better man on the ground if he couldn't do it in the air. Given Nancy's limited intelligence, he could almost forgive her, but Brax disappointed Hank. Winty was something else. He couldn't figure why the she might be willing to go along with Brax's and Nancy's scheme to humiliate him.

Hank went to Winty, whose expression was opaque. He frowned at the age of the Harley, a good three years older than Brax's.

"I know what my sister is up to."

"So do I. But why are you letting me use your bike?"

"They won't let me race. I could beat them all, too."

"I'm sure you could." Hank meant it.

"So, you'll have to do it for me on *my* Harley." She patted the seat. "I've taken excellent care of her."

A quartet of locals on motorcycles roared past Brax and splattered him with dirt. They resented the flashy cadets who took away their girls and provoked brawls whenever they had an edge in numbers. Brax was ready to take them on. Hank had second thoughts. He'd never backed away from a fight, but preferred to avoid them if possible. They were outnumbered by one, but he figured Monahan, who was the strongest cadet at Randolph, could handle all four with little trouble.

"Brax, a fight might cause us problems at Randolph."

"I ain't going to chicken out with that trash."

"Then we'll show them who's best in the race."

"Great idea, Hank. Us against them. Me as leader and you as wingman."

"Or more likely the reverse."

Brax hadn't heard Hank.

Nancy introduced the cadets to their competition and flirted with Brax to annoy her admirers. One in particular, Jody Pritchard, a rancher's son, seemed unsure on his bike. Hank was unfamiliar with the course. It didn't bode well either when he overheard a local tell Nancy those big mouth cadets would get theirs at Iron Maiden Narrows or The Devil's Twist.

As if to illustrate the threat, a quartet of musicians on a truck bed sang:

"The race through life's on wicked roads to be
    avoided well,
Its curves and turns and the Devil's Twist will lead
    you straight to hell.
Watch, watch, watch out for the Devil's Twist.
Watch, watch, watch out for the Devil's Twist.

My true love tried to hold me back; she looked into
    my eyes,
She stroked my cheek, she didn't speak, but I heard
    her silent cry.
Watch, watch, watch out for the Devil's Twist ....

I started out upon the road without a look behind,
The warning signs along the way to them I paid no
  mind.
My speed along the road increased, I raced without a
  care.
And ignored my true love warning me, 'My darling,
  please beware.'
Watch, watch, watch out for the Devil's Twist ....

Then came the curves, the forks, and bends, I never
  slowed a lick.
The Devil laughed, I heard him not, my speed too
  high a kick.
The warning flag, the last, the last was waved before
  my face,
'Turn back,' it said, 'You'll never win, not at your
  reckless pace.'
Watch, watch, watch out for the Devil's Twist ....

Then suddenly! The Devil's twist! I flew far off the
  road,
I plunged through space and fell below to bear my
  eternal load.
Yes, the race through life's on evil roads to be
  avoided well,
Their curves and turns and the Devil's Twist will take
  you straight to hell.
Watch, watch, watch out for the Devil's Twist.
Watch, watch, watch out for the Devil's Twist"

***

Brax entered and won a preliminary wheel-walk
challenge, while Hank checked out Winty's bike. The older

powerful engine hummed a sweet melody as it drank high-octane gas. Hank wanted to speak with Winty before the race, but she chose to work in silence, tightening bolts and screws until satisfied the Harley was ready to go.

Before Hank rode toward the starting line, however, Winty blocked his way. "I've another reason for loaning you my bike. I want to see if you've got the right stuff."

The race began with much jockeying for position. Hank laid back, but not too far from the leaders, in order to become familiar with the twenty-four mile, three-loop course. It snaked over rough ground through groves of mesquite on a limestone plateau. He would need quick reflexes to avoid a wipeout.

Hank took the ungraded hairpin curve and knot known as the Devil's Twist that swung around to a treacherous part of the straightaway. It narrowed to a body's width between mesquite that created an arch four feet in height. After that lay more suicidal bends and twists before the open last half-mile where the flagman waited to wave them onto the next loop. By then Hank had seen Brax force two bikers into mesquite and rock.

At the start of the second loop, Hank increased his speed and caught Brax, who was a few yards behind the leader. They left the remaining nine competitors farther behind.

The three Harleys roared in a tie along the rocky trail and approached the hairpin turn. Brax made a bid for the lead, and Hank accelerated to avoid getting run off into the meaquite. He took the lead and held it. Hank's other rival made it less of a challenge when he slowed on the inside of a curve at a safer speed. Brax also decelerated and edged toward the local, who dropped back to avoid a collision.

Hank slipped through Iron Maiden Narrows with Brax a bike length behind. The flagman waved them on to the third and final loop, and Hank raced with flawless rhythm. He slalomed between the mesquite and took every rise at full speed. Each time Hank soared through the air he felt the same sensation as flying, ultimate freedom and oneness with a powerful machine. Then he saw a dawdler loping ahead of Iron Maiden Narrows. To avoid a collision, he'd have to slow and let the tail-end Charlie pass through the Narrows first. Thanks to Winty's high-octane fuel, Hank had enough lead on Brax to win.

Hank recognized the dawdler as Jody Pritchard, the boy who adored Nancy McCabe, and he shouted at Jody to get off the track. When that failed, Hank slowed. He hadn't entered the race to injure anyone.

Brax didn't hesitate. He pressed his bike to the limit and screamed a rebel yell as he passed Hank, who shouted at Pritchard to get out of Brax's way as both converged on the Narrows.

Pritchard rode on, oblivious to the danger. Moments later, Brax forced Pritchard off the course into a thick growth of mesquite and shot through the Narrows alone. Enraged by the brutal, unnecessary wipeout, Hank accelerated and pushed Winty's bike beyond its presumed capacity and gained on Brax. His sole desire in life at that moment was to beat Brax to the finish line. Hank's natural balance and instincts saved him from wiping out. He raced along the final straightaway and caught Brax at the finish.

Unaware that Hank had tied, or perhaps won, Brax upped the front of his bike and went into a triumphant wheel-walk to receive the accolade of adoring fans. Except for Nancy, Winty, and Monahan, all racers and spectators ran toward Pritchard.

Hank returned the borrowed Harley to Winty, who was crying. Before Hank could explain he had nothing to do with the brutal wipeout, Winty jumped onto the bike, gave a look he couldn't interpret, and left in an explosion of dust.

Brax rode to Hank. "Hey, where's everyone going?"

"You might have killed Pritchard." Hank saw several competitors helping the boy to his feet. "Looks like he's got only cuts and bruises … no broken bones."

Brax guffawed. "Bet he'll be tweezing plenty of branches and leaves out of his butt."

Nancy hugged Brax, but said, "Poor Jody."

"He asked for it. Say, you weren't too bad yourself, good-buddy." Brax lit a cigar, motioned for Nancy to sit beside him in the passenger seat of her truck, and threw Hank a set of keys. "Y'all take care of my bike."

Monahan frowned at Brax. "He's got a great killer instinct."

"Sure, Brax won't let anything stand in his way."

"He'll never believe you won the race, Hank."

Hank mounted Brax's Harley. "Let's get of here."

Monahan sat behind Hank. "Where to?"

"Where I should have gone in the first place today."

Hank headed toward McCabe's airfield. He needed to get up alone into the purity of the sky and sort out how best to deal with Brax's ruthless behavior, all over a transient roll in the hay with a faithless female. Hank's good humor returned when he imagined all the ironing Miller would be doing on their dusty uniforms after they returned to Randolph.

***

Hank saw it coming before anyone else. As Monahan began a take-off roll in a PT-13, a West Point second lieutenant student-officer in a PT-11 misread the landing tee and came in ninety degrees off-wind. Monahan forced the PT-13 into the air to avoid the PT-11. It responded barely above stalling speed and mushed tail-low toward the other plane. The PT-13 lacked enough power to take Monahan high enough in time. Its landing gear caught the top wing of the PT-11, much like a person tripping over unseen wire. The nose of Monahan's trainer flipped down, the propeller dug into the ground, and the PT-13 burst into flames. The student-officer continued the landing roll, taxied to a stop, and waited for further instructions.

Hank led the charge of classmates and instructors to the burning PT-13. Disregarding the danger, he pulled Monahan from the cockpit and rolled his roommate in the dirt until the last flame was out. Ignoring the stench of cooked human flesh, Hank cradled Monahan's charred remains.

Kilrain kneeled beside Hank. "I know it's rough, Milroy, but get used to it. You're going to do more than fly. You'll command men. I wrote plenty of letters to families of boys killed in my squadron. Good men, all of them. Like Monahan here. Looks like his neck snapped on impact. At least he never felt any pain."

"Do you ever get used to it, sir?"

"Some extra advice, Milroy. Have buddies you can rely on in combat, to drink and carouse with between sorties, but don't get too close to them. When things like this happen, it'll wrench out your guts."

***

That night Hank wrote a letter to Monahan's parent's. Brax paced the floor and reflew every second of their roommate's fatal take-off.

"You know, Hank, it's tough about Monahan. Still, I'm pretty sure if I'd been in his trainer, I'd have avoided that PT-11."

Hank said nothing. Brax could be damn unconscionable and callous.

Miller had yet to solo. "What would you have done, Brax?"

"I'd have made sure that Yankee got fried instead of me. What's the matter with those West Pointers?"

Brax's last comment underscored something that had bothered Hank ever since he learned their pampered classmates would be quartered some distance from the cadet barracks; as if to avoid contamination by the "peasants." A few turned out to be regular guys; but the majority of the West Pointers acted as if they were superior beings.

"That's the greatest inequality of our training program, Brax. When a regular cadet fails to meet Air Corps standards, he's washed-out. Unlike the cadets, those student-officers from West Point are commissioned second lieutenants. They're given extra chances because the higher-ups are determined to get more regular army officers into the Air Corps at any price."

"But what happened today ought to finish him."

Hank sealed the envelope destined for Mr. and Mrs. Monahan. "No way. He's already been reinstated."

Brax faced Hank. "The way Monahan got fried and his face melted, he'd have been one ugly mess if he'd lived. And in pain the rest of his miserable life. Hank, old-buddy, if we ever serve together and I survive a crash but end up burned like Monahan, or paralyzed like a vegetable, promise me you'll pull out your sidearm and put me out of my misery."

"It'll never come to that, friend-o. You're the star of your own movie."

"Promise me."

"Sure, Brax."

Miller peered into an open locker. "What'll we do with Monahan's things?"

Hank also looked at its contents. "In the Great War, pilots divvied the personal items of a buddy who'd bought it, but we should send them to his parents."

Brax rummaged through Monahan's effects. "Maybe there's a little black book I can use if I ever get out to Californy."

***

Before the four months of A Stage came to a close, more crashes followed, with one other fatality. A different student-officer landed his trainer on top of a plane and killed the cadet in the cockpit with the propeller. As predicted, half the class washed-out. Ninety men survived to go on to B Stage, Hank and Brax among them.

Last in the class to solo, Miller had watched, copied, and learned from Hank, Brax, and Monahan. During the preceding weeks, Hank discovered another quality that would stand Miller well if he made it into the USAAC. An amiable, puppy-like aggressiveness caused people in high places to like him. He helped several officers' wives with their groceries, walked their dogs, and sat in for games of bridge.

After the Recognition Day parade and ceremonies, Hank and Brax groomed themselves for a big afternoon and night on the town. The Texan had two hot dates lined up and was open to anything else he could find in between. Hank won big at the last two poker sessions and planned to spend the winnings flying one of Roy McCabe's planes.

A pilot-instructor's wife arranged a blind date for Miller with the daughter of a regular Army Air Corps Major. Hank now believed Miller might go farther than any of them in the USAAC.

Brax interrupted Hank's musings. "Good-buddy, the worst is over. B Stage is going to be a turkey-shoot."

"Don't count on it. Flying in B Stage is also going to be more exacting."

"Why?"

"Because now we'll be taught formation flying, night flying, cross-country, and instrument flying, under-the-hood."

"What's that?" Miller asked.

"We sit blind in the back seat of a BT-9 with an instructor in the front seat. Then there's also the Link Trainer to simulate instrument flying." He anticipated Miller's next question. "The Link is a training device that never leaves the ground."

"No worries," Brax said. "We'll be in Pursuit at Kelly Field, and then second lieutenant pursuiters. Hot damn, boy." He slapped Hank's back. "With me as leader and you as wingman. I'll lead. You follow. We'll tear 'em apart. I'm going to be the top ace in the next war, and erase Rickenbacker's record of twenty-six kills."

Hank did not get a chance to set Brax straight about who was going to lead whom. Cadet Captain Chilton and Squad Leader Ashley entered their room and barked, "Attention!"

The three cadets froze. Chilton and Ashley turned to the empty bunk Monahan had occupied, saluted, and faced the survivors. Chilton gave them at-ease. "Gentlemen, we lost a mighty good man there, but life goes on."

Hank shook hands with Chilton. "I think it's great you made it to Pursuit at Kelly."

Brax also shook hands. "I envy y'all becoming fighter pilots already. Suhs."

Ashley shook his head. "Not all of us. I have to settle for Bombers."

That horrifying possibility dampened the cadets' festive mood until Miller asked, "Is it true there's no more hazing?"

"Now it's your turn to harass the new Dodos," Chilton said. "I hope you'll approach hazing as we all did. There was nothing personal during the four months I dished it out."

Brax looked forward to charging into the new cadets with upper class rank insignia worn on his sleeves: black mohair chevrons on slate blue backing to indicate ranks from cadet corporal to captain.

Hank worried hazing might take valuable time away from academics, even though he needed to have experience in leadership, which included giving orders, commands, and instructions. He thought about Brax's comment about the next war. Did the Germans and Japanese have similar training methods?

# Chapter 4
## Karl

Karl, Fürst zu Pfalz von Teuffelreich, had been granted a rare weekend pass to celebrate Der Führer's bloodless triumph at Munich on the previous Monday, 29 September, 1938, and the Wehrmacht's occupation of the Sudetenland two days later.

Wearing a Luftwaffe cadet's uniform, Karl froze when he saw Uncle Leopold, Graf von Osterwald, seated at a desk in the study at the family's Berlin mansion.

*This is no longer my home.*

Poldi had become Karl's legal guardian three years earlier, after Prince Friedrich and his brother Wilhelm died in a crash on a narrow Alpine road. Poldi was different from Karl's beloved father in every respect. Friedrich's contemporaries had referred to their "Fritz" as the Bohemian Prince, not in the geographic sense, but because he preferred the company of people in the arts, including talented Jews, and was himself a respected lyrical poet.

Without consulting Karl, Poldi had purged the library of all Jewish, Bolshevik, and other literature decreed by Goebbels to be decadent, Jewish, or anti-Nazi. He decimated Prince Friedrich's extensive music collection for the same reasons.

Karl resented his uncle for living instead of his mother, Poldi's twin, who had died ten years earlier of ovarian cancer. From earliest memory, he had been put off by the slight of build, over-cologned uncle with his mother's features. An instinctive child's dislike developed into contempt after Poldi joined the Nazi Party, associated with commoners, and became an officer in the black-uniformed Schutzstaffel, the dreaded SS. Now he had made the Pfalz-Teuffelreich mansion his Berlin base of operations.

Poldi interrupted Karl's private thoughts. "I am delighted you have matured physically, but I have reservations about your emotional growth and judgment. I am receiving too many reports of your blatant arrogance toward classmates and instructors not of your caste. I am concerned about your lack of reverence for our Führer."

"So, you have set spies on me."

"Not spies. Eyes and ears. Karl, you are the last Pfalz-Teuffelreich male, my dear sister's son. My sole heir as well. Your person and interests must be protected."

"My interests? You and your Nazis have militarized the proletariat and the peasants. They make war against their political enemies and the racially inferior. They thrive on bloodlust and power. After the Bolsheviks and the Jews, the anti-Nazi clergy and the Gypsies, the deformed and the demented, do not be surprised if Der Führer will next populate the concentration camps with fürsts, grafs, and vons."

"Use your head. Am I not a Graf myself?"

"A red Graf in a Nazi uniform."

"Karl, those workers and peasants are members of our Master Race, pure Aryans, our splendid blond beasts, who will conquer the world and purge it of mongrels."

"Please, spare me your party line drivel, Uncle. I also have read my Nietzsche, the volume in my father's library you purged, not the doctored version we get in school. One does not become an Übermensch by accident of German birth. No foaled farm boy, slum dweller, or mealy-mouthed clerk shall ever be my equal. I am geboren, superior to them through heredity and by my own will, not by decree of any führer. Am I not outstanding at my studies and first in my cadet class? Am I not certain to represent Germany in sabre and épée at the Helsinki Olympics in 1940? Do not equate me with swinish, vulgar commoners."

"Karl, you will do well to keep those ideas to yourself. Better yet, discard them. I will recite some names for you. Adolf Hitler. Josef Goebbels. Heinrich Himmler. Shall I continue?"

"What is your point, Uncle?"

"Where are our brother aristos and princes among our Reich's leaders? What happened to your father's fantasy of a constitutional monarchy? Our Führer told the Crown Prince he will never permit a restoration of the Hohenzollern monarchy. We dare not mention the old Kaiser who now resides in Holland. Face one fact. Low born they may be, the Nazis hold absolute power in Germany today."

"I remember conversations when you and your pompous friends boasted how the aristos and industrialists would use the Austrian peasant as your cats' paws to take power. Hitler outfoxed you."

"A reality I have understood and accepted for some time."

"Yes, your Nazis control Germany, but don't you see the irony? If the communists had won the elections in 1932, those same *pure* Aryan farmers and mechanics would be wearing red armbands and marching down Tiergartenstrasse singing the Internationale under the hammer and sickle. And they'd be after our aristocratic throats as if we were no different from Jews. Tell me, Uncle. How much time do we have before they come after us?"

Poldi's expression hardened. "If you behave, the respite will be longer than if you do not. We cannot predict how long the Fürst zu Pfalz von Teuffelreich will have immunity."

"And a Graf von Osterwald?"

"Longer than certain other aristos at the top of our enemies list."

Karl caught Poldi's meaning. His best friends' fathers supported a clandestine visit to England by emissaries of an opposition group. From what Karl pieced together, the anti-Nazi Germans pleaded with the British Prime Minister not to give in to Hitler's demands at Munich. Had Neville Chamberlain held firm, Der Führer might have lost enough popularity at home for a coup against him and his Nazis to succeed.

"Now then, Karl, listen to me. We have new neighbors who confiscated that Jew estate across the street. Hermann Bauer is Number Four in the Gestapo. I have invited the Bauers and others of high rank in our Reich for a banquet tomorrow evening for the specific purpose of meeting you."

"I refuse to sup with commoners."

"It is for your own good. In any case, I have promised your participation."

"Hear me, Uncle. You will never again commit me to anything in advance of obtaining my consent."

"I had no choice. The Party has been applying pressure."

"Mein Gott, you do fear your own Nazis. Tell me, with what did they threaten you?"

"They did not threaten me, Karl. The Party favors those who cooperate. It punishes those who do not. Undoubtedly, they will allow athletes to compete in the next Olympics only if they are obedient and loyal to our Führer."

"So, I must appear at Party functions or forget the Olympics."

"And behave with absolute political correctness if you hope to fly in the Luftwaffe."

That last threat silenced Karl.

"It will not be so unpleasant. The Party leaders will be accompanied by their families. In our new Germany, you would be wise to court and marry one of their healthy nubile daughters. With your perfect Aryan blond looks and blue eyes you can choose ...."

"Choose among a litter of peasant sows? Impossible. You go too far. The best you can expect from me tomorrow will be formal politeness, unless I am provoked."

***

That afternoon Karl's mood improved when he met his dearest friends at a crowded café on festooned Tiergartenstrasse. Bruno von Strachwitz, Karl's taller and older anglophile cousin, worked in the Abwehr, German intelligence. Oberleutnant Albert von Wittelsberg was a lean and tanned Panzer officer. Albert's ursine younger brother Gerd had been Karl's classmate and member of his dueling fraternity at the university. So had Walti von Frankenthal, another classmate taller than Bruno.

They sat at an outdoor table and admired the better class of women seated at adjacent tables and promenading along the crowded boulevard in their stylish autumnal best. When a waiter poured the wine Karl ordered, a Schloss Teuffelreich Spätlese '36 from one of the family estates on the Moselle, Bruno raised the glass to admire its straw color before they toasted each other and drank.

"An excellent vintage, Karl."

"Speaking of vintages," Gerd said, "this year will go down in history as one of Germany's greatest. Our Anschluss, the union with Austria, was something Bismarck failed to accomplish, and we have acquired the Sudetenland without a shot being fired."

Walti offered another toast. "To the rest of 1938. May this year continue to be productive for our beloved Fatherland."

"It well may be," Bruno said. "There is talk of recovering Danzig and taking back the Corridor from Poland. Have you heard anything from the military side of things, Albert?"

"One hears all kinds of rumors these days."

Karl savored the wine, elegant and refined with a subtle suggestion of spritz. "Does the Abwehr believe the English will let us have all that?"

Bruno dabbed his moist blond mustache with a napkin. "The Sudetenland, Danzig, and the Polish Corridor are peopled by Germans. The British will not fight because their Prime Minister,Chamberlain says Czechoslovakia is not a top-drawer country."

Karl had complicated blood relationships with the House of Windsor, formerly Saxe-Coburg-Gotha, and was well acquainted with the royal and noble British mentality. "The Englanders can become idealistic and emotional. Keeping their word is a point of honor. Remember Belgium and scraps of paper? And last May the English began to mobilize when they believed we were going to invade Czechoslovakia."

"You have well described the Anglo-Saxon fascination with honor," Albert said. "However, there is a generous spirit of revisionism among our former enemies. They are willing to allow us to reverse the iniquities of the Diktat imposed at Versailles in 1919 because they fear the Soviets more than a resurgent Germany. I am convinced the British will not fight for the Czechs or Danzig. It is possible Herr Hitler can get them to think twice before they object to anything we might do regarding Czechia and the Poles."

"You may be right, Albert," Bruno said. "Most amazing, the students at Oxford voted in a significant majority never to fight again for England, even if attacked."

The Panzer officer snorted. "And the French dare not act without the British, whom they hate more than us. On the other hand, I expect the Poles will fight. Their excessive romanticism blinds them to brutal reality. Are they not supposed to have the best cavalry in Europe? How I would like to see them mount a charge against our Panzers."

Bruno spoke over their laughter. "They may yet do so. Colonel Beck, the Polish Foreign Minister, promised, *if the Germans give my country any trouble, our cavalry will charge into Berlin with our sabers.*"

"When the Poles rattle sabers, they really mean sabers," Alfred said, which brought on more laughter.

"Perhaps we should forget about the Poles and leave the east to the Slavs," Walti said. "But then, will the Slav be content to stay in the East?"

Gerd patted his ample belly. "If war does come, I know I won't be able to fit into one of my brother's tanks. I'll go into the navy. A battleship ought to be big enough to hold me."

Walti laughed at the image. "You'd capsize any ship they'd be foolish enough to let you board."

"Walti, you're so tall, you'll be an easy target no matter where you go. Now tell us, Karl, how is your training going? Have you flown yet?"

"No, and I will not until I transfer to Berlin-Gatow in November for Basic Flight Training."

"Then what have you been doing since June?"

"Gerd, one would think I joined the infantry. I never thought we would have to suffer through Prussian close order drill and manual of arms. Their idiotic goose-stepping has damn near given me shin splints. The academics have been tolerable; I enjoy my studies in History of Aviation, Theory of Flight, Aeronautical Engineering, Design, Construction, Aeronautical Engineering, Strength of Materials, Aerodynamics, and Meteorology."

"A full plate," Bruno said.

"Regrettably, the Nazis have ensured the Luftwaffe will no longer be an elite dominated by vons. Through its Hitler Youth, the Party has given all boys a chance to fly in a glider program, regardless of social station, to stimulate an interest in flying. And so, I must live among commoners. I cannot tell you how appalled I am to be taking orders from lowborn louts because of the classless spirit infesting the Third Reich. Nor do I look forward to commanding them."

"A necessary evil," Albert commiserated.

"As a fighter pilot, I can still become a knightly lone-wolf ace in the next war like my father."

Bruno opened a crested cigarette case and offered his friends English Ovals. "Speaking of family, Karl, has your uncle left yet for the Sudetenland?"

"An hour ago. All of you should know this. He demanded I sever all relations with you and your families, and he deliberately dropped the von each time he mentioned your names. Of course I refused."

Bruno tensed. "Did he say why?"

"The usual reports of disrespectful, near treasonous utterances. Of course I told Poldi he must never dictate to me who should be my friends. He had the gall to suggest I select a wife from among the daughters of low born Nazi Party members."

"I didn't know your uncle was a democrat," Bruno said.

Karl sneered at the absurd image. "Poldi wants me to attend a dinner tomorrow for our new neighbor, a high muckety-muck in the Gestapo, who is supposed to have a healthy, nubile daughter. Their family name is Bauer. *Bauerin*! Can you imagine farmers dining with me as equals?"

"The Nazis hope to marry off all their spawn to aristos and legitimize their bastard regime," Gerd said. "Still, she might be worth an hour between the sheets. I can already hear Fraulein Bauer commanding you to perform or face a Gestapo cell."

Karl did not have to remind his friends how much he enjoyed cavorting among the extensive herd of females available throughout Europe the past two years: American debutantes hunting for titles, actresses, ballerinas, promiscuous daughters of aristos, and a lusty servant girl on occasion. "I have plenty of time to select a wife."

Albert lit Gerd's cigarette. "Perhaps, Karl, but our father says that as the last surviving male of your line you do have an obligation to produce an heir."

"I have a temporary solution," Bruno said. "Why not pretend to settle on one girl and nip in the bud any ideas your uncle might have about gifting you with Gestapo in-laws?"

"If I could find someone among the acceptable young ladies to hold my interest beyond a few minutes I might take your advice."

"Perhaps you will meet a beautiful femme fatale, with the right pedigree of course, at my sister's engagement reception this evening," Walti said.

"Uta marrying? Wonderful. I didn't know. Who is he?"

"Grand Duke Pavel Romanov."

"The Grand Duke is old enough to be Uta's grandfather. "Why would she wed old Pavel?"

"My sister panicked, Karl. Uta's no beauty, you know. After she reached age thirty, she believed no man would ever ask her to marry. Now she'll be a Grand Duchess, with greater ambitions. My future brother-in-law is an ardent Nazi sympathizer and worships our Führer more than God. So does Uta. Women. They get so emotional about Der Führer. Uta believes everything our leader says. She expects one day to be Empress of all the Russias when the Grand Duke is made Tzar by our Wehrmacht."

"She would not be the first German girl to boss those muzhiks. But why would an elderly Grand Duke marry your sister? Yours is not a hereditary ruling house like mine."

"Money. All those Russian royals think about is money."

Gerd patted his enormous stomach. "It must be near impossible to wean oneself away from caviar."

A stylish brunette passed their table and mouthed a silent thank you at Bruno before hurrying away.

Bruno nodded with the appreciation of a connoisseur. "Such elegance and grace."

Gerd agreed. "Who is she, your secret love?"

Bruno's expression turned Basset-miserable. "She was until the Nuremberg Laws. It has taken my father and I since then to arrange visas for Lisa and her family. They leave for Hamburg tomorrow, then on to the Dominican Republic."

Karl thought himself fortunate not to be involved with a Jewess like Bruno and other aristos he knew. When Hitler became Chancellor, Karl's father anticipated what the Nazis intended for the Jews and arranged for his longtime mistress, actress Mitzi Landau, to emigrate for the United

States. Now she was a star in Hollywood. No Jew, no commoner; Karl vowed he would marry a royal or no one.

# Chapter 5
## Mariya-Xenia

Karl stood with Albert and Gerd at the entrance to the von Frankenthals' crowded reception hall. Most of the men were in uniform. Those in white ties and tuxedos wore glittering medals, orders, and bright sashes. Their women flaunted jewels and wore stylish formal gowns. An orchestra played trite, Party-approved Strauss waltzes.

Karl recognized many generals, admirals, and diplomats. Bruno, Gerd's father and other aristos, whom Poldi mentioned as disloyal to the Führer, conferred in a corner with Admiral Canaris, head of the Abwehr.

The friends took glasses of champagne from a tray held by a servant and mingled. Karl exchanged light conversation with several young ladies he thought to be beyond boring, damn near anesthetizing with their persistent gossip, catty remarks, and talk of shopping excursions. Then he saw among the von Frankenthals and their guests a tall, elegant ash blonde.

At the reception line, the von Frankenthals introduced Karl to the Russians, each of whom wore swastika armbands. Grand Duke Pavel was in the middle of a publicized battle against other Russian royals to be declared head of the Romanov family, pretender to the throne, and heir to the enormous Tzarist wealth scattered among banks throughout the world. Karl thought the slight, white bearded old man regarded him with unwarranted arrogance and condescension. Pavel had no money and no country.

Karl forgot about the Grand Duke when Walti introduced the ash blonde. She stood in a white silk brocade gown as if she were a fashion magazine model. For the first time, Karl did not mind standing with a girl several inches taller.

"You are one of the few younger men I have met during my visit."

She had no noticeable Russian accent, and Karl admired the young woman's poise and confidence. "There was too much commotion for me to hear your name when we were introduced."

"I am Mariya-Xenia Dimitryevna Narishkyn. My friends call me Zizi."

"If you do not mind, I prefer to address you as Mariya-Xenia."

"I do not mind, but may I ask why?"

"Zizi is a name better suited for a small soubrette, not for a tall, elegant blonde."

"And how are you called? I couldn't hear your name either."

"Karl, Fürst zu Pfalz von Teuffelreich." He offered Mariya-Xenia a cigarette from a crested gold case. "And you are from?"

"Estonia."

Karl was familiar with the background of émigrés like Mariya-Xenia. After the Bolshevik Revolution, hordes of Russians had relocated to Europe, but they were not brutish Slavic and mongoloid degenerates dreaded by all Germans.

It had been a "white" invasion of royals and aristos, more of German blood than Russian. Some, like Grand Duke Pavel, embraced the Nazi party from the start; and those with money financed Hitler during the early days of the Party with the expectation he would return them to power after Germany invaded the USSR and defeated the Bolsheviks. Cossack General Krasnov and other former Tzarist officers volunteered to form fighting units made up of White Russians ready to aid the Reich on the day Hitler carried out his ambitious plan to conquer the Heartland, as described in *Mein Kampf.*

Russian aristos wandered all over Europe as guests of this relative or that, from season to season, year after year. Others remained in the east and settled at their estates and homes in the new Baltic States of Estonia, Latvia, and Lithuania, former Russian possessions. After the recent Munich Conference, rumors circulated about a German rapprochement with the USSR, and a division of Eastern Europe between Hitler and Stalin. The anti-communist Russians living in the Baltic States feared for their lives in the foreseeable Soviet annexation. Consequently, many with exalted titles sought sanctuary within the Reich.

"Mariya-Xenia, are you a princess, grand duchess, or countess?"

"Princess." She accepted Karl's offer of a cigarette, placed it in a long holder, and waited for a light. "Ovals. You must admire things British."

"Rather." Karl was delighted to have someone with whom to practice. "Where did you learn to speak such flawless English?"

"School, my travels. I have a knack for picking up languages. I am fluent in Russian, German, French, Italian, Finnish, and Swedish. Balt too." Mariya-Xenia took Karl's arm. "I believe we are cousins."

"Are you sure? I recall no Narishkyn among our genealogical charts."

"When was the last time you saw them?"

"It has been years."

Mariya-Xenia led Karl into the von Frankenthals' library. "I'm sure there's an *Almanack* here somewhere."

Karl watched the regal blonde search along the shelves. He admired her form and line and the way she moved with the airy grace of a ballerina. Karl analyzed his feelings toward Mariya-Xenia. Instant attraction. Lust. If love came later, so be it. He could do much worse than Mariya-Xenia, likely no better. She would be the perfect female to prevent Poldi from forcing a Gestapo peasant's sow on him.

Mariya-Xenia lifted a heavy gold-embossed volume and placed it on a table. Karl recognized the *Almanack*, which traced and certified the lineage of royal and noble families. The Pfalz-Teuffelreich pedigree went back to tribal kings and Roman senators. He was a hereditary prince of the Uradel, the ancient aristocracy whose rank and titles predated the thirteenth century; he counted among his forebears Crusaders and Teutonic Knights who had Christianized the pagan Slavs.

Mariya-Xenia opened the *Almanack*. "I shall now prove we are indeed related."

Karl savoured Mariya-Xenia's delicious fragrance and watched her turn the pages. "I hope not too closely."

"Jolly good. I can tell you how we are cousins. Your paternal great-grandmother's sister married a Hesse-am-Rhine Grand Duke. One of their daughters married my maternal grandfather. And in the eighteenth-century, another of my maternal antecedents married a younger son of the house of Teuffelreich-Durkheim."

Karl and Mariya-Xenia continued to review their extensive pedigrees and laughed each time they touched as cousins. She would be the perfect match, and he saw no obstacles to winning her family's consent to marriage. They had little money, and she needed the protection of nationality. Mariya-Xenia was stateless, her family no longer Russian subjects of the Tzar, nor had they become citizens of the USSR or Estonia, that fragile new nation bordering the voracious Soviet Union.

Another plus from Poldi's point of view, Mariya-Xenia's father, older brother, great-uncle Grand Duke Pavel, and two other uncles were active Nazi sympathizers. But what were Mariya-Xenia's politics, if she had any?

Mariya-Xenia found in the *Almanack* other aristo and royal cousins who had played host to her family during extended visits in the west. "We live as blue-blooded gypsies. The older Russians have no marketable skills. My generation is about to come into its own, but we must make our own careers or professions if we wish to thrive."

*Or marry well.* "And what will you do, Mariya-Xenia?"

"If I had money, I would study to become a teacher of languages at a respected university. I know I can get work as a translator, but in a war, I would rather be a nurse."

"That is admirable."

"I am curious about something, Karl. If war comes, for which side will you fight?"

"Why do you ask such a question? Is it because I'm not wearing a swastika?"

"No, you are of the Blue Internationale, as I am. Doesn't dynastic self-preservation come before loyalty to any nation? I have cousins in the armies of Germany, France, and Great Britain, and another who would serve with the Americans, should they become involved in another European war. If you are typical, you must own property and estates throughout Europe. Which will you fight to protect?"

"I am a German prince. Both my grandfathers stood with Bismarck and Wilhelm I of Prussia in the Hall of Mirrors at the Palace of Versailles when the German Empire was proclaimed atop the corpse of a defeated France. My father flew in the Great War and had 49 Luftsiegen."

Mariya-Xenia took Karl's hand. He did not let on how much her touch excited him.

"Be careful, Karl. You may end up fighting not for Germany but for Hitler. I love Russia, but I would never fight for Stalin."

"For which nation would you fight if you were a man?"

"I think that will be decided for me wherever I am living when war begins. To be honest, I prefer it not be Germany."

Karl lit another Oval for Maria-Xenia. "How do you come to have political views so different from your family?"

"I suppose it is because I am better educated. I would not presume to say I am more intelligent."

Karl had never discussed politics with any female, and he felt awkward doing so with Mariya-Xenia. She was indeed intelligent. "Perhaps there will be no war."

"Then what will you do? We aristocrats no longer rule, and we are becoming less decorative. The masses prefer the royalty of cinema stars. Will you spend your life hunting, caring for your estates, going to endless rounds of parties?"

Karl understood Mariya-Xenia was testing him. "I shall fly and produce the greatest German wines." Karl came to a decision. Mariya-Xenia would be the perfect consort to help oversee the Pfalz-Teuffelreich domains and breed sturdy heirs. "Mariya-Xenia, tomorrow, will you attend a dinner party as my hostess?"

"Thank you, Karl. I am honored."

Still alone in the library, he embraced Mariya-Xenia. Or was it she who had been the aggressor?

# Chapter 6
## Seth

On a windy January Saturday morning in 1939 at a private South San Francisco airfield, Seth approached a Jenny for another lesson, but Coach DeLuca guided him to a different plane. "No, kid, not the Jenny." He walked Seth to his Spad XIII. "I want you to solo first in my bird. Show me what you can do."

Seth didn't need to be told twice. He adjusted his goggles and worn leather helmet, stuck the wad of gum he'd been chewing next to the Hat-in-the-Ring Squadron logo on the camouflaged canvas fuselage, mounted the Spad, and thanked DeLuca for letting him fly the precious Great War relic. At five-ten and two hundred and five muscular pounds, Seth hoped the modern fighters being developed had more room, otherwise he might be deemed too big to fly one; DeLuca was around five-six.

In the cockpit, Seth checked the joystick, ailerons, and rudders. After the 220 hp Hispano-Suiza engine turned and DeLuca removed the wheel chocks, he began the take-off roll and lifted the venerable biplane off the runway. The Spad climbed for altitude, and he gaped at the spectacular aerial view of San Francisco and the Bay below.

Much had changed since Seth's first flight in the Trusty at Chrissy Field with Lt. Kilrain back in 1928. A vermilion bridge now spanned the Golden Gate and had become the great identifiable symbol of the city. A longer grey bridge connected San Francisco to Oakland, and off its middle next to Yerba Buena Island, a sliver of land had been reclaimed for a World's Fair scheduled to open next month. Alcatraz lay below, unmoving amidst the choppy water, surrounded by sailboats and ferries still traveling back and forth across the bay between San Francisco, Sausalito, and Oakland.

At ten-to-fifteen thousand feet, Seth flew the Spad through Immelmanns, chandelles, and other aerial acrobatics DeLuca had taught him over the years. He imagined what it must have been like flying with the Coach and Rickenbacker and dogfighting against Luftwaffe aces. He'd soon find out.

A bright red Fokker DrI Triplane came into view a few thousand feet below and unaware of the Spad. A trophy from von Richthofen's famous Flying Circus, the German pursuiter was a permanent fixture at the airfield. Like DeLuca, its owner, whom he'd met through the coach, was a veteran ace of the Great War.

Seth recalled a fighter pilot maxim DeLuca had drummed into him: when flying a slow, sharp-turning plane against a faster enemy, draw your foe into a turning dogfight. When flying a fast plane against a slower adversary, keep the speed as high as possible and hit-and-run. Never stay and fight.

Seth took the Spad to fifteen thousand feet and flew a position on the perch. He dove at the red triplane from the above-and-behind position until he was several hundred feet from his prey at a Great War speed of about 125 mph and leveled into a blind spot behind its tail. Seth's competitive juices surged when he had the other plane in his sights and scored a mock aerial victory. When he flew alongside the Fokker, its pilot acknowledged Seth's victory with a gracious salute.

Seth peeled away for a descent to the airfield and made a bouncy but competent touch down. After the last rev died, he leaped from the cockpit and pulled off his helmet and goggles when he met DeLuca at the hard stand.

"A great hit-and-run bounce, kid, but I thought you'd have preferred the romantic challenge of a classic dogfight."

"I had to use the element of surprise. He's an ace like you."

"Good thinking." DeLuca pointed at one of the monoplanes nearby. "Now it's time you earn your pilot's license and fly one of those modern crates."

"School and athletics take up most of my time. I'm lucky to get away when I can."

"Well, I know one thing. You're a natural born pursuiter. I saw it back in 1928, the day of our excursion to Chrissy Field."

"I'll never forget it, Coach, and thanks again for letting me take up your bird today."

"Any time, kid."

At the ops shack, Seth bought a coke. DeLuca took a pint of I.W. Harper from his jacket and swallowed a belt of the bourbon. "It's always good to get away from the women."

DeLuca's profile reminded Seth of those Renaissance condottieri he'd seen illustrated in history books. Andy had no sons. Three of DeLuca's daughters had married, and the youngest still lived at home. This morning Carla had given Seth a big hug and wet kiss. The nubile thirteen-year-old made no secret of her crush.

"My Carla, she's already driving the boys crazy. Me too, with worry, but enough of my problems. I want to speak to you about the coming war."

Like all young men who followed the news, Seth did not doubt a major war loomed on the horizon, and the History courses he took at Cal gave him a broad perspective on international relations. "I'd love to see Hitler and all those Nazi bastards get theirs, but I don't think the British and the French will defend Danzig or what's left of Czechoslovakia."

"Maybe they will. They fought heroically in The Great War. I saw it. I was there."

"Sure, but now they want a strong Germany to fill the power vacuum in central Europe, to stop Soviet-backed bolshevism from spreading. The British and the French let Hitler rearm Germany, remilitarize the Rhineland, annex Austria in violation of the Versailles Treaty, and the Sudetenland too with the great Skoda munitions factories. They'll let Hitler gobble up the rest of Czechoslovakia any time he wants."

Seth heard himself lecturing but was so wound up he couldn't stop. "As for the French, at the beginning of the Spanish Civil War in 1936, they had a leftist coalition Popular Front Government, the same as the Spanish Republic, yet they did nothing to help their neighbor."

"I knew a different France," DeLuca said. "I remember the French spirit during the Battle of Verdun in 1916 and their cry: 'They shall not pass.' It's a bleak world situation, and you've got to make contingency plans."

Seth simulated a dogfight with his hands. "If war comes, I'll fly pursuiters, like you. My mock victory today has made me hungry for the real thing."

"Whatever you do, stay away from the infantry, armor, or anything else on the ground. Trench warfare is all muck and blood. You get a different combat perspective up in the purity of the skies. There a guy can feel clean, detached from the violence below."

# Chapter 7

## Gershwin Lady

First Sunday morning in June 1939 at the San Francisco Marina, Seth finished spar varnishing the top step in the family's 23 foot sloop. The thermometer indicated a deceptive 65F. The chill wind made it feel like 40 and the Bay too rough for a pleasant solo sail to Sausalito.

The deteriorating situations in Europe and China weighed on Seth's mind. The victors who drew the map of Eastern Europe after the Great War amalgamated mutually hostile ethnic peoples into new nations. Now greedy Hungary and Poland joined Hitler in partitioning out of existence Czechoslovakia, instead of allying with their neighbor against the Nazi menace. They believed Hitler would not invade Poland, or if he did, that the Poles could defeat the Wehrmacht.

In Asia an inevitable showdown with Japan loomed closer on the horizon. Unable to affect the course of world affairs, Seth considered a more immediate challenge over which he had some control.

Girls. Interchangeable and predictable girls, some beautiful, many pretty, all of them potential decent wives and mothers, whom Seth dated or knew in high school and now at Cal. No matter which one he might woo and wed, Seth saw the rest of his life flashing before him: weekly dinners with family, in-laws, and identical couples watching the years go by in a succession of births, marriages, football seasons, and Friday night poker games with friends in the same circumstance.

Okay, he'd lived that life to its conclusion in his mind, but Seth wanted more. More included adventure, and the unpredictable, and romance with someone unlike all the girls he knew and had known. Most of all, more meant flying.

Seth locked the varnish and brush in a storage bin on deck, zipped his heavy blue and gold trimmed Cal Jacket to the neck, and stepped onto the windswept dock. He looked toward the family home on Bay Street across from the Palace of Fine Arts. The Marina District had been built on the site of the 1915 Panama-Pacific International Exposition that celebrated the rebirth of the City nine years after the great earthquake and fire of 1906, and the PFA remained the one surviving structure.

Seth's parents and younger siblings had gone to the World's Fair on Treasure Island, and he'd decided to stay home instead and study in the afternoon for finals week at Cal. On instinct Seth looked toward the Bay, and he saw a girl at the far end of the dock, back to him, hair metallic bronze under the sun falling in ringlets to the shoulders of a plain sleeveless coral linen dress clinging to her curvaceous body.

When Seth took a first step toward the girl, she turned at the same time and flashed a fetching smile more brilliant than the sun. They closed the distance between them. Never shy with the ladies, he introduced himself. "I'm Seth Braham. I saw you standing in the sun."

She fixed her eyes for a moment at the Cal logo on his jacket. "Hello, College Boy. I'm Miriam Keramopoulos."

"You're chilled." He unzipped his jacket and wrapped it around Miriam's shoulders. She didn't resist. "You must be from out of town. You aren't dressed for the weather."

"I didn't expect it to be this cold on so bright a day. It's June. Almost summer."

"As Mark Twain supposedly said, 'The coldest winter I ever spent was a summer in San Francisco.' Where are you from?"

"Brooklyn, College Boy."

"But no accent."

"And I never lived on toid and tirty-toid street where they berl ersters in oil. I learned how to speak better by watching movies."

"Are you and your family in town to see the World's Fair?"

"No. Why are you staring at me like that, College Boy?

"Because you like me as much as ...."

"I like you after only a minute? What makes you think that?"

"You call me College Boy. You're teasing, mocking me, not brushing me off. A good sign."

"Well, maybe you are different from most college boys who think they're superior to girls who work and can go all the way with them. I'll put you on probation for now. But tell me. Why do you look at me like that?"

"Difficult to explain. Standing here with you, I hear George Gershwin, minor key stuff. I see you as a Gershwin Lady. And if you are, oh, lady be good to me."

"The lyric is Ira's, but that *is* an original line. Odd you said that, though. I do sing Gershwin. I had a gig with a combo that ended last night."

"You're a singer? Damn, I'd have gone to see you."

"They wouldn't have let you in without a fake ID. The club has strict rules about its patrons having to be twenty-one or older."

"You don't look twenty-one either."

"I'm sixteen, but with makeup, the right clothes and attitude, no one bothers to ask."

*Only sixteen.*

Seth had assumed Miriam might be around his age, give or take a year. Across the Bay lay a famous prison. Miriam was San Quentin quail, underage jailbait. It didn't matter.

Seth checked his watch. "Have you tried abalone?"

"Everyone knows what baloney is."

"No, abalone. It's seafood. You'll have to try it when I take you to lunch at the Wharf."

***

By the time they walked to Alioto's on Fisherman's Wharf and finished lunch, Seth learned much about Miriam, who spoke as if a secretary were typing 160 words a minute and wisecracked better than he. Her background explained much. Miriam left home at age fourteen to get away from a verbally abusive step-father and a weak-willed mother. Blessed with perfect pitch, she sang professionally with local trios and quartets. Miriam had left the combo because she had opportunities to audition with two big bands and was taking the Greyhound bus at six-thirty in the evening for L.A.

"Can't you stay here in the city for at least another day?"

"I wish I could. You're not so bad for a college boy, but I can't pass up any audition. It might be my big break."

"I'll give you my address. You can write and tell me which band you sign with so I can follow your career." *And follow you after I graduate.*

"You won't know who I am. Everyone tells me I'll have to change my name. Keramopoulos is too ethnic, they say. It's a Greek name. My birth father, may he rest in peace, and my mother came from Salonika. We are Jews."

Seth liked the way Miriam said it with pride and defiance.

"I guess I'll let the band leader or my agent choose my name. Did you know that Bea Wain who sings with the Larry Clinton Band was Beatrice Weinsier and Helen Forrest who's with Artie Shaw was Helen Fogel? Shaw had to change his name too. Why are you shaking your head?"

"Unbelievable. You're a Jewish male's ideal, a non-Jewish looking Jewish girl."

"Seth Braham, you don't look Jewish either, more like that actor Spencer Tracy."

"There's a reason why. I used to date his mother."

Miriam's wry grin and tone of voice indicated she got it. "Of course you did. I like that response. Anyway, you're better looking than Tracy, but are you really an M.O.T?"

"Member of the Tribe? Sure, on my parents' side."

Seth told Miriam his grandfather Joseph Vitebsky came from a family of foresters in Tzarist Podolia. In 1877, at age twenty, he came to the USA with his older brother, wife, and infant son. They settled in Montgomery, Alabama, established a hardwood lumber business, and moved to the City during the rebuilding boom after the Great Earthquake of 1906. That was when Seth's nonobservant grandfather Anglicized the family name to Braham in honor of his father, Abraham, with each grandchild given a middle name that began with the letter A. Seth's was Arthur.

He also related how his maternal great-grandfather Solomon Rhinelander emigrated at age eighteen from Frankfurt after the failed liberal German revolution of 1848 and arrived in the City at the peak of gold rush hysteria. He prospered and married a cousin of Josephine Marcus, Wyatt Earp's common law wife.

"Miriam, I'd like to hear you sing."

"A Gershwin tune?"

"From a Gershwin Lady."

"I'll sing anywhere, any time, but there's no piano here."

"We have one at home, and I can play what some call a full piano."

"That line is better than showing etchings or cute puppies."

"No line...."

"But I'll tell you something, College Boy. Beware. I've taught bitter lessons to men tougher than you. I think I can keep you at arm's length."

***

Miriam took in the double ambiance living room with a view of the Palace of Fine Arts across the street and beyond to the Bay. "So, you are a rich and privileged college boy."

"Relatively. I'll still have to make my way in the world because I don't want to go into any of the family businesses. My father and uncle sold all their stocks and bonds several months before the Crash of 1929. They sensed something bad was about to happen."

Seth riffed at the piano and Miriam sat atop the Steinway.

"Name your tune, College Boy."

"*They Can't Take That Away from Me.*"

"Very good ... you're vamping like Eddy Duchin. '*The way you ....*'"

Miriam sang the lyrics in a smoky voice with perfect pitch, and her features changed to those of a woman far beyond sixteen years of age.

"Gee, Miriam, that was swell. I could listen to you for hours."

"You will one day after I record a slew of tunes." Miriam left the piano. "College Boy, it's been great."

"Hope it's not like the lyric from 'Just One of Those Things'."

"I wonder ... might be better if it is. Anyway, gotta' go. Remember, I'm taking the milk-run bus to L.A. at six-thirty. Have to pick up my suitcase I left at the hotel."

"The train would be more comfortable."

"Can't afford a train."

"I could pay ...."

"And think you own me? No sirreee."

"It's still only three-fifteen. Let me show you the City until your bus leaves."

"What's that sound?"

"Fog horns. It often rolls in about this time of day."

"I could sing some great Blues to it, but we'd better leave. I don't think it's a good idea for us to stay alone in your home. I like you too much, College Boy. I might not want to hold you at arm's length after all."

***

Seth brought a camera and showed Miriam the Cliff House, drove through Golden Gate Park in his '34 Chevy

71

sedan, and took her to Coit Tower. Everywhere they stopped he shot a roll of film of Miriam by the landmarks, and strangers took several photos of both. Despite the life associated with bands, combos, and night clubs, Miriam swore she never smoked cigarettes or reefers, nor did she drink alcohol. Miriam also assured Seth she did not sleep around.

At New Joe's on Broadway Street in North Beach, Seth introduced Miriam to the restaurant's "special," an omelet of egg, spinach, ground beef and onion. From there, they stopped at her hotel, collected her suitcase, and drove to the terminal at Mission and Howard fifteen minutes before the bus was scheduled to depart.

They sat on a bench silent for a minute until Seth said, "Miriam, I feel like a guy I saw in a magazine illustration for a short story."

He described how a couple sat on a bench in a park. The girl looked toward the sky after informing her admirer she was leaving their small town and going to New York City to be an actress. The young man who loved her stared the ground disappointed.

"He loved her, you say? Don't beat around the bush. Do you think you love me, College Boy?"

"If it isn't love, I don't think I could deal with anything more intense."

"I have strong feelings for you too, College Boy. First time for me too. I never believed it would happen so soon in my life. Glad we're in a public place."

A Terminal clerk announced the bus to Los Angeles was ready for the passengers to board.

Seth stood with Miriam. "You have my address. Please write and let me know where you are, how you're doing. I'll send you copies of the photos after they're developed. We must never lose touch."

"No, College Boy. It'll do us no good. We have to get on with our lives. You have to finish your education and decide what you want to do. I must make my way as a singer. If anything more is meant to be, we'll meet again. Now, I've got to go, and thanks for a nice day."

Miriam dropped her bag, placed her hands on Seth's face and kissed him, at first light and perfunctory, but he did not disengage, and she responded with a warmth and softness beyond any other experience.

"There, now you'll never forget me even if we never meet again, and... oh, damn you, Seth, we've met too soon in our lives. I like you so very much."

"Miriam...."

Too late. She carried her suitcase into the bus and did not look behind or out the window.

Seth waited until the bus drove out of sight. Odd, not once did he mention his love of flying to Miriam. He touched his lips where the pressure of her kiss lingered. Yes, it had to be. They would meet again.

# Chapter 8
## Kelly Field

"Don't push."

"I can't see my name,"

"Learn to read."

It was the end of February, 1939, and Hank swam in a sea of 39B cadets crushing against the bulletin board at the Administration Building. B Stage had ended, and the men were about to be separated from the boys.

Who would be future fighter pilots in Pursuit? Who would be shunted off to Bombardment, Attack, or Observation? The cadets had been allowed to state their preferences for Kelly Field, home of the Army Air Corps Advanced Flying School. The majority put in for Pursuit. Most would be disappointed.

Brax let out a rebel yell. "I made it!"

Hank shouted louder. "So did I!"

Hank and Brax shook hands and pounded each other on their backs. Many classmates cursed, some cried, over their failure to be chosen for Pursuit. After he returned to his room and packed for Kelly, Hank reviewed the Air Corps' selection process.

With few exceptions, the vibrant, quick, impulsive, somewhat immature, and youngest in looks were going to Pursuit. The quiet, slower moving staid types went to Bombardment. Observation got the most lethargic cadets. Wayne Miller was going to Observation.

***

No more T's after the P's, Hank settled into Pursuit training as if born to fly the Boeing P-12E and Seversky BT-8, and his favorite the P-12. Back home, he had built models of the biplane. Seeing a real P-12 on the flight line all blue and gold, he thought it had the lines of a thoroughbred, but the newer P-35 and P-36 fighters with 125 mph more speed made it obsolete.

The open cockpit fighter gave him the feeling he had a motor in his lap and a feather in his tail. In the air, the P-12 was so sensitive to the pilot's touch a cadet needed to make several flights before he could master the soft technique required to fly it. When Hank flew straight and level, he could extend one hand out in the slipstream and cause the plane to turn, but during mock combat, take-off, and landing he had to grab the stick to control the bird.

There was more to the P-12 than aesthetic appeal and sensitivity of response to pilot demand. Blowers like Hank got a measure of revenge when they watched the High-Pockets sitting head and shoulders out of its small cockpit in the slipstream at high and bitter cold altitudes.

Hank and Brax continued as roommates at Kelly, and they sneaked in some fun practicing aerial combat in the P-12. Acknowledged as the best in their class, they outfought their classmates and drew even when they challenged each other. Their dogfights were furious, and after landing both cadets would be drenched in sweat. Hank was the wilier of the two. Brax flew more on instinct, and pushed each plane to limits no rational flier would attempt. Hank conceded one point: If Brax had been in Monahan's plane that fatal day at Randolph, he would have been able to avoid the careless West Pointer.

In Hank's book, Brax was the flyer with at once the most potential and the most harmful weaknesses. Brax drank more than any cadet or officer at Randolph, and Hank worried the Texan might wash out for breaking serious rules of conduct. Brax always had a flask of whiskey stashed somewhere. He said it relaxed him when he couldn't have sex, which he seemed to need twenty-four hours a day. Brax wanted to get into every woman he encountered. Hank felt the same way each time he saw a new fighter. Brax needed to lay them all. Hank had to fly them all.

***

The roommates went separate ways each weekend. Brax cavorted with an extensive harem of females. Hank sampled from a buffet of de-icers, as women were called in the *Smilin' Jack* comic strip, but he preferred to spend more time at Roy McCabe's airfield, where he flew everything from the Piper to Kilrain's Dolphin. Winty never came to the airfield when Hank was there. Roy McCabe said she still worked on the planes and flew often. How would he ever be able to understand older women if he couldn't figure out a sixteen year old?

Kilrain, who did not instruct at Kelly, treated Hank as a protégé. On a Saturday afternoon in March, he lit a cigar and one he had given Hank outside McCabe's office. "Nothing changes. All you kids get to fly at Kelly are the P-12 and BT-8."

"At least it's a bit more than what we did at Randolph, sir. We get instrument and night flying, Link Trainer simulations, cross-country, and acrobatics, singly and in formation. But we're not going to receive aerial gunnery training until we reach our tactical unit of assignment after graduation in June."

"Incredible, isn't it? You'll have had one year of training as a fighter pilot and no experience in air-to-air gunnery."

"And less than six hours of air combat maneuvering at Kelly. Captain Kilrain, I can't believe the Air Corps is unaware the Germans have honed their shooting eyes and improved their fighters in Spain with the Condor Legion. And the Jap pilots are cutting their teeth in China."

Roy McCabe came outside to join them. "Is it as bad as he says, Leo?"

"The training syllabus and Pursuit criteria used by the Air Corps hasn't changed since 1935." Kilrain used his hands for emphasis. "They don't understand the most difficult part of fighter aviation is not learning to get a pursuit plane off the ground. Nor is it flying from point A to point B and making a safe landing. It's the ability to fire guns from a moving platform and hit a moving target. That should be the number one objective for all fighter pilots."

"Captain Kilrain, can you explain why Air Corps thinking is so muddled?"

Kilrain's reply distressed Hank. The captain described how the top brass believed pursuit aviation was a dead issue and of no value in future warfare. Instead, the Air Corps had put all its metal eggs into one basket, bombardment. The new bombers were supposed to be faster than any pursuit plane, and so well armed they'd be able to shoot down every fighter that managed to intercept them. Kilrain alerted Hank to the British Air Staff's theory that the best defense against bombing was counter-bombing enemy bases and factories. Fighter defense was not a factor according to something called the Trenchard Doctrine.

Hank would never accept their reasoning. "Someone's got to make them change their minds."

"Maybe you'll be the one to do it." Kilrain turned to McCabe. "And Roy, you must run for Congress and kick those isolationists' butts."

"I just might surprise you."

"Well, at least I'm getting some great dogfighting lessons from you, sir. It helps me stay on top of my classmates whenever we take a chance to go at each other without the instructors knowing."

"A lot of good that'll do you when we go to war. At Kelly, you're doing mock combat at around 180 mph, but the best fighters manufactured today blast away at well over 300 mph. Milroy, I may be doing you a disservice with our mock combats. It's great sport, but not the best training for contemporary aerial combat. It's suicide for a pilot in a fast plane to dogfight with an enemy in a slower, more maneuverable fighter. It's time to forget dogfighting. Concentrate on the hit-and-run bounce."

"But as I understand it, after we get our commissions, the Air Corps will train us to fly the speedy P-36 and at the same time teach us to dogfight as you did in the Great War."

"Maybe things will even out by the time they send you youngsters into combat. Hells-bells, I wouldn't mind buying it in my fighter if I could have another go at the krauts and score a few more. Roy, I envy kids like Milroy here. He'll be flying faster, sleeker beauties in combat, and when the next war comes, I'll be too old to maneuver anything but a desk."

McCabe frowned. "You think we're getting into another war, Leo?"

"Very soon, no matter what those daydreaming isolationists say."

"We did it before. We can do it again."

"It'll be tougher next time. The Germans are good, very good, and they're getting a big experience edge over boys like Hank here in Spain."

Hank had been thinking the same thing. "You flew against them, sir. What are they like?"

Kilrain looked at the sky. "Pursuiters are alike no matter the country. The krauts are no different from you and me. Except there are the vons, their nobility. During the last day of the war, one of them, a goddam prince at that, had a chance to shoot me down after I ran out of ammo. Instead, he saluted me and broke away. Those flying vons were a breed apart."

***

Throughout the night before their graduation from 39B, the cadets speculated about their postings. Everyone except Hank expressed surprise Miller survived to become a USAAC second lieutenant. More astounding, the simpleton became engaged to a regular Army officer's daughter.

*By golly, the boy was going to go far.*

Brax was subdued for the first time and sat at his desk writing a letter.

"What's bothering you, friend-o? Is it a let-down?"

"No way. Like you, I can't wait to get my wings, a fighter of my own, and jump into my officer's pinks to excite the ladies." He put the letter in an envelope and sealed it. "Hank, old-buddy, I guess it's time I told you about Wilma Lee. But you have to promise me you'll never mention what I tell you to anyone else."

"Sure, whatever you say, Brax." Hank sat alert on the edge of his cot. For eight months, not a night had gone by without the Texan crying out for Wilma Lee.

"Back in January 1938, I married her."

"Brax, you can't be a cadet if you're married. How have you been able to keep it a secret?"

"I outsmarted everyone."

"But you lied on your records. If anyone finds out ...."

"They won't."

"For your sake, I hope you're right. Gloryosky Sandy, I never thought that you of all the guys to be shot down so soon by a woman."

"I had a goddam shotgun rammed up my ass."

That sounded more like Brax. "You couldn't get out of it?"

"She was a good girl and four months pregnant. Her daddy was rich, powerful and a big-time alum. He showed me how they turn Roosters into capons."

"A convincing argument."

"Still, Wilma Lee is a pretty little thing and a hot lay. Here's her picture."

Hank took the photo. She was gorgeous, with long straight black hair like a Cherokee, perhaps blue eyes too, but it was difficult to be sure of the exact color in black and white. "I can't blame you, Brax. She is a looker."

"So's my little girl, Melissa."

Hank glanced at a snapshot of a baby. They all looked alike. "So that's what happened to make you give up your great football career."

"Two months after the wedding, Wilma Lee's daddy died of a heart attack, worse than stone broke, drowning in debt. How the hell was I going to play football and support a wife

I never wanted and a child too? I'd been living high off the hog, but the alumni association was too cheap to let me keep it up. Do you know what it's like to be poor?"

"Hell, Brax, we are in the middle of a depression. Everyone's got it rough. My parents are barely breaking even."

"That's not what I mean. It's one thing to be poor when everyone around you is in the same boat. It's different with me. I ain't no trashy white. I come from an old family that includes generals who fought for Dixie. We still got social standing in the county."

Hank squinted at Brax. If they hadn't gotten to know each other as roommates, would the Texan have thought him trashy too? "What happened next?"

"I ran into an old buddy who graduated Kelly with the class of 37C. He was an ordinary looking yokel, but you should have seen the girls flocking to the guy in his officer's pinks. That's when I got the idea to join the Air Corps."

"Even though you were still married to Wilma Lee?"

Brax laughed nastily. "I painted a bee-yoo-tee-full picture showing Wilma Lee what a great life we'd have in the Air Corps, and she went along with my suggestion of a temporary divorce."

"So you didn't lie about being married on your application." Hank liked happy endings. "Then after you get your commission and wings tomorrow, you'll remarry her."

"No way." Brax handed Hank a sealed envelope. "I wrote Wilma Lee that I will not marry her again. If she shows up tomorrow and I have to make a hasty exit, do me a favor and give this to her."

"Brax, she's got a child, your child. That's a rotten thing to do."

"So was forcing me to marry her. Come on, boy, take it. Shucks, I don't expect Wilma Lee to show up anyway. She'll be waiting for me at Plainview. We're legally divorced now, and she ain't got no daddy to push me around anymore."

Hank resented being asked to shovel Brax's manure. "I can't do it. I won't do it."

"No matter, good-buddy. I'll get Miller to do it. He'll think it's a love letter."

***

Graduation Day dawned bright and glorious. Aside from the usual parade and speeches, the program required the cadets and student officers to fly a gigantic formation over Kelly Field's flight line. The slow Observation planes led, followed by bombers, A-12 attack planes, and last the P-12s and BT-8s of the Pursuit Section.

After Hank landed for the last time as a Flying Cadet, he sat as if in a daze throughout the ceremony inside the Post Theater. Having received a diploma, gold bars as a second lieutenant in the Air Corps Reserve, and silver wings, Hank still couldn't believe he had at last become one of a select few. Thousands of young men applied for the 39B training cycle. Two hundred had been accepted. Less than one hundred survived to graduate, and a mere few dozen of them qualified for Pursuit, the cream of the class.

After the ceremony, a mob of relations and friends swallowed the new officers outside the Post Theater. Hank stood alone and ignored while excited fiancées and family members pinned wings and bars on the new officers. His parents had been unable to make it. They needed to save every penny to keep the ranch going. He hadn't seen them for a full year. There'd be longer separations if the United States got into a war.

Hank turned in the direction of loud female voices. Nancy McCabe was among a gaggle of flirtatious females surrounding Brax. They kissed and vied for the honor of putting on the Texan's bars and wings. Brax was the most charming rogue Hank had ever met. A man's man, the Texan made many friends among the cadets. At the same time, he'd managed to romance a gaggle of girls without getting them angry. Somehow, Brax had succeeded in convincing Wilma Lee to wait with their daughter in Plainview.

Hank's spirits rose when he saw Winty wobbling in heels, probably the first time she wore them. The girl looked so appealing Hank thought she might be wearing makeup. When the petite blonde came closer, he saw she wasn't and didn't need any.

Winty blushed when she kissed Hank on the cheek and gave him a wrapped present. Tears came to Winty's eyes when he asked her to pin the three-inch silver wings on his chest above the left breast pocket. After Winty complied, Hank looked down, and they seemed a yard wide. Before he asked Winty to attach the gold bars, she hurried away and disappeared into the sea of humanity clustering around the new officers. Hank opened the package and took out an elegant white silk scarf.

An excited graduate shouted, "The lists are posted! The lists are posted!"

To a man, all the new second "looeys" rushed to be first in the orderly room to read their names listed on a bulletin board. One paper ordered the entire class back to Randolph Field on permanent duty for two weeks to circumvent an Army regulation forbidding travel pay for a new officer going to his first station. That allowed them to receive a generous six cents per mile allotment when they did travel to their assigned bases.

The second bulletin contained the all-important list of new officers, locations, and units to which each had been posted, PCS effective two weeks hence. Hank read he had been assigned to Mitchel Field, Long Island New York. He looked forward to seeing for the first time the greatest, most exciting city in the USA, if not the world, until the name and number of his new unit sunk in.

*Bombardment. Bombers. Not fighters.*

He had been assigned to the 9th Bombardment Group.

It had to be an error. He had just spent four months in the Pursuit Section here at Kelly Field. He was a pursuit pilot. So were all the other disappointed new officers. Yet, to a man, they had been assigned to Bombardment units.

Sick at heart, Hank went outside and found Kilrain. "What happened, sir? It must be a mistake."

"No, it was a deliberate decision to assign everyone to bombers, Lt. Milroy, of that you can be sure."

"But why?"

"The bomber units are short-handed. They need co-pilots. Their brass talked the Chief of the Air Corps into giving them their choices among your 39B class. He's a dyed-in-the-wool bomber man who firmly believes in the Trenchard Doctrine and is convinced pursuit flying is obsolete."

"Is there any chance we'll be reassigned in the next two weeks?"

"No, and not in the foreseeable future."

Never had Hank envisioned being at the controls of any plane other than a trim little pursuiter. What had started out to be the greatest day of his life had become a nightmare. Then Hank realized he hadn't seen Brax's name on the bomber list. A loud, sustained rebel yell, and 2nd Lieutenant Braxton Hale Mobley announced to one and all he had been assigned to a fighter group based at Barksdale Field, Louisiana, the only cadet of the Pursuit Section not going to bombers.

Hank almost choked on the words when he congratulated Brax in front of the orderly room. "At least they picked the best stick-and-rudder man in our class."

"I wish they'd had room for just one more, but better me than you, good-buddy."

Kilrain offered Hank a cigar. "Listen to me, Lt. Milroy. I know how you feel. But stick it out. Do the best you can at each of your assignments. When war comes, and it will, I promise you this, if I am in a position to place you in a fighter unit, I'll damn well do it. You're tops in 39B and one of the best I've ever seen."

Hank thanked Kilrain, and as he accepted Kilrain's light he heard a familiar roar. Brax wheel-walked his Harley past the cadet barracks, saluted Hank and the other stunned pursuiters, and tooled by them out the main gate toward Randolph Field.

Hank watched until Brax disappeared from view. In two weeks he'd report to a bomber unit as a co-pilot. He prayed Germany and Japan, America's inevitable antagonists in an approaching war, wasted their fighter pilots the same as the United States Army Air Corps.

"Nothing makes a man more aware of his capabilities and of his limitations than those moments when he must push aside all the familiar defenses of ego and vanity, and accept reality by staring, with the fear that is normal to a man in combat, into the face of Death."
—*Major Robert S. Johnson, USAAF*

# PART TWO

## Raptors

## 1940—1943

"There are pilots and there are pilots; with the good ones, it is inborn. You can't teach it. If you are a fighter pilot, you have to be willing to take risks."
—*Brigadier General Robin Olds*

# Chapter 9

## Human Beast and "Little Beast"

Wearing wings and rank of Leutnant on a blue Luftwaffe uniform, Karl drove his 1933 Hispano-Suiza Cabriolet toward the family manor located outside the village of Eppelborn. Mariya-Xenia sat in the passenger seat holding Elsa, the White German Shepherd that was a graduation gift from an instructor. She respected Karl's silence and gave attention to the puppy on her lap.

Karl wished his friends could have attended the graduation. Albert was playing the conqueror in Paris. A Party member who hated aristos had assigned Gerd to a submarine and Walti to a Wehrmacht infantry unit based in Poland. Bruno had made trips to neutral Portugal, Switzerland, and Turkey for the Abwehr, and God-knew-where he was today.

One of a select few sent to the coveted fighters, Karl had been assigned to the Luftwaffe's best fighter wing, Jagdgeschwader 26. Other classmates would be going to yet another school to learn how to fly the larger and more complex bombers. In spite of its many faults, the Luftwaffe's selection process made sense to Karl. The most impetuous, alert, and independent types with the quickest reflexes and situational awareness made it to the fighter Gruppen, even if some of them were low born.

Karl broke his silence and discussed with Mariya-Xenia the events of the past year. Although Germany's invasion of Poland brought England and France into the war, they had failed to launch an all-out attack. Instead, the combatants settled into a passive war of propaganda with names in three languages: The Phony War; Sitzkrieg, the sitting war; and Drôle de Guerre, a Peculiar War.

While the French Army sat behind the Maginot Line, their anti-communist government considered sending troops to fight for Finland after the USSR attacked that gallant country in November 1939. At the same time, the British limited their air activities to bombing military targets along the coast and dropping propaganda leaflets inland.

Karl shared a laugh with Mariya-Xenia over the naiveté of the English. When a Member of Parliament suggested Bomber Command strike at the Black Forest with incendiary bombs to destroy German timber reserves and factories, the Air Minister refused to allow such raids because it was unthinkable to destroy private property.

Aside from an occasional ship-to-ship battle at sea or dogfight in the skies, all had been quiet on the Western Front until April 1940, when the Wehrmacht blitzed through Denmark, Norway, the Low Countries, and attacked France. The week before Karl's graduation, France capitulated to Germany on the twenty-second of June and signed an armistice after a short forty-six days of combat. The British army escaped from Dunkirk, but was no longer a fighting force. Most Germans thought the English would sue for peace within a short time, but Karl and Mariya-Xenia believed they would never admit defeat.

Karl worried more about a greater threat looming in the East. Hitler and Stalin had partitioned Poland out of existence according to terms of their non-aggression treaty. He appreciated the necessity of keeping the Soviets neutral but was uneasy; they had encroached more kilometers westward into Europe and now shared a long border with the Fatherland. Both Karl and Mariya Xenia worried if secret clauses in the treaty might affect her status in the Reich.

What would the Führer do if the Soviet commissars demanded the return of all Russian royals and aristos residing in the Reich? The USSR had forced Estonia, Latvia, and Lithuania to sign mutual assistance pacts and established garrisons in those Baltic countries without protest from Germany, a transparent prologue to annexation.

Karl felt Mariya-Xenia squeezing his hand. God in heaven, she was gorgeous today, more desirable than ever in a straw yellow and pale blue silk print dress. Karl wanted to make love before he reported to JG-26. He had no idea how long he would be away from Mariya-Xenia. She had taken residence in Berlin, working as a translator for the Abwehr, and had leased a flat.

"I am delighted you will not return to Estonia, but why do your father, brothers, and uncles stay there? Do they not see the inevitable?"

"They are too filled with hatred for Bolsheviks, whom they blame for the revolution and their ruined lives, and the Jews, whom they blame for that and everything else. They worship Hitler as their savior and are conspiring to establish a pro-Nazi fascist government in Estonia. I abhor their politics, but they are my family. It is a terrible world, Karl, when the only choice is between a Hitler and a Stalin."

"And we must adjust to it."

"Can we, really?"

Karl had no answer.

***

Mid-afternoon they arrived at Karl's English style manor outside Eppelborn near the Prins River in the Saarland, fifty-five kilometers northwest of Pirmasens and thirty kilometers from Occupied France. They would be alone. The older servants now worked in agriculture and industry, and the younger had joined the military.

During a tour of the manor, Karl showed Mariya secret entrances to hidden rooms. One was a comfortable well-ventilated cellar bedroom and library suite filled with valuable furniture and rugs, shelves of rare books, and racks of collector's weapons: rifles, shotguns, pistols, swords, and crossbows. An adjacent closet had been packed to the ceiling with cases of old wines and rare cognacs.

"My grandfather built this sanctuary, and my father later improved it to preserve our valuable possessions during the French occupation after the last war. None of my friends know about these rooms and passages. Be assured that Poldi is unaware of them."

"That is a good thing."

Upstairs, Mariya-Xenia lingered over a large bathtub. "I may stay in here all day. Karl, I do not know how it is at your bases, but the Government decree of 15 January restricted civilian bathing to Saturday and Sunday. It is much worse in a big city like Berlin where one gets so dirty. You would think we'd lost the war. What bothers me most, along with the bathing restrictions, is that women receive half the ration of tobacco given to men. Our special smokers' cards are stamped H for Herren and D for Damen, as if the officials cannot tell the difference."

Karl commiserated with Mariya-Xenia. "Yes, I am familiar with the Nazi slogan, *A German Woman Does Not Smoke.*"

"Another absurdity we must endure."

Maria-Xenia described how severe the rationing, which began the previous August, had become. It included all the necessities of food, fuel, clothing, leather, textiles and soaps, and substitutes such as margarine. Yet expensive luxuries like crayfish and caviar were not rationed. The long lines drove everyone crazy. If one did not work, no ration card was available, thus giving the government total control of the population. It taxed salaries at a minimum of thirty-five percent, and prices continued to rise.

Karl tried not to listen to Mariya-Xenia's complaints. He guided his fiancée into the master suite and opened the doors leading to the patio and view of a lush garden below. A breeze wafted the redolence of garden flowers. Karl desired Mariya-Xenia as no other female before, but he was not sure if he loved her, whatever love was. Karl did know he wanted to tear away Maria-Xenia's clothes and have his fiancée now.

"Karl?"

*Love.* That word had meaning in so many different ways. He loved his vineyards and flying. Those he would never give up for any woman. If he did have a true love at this moment, it was the Me-109. But love a woman? Love Mariya-Xenia? One day perhaps, not now. Karl read Mariya-Xenia's mind. She wanted to hear the magical word that would make everything all right. He felt desire, lust, physical passion—and contempt. Yes, contempt for Maria-

Xenia because she would believe the lie when he spoke the words she wanted to hear.

"Mariya-Xenia, I love you. From the first moment I saw you, I wanted you, as I do now." How flat he sounded, how unconvincing. Yet he must play the charade to its inevitable denouement.

Karl led his hesitant fiancée to the bed and sang the soldier's eternal seductive song, "I cannot wait until we are married. Can you? I leave tomorrow for my Geschwader on the Western Front. There is always the possibility I may never come back."

Mariya-Xenia anticipated a gentle kiss, but an uncontrollable perversity overcame Karl. He crushed his lips against Mariya-Xenia's mouth. No preliminaries, no tenderness, with brute strength and a violence she had not anticipated, Karl assaulted Mariya-Xenia.

When he finished, Mariya-Xenia spoke one word in a tone that shriveled Karl's genitalia.

"Beast."

***

July 1940, Karl reported to Adolf Galland's III Gruppe of Jagdgeschwader 26 based at Caffiers France. Galland offered Karl advice based on his own recent combat experiences:

*The first rule of all air combat is to see the opponent first. Like the hunter who stalks his prey and maneuvers himself unnoticed into the most favorable position for the kill, the fighter in the opening of a dogfight must detect the opponent as early as possible in order to attain a superior position for the attack. As a fighter pilot I know how decisive surprise and luck can be for success, which in the long run comes only to the one who combines daring with cool thinking.*

*It is true to say that the first kill can influence the whole future career of a fighter pilot. Many to whom the first victory over the opponent has been long denied either by unfortunate circumstances or by bad luck can suffer from frustration or develop complexes they may never rid themselves of.*

The pilots of JG-26 flew the Me-109E for Emil, affectionately known as the "Little Beast." It had two machine guns mounted on each side of the engine and three 20mm cannons, one on each wing and a third between the cylinder banks of the engine, which, unlike earlier models, produced no vibration when fired through the prop spinner.

Karl was well aware of the fighter's faults. Not as maneuverable as the RAF Spitfire, the 109's limited range would hamper its effectiveness if the war expanded beyond countries adjacent to the Reich. The pilot's armor protection began 1.25 meters behind the cockpit, with the glycol, radiator, and oil coolers exposed to attack from below. Because of its narrow landing gear, the Me-109 had a built-in ground loop if one of the struts collapsed. The Messerschmitt's large motor in an oversize fuselage blocked the pilot's view during take-off, which required Karl to taxi on the runway in ess curves so he could see ahead through the side windows. An alternative was to have the crew chief ride on the wing and direct him to stay on a straight course.

Karl's instructors drilled the new pilots in the safest technique to land the little beast. Speed down to the final approach path was essential, with touch down on the front wheels and the tail wheel about twenty-five centimeters above ground. Karl learned to hold slight forward pressure on the control stick without braking until the tail touched down, and to maintain directional control with the rudder. The tail would lower of its own accord at about 45 knots, and at that moment, the plane would begin to swerve left or right. He had to be quick on the brake to keep the 109 going straight. Too much correction forced the fighter to turn in another direction, and over-control might cause a ground loop or nose-up. Many 109 pilots lost their lives in such accidents during landing.

Karl added his personal logo to the fighter's JG-26 emblem, a black gothic S in a yellow shield, and identification number 23 among iron crosses and swastikas. Gruppenkommandeur Adolf Galland had a cigar smoking, bellicose Mickey Mouse on the fuselage of his 109. Other pilots chose symbolic animals or aces from card suits. Karl decided to copy neither them nor the others who honored their wives or fiancées on the fuselage. Instead, he had the best artist in the Gruppe paint on each side of the Emil a bottle of sparkling wine containing the Pfalz-Teuffelreich crest and beneath it in bold letters, SPRITZ.

Karl's CO assigned him as Kaczmarek, wingman, to one of the combat-experienced pilots. His principal duty was to protect the Rottenführer who did the shooting.

The Luftwaffe evolved a successful combat tactic late in the Spanish Civil War called the double-attack, or finger-four formation, because it resembled the four fingers of an outstretched hand. The finger-four allowed more flexibility and mutual protection than the RAF three-plane Vic and other, more primitive formations.

A leader and his Kaczmarek made up a Rotte. A Schwarm was a two-Rotte formation. Three to four Schwarmen made up a Staffel. When a twelve- to sixteen-plane Staffel charged into a melee, the Schwarmen broke into their flights of four, with individual Rotten elements moving out in pairs. Each Rotte protected the other, and at the same time maintained optimum tactical integrity and protection of leader and wingman. Karl had no desire to be a Staffelkapitän, but he did want to become a Rottenführer and have more opportunities for aerial victories.

Throughout July and August 1940, Karl mastered the idiosyncrasies of the finger-four formations. On each sortie enthusiastic ground crew sent their pilots away with shouts of *"Hals und Beinbruch!"*, *break your neck and leg*, in the hope the opposite would happen. As a wingman, he had yet to shoot at a RAF opponent. For an ambitious and competitive fighter pilot it was a most inauspicious beginning.

# Chapter 10
## Wasted Talent

"Bail out, Milroy."

On instinct, Hank struck the lapel of his tuxedo then recovered. "What the hell?" When he turned in the crowded bar at *The Stork Club*, he faced a grinning redhead in a RAF uniform with a flaming RAF mustachio and an empty left sleeve. Hank took a longer look at the redhead.

"Chilton? Bob Chilton?"

"On target, Mister."

Hank and Chilton shook hands, and he made room for the former cadet captain at the bar. "What are you having, Bob?"

"Scotch neat. A habit I picked up across the pond flying with the Eagles." Chilton frowned at Hank's tuxedo. "Bloody hell, I never thought I'd see you of all people wearing civvies."

"It's a long story, Bob, but I'd like to hear yours first."

"Sure, as long as you're buying."

"How did you end up with the Eagles? I thought you were ensconced in a fighter unit."

Chilton touched glasses with Hank. "I got disillusioned with the lack of flying time and the promotion system. As you know, in the Air Corps, pursuiters are the men least likely to rise to high command."

Hank couldn't have agreed more and told Chilton he'd received a letter at the end of 1940 from Wayne Miller, which underscored the unfairness of the Air Corps promotion system. The untalented cadet, whom everyone had expected to wash out, had married a Regular Army major's daughter. Miller was promoted to 1st lieutenant ahead of everyone else from 39B and now served as an aide to a brigadier general at Langley Field, Virginia.

They reminisced about the hazing at Randolph and how the upperclassmen did everything possible to make Miller wash out. Instead, Brax became the survivor with the most gigs.

"It was always obvious when we were cadets, Hank. The will-do, can-do aggressive guys seldom make it to high command because the practice in upper military circles is never to rock the boat. That's why Kilrain is still a captain."

"You said it, Bob. Brilliant visionaries like Billy Mitchell and Claire Chennault are either court-martialed or hounded out of the service. Now tell me. What happened after you left the Air Corps and joined the RAF? Did you score any victories?"

"It was great while it lasted. I scored two kills, a 109 and a 110 on my first sortie. Then some hotshot kraut holed my Spitfire over the Channel. I tried to make it back to base, but crashed past Dover and lost most of my left arm. That ended my career as a fighter pilot. I was a good enough shot to have become an ace, but I can't complain. At least I survived in better shape than many with more severe wounds and multiple amputations."

Hank admired Chilton's positive attitude. "And your RAF proved the Trenchard Doctrine wrong too."

"The Bomber Will Always Get Through? We sure busted that theory to hell."

"You still look fit enough to get back into a cockpit, Bob."

"Tell it to the RAF. And the friggin' Army Air Corps too. They won't let me fly a desk or teach tactics."

"What will you do?"

"I lost my arm mid-bicep, and I've got a prosthetic device that should be ready for me to try in a day or two. Then my amputation won't be so obvious at first sight if I keep the hooks in my pocket. On Monday I'm going to D.C. I'm fluent in French, German, and Spanish, and a cousin who is a senior official in the State Department has arranged for me to be considered for a position as Assistant Counsel in some friendly or neutral country."

"Cloak and dagger stuff?"

"Hope so, but too early to know. Now tell me, Hank. What happened to you? You were the best pursuiter in 39B."

"After Kelly, they assigned me to the 9th Bomb Group as a B-18A co-pilot."

"You poor bastard. Say, whatever happened to that Texas tornado you roomed with? I'm waiting to hear he'd been shot by a jealous husband."

"The last I heard, the lucky s.o.b was over in Toungoo, Burma, flying P-40s for Chennault in the AVG."

"He must have believed their sales pitch. Four hundred-and fifty bucks a month, two cases of Scotch, and a concubine."

"And a five hundred dollar bonus for each plane he shoots down. I'll bet the moment they see combat, he'll bag a batch of Japs. And a sack full of women."

"But back to you, Hank. What was it like in bombers?"

"We were given a measly four hours a month flying time at Mitchel Field."

Hank and Chilton reviewed how most Americans, including those in Congress who controlled military budgets, opposed getting involved in the European conflict during the Phony War. They believed the Sitzkrieg was a prelude to a negotiated peace. The Department of Army became so sanguine about peace it made economic burps and restricted pilots to flying no more than fifty hours a year, even though ten to fifteen hours per month was considered the absolute minimum number necessary for them to master the bigger, faster, more complicated aircraft.

"We all flew extra time, of course, but it was never enough. That's why I resigned from active duty in March of 1940 and joined Trans World Airlines. The pay was better, and they guaranteed me eighty hours a month in the air."

"Holy cats. You're with TWA? That's one hell of a surprise. At least you've had plenty of attractive stewardesses to prang."

"That too. And what about you and the lovely English roses?"

"If I'd stayed there a bit longer, I might have wed one of the long stems."

Hank ordered another round and moved closer so he could be heard above the noise at the jammed bar. "Bob, there's a lot more. TWA sent me to Captain's school in Kansas City at the same time President Roosevelt signed the Lend-Lease Agreement."

"Which saved England's ass."

"And reamed mine. TWA sent all their new DC-3s to the Brits and no longer needed more captains. Rather than go back to co-pilot status, I signed a contract with the Canadian Pacific Railroad Air Service to ferry planes to England at a thousand bucks per flight, fifteen hundred for more than one trip within a month. Because I had more than sixteen-hundred hours flying time in twin-engine B-18s and DC-3s, plus five-hundred more in the four-engine Boeing 307B Stratoliner, I qualified to fly Lockheed Hudsons and LB-30 Liberators across the Atlantic."

"You always impressed me as a balls-out flyer who'd have found a way, any way, to get into the shooting war as a fighter pilot, Hank. Why didn't you try the AVG or the Eagles?"

"I learned too late that Chennault recruited hush-hush from the fighter squadrons for his American Volunteer Group. They'd never have taken me."

"The Eagles would have for sure."

"That possibility came right after I committed myself by contract to the Ferry Command."

Chilton didn't say anything, and Hank guessed what the redhead must be thinking. He could have broken the ferrying contract any time and enlisted in the Eagles to fly for the RAF. Why hadn't he? Hank rationalized he could not bring himself to put on the uniform of a foreign government.

Bullshit. Truth be told, Hank had been lethargic about getting into fighters for the first time in his life for two other reasons. He was earning big money, which helped his parents out of an economic mess and kid brother Doug Jr. to afford college, and war might come to America at any moment. The United States had cut off trade with Japan, frozen its assets, and threatened war if they continued their aggression in the Far East. German U-boats had sunk U.S. ships. War with the Axis was inevitable. In a December, 1940 speech, FDR had said:

> "If Britain should go down, all of us in America would be living at the point of a gun. We must be the great Arsenal of Democracy."

When Japan, Germany, or both attacked the Arsenal of Democracy, Hank believed the Army Air Corps would welcome him with open arms and place him in fighters.

Chilton followed Hank's eyes toward the entrance. "Expecting someone?"

"A chorus girl from the Cole Porter musical, *Panama Hattie.*"

"Now you're talking like a pursuiter. Any chance she'll bring a friend?"

"Lucky you, she's brought several. Look, here they come."

# Chapter 11
## Unheeded Advice

During an escort sortie high above a Staffel of lumbering Stukas over the Channel, Karl spotted far below a pair of Hurricanes diving to the attack. The RAF pilots forgot everything else in the sky and concentrated on the dive-bombers. Karl and his Rottenführer fell in behind the Hurricanes and at sixty meters away fired their guns in short bursts to blast the Englanders out of the sky.

Karl had no time to exult over his first Luftsieg. He saw a pack of Spitfires through a break in the clouds and called his Rottenführer to meet the attack as the Stukas maneuvered into a Lufbery circle sixty meters above the waves of the Channel to protect each other's tail. Karl dove into the RAF pack and shattered a Spitfire. He continued his dive and snapped a shot at the squadron leader with no time to zero-in the gun sight and missed his target. Flying close to the water, Karl sustained full speed for about ten kilometers before zooming 3,000 meters into a broken cloudbank. He turned back to the attack as the Stukas left their Lufbery and snaked to Krefeld until two new Spitfires burst onto the scene.

Karl dove after the rear Spit, whose leader began a sharp right turn. His target continued straight ahead. At 250 meters, Karl fired and saw hits and smoke coming from the Spit's engine. He closed to fifty meters and fired the 20mm cannon. The Spit's canopy and left stabilator flew away, and the Englander plunged into the Channel. On pullout, Karl looked behind and saw the other Spitfire about 700 meters behind. He pushed right rudder, causing a skid that enabled him to avoid the Spitfire's bullets. When Karl zoomed for altitude, the RAF pilot cut across the circle, closed to 600 meters, and fired again, riddling the 109E's's right wing. More bullets made thwanging thumps on the armor plate behind Karl's head, and he flew for safety into the clouds. Turning toward home, Karl smelled leaking hydraulic fluid and glycol. He made an emergency landing at Le Touquet Airfield, but his fighter was no longer flyable.

When Karl returned to Krefeld that evening, the Staffel and the Stuka pilots confirmed his three Luftsiegen in one sortie. Better yet, Galland promoted Karl to Rottenführer. As a leader, he would soon become an ace.

Flying his new 109, Karl added two Luftsiegen on subsequent sorties to achieve acedom. Champagne flowed that evening during celebrations, but he maintained a patrician reserve. By then he had become known as a loner and a perfectionist in the Geschwader. Karl's Emil had to be in top condition, the guns well prepared, and the engine tuned to please his critical ear. He never used exhaustion as an excuse to dress slovenly or to be unshaven, as happened with so many others. He demanded the same from his Kaczmarek and crew. With five Luftsiegen, still a long way to go before he equaled his father's totals, and impatient to become top ace, Karl protested but could not disobey orders to take a required weekend leave from the front.

***

In the great room of the Berlin mansion, Karl sat opposite Mariya-Xenia, wrestled with Elsa, and sipped his best Schloss Teuffelreich wine. Mariya-Xenia smoked through a decorative cigarette holder and crocheted a heavy white turtleneck sweater for Karl. They would have tied in a contest to determine who had lost the most weight and had the darkest shadows under the eyes. After the RAF retaliatory raids on Berlin began at the end of August 1940, Karl changed his mind about Mariya-Xenia sitting out the war in Switzerland. He now thought it best she reside at Eppelborn or at the family castle near Bad Dürkheim where she could manage the Pfalz-Teuffelreich estates and vineyards.

Karl had not seen Mariya-Xenia since the day he deflowered her. This time he intended to demonstrate he could be a gentle and romantic lover. But first, he must face reality and break through the glacial barrier she had erected between them. Mariya-Xenia had not looked at him from the moment he entered, nor had she spoken. They were like two chess masters deliberating strategy and tactics before a first move. Karl had no choice but to initiate.

"Do you wish to end our engagement?"

"No."

Mariya-Xenia's instant response surprised Karl. "Why not? Your beauty attracts other men."

"I do not love other men."

"Do you love me, Mariya-Xenia?"

"Not as much as I did before you ...."

"I apologize, Mariya-Xenia. Forgive me. It will never happen again."

"I have not forgiven you. But know this. You shall never again touch me like that. Never. I am not a Stachelschwein who can be abused by anyone in uniform."

Where had Mariya-Xenia learned the Luftwaffe pilots' disparaging word for a promiscuous woman, that if all the pricks she accepted were to stick out of her, she would resemble a porcupine? During another extended frigid pause, Karl asked himself why Mariya-Xenia had not ended their engagement. The answer was obvious. A stateless non-citizen, Mariya-Xenia's resident status could be revoked instantly. Because of the non-aggression treaty with the USSR, the authorities might deliver his fiancée to the Soviets on a whim.

Karl had no wish to break off their engagement either. In the traditional dynastic scheme of things, love did not matter, and Mariya-Xenia was the best woman available, a stunning decorative beauty with a maturity far beyond her mere twenty-one years, and enough intelligence to manage his estates.

Karl needed something stronger than wine. He left his chair, hunted for a fine cognac, and returned with a bottle and an oversize crystal snifter. "Then we shall wed in June as we planned, though you hate me now."

"Not hatred, it is more a matter of disappointment, which I hope will pass. It must pass. You could be killed in combat. You still run that risk."

"We flyers see ourselves as immortal."

"You might think differently if you sit for five hours in a foul cellar at night while the city is being bombed, dreading you might be next to die in a direct hit. Karl, where is the Luftwaffe? Is there a good reason why you fighter pilots cannot stop the RAF?"

"You sound like Hermann Göring."

Mariya-Xenia crossed herself in the Russian Orthodox manner. "God forbid. Why say such a thing?"

"Surely you must know Göring blames the fighter wings for their inability to prevent the RAF night bombing raids. He has weakened fighter pilot morale by referring to us as cowards and placing all responsibility on our shoulders for not destroying the RAF."

Mariya-Xenia chain lit another cigarette. "Yes, his propaganda has been quite successful among the populace. The masses believe the Fighter Arm is indeed made up of cowards."

"My commanders say Göring will do anything to cover his fat ass because he ignores their requests for better night equipment and tactics to halt our high attrition rate."

Karl told Mariya-Xenia that at the beginning of the war Göring rejected the concept of night fighters. He could not imagine anyone hitting a moving target from a moving platform in the dark, even after several Luftwaffe bombers returned from their missions over France damaged by the British night fighters. Göring often said, "Who can hit anything at night? Better yet, who can find anyone at night?"

"Because Göring and his toadies will not admit to mistakes, their policies are nothing less than pure murder of night fighter pilots."

"It seems, Karl, your greatest enemy is not the RAF. It is Hermann Göring," Mariya-Xenia remarked.

Why would she not look at him? "That is what I cannot understand. He was a fighter pilot with twenty-two Luftsiegen, and he won the Blue Max among his many awards."

"That was another war."

"Is there no one in your Abwehr to advise Göring?"

"They have tried, but he has overweening self-confidence combined with a forceful and aggressive personality."

"An ego which demands total conformity is diametrically opposed to the individualistic tendencies of fighter pilots." Mariya-Xenia was as well informed as Bruno, so he continued. "I suspect you know more about Göring than I do. I have heard rumors he has been dependent on drugs for many years because of several war wounds. Is that why he has a warped view of reality?"

"Drugs can intensify one's inadequacies. My Chief, Admiral Canaris, says that although Göring dominates his subordinates, he has become a yes-man to Hitler and allows Der Führer to dictate all air planning and strategy."

Karl poured another cognac. "Inconceivable. How can any country win a war when its political leader tells the military what to do without asking for their opinions?"

"How, indeed."

Another long, cold silence. "Mariya-Xenia, you must move to Eppelborn."

"Impossible. I have important work to do for the Abwehr."

"What can be so important? There are other translators."

"I am the best."

"Please, do as I have asked. Quit the Abwehr."

Mariya-Xenia looked at Karl for the first time since his arrival, her face blank as unused paper. "I have received so few letters from you. I would love to hear about your flying experiences. I have not yet congratulated you on your victories and becoming an ace."

Mariya-Xenia had changed the subject. No matter. He might as well spend the rest of his brief leave talking about flying. "My victories have made me hungry for more. I want to surpass my father's 49 Luftsiegen and become the top ace of this war."

"I would be proud for you to achieve your goals, but have the implications of it all occurred to you?"

"The dead opponents?" Karl shrugged. "Fortunes of war. Anyway, some of them do get good chutes."

"I meant something else. You can become a top ace only if the war continues for many years."

Karl swirled the cognac in his glass. "A long war is likely."

"I am sorry, Karl. Perhaps I should not speak so pessimistically. Flying many sorties each day in combat must be wearying. How much of it can you take?"

"At least we can fight back. I do not mean to insult you, Mariya-Xenia, but you look as worn as our most fatigued pilots. I repeat again, make my manor your residence. I need you in Saarland, in the Pfalzland too. As my wife, you will have the authority to administer the estates and vineyards."

"I told you, I have my work with the Abwehr."

"Why is that so important to you?"

"It takes my mind off the air raids."

Her answer did not satisfy Karl. He believed Mariya-Xenia might be doing more than translating for German Intelligence. The Abwehr was reputed to be less than loyal to the regime. If the vons were plotting to overthrow Hitler and the Nazis, Karl did not want to know anything about it.

Mariya-Xenia cut the last piece of yarn and handed the sweater to Karl. "Here, it will fit. You may need to wear this soon."

Karl draped the sweater of his knees. "Very well done. Heavy too. I thank you, but why now? It is still spring, and I certainly will not need it during the summer."

"Our brilliant leaders are not producing proper seasonal wear for our Wehrmacht and Luftwaffe. Winter comes early and brutally in the East."

Yugoslavia, Greece, and Albania had fallen to the Wehrmacht the previous month. Germany was poised to strike at the Suez Canal, take the oil fields of the Middle East, and threaten India. But England refused to sue for peace, and the Americans were likely to enter the war, given the right provocation. It would be madness to attack the Soviet Union at any time. Did Mariya-Xenia know of specific plans to invade the USSR?

Karl chose not to ask for clarification. "Do you see our friends?"

"Walti is an infantry Leutnant somewhere in Poland. Albert is with Rommel in North Africa. Gerd is at sea. I see Bruno on those infrequent days when he is in Berlin."

"What news of my uncle Poldi?"

"He is participating in horrible atrocities throughout the conquered lands."

Karl tried not to listen when Mariya-Xenia described the sanguinary activities of the SS and Gestapo. Yet, he could not avoid imagining Poldi strutting before a cowed populace. Karl thanked the gods of war he could climb into a fighter and soar to the clear purity of the blue skies. Above the clouds, the war was still clean and honorable.

***

Mariya-Xenia must have known, and her gift of the heavy sweater had been her way of alerting him. On 22

June, Hitler launched Operation Barbarossa, the invasion of the USSR and the Baltic States, which took Stalin by surprise. Four days later at dawn 26 June 1941, a pack of RAF Hawker Hurricanes crossed the narrow part of the Channel to chase four Heinkel 111s and another Schwarm of Me-110s attacking a convoy. Karl led his Rotte out of the clouds in good position for a successful bounce. When British radar painted the two Me-109s joining the fray, the Hurricanes broke off their attack and headed for altitude.

Karl told his Kaczmarek to meet the first fighter head-on and got off a short burst on the second, and saw flashes on the RAF plane. He banked into firing position behind another Hurricane flying below in a lazy left hand circuit. He held down the tit in a long burst and saw the Hurricane's ammunition panel blow away and its wing flaps go down for his sixth Luftsieg.

Karl overshot his quarry and half-rolled into a split-ess to seek another target. The low morning scud had turned bright because the sun glared fifteen degrees above the horizon, and the sky was empty except for the last Hurricane he had hit.

Karl's Kaczmarek broke radio silence. "Beware. Achtung."

The windshield and part of Karl's instrument panel disappeared in a crescendo of ripping metal. He yanked the stick all the way back. The 109 responded, then stalled.

Karl's altitude was too low to recover from a spin. He unfastened the seat belt, catapulted through the open cockpit as the plane whip stalled, and pulled the parachute's ring. After three never-ending seconds, it opened. Karl floated earthward through the scud and landed hard on his back atop a stone wall surrounding a French farm house.

***

A dark angel, but no messenger of death. Sun-bronzed skin against nurse-white uniform. Raven-black hair. Brown eyes. A warm smile to melt the heart. Trim as a 109. A touch to soothe the body. A heartfelt yearning for something, someone indefinable.

Each day in the hospital, Karl looked for the petite, dark young woman. Had the beautiful Schwarze Engel been real, or a product of morphine induced delirium? He had no way of knowing. He did not know her name. If she were real and his nurse, the world might not seem so bleak.

***

A broken back ended Karl's active status. He and Mariya-Xenia postponed their wedding, but she agreed at last to manage the Pfalz-Teuffelreich estates. The bombing raids and severe rationing had taken a heavy toll. Mariya-Xenia was thinner, skin pale as alabaster, eyes red and lids shadowed. The exhausted ash blonde appeared to be on the edge of collapse. Yet he could not convince Mariya-Xenia to take permanent residence at Eppelborn or the Schloss. Nor had they resolved the matter of religion. He preferred a traditional Lutheran ceremony. She wanted a Russian Orthodox prelate to marry them.

During visits Mariya-Xenia tried to cheer Karl with caustic Berlin jokes. One of them about Hitler's deputy appealed to Karl's sense of humor and opinion of the Nazi regime:

"With the loss of Rudolph Hess, the Thousand Year Reich has become the Hundred Year Reich, because Germany has lost one of its biggest zeros."

Mariya-Xenia aborted Karl's laughter with news of Poldi. "Your uncle has been appointed commander of an Einsatzgruppe, a special Baltic task force made up of SS, Gestapo, and collaborationist police, whose mission is to liquidate all Jews, Bolsheviks, and anti-Nazis. He did manage to confirm that the Soviets executed my father, brother, and uncles along with thousands of anti-Bolshevik and intellectual Estonians."

"I am sorry, Mariya-Xenia."

"It did not surprise me. I wish I could have been with mother when she heard about their deaths." Mariya-Xenia arranged the fresh flowers she brought in a vase on the nightstand. "The anti-Bolsheviks were slaughtered by the Reds, and now the anti-Nazis are being massacred by Poldi and his ilk. Were they alive, my father and brothers would be supporting his bloodbath. I loved them, but given the game they played, they got what they intended to dish out. It is a wicked world, Karl."

***

Each time Mariya-Xenia visited she wore the same drab brown suit but with a different hat. Because of a bureaucratic mistake, hats were not rationed. She described how life in Berlin had become worse and made serving in combat seem more desirable than being a civilian. The government forbade the wearing of make-up and dancing in public. Food was still difficult to obtain, except for luxury items. Good beer was almost impossible to get, yet champagne from France flowed freely.

Mariya-Xenia's descriptions of the relentless RAF bombing raids made Karl all the more eager to escape his white prison. During August of 1941, he remained still hospitalized. Several doctors believed he would never return to combat. If he did heal well enough to fly again, everyone assumed the war would be over by the end of the year. Not Karl. In spite of the great successes of the Wehrmacht and the Luftwaffe in the Balkans, North Africa, and now the Soviet Union, he no longer believed it would end so soon. The June invasion of the USSR had made a long conflict unavoidable.

Given the Americans' behavior, it was inevitable that the United States with its awesome resources and great population join in the war. Hitler's uncharacteristic restraint in not declaring war against a country behaving so provocatively puzzled Karl. In addition to supplying Britain with food and war materiel, on 16 June the United States closed all German Consular offices and expelled the diplomats and staff. Eight days later, Roosevelt promised aid to the Soviet Union. On 7 July, U.S. troops landed in Iceland to free British forces there to fight against the Reich. 14 August, Roosevelt and Churchill met on a battleship and called for the defeat of the Axis powers.

When would Hitler act? Was Der Führer waiting for the Japanese to do something first in the Pacific? Most important of all, when could he get out of bed?

Karl cursed the feats of his rivals when a voice interrupted the music coming from the radio beside the bed. The speaker enumerated the most recent advances of the German armed forces along the Russian Front where, during a short two months, Luftwaffe aces were setting awesome records. Heinrich Hoffman reached 60 Luftsiegen; Hans Strelow 33; and Hermann Graf 20. In the West, Assi Hahn had 50.

Karl thrashed dismayed. He was missing hot combat against Spits and Hurricanes in the West, Migs and Laggs in the East, and skimming over the azure waters and golden sands along the coast of Libya and Egypt in aerial combat against the RAF. He could not imagine anyone having a better summer than those aces scoring record Luftsiegen.

# Chapter 12

## Time Out of War

"Damn."

That pesky rear window shade rolled down again. Seth Braham parked the 1934 black and forest green Chevrolet sedan on a soft shoulder a dozen miles beyond steaming hot Los Gatos. He adjusted the shade for the fourth time since leaving San Francisco and opened the hood. Seth took a handkerchief from his pocket, unscrewed the carburetor cap, and checked the water temperature with his fingers because the gauge did not work. The Chevy had come close to overheating, but now that he'd passed over the Summit, it would be a cool downhill run to Capitola-by-the-Sea.

Seth's parents gave him sole use of their bungalow on the Soquel River across and up the road from Watson's Cottages, a short walk from the beach for a last vacation until the coming war ended. He would have it the entire last week of August and through Labor Day weekend.

For more than fifteen years, Seth and his family had vacationed at Capitola, eighty miles south of San Francisco and situated five miles beyond Santa Cruz at the north end of Monterey Bay. He aired the rooms and the homey hodgepodge of aged wicker furniture and comfortable overstuffed floral-pattern sofa and chairs in the living room.

Seth greeted shopkeepers and regular vacationers he'd known for years, but he didn't go anywhere that night. He drank beer, sat on the rocker on the front porch, and brooded over news about the war in Europe, none of it good.

He reviewed all that had transpired during the months since he graduated from Cal. He'd inquired about enlisting as a flying cadet but changed his mind when he learned the Army Air Corps wanted a large number of pilots for multi-engine bombers. That would have made him no different from the Nazi murderers he intended to blast out of the skies.

Coach DeLuca had come through and introduced Seth to a young pilot who'd washed-out in C Stage at Randolph back in 1937 for buzzing a girlfriend's house with his BT-9. Freddy "Buzz" Parker taught Seth to fly for twenty dollars an hour and included in the lessons meteorology, engine and aircraft maintenance, navigation, and map reading, pretty much the entire Randolph Field curricula. Seth soloed after five hours of dual instruction in a Travel Air Speedwing.

After Parker's instruction, Seth had two options: enlist in the USAAC with no guarantee he would get into Pursuit, or join the Civilian Pilot Training Program and be deferred from the draft until he qualified as a pilot. Seth chose the latter. The civilian head of the school could not promise any flyer a future in the military as a pursuiter. Most of the CPTP grads had been obtaining instructor positions. Some signed with the new Canadian Ferry Command, which delivered American-built bombers to the British.

By the middle of August 1941, Seth had completed the Primary, Secondary, and Cross Country stages of CPTP training and flown the Waco, the UPF-7 biplane, and the Luscomb, a small high-wing monoplane. The next phase of CPTP training was to have been the Instructor's Course, which Seth avoided. If he qualified as an instructor, he'd end up at a training base, a dead-end career for an aspiring fighter pilot.

Then the Air Corps surprised Seth. After encouraging qualified flyers to leave the service for airlines, the Ferry Command, Claire Chennault's American Volunteer Group flying for the Chinese, and the RAF Eagle Squadrons, the USAAC reversed gears. It sent teams to the CPTP schools to offer the students Service Pilot ratings if they would sign up for additional training, provided they passed flying tests and a rigorous physical examination.

With a reserve commission in the USAAC, Seth could stay at Mather Field in Sacramento until he earned a Service Pilot rating. Then he'd apply for a change of rating to Regular Pilot and an assignment to Combat Crew Training School, end up in Pursuit, and fly against the Germans. Seth read yet again the official notice accepting him for Service Pilot training with orders to report 3 September at Mather Field.

It would be swell if he found Miriam, his Gershwin Lady, before he received his commission; she'd be there to pin his wings and bars.

***

His first full day at Capitola, Seth fell into the routine he'd established as a child, with added privileges entitled by adulthood. He rose at seven, drank several mugs of coffee, and read the paper. Then he took a trout rod to the long pier to fish for jack-smelt until the summer morning fog dissipated. Seth did eat fish, but preferred shellfish. He caught jack-smelt for the play and always tossed the exhausted fish back into the bay.

If he wanted something larger, he could always rent a boat and row to the kelp beds for cod, or a few hundred yards down the coast for halibut. Over the years, he hooked an occasional baby shark or sting-ray.

After the sun broke through the fog, Seth returned to the bungalow, changed into his trunks, and ambled to the beach. He smoothed an oversized towel over a sandy rise at the water's edge. Swimmers rode the waves, children made mud castles, and athletes played football between the Soquel River, which emptied into the bay, and the pier where he'd fished earlier in the morning. Seth felt the strong sun warming his back. He tanned well except for the nose, which he protected with glaring white zinc oxide.

Time stood still at Capitola. The resort was the same as it had been every day of each summer since he was a child. Seth listened to music and amusing comments blaring from loudspeakers a block away at Doug's Roundhouse. Doug announced birthdays and anniversaries between hit songs while he dished out hotdogs, burgers, ice cream, and soft drinks.

After a swim, Seth joined athletes he saw each summer from high schools and colleges at "the mound", as he liked to call it. Younger boys and girls sat on the periphery, and as they became older, they moved toward the center. Seth reached the center core after his sixteenth birthday.

A bevy of teenage girls who grouped around the athletes admired Seth's physique. He kept them at a distance. Tanned and shapely, they were San Quentin Quail, underage jail bait. So was Miriam when they'd met. She'd be eighteen now. Where the hell was she singing now? None of the big bands had a singer with any name that suggested hers.

Seth watched young boys and girls stand in a respectful semi-circle across the river at the boat rental dock where Bill Deane, the great Hawaiian Olympic swimmer, gave lessons. Whenever Seth saw a young couple holding hands or kissing on blankets or the benches along the beach walk, oblivious the world was going to hell, he couldn't blame them. On a glorious, peaceful summer day, who wanted to be reminded that the Germans had conquered the Continent of Europe, the western USSR, and North Africa, and that the Japanese had taken most of China and now Indo-China too? He had a surreal image of Congressmen in seersucker suits on the beach with their heads in the sand. Despite the Axis's successes, there was still strong resistance to the first peacetime draft in American history. Its renewal in October was not guaranteed.

At the food and drink stand adjacent to the casino, Seth ordered his daily lunch of cheeseburger, fries, and a chocolate shake. He returned to the beach until five. At the cottage, he shaved, showered and changed clothes, then ate dinner at Coleman's, a family operated restaurant with a different specialty each night and the best pies. Afterward, he launched his kayak and paddled up the narrow trout-filled Soquel River, which ran through the town and split the beach to empty in Monterey Bay.

Families waved from rented canoes and porches of their summer homes, all with cute names like Dew Drop Inn. A half mile up river he could still hear music coming from The Roundhouse: "Up a Lazy River" sung by the Mills Brothers.

Up the lazy Soquel River at dusk, Seth had only minor concerns. Would the trout bite? Which escapist film should he see in Santa Cruz? *Sun Valley Serenade* or *Down Argentine Way*?

At night, Seth strolled to the Casino, where he played penny pinball machines and racked up dozens of free games, having perfected that skill over many summers. Young boys surrounded Seth. They knew he would leave them a machine loaded with free games before he went into the adjoining room to sit in for an hour of bingo.

After bingo, Seth went next door to the Edgewater Bar for a couple of drinks and watched interplay between the sexes. He did not respond to any of the flirtatious married women from the City, Fresno, and San Jose, whose hard-working husbands visited only on weekends.

In Capitola a young man could become a cynic when it came to the opposite sex. Many wives went into action the moment their men drove back home Sunday night. Most hoped to get someone to take them dancing at the ballroom in Santa Cruz. A few let Seth know they were available for intimacy. Seth kept away from those women. He preferred his memory of Miriam and what might be some day to any current reality. Seth's evenings ended early when he returned to the cottage to read and drink a scotch nightcap or two before falling asleep.

***

The last weekend in August Seth varied his routine, because vacationers arriving for a Labor Day weekend holiday swelled the population. No fishing; he swam each morning a quarter-mile parallel along the pier to a raft near the kelp beds. It was connected by a thick cable-rope to a post on the beach with eight floats that aided weaker swimmers who needed to rest.

In the afternoon Seth drove to Santa Cruz, played games on the Boardwalk, and rode the Big Dipper roller coaster, which failed to approximate the sensation of flying. After dinner he chose not to connect with any of the flirtatious young women. He saw several movies to forget about the

German encirclement of Leningrad and Japanese threats to take the Dutch East Indies. At night, he brooded over the implications of the barbaric Nazi decree to go into effect September 1st, which would force all Jews in Germany to wear a yellow six-pointed star on their clothing. Time marched backwards. Medieval madness heralded a second Dark Age.

September 1st, Labor Day, Seth slept in, made his own breakfast, and read the newspaper on the porch. He decided to drive back to the City the next morning instead of this evening because the roads would be clogged with vacationers rushing home.

Before noon, Seth ambled toward the beach, but stopped when he saw a girl standing on the bridge over the Soquel River and facing Monterey Bay. Bronze blonde hair, trim figure, she had to be his Gershwin Lady. The moment he crossed the street, Miriam turned as if by instinct.

"College Boy?"

Seth embraced Miriam. She responded to his kisses.

"You were right, Miriam. We were meant to meet again, but what brings you here to Capitola? You're not with anyone else, are you?"

"No, and because of you, there's been no one. But does College Boy have a College Girl?"

"No. I think you've ruined all other women for me."

"I hope so, I really hope I have."

***

Over cantaloupe and coffee in Seth's cottage, Miriam related how an audition landed her a spot as the lone female singer with four men in a group similar to Glenn Miller's Modernaires. They sang with the Mac Herlihy Band, and the leader gave Miriam a new name, Mimi Kay, close enough to

Keramopoulos. The Herlihy Band hadn't yet reached the same popularity as Goodman, the Dorseys, Shaw, and Miller, whose records sold in the hundreds of thousands and filled dance halls across America.

"We open in Santa Cruz tomorrow night. I remember you mentioned a summer home in Capitola, and I took the bus hoping I'd find you here."

"Dammit. Unsynchronized again."

"What's wrong, Seth?"

"I have to drive home tomorrow for a farewell dinner. I report to my training base the day after on September 3rd."

"Training base? You've been drafted?"

"No, volunteered." Seth brought Miriam up to date about his passion for flying. He described his flight training and plans to earn a commission in the Army Air Corps. "But at least we can be together all day and night through tomorrow, when I drive you to Santa Cruz, that is, if you want."

"I want, Seth. I made a big mistake two years ago when I left you without staying in contact. I paid for it. I tried, fought it, fought it hard, but I couldn't get you out of my mind. I was a kid then, only sixteen, but trying to act older. Forgive me?"

"Nothing to forgive. Everything worked out for us after all."

"Then understand this, Seth. I'm still untouched. I've waited for you to be my one and only."

Seth reached across the table and held Miriam's hand. "Then you must have known how I felt about you."

"I did, and it frightened me then. But I'm not frightened now."

***

After showering, Miriam came out of the bathroom in Seth's robe and ran to his arms. He didn't know what to do first because he wanted to do everything at once. For the first time, Seth appreciated the joke that explained Einstein's Theory of Relativity: Five seconds on a hot stove can seem like five hours; five hours with a beautiful woman can seem like five seconds.

Five seconds later, the clock the nightstand showed four in the morning. In the moonlight slanting through the shutters, Seth saw Miriam staring at him with tears in her eyes.

"I have something to tell you, Seth, and I mean it. Whenever you hear me singing on radio or a record, know that each word of every lyric is for you, for my College Boy. It's been that way since the first day we met. You are the man I love. The someone I need to watch over me. I'll always be your Gershwin Lady."

"That'll help get me through the lonely nights. God knows when war will come and how long it'll last."

"I know one thing. We'll survive, and at the end, you'd damn well better marry me."

"I don't have a ring for you, but right now I consider us to be engaged."

"I need no ring, Seth. We'll declare our love and commitment on the back of those photos you took the day we met and every letter we write each other."

Later at noon, before they drove to Santa Cruz, Seth wrote his parents' address and phone number on a slip of paper. "Keep this, Miriam. Contact my mom and dad regularly to learn where I am. Write me in care of my parents and they'll forward your letters to me. If you're in the Bay Area, you can stay with them. When I earn my commission, I'll want you there so you can pin my wings and gold bars. I'll have an engagement ring for you by then."

***

Seth's parents invited his aunts, uncles, and cousins for his farewell dinner. Before they arrived, he laid out the photos of Miriam he'd taken the first day they met. Seth's father, brothers and sisters praised her looks and congratulated him, but his mother made one comment.

"She's a schicksa."

Seth had difficulty convincing his mother that Miriam's parents were Jewish. "Dad, here's two rolls we took in Capitola. Can you get them developed and send the photos and negatives to me at Mather?"

"Sure, son."

"I gave Miriam our address and phone number. Read the back of these photos. We are engaged, minus a ring. I told Miriam you'd welcome her if she's in town. Please do so and treat my fiancée as if she's already your daughter-in-law."

***

After the meal, the men set up a game of poker, and the women arranged folding tables for mah-jongg. Seth wanted to be alone and left everyone downstairs with the excuse he needed to finish packing. In his bedroom, he took from his bookcase a rare book in German he'd purchased from a refugee, *Jüdischer Flieger im Weltkrieg*, Jewish Flyers in the World War, by Dr. Felix A. Theilhaber.

One photo showed 15 victory ace Edmund Nathanael looking Prussian stiff. In another, Willi Rosenstein, who had 9 kills, sat with his squadron mates horsing around, smoking cigars and drinking cognac. Rosenstein escaped from Germany in 1936 and now lived in South Africa.

Seth next looked at photos of handsome Leutnant Wilhelm Frankl, who'd earned the coveted Blue Max. A separate postcard commemorating his heroics was inscribed: *Unser erfolgreidister Flieger, Leutnant Frankl*, our most Successful Flyer. He was shot down in 1917 after achieving 20 victories.

For France, Jaques Louis Ehrlich had 19 victories and Marcel Bloch 5. For England, Solomon Joseph had 13 kills. Jaques Swaab had 10 for the USA.

*Will I come close to their records in the coming war?*

Seth stared at framed photos on the walls. In one, he was age eight and standing between Coach DeLuca and Lt. Kilrain in front of the Trusty that glorious day he took his first flight at Chrissy Field. Next to it, a prized and signed photo with DeLuca and the great Eddie Rickenbacker, with "the ace of aces" Spad XIII in the background.

Seth put away the book, photos, and postcard. He scanned the walls again as if trying to memorize everything on them: club, high school, and college pennants; photos of football and boxing teams; and snapshots of himself in boxing gear and three-point stances. Trophies and medals lay on display atop the bookcases and along the shelves.

He bade a wistful farewell to the books of his childhood, his favorite being the four-volume Scribner's Brandywine Edition of Howard Pyle's version of *King Arthur and the Knights of the Round Table*. Until he met Miriam, Seth often speculated if he might encounter a tragic Fair Maid of Astolat, an ill-tempered Lynette to tame, become willing victim to a wicked Morgana le Fay, or fall in love with an Aleta, Queen of the Misty Isles, as drawn in Hal Foster's comic strip set in the days of King Arthur, *Prince Valiant*.

Not anymore. The reality of Miriam erased all fantasies. Seth packed all the photos taken the day they met. He'd enlarged the one he liked best, all of which she'd signed the previous day. Miriam looked adorable in his Cal Jacket with a smile meant for him and no one else. He looked forward to seeing how those rolls he shot in Capitola came out.

Seth's romantic speculations ended when he saw his younger brother Alan watching from the doorway. Any gulf between them was of his own making, not Alan's. True, he was five years older, but that wasn't much of an excuse. Seth had been too self-absorbed working hard academically, playing sports, and flying.

Alan turned out to be a pleasant surprise. At sixteen, he had grown taller than Seth to more than six feet in height. A talented athlete, he stroked for the Lowell High School Crew and would start at forward on the varsity basketball team.

Seth motioned for Alan to enter, and his brother smiled gratefully. For the first time, he realized the boy hero-worshiped him.

Alan picked up Seth 's fraternity drinking mug with the nickname, BRUISER, printed across it. "Aren't you taking this with you?"

"Only what few brains I have." Seth gestured to take in the entire room. "Consider all this stuff yours while I'm gone. Like holding it in trust."

Alan's eyes widened. "Gee, that's swell. I'm really going to miss you, Seth."

Touched by his brother's declaration, Seth wondered what Alan's dreams and aspirations might be. Did he have any aspirations of his own, or would he become a doctor, a lawyer, or go into the family business like their older brother Dave to please mom and dad? Would Alan become a schmuck to avoid, or a mensch with whom he could become friends? Regardless, Seth promised himself to behave like a real brother from now on.

"Say, Alan, put down that mug."

"Did I do something wrong?"

"No, it's time I showed you some great boxing moves."

Seth thought if Alan's grin were any wider, it would have pushed his ears back.

# Chapter 13
## The East

During the last stages of Karl's recovery from a broken back at the end of 1941, he wrote and phoned every senior officer who had served with and remembered his father to certify him ready for combat. Freed from the back brace in January 1942, he married Mariya-Xenia in a perfunctory civil ceremony.

Karl requested a return to JG-26. Instead, he was sent to the dangerous Russian Front for an indefinite period. He suspected Poldi arranged the assignment. His uncle would shed no tears if he died in combat or froze to death.

Karl reported to III/JG-3 headquarters at Pleskau, a sea of crude tents and small wooden shacks, a miserable place during any Russian winter. Gruppenkommandeur Major Werner Andres greeted Karl in the primitive ops office and introduced Staffelkapitän, Hauptmann Erich Lienau, who had 32 Luftsiegen. Experienced veterans of the campaign against the Soviets, Andres and Lienau, were mummified with extra sweaters, gloves, and scarves, and the latter commandeered the best position by an inadequate potbelly stove. The mercury had dropped to -20°C outside, and it was around zero inside. Relentless winds lowered the effective temperature. An icy chill knifed through Karl's garments, which included the sweater Mariya-Xenia had crocheted for him He vowed never to show discomfort or let the weather affect his performance.

Andres pointed across a map. "Our Gruppe is charged with protecting the Junker-52 transport planes from here at Pleskau to the Wehrmacht's X and XI Corps trapped in the Demyansk and Kholm salients, about two hundred kilometers east of the Latvian border. Our Me-109s will intercept the increasing number of Soviet aircraft harassing the Ju-52s as they land, unload supplies, and take-off again."

Lienau showed Karl photos and drawings of the Soviet manufactured aircraft. "The enemy flies the Mig-3 and Lagg-3 fighters, and IL-2 dive bombers. The Mig-3 can reach between 375 and 550 kph, depending upon altitude, but it lacks the speed, maneuverability, and firepower of our Me-109 and FW-109."

Andres pointed at the Lagg-3. "This baby is showing up in an improved Lagg-5 model with a top speed of 620 kph and two 20mm cannon. Because they perform best at low altitudes, our tactic is to lure them up high out of their optimum performance envelopes." He handed Karl another photo and a set of drawings. "This is the Il-2 Sturmovik, a ground-support dive bomber, similar to our Stuka, except that its pilot and rear gunner sit in cockpits protected by armor plate, like big bath tubs. Either blow off the canopy and freeze the pilot and gunner, or go for the cooler underneath the big bird."

Karl studied the Laggs and Migs. "Nice designs. What about their tactics and idiosyncrasies?"

Lienau replied, "The Russian pilots are aggressive when they fly in formations of four or more aircraft. Individually and in twos, they always run to join the nearest large formation or flee to home base. Their experienced pilots lead the formations, and we try to break them up by shooting down the leaders on our first pass. When we're successful, the Reds scatter, and we score Luftsiegen at will."

Andres ran a gloved forefinger across the map. "The Soviets have spread their defenses thin to cover the entire one hundred-and-sixty-eight kilometer front in the Demyansk-Kholm sector. Our pilots accumulate Luftsiegen at an unbelievable rate because they're sending inexperienced pilots fresh from their short-course flying schools to do the job."

Lienau cautioned Karl, "It may be easy to shoot them down, but do not let that make you careless. Here in the East, a pilot does not live long if he becomes overconfident. We have lost seven men in the last four days."

Karl promised himself to remember their advice at all times. He intended to attack as if each Soviet plane held the best combat flyer in the world. That would insure survival against any master pilot or lucky fool who might appear on the scene.

Left alone with Karl, Lienau lowered his voice. "The boss does not approve, but by chance did you bring any Pervitin tablets with you?"

"No."

"It has proven to be a miracle pill."

"I disagree. It's an addictive amphetamine."

"Perhaps, but you may change your mind after a week of flying five or more sorties each day."

***

On his first mission over the USSR, Karl clobbered a Mig-3. The next day he shot down a Lagg-3, and another Mig. Carried away by those easy successes, he forgot all resolutions. On the way home from his third sortie of the day, he bounced a snake-formation of Il-2 Sturmoviks. An opportunistic Soviet rear gunner put some lead into Karl's Me-109 and holed the windshield, one bullet coming within centimeters of his head. He rebuked himself for fighting with muscles instead of his brain, and the following day he knocked an Il-2 out of the grim winter sky.

Despite those victories, Karl was still far behind the leading aces. Many of the top guns had gone well beyond fifty. The combat inflation also affected the awards. In the West, 25 Luftsiegen earned the pilot a Ritterkreuz, the Knight's Cross. In the East, the ante had been raised to 40. Then, because the High Command believed victories came easier against the Russians, it initiated a point system in the West so the Ritterkreuz would be awarded for forty points instead of any set number of kills. A single-engine plane shot down earned the pilot one point. He earned two for a twin-engine and three for a four-engine aircraft. Under that system, if a pilot in the West shot down a single engine, two-engine, and four-engine planes, he would have three kills and six points toward his award. In the East, a pilot would have three Luftsiegen, but only three points toward the Ritterkreuz.

Karl ignored the point system. He was not interested in which total earned what award. He intended to shoot down as many planes as possible in the race to become the top scoring ace of the Luftwaffe and let the awards take care of themselves.

***

Flying became the easiest part of combat in the East. The barbarous state of the so-called Soviet workers' paradise and the vicious long winter took a heavy toll. Good roads were scarce and service facilities few, which forced the invader to rely on extended and vulnerable supply lines. The brutal weather along the dreary Russian steppes played havoc with airplanes and humans alike. Tires went flat, hydraulic seals leaked, fuel lines froze, and radios malfunctioned.

Many pilots and mechanics became ill or suffered from frostbite. On average, one out of every four fighters could be readied for combat each day. During the coldest hours, the Gruppe seldom sent more than eight planes airborne.

The pilots' physical appearances deteriorated too. Many let stubble mar their faces. Not Karl. He earned a reputation for being more glacial than the climate. Unlike many colleagues, he shaved daily, combed his hair, and wore creased garments. He looked upon it as a contest of will, a duel against the elements he intended to win.

Like most Germans, Karl became depressed by the sere flatness of the monotonous countryside made yet more inhospitable by the Soviets' Scorched Earth Policy. When the Red Army retreated in the summer and autumn of 1941, their soldiers burned farms, barns, wheat fields and orchards. They slaughtered all livestock and draft animals they had to leave behind.

Battling against the Soviets and General Winter, Karl also struggled with a devastating personal problem, the cause of which he blamed on Mariya-Xenia. The evening of their wedding night, Karl had approached his bride with respect and tenderness in a sincere attempt to erase the memory of what he had done before. To his dismay, Mariya-Xenia kept her eyes closed, body tense, fists clenched in anticipation of another painful assault. She would not respond to soft words, gentle kisses, and affectionate caresses. Worse, he could not become aroused; nor had he the slightest erection since.

Karl considered and rejected an annulment, which would have left Mariya-Xenia stateless and unprotected. He did not feel vindictive toward his wife, and Poldi had become suspicious about Mariya-Xenia's loyalties. He mistrusted everyone who worked for the Abwehr. That was reason enough to stay married for the time being. After the war, they would resolve their problems one way or another.

***

The Russian thaws arrived. Rivers overflowed their banks. Roads and airfields became mud bogs. Cold, wind-driven rains lasted for days, cutting through clothing and saturating interiors of leaky huts used for shelter and quarters. In that miserable climate, Karl flew in damp, sometimes wet clothing, which froze when he climbed to high altitudes. The 109's heater was inadequate, and Karl despaired of ever shaking a persistent cold. He emerged from each flight pulling at his trousers like a toddler with a wet diaper.

Because of the foul weather, Karl had a pathetic 19 Luftsiegen at the end of March 1942. Early April, however, was another story. He scored well because the Soviets sent into the fray tyros fresh from their flying schools. By the latter part of the month, he had a rhythm regarded as supernatural by all who kept track of his run. At the same time, he was astonished to find himself aroused in combat. In the brothels, prostitutes had tried every trick to excite Karl with no success, and he left them ashamed and disgusted. In his fighter, Karl felt more like a man when he heard the love song of the revving engine and breathed the inebriating, erotic aroma of cordite in the cockpit when he fired his guns.

***

On 22 April, Karl used a high-speed yo-yo maneuver, a vertical loop, to come from high through a formation of enemy Pe-2 bombers. He hit one on the first pass and shot down another when he zoomed back and up under the gaggle. He repeated the maneuver to blast victims three and four out of the sky, and the other pilots of his Schwarm accounted for five more bombers.

But then more advanced Soviet aircraft appeared on the scene, and many of their pilots who survived early combats gained experience and confidence. Veteran Luftwaffe pilots commented on the increased aggressiveness and tenacity of the enemy.

Losses occurred too. Lienau had increased his dosages of Pervitin and flew sweating like a horse with dilated pupils. High on the drug, he became careless. One evening, Karl joined his comrades in a fighter pilot tradition and participated in the division of their commander's personal effects. He selected Lienau's scarf.

Flying two to four sorties each day to the end of the month, Karl reached 51 Luftsiegen with a trio of kills and passed his father's 49 from the First World War. After Karl's 57th victory, the Gruppenkommandeur summoned him.

"Fürst, tomorrow, Luftflotte Chief Colonel General Wolfram Freiherr von Richthofen will be here. He knew and respected your father and personally wants to award you your Ritterkreuz. You will receive your decoration during a short ceremony on the flight line."

"Very short, I trust."

"You must rest. You resemble a walking corpse, albeit an elegant and well groomed cadaver. You have lost too much weight. The circles under your eyes grow larger and darker each day."

"But ...."

"No, do not protest. In sixty days, you have flown 132 sorties and scored 57 Luftsiegen. You have earned a two week leave."

Karl panicked. Two weeks leave could cause him to miss another ten to twenty Luftsiegen. "Major Andres, I appreciate your concern. However, as we are now winning at Demyansk and Kholm, I would like to see the battle through to its conclusion. Then I'll take my rest."

"Damn it all, Fürst, I'd hate to lose you in combat the same as Lienau because of fatigue."

***

Karl's victory streak continued between bouts of bad weather until 18 May. Later he attributed its end to lack of concentration. When he came in for the landing, he bounced on touchdown and ground-looped, which resulted in one of those maddening, freak accidents so frequent in war, which broke his collarbone. The injury was painful, knowledge he would be hospitalized again horrifying, the loss of another plane humiliating.

At dawn, Karl flew as passenger on a transport to Berlin and a hospital. Over Warsaw, the left engine popped, and he prepared for the worst. As the pilot set up an approach to the main Warsaw airport, the engine popped again and went silent. He attempted a go-around, but the underpowered engine could not regain sufficient airspeed. The transport went into a half stall, dropped, and hit the ground. It skidded three hundred meters beyond the airport fence, stripped both landing gears, and piled into a shallow ditch before coming to an abrupt halt and catapulting Karl across the cabin toward a bulkhead.

*No, not again.*

# Chapter 14

## Season of Discontent

Late in September 1942, Hank piloted a twin-engine Douglas Boston Mk III attack light bomber and night fighter for a test flight from Wright Field, Ohio, to Twenty Nine Palms, California, with a two-man crew. That gave him plenty of time to review his military career from December 8, 1941, when he reported to the Air Corps, now called the United States Army Air Force, for active duty. A reserve officer, Hank came back in the same rank he held in 1940, second lieutenant. At first the USAAF assigned him to bomber testing at Wright until April 1942, when he was promoted to first lieutenant and transferred to a comparative fighter and attack bomber evaluation program. That was the best duty for a pursuiter short of being placed in an active combat group.

Hank flew every available American, Allied, and captured, often repaired, Axis-made plane to determine the best in different phases of aerial warfare. Against all United States manufactured fighters, he tested the German Me-109 and FW-190, the RAF Spitfire and Hurricane, a Japanese Zero, and the Italian Macchi. Hank won most of the mock combats and was regarded as the most skilled fighter pilot in the program.

He concluded the most superior dogfighter was the Zero, with the Spitfire a close second. Among the Army Air Force's planes, the Bell P-39 and Curtiss P-40 were inferior in performance to the German fighters. The Lockheed P-38 Lightning flew well against the Zero, but it was unwieldy with too many blind spots. In a Me-109 or FW-190, Hank could whip the P-38 without breaking into a sweat. One American-made fighter, the P-51 Mustang, was the best for hit-and-run bounces. Not yet ready to be sent overseas, it had the potential to handle anything one-on-one the Axis could throw at the Allies. If there had been no war, Hank would have accepted the fighter evaluation program as the apex of flying.

But there was a war, a big war on two fronts. The United States had gone on the offensive in the South Pacific and was preparing to liberate Europe, but he, Henry Clay Milroy, who had the potential to be one of America's greatest fighter pilots, was stuck Stateside and untested in battle. Each time Hank applied for combat duty, his C.O. said he was too valuable a pilot for the evaluation program to lose.

***

Hank looked down at dusty Army tank maneuvers in the desert below and made a mock bombing and strafing run before he landed the Douglas Boston Mk III at Twenty Nine Palms and ambled to Operations. In the middle of his report to the Duty Officer, the man turned white, gasped for breath, and sprang to attention. Hank also snapped to rigid attention. A tall, lean and hard man had entered wearing a shiny helmet and a belt with a pair of holstered ivory-handle and filigreed Colt .45 Revolvers.

General George S. Patton had entered Ops with several tank commanders. He ignored the Duty Officer and faced Hank. "At ease. You the pilot who brought in that crate out there?"

"Yes, sir."

"I like its glass nose. What's your name, Lieutenant?"

"Henry Clay Milroy, sir."

"Milroy, get the ground crew to refuel it. I want to see what a strafing run on my men looks like from the enemy's perspective."

During take-off, Patton removed his helmet, stretched out on the floor, and pressed his face against the glass nose the entire time Hank buzzed over troops and tanks at low altitude.

After Patton had enough, he sat beside Hank in the co-pilot's chair. "Poor fuckin' bastards, the krauts, I mean. You fly-boys will be strafing their goddam balls off during air support."

"Yes, sir."

Patton checked the fuel gauge. "Got enough gas left to fly me over the Grand Canyon?"

"Yes, sir."

"Then let's go."

Hank obeyed and headed on a course toward the great chasm. On the approach, it appeared majestic in purples, pink, and gold under the bright sun.

"Beautiful view, sir."

"Lower."

Hank took the Boston lower a thousand feet.

"I said lower. Goddammit, man, take me into it."

Patton left the co-pilot's seat, and as he had done during the mock strafing runs, removed his helmet and lay prone with his face pressed against the nose glass.

The challenge of flying into the canyon was difficult enough without a valuable passenger. Hank obeyed Patton's command and dropped the Boston deeper into the maw. Downdrafts almost caused the plane to scrape the canyon walls, and he needed all his skill and concentration to fly level above the raging waters of the Colorado River.

Patton paid no attention to the near misses. Hank guessed the general was having the sightseeing time of his life viewing the canyon and Colorado River through the glass nose.

"Holy shit."

"Sir?"

"Holy fuckin' shit. It's awesome, goddam fuckin' awesome."

Soaked with sweat by the time he lifted the Boston out of the Grand Canyon, Hank took it to sane altitude. Patton returned to the co-pilot's seat. The general's facial muscles and jaw went slack, and he sat silent during the flight back to Twenty Nine Palms.

After they alighted from the plane, Patton came to life again. Hank felt a slap on the back so hard if he had false teeth they would have sailed across the airfield.

"A goddam great flight. Milroy, you should have gone into the caval ... uh, tanks. How'd you like to be my personal pilot?"

Hank panicked. He did not want to sit out the war as anyone's aerial chauffeur. "Sir, I thank you for that honor. But what I really want, and I'd be eternally grateful, if you could get me assigned to an 8th Air Force fighter group."

"I like your attitude, Milroy."

***

Hank was not the only talent wasted by the USAAF. He'd heard through the grapevine that Brax shot down five Japanese planes with the American Volunteer Group in Burma. After the AVG was disbanded and its pilots and planes absorbed into the USAAF, *The Powers That Be* assigned Brax to Nellis Field, Nevada, as a pilot instructor instead of sending the ace to a combat unit. Hank had contacted Brax before he left Wright, and they coordinated their three-day passes to meet in Hollywood for the first time since graduation day at Kelly Field.

Brax reserved a suite at the Hollywood Plaza Hotel on Vine across the street from the Brown Derby, where they were to rendezvous with two starlets for drinks and a romp between the sheets. That would be a change from the V-Girls, those secretaries, coeds, telephone operators, and department store salesclerks who visited the bases on weekends for morale-building dances. More often than not they bestowed their favors on the young men who might not return from overseas combat.

Brax paused in mid-narrative and flushed the toilet in the bathroom of their suite at the Hollywood Plaza. "Too bad for you, Hank, stuck here in the States and all that, but for me it was great while it lasted."

Shaving bare-assed naked, Brax bragged about his experiences with exotic Asian women. The Texan's monologue ended when he stepped into the shower. Brax showed no interest in hearing about Hank's experiences or what happened to Cadet Captain Chilton, Miller, and other cadets they knew at Randolph.

Hank waited in the sitting room, smoked a cigar and reviewed how the AVG came into being. During the 1930s, visionary Claire Chennault had lost the argument with the top brass in the Air Corps about the role of fighter aircraft in the coming war. He retired from active duty and became the civilian adviser to the Secretary of Aeronautical Affairs of the Republic of China, none other than Madame Chiang Kai-shek.

From the moment the so-called Undeclared War began in 1937, the Chinese took a shellacking from the Japanese. Early in 1941, Chennault returned to the United States and convinced President Roosevelt's aides the last hope for China in the air was an American Volunteer Group made up of service reserve pilots. He won his point and received contracts for one hundred military trained fighter pilots and a hundred Curtiss P-40 Tomahawks.

After Brax dried himself and got into a pair of pressed boxer shorts, he sat on a chair opposite Hank to buff a pair of shoes and continued his autobiographical soliloquy. "You know the War Department cut back our flying time to a stupid-ass fifty hours a year on the absurd assumption that we could go a long time without flying yet maintain proficiency. And all the time it was obvious that a big war was a-comin'. I ain't interested in all that history crap like you, Hank, so I don't care who we fight or why. Tho' if I had my 'druthers, I'd like to have a go at the krauts. They've got the top reputations. Hells-bells, good buddy, I'd have flown with the French in '40, but they didn't have a Lafayette Escadrille like in the last war. They didn't fight as long either."

Brax would have joined the Eagles if FDR hadn't issued that Executive Order on April 15, 1941, allowing officers and enlisted men to join the American Volunteer Group. "They offered us one helluva a contract with some dummy outfit called CAMCO, the Central Aircraft Manufacturing Company of Toungoo, and salaries up to seven hundred-and-fifty dollars a month with plenty of fringe benefits. Free travel and housing, a generous food allowance, whiskey, a five hundred dollar cash bonus for every confirmed enemy plane shot down. And boo-coo concubines. We went by boat across the Pacific and reached Rangoon in September, 1941. Then came a miserable trip by rail through the jungle to Kyedow Airfield at Toungoo, a shit-hole primitive base loaned to Chennault for home plate. At first, the only fighting I did was against thick swarms of flies and mosquitoes. But thank the Good Lord for all that poontang."

Brax admired himself in a mirror, finished dressing, and bragged again about the women he'd had: Asians, Las Vegas showgirls, movie starlets, nurses, WACS, and wives of fellow officers, until Hank steered the conversation back to flying and confirmed what he'd concluded about the relative merits of the P-40 and the Zero.

"Our P-40 had the same speed, about 350 mph and an extra three hundred and twenty-five miles of range. Armament-wise, we had a pair of .30s and two .50 caliber machine-guns against their two 20mm cannon. But the Jap plane was more maneuverable for dogfighting. Chennault drilled it into us that the P-40 was more rugged, could take more punishment, had a higher ceiling, and was faster in a dive than the Zero. He said the Japs had superb flying abilities, but their flaw was a tendency to fly set patterns without deviating. He wanted us to be flexible. Chennault taught us to work in pairs and use the diving speed advantage of the P-40 to full capacity. He emphasized hit-and-run. It ain't the romantic, chivalrous one-on-one combat y'all always talked about at Randolph and Kelly, but it sure as hell increased our chances to score kills."

Brax explained why shark's teeth had been painted on the P-40 noses. One of the pilots saw a photograph of a Luftwaffe Me-110's nose from the Haifisch Gruppe painted like that. Another volunteer had a friend in the Disney Studios design an insignia for the group, a winged tiger leaping through a large V. Those shark's teeth and tiger insignia caused the AVG to be known as The Flying Tigers.

"Great for morale." Brax handed Hank a photo. "One of my AVG buddies, Bert Christman, used to work for Milt Caniff on that comic strip, *Terry and the Pirates*, and I got him to paint my bird."

The artist had painted on the fuselage of Brax's P-40 an officer in Confederate uniform waving a rebel flag and brandishing a cavalry sword. Predictably, the Texan named his fighter STUDS. Hank searched for the five red circles representing Brax's kills.

"Where are your meatballs?"

"That photo was taken before we saw any action. We were combat-ready when the Japs hit Pearl Harbor, but I didn't see my first action until December 23rd, after we moved to Rangoon to help the RAF defend the city. Let me tell you, Hank-buddy, flying a fighter in combat is the same as pranging a piece of poontang. You get inside the broad three to five times a day and take her up to heaven."

Brax described how he scored five victories and achieved acedom against the Japanese with the P-40 as an element leader in Arvid Olson's Hell's Angels 3rd Pursuit Squadron. "Then I got careless, and my P-40 took a lucky hit from some sneaky Jap. Never would have happened if you'd had been my wingman. I caught a good chute, but broke my leg when I hit the ground. After I recovered, the Air Force gave me a diabolical screwing. Instead of returning me to a fighter unit, the bastards assigned me to Nellis as an instructor. Now, with all those sweet wars going on in Europe and China, a fighter ace like me is forced to watch on the sidelines."

"You and me both."

"But at least I've managed to make Hollywood my home away from home. I've already got me a screen actor's agent to lay the groundwork for my postwar movie career." The phone rang and Brax answered it. "Goddammit, I told you to leave me alone. It's over. For good."

He slammed the receiver. "Say, Hank good-buddy, can you do me a favor?"

"What? Who called?"

"Wilma Lee. I don't know how she tracked me here. She's downstairs with her little brat."

"She's your daughter too."

"Ain't never seen her. Ain't going to."

"Aren't you divorced?"

"Wilma Lee don't believe so. You talk to her."

"Why? What do you want me to say?"

"Wing it for a minute or two. I'll sneak out the back way and meet you over at the Brown Derby."

Hank hesitated. Now he wished he'd accepted his sister's invitation to dinner in Burbank. "I don't want to get involved."

The Texan put an arm around Hank's shoulder. "I'll do the same for you one day, good-buddy."

Hank doubted he'd find himself in a similar situation, but he was curious to see in the flesh the woman whose name Brax had called out every night at Randolph and Kelly.

***

Hank stepped out of the elevator into the main lobby and recognized Wilma Lee from the photo Brax had shown back at Kelly. The tanned, voluptuous brunette had unusual turquoise eyes set beneath a broad forehead and lustrous, straight hair. Hank had never seen Brax with a better looking woman.

Wilma Lee's five-year-old had Brax's coloring, symmetrical features, and curly blond hair, all the potential to be a great beauty. For a moment, Hank regretted not having a family of his own with a pretty daughter like Melissa.

The girl clutched a Raggedy Ann doll and stared at Hank with large eyes. "Are you my daddy?"

"Wish I was your daddy. Wilma Lee, I'm Hank Milroy. I roomed with Brax at Randolph and Kelly."

"And he sent you to tell me to stay away."

"Yes."

"I assumed as much. All right then, you tell Braxton Hale Mobley for me that I don't need him. I don't want him anymore. And you also tell Brax I've moved here to Hollywood, and one day, my M'liss will be a famous movie star."

Wilma Lee turned and walked out of the hotel. Hank figured she must have learned of Brax's plans to be in pictures and gambled he'd be consumed with jealousy if his daughter became a star and he did not. That, Hank mused, was one combat zone to avoid.

# Chapter 15

## Head in the Clouds, Feet in the Snow

Taken out of combat again, this time with a broken collarbone and ankle and severe lacerations across his shoulders, Karl's release from the hospital did not come until July of 1942. Needing a cane to support his tender ankle and foot, he reported to Luftwaffe headquarters in Berlin, where one of the Reichsmarschall's staff officers handed him a box containing a Knight's Cross and Oak Leaf, without ceremony or publicity. Exiled Kaiser Wilhelm II had passed away in Holland, but the Nazis continued to be concerned about popular sentiment for a monarchist restoration, which was why they ignored heroics by royals and nobility.

Despite the RAF night bombing Karl's Berlin home still stood untouched, and he would not be seeing Poldi. His uncle was on an extended tour of occupied countries, murdering enemies of the Reich and confiscating fine art.

Mariya-Xenia resided in Karl's home and cared for Elsa during his hospitalization. She expressed concern about his wounds but otherwise offered no affection, nor did he. When Karl inquired about his friends, Mariya Xenia told him what she knew. The Abwehr had posted Bruno to

Spain. Albert served as a regimental tank commander with Rommel in North Africa. In April, Walti von Frankenthal had been reported missing in action on the Russian front. Combat and bombing raids were taking the lives of other acquaintances and schoolmates.

Gerd alone of Karl's intimate circle resided and worked in Berlin, a civilian again. On leave, he'd lost an arm during a bombing raid. He looked a generation older. He had gained fifty kilos, as if to compensate for his missing limb, and grown a walrus mustache and goatee so that he resembled a Bürgomeister. Discharged from the Navy, Gerd worked as an assistant to the Vice-Commissioner of Berlin, Graf Fritz-Dietlof von der Schulenberg. The Vice-Commissioner's brother, Graf Friedrich Werner von der Schulenberg, had been the German Ambassador to the USSR from 1934 until 22 June 1941, the day Operation Barbarossa began.

***

On a Sunday afternoon, Gerd embraced Karl with his good arm and kissed Mariya-Xenia's hand. The trio settled in the library. Karl opened a bottle of wine, poured, and sat with Elsa at his feet.

Gerd raised the fine crystal glass half-filled with Schloss Teuffelreich Riesling Kabinett Spätlese *1939*, and admired its familiar clear straw color. "Karl, I am relieved you did not acquire an addictive taste for vodka. Prosit."

"Prosit, Gerd. No, we preferred to use vodka as anti-freeze for our Daimler-Benz radiators."

While Karl described his combat experiences, Gerd seemed preoccupied. He leaned forward and interrupted in a whisper, "Did you do more than fly fighters?"

"I had no time to do anything else. Of course the single fellows, and some who were married, strafed the Strasse."

"I didn't mean that." Gerd glanced toward the door, an unnecessary gesture, Karl thought, because all servants had gone into war-related work. "What did you see or hear about the activities of the SS and Gestapo?"

"I was flying four to five sorties a day in freezing temperatures. Seldom sleeping. I had time only for myself and my Me-109."

Gerd stood. "There are things I must tell you. Let us go for a stroll in your garden."

Karl limped outside with Gerd with Elsa at his side. Mariya-Xenia followed with another bottle of wine. They wandered through the untended garden in silence, alert for the sounds of bombers. The sun of a rare, clear day streamed through the trees in shafts of light and illuminated bright summer flowers between the weeds.

"What is it, Gerd? Given your positions, Mariya-Xenia and you are better informed than I."

"Then listen to what I have to say, Karl. Early in the war, I had heard rumors too incredible to believe. Then, after I became an assistant to Graf von der Schulenberg, I met eye-witnesses. Walti was one of them. On his last leave in March, he told me the most horrible stories of what Gestapo and SS units were doing behind the lines."

Mariya-Xenia offered more wine. "I have also seen evidence of their unconscionable sadistic acts."

Gerd accepted a refill. "Of course, it was justifiable to take back what we lost because of the Diktat. We needed defensible borders and restoration of our traditional lands. No one was for that more than I. Do you remember, Karl?"

"I remember."

"But I cannot condone their monstrous crimes."

"Gerd, will you please speak coherently?"

"Sorry, Karl. The atrocities ...."

"Ach, those." Karl gestured as if to dismiss them. "Gerd, every war breeds the most incredible stories, some of them true, of course, and unavoidable in the heat of combat. Other tales are false, the purpose being to discredit and create hatred for the enemy, as with the fabricated Belgian atrocity stories of the last war, that our soldiers raped nuns and tossed infants in the air to be caught on bayonets for sport."

Mariya-Xenia touched Karl's arm. "It has gone far beyond that."

"Of course it has, thanks to modern weapons. Everything now happens on a greater, more efficient scale. The English bombed our cities, so we did the same to London. Now they are doing worse to us. Machine guns and cannon are more efficient. Noncombatant civilians are perishing on both sides. Kismet. I have seen terrible things done by the Soviets under the stress of combat, and by some of our men too, decent fellows all, until they go berserk from fatigue or desire for revenge because a comrade died."

"What Mariya-Xenia and I are speaking of is different. I pray we survive this war and all that will follow. We must be able to hold up our heads high in pride after our defeat."

"Defeat? Gerd, how can you speak such nonsense? We're advancing on all fronts in Russia. In Africa Rommel will soon take the Suez Canal, and after that the rich oil fields in the Middle East. The Americans are beaten everywhere by our Japanese allies. And you talk defeatism?"

"Yes. It is true we are winning at the moment. That is why now would be the perfect time for us to negotiate from strength, not later from weakness."

Mariya-Xenia chain lit another cigarette. "Regarding our ally in the Far East, the Abwehr now has the details of how the U.S. Navy defeated the Japanese fleet in a decisive battle at Midway Island, which Goebbels has so far suppressed. The Americans will be taking the offensive in the Pacific in another month or two. Next year, perhaps sooner, our Wehrmacht and Luftwaffe will have to face the full industrial might of the Americans, with their improved weapons and manpower greater than ours; for a second time in this century."

Karl stared at Mariya-Xenia as if seeing her anew. She did not speak in a whine but with the authority of one who had all the facts. His wife had to be doing more in the Abwehr than translating. Whatever it was, he did not want to know.

Gerd moved closer to Karl. "The problem goes beyond debate over military strategy and tactics. Our Darling is mad."

Karl led them away from the garden wall. An informer might be listening on the other side. "It is true there have been many questionable military decisions, but that can be attributed to poor judgment, perhaps to poor advice, but not madness."

"All military decisions are now made by Der Führer. He does not trust a single general anymore. In 1941 after the Smolensk victory, he praised the marshals and generals, but once everything went wrong this past winter and the Wehrmacht failed to take Moscow and Leningrad, Hitler lost all confidence in them. It is now a one-man show." Gerd went to a table on the terrace where Mariya-Xenia replenished their glasses. "It is well known that Der Führer ignores the generals and often bases his plans on what he hears from junior officers. Then he orders the Wehrmacht to hold untenable defensive positions to the death. He will not let our generals win the war."

"Then let the generals do something about it."

"There's more and worse. Hitler ordered Reichsführer Himmler to establish a special task force on the Eastern Front."

"Your point?"

"Surely, you have been aware of your uncle's Einsatzgruppen terror squads. They are murdering communists, thousands of helpless civilians in retaliation whenever a German soldier is killed by the resistance or partisans, and every Jew they get their hands on, man, woman, and child. That is what I thought you might have observed in the USSR."

The previous year, Mariya-Xenia told Karl about Poldi's mission in the conquered Baltic republics. He had not thought about it since. "Flying combat in the East in vile weather is so damn debilitating. I had time for nothing else."

"Yes, I suppose you have your head in the clouds in more ways than one. It's all sport for you fighter pilots. You keep score and can afford the luxury of treating your opponents as equals with cognac and carousing. You ought to experience the real side of the war, on the ground, where all hands are dirtied."

"Gerd, this is taking us nowhere."

"As the nephew of SS Gruppenführer von Osterwald, are you condoning his atrocities and those of the Gestapo and SS?"

Karl reacted as if he had been slapped. "Gerd, you're my best friend. I have no wish to fight with you."

"I apologize, Karl, Zizi. I was unfair. You must understand that I can vent my outrage only to the very few I can trust. But you must know this. Hitler is more than a madman. He is insane, criminally so.”

“I have read *Mein Kampf,* seen *Der Stürmer.* They reflect views held by a large segment of our population. Is everyone mad?”

Mariya-Xenia poured the last of the wine. “Hypnotized might be a better word. You saw the effect Hitler has had on Uta, Walti’s sister ... my father, brothers, and uncles ... your uncle too. Poldi’s boss, Heinrich Himmler, supervises more than the SS and the Gestapo. He is in charge of the Race and Resettlement Bureau. Concentration camps....”

“Which are becoming extermination camps,” Gerd finished for her. “And we know where they are.”

Karl did not wish to know anything about atrocities on the ground. He could do nothing about them.

“Before it is too late, we must carry out a successful coup against Hitler and the Nazis. Karl, it is your duty as a hereditary prince to join us.”

“Join what, Gerd? Are you telling me there is an organized conspiracy against the Nazi regime?”

“Not yet, but soon.”

Gerd whispered the names of field marshals, generals, diplomats, and administrators, all of them aristos, who were anti-Nazi. Despite that impressive list, Karl doubted any coup could succeed. The masses believed in Der Führer as a god. Fanatic SS divisions, the Gestapo, and many officers and men in all branches of the military would fight to the death for Hitler. Spies lurked everywhere. With few exceptions, no one could be trusted.

For the time being it was all talk. More than anything else, Karl wanted to soar above the clouds in his Me-109.

***

August 1942: Karl persuaded a flight surgeon he was fit for combat, and the Luftwaffe assigned him to JG-52 operating out of Taganrog at the northeast corner of the Sea of Azov. On his first sortie, Karl took a southeastern course over the Caucuses Mountains where majestic Mount Elbrus topped the horizon as the main landmark. The long layoff had not hurt him, and he scored a quick victory against a SB-RK twin-engine Soviet dive bomber with four men aboard for his 72nd Luftsieg.

Four hundred-and-eighty kilometers to the north, the Wehrmacht's VI Army attacked Stalingrad for the first time on 19 August. The tempo of fighting increased on the Kalmyk Steppe to the south of the besieged city, and Karl's unit had to move forward to a new base two to three times a week. Because the Soviets learned well from earlier disasters and improved their weapons, Karl had more difficulty scoring. Not until the end of September when he hit a Lagg fighter over Modzok almost in sight of the Caspian Sea did he get his eighty-first victory.

At an earlier time, Karl might have been beside himself with joy to have surpassed von Richthofen's immortal record from the First World War, but too many flyers had gone well beyond that legendary total. He would need more combat time and luck to stay out of hospitals to catch them.

Karl also faced a new factor in combat, increasing numbers of American-made aircraft flown by Soviet pilots. On 1 October, he shot down two Curtiss P-40s. The next day he hit a speedy A-20 Havoc and sent it to a fiery crash. Then he blasted out of the sky a Bell P-39 Airacobra. Karl's morale soared at getting four Yank-built fighters until he realized the significance of it all. America was bringing the full might of its industrial capacity into the European war. Could its great reserve of manpower be far behind?

***

General Winter made an early appearance in the USSR. October ended with visibilities of seven hundred-and-fifty meters and temperatures of minus twenty degrees centigrade. The snows came with a white fury that grounded all planes, and the temperature dropped lower when the sky cleared.

On one of those rare mornings when the Staffel was able to function, Karl flew at first light toward Stalingrad. He spotted movement in the southeast where the sun was low over the horizon and led his Schwarm toward a mass of Migs and Laggs attacking four 109s. On the first pass through the Russian fighters, Karl shot down two Laggs for his 100th and 101st Luftsiegen. He had no time to exult. A Lagg latched onto Karl's tail, chased by his Kaczmarek, and behind flew yet another Lagg in a short daisy-chain.

Karl pulled eight Gs in an attempt to square the circle and get behind the Lagg chasing his Kaczmarek. Karl's 109 bucked once and flipped out of control with a deafening sound. It went into an inverted spin, tumbled, and spun again.

Someone screamed over the R/T, "Get out, Fürst. Get out!"

Karl glanced at the tail assembly. Everything behind the cockpit had been shot away. At sixteen hundred meters altitude, he jettisoned the canopy, unfastened his seat and shoulder belts, and fell into the bitter cold air. He opened the chute and floated downward into a forest area where he landed between trees in a soft snow drift. Visions of a return visit to a military hospital haunted him.

Karl could not extract himself out of the drift. He pulled at the parachute and planned to stuff it in the snow beneath as a step. As he gathered in the silk and riser cords, he saw movement in the woods about fifty meters away. Four Red Army soldiers emerged with guns at the ready and swept through a clearing about sixty-five meters to the left.

Karl noted the direction of the sun before he burrowed deeper into the snow. He marked a niche in the snow-coffin to indicate north and pulled the white chute into the hole over his helmet. Karl stood motionless. Either he had drifted into enemy territory, or they were part of an advance unit trying to encircle German troops.

Certain the Soviet soldiers had moved on, Karl freed an arm so he could look at his wristwatch. 0930. He could not afford to wait for night. Karl extricated himself, muscles stiff, hip sore. Despite the colder temperature outside the snowy womb, he lowered his pants to relieve himself. Karl's hip was bruised but not broken.

He cut the silk parachute into strips and wrapped them around boots, arms, gloves, neck, and head. He made a hole in the largest piece and pulled it over his helmet. The Reds would have difficulty seeing a downed camouflaged pilot against a snowy background.

Hours later when Karl staggered into home base at Mineral'nyye Vody, he took his comrades by surprise. They'd assumed Karl had died and already divided his belongings according to pilot custom. He did not expect to be flying in the near future and told the pilots to keep whatever would help them shoot down Soviet planes.

Karl's fingers and toes were frostbitten, and his nose went through the entire spectrum of hues before its condition cleared. The base physician ordered Karl evacuated to Germany for treatment of the frostbite.

"How soon will I be flying?"

"Ach, Fürst, I suspect the war is over for you. You need fingers to fly fighters, and you may lose them all, except your thumbs. Another day or two out there, and you would have been...." He forced a smile. "At least your Vögel is undamaged."

Karl was so disheartened by the prognosis he would have traded his non-functioning schwantz for healthy hands and feet.

# Chapter 16
## Strange Bird

Insignificant in the great scheme of things, Hank assumed General Patton forgot about his request for transfer to an overseas combat unit. November 1942, the Americans landed in North Africa, and by the spring of 1943, Old Blood and Guts was leading the tank boys toward Tunis.

During those crucial months, Hank made more appeals and efforts to transfer overseas. He connived, played politics, and appealed for help from Kilrain, now a Brigadier General with 8th Air force in the ETO, and other instructors who taught at Kelly and Randolph. He learned to play a decent game of bridge to charm the wives of his superiors, a lessoned learned from Morrison of all people.

One of Hank's tactics must have worked. At the end of April, he received a promotion to captain and assignment to Combat Crew Training School at Fort Sumner, South Carolina, to prepare for an overseas assignment. Did Patton or Kilrain come through, or had someone else of high rank realized he was needed in the war zone?

That Wayne Miller was now a major bothered Hank not at all.

For his last assignment at Wright, Hank tested a new version of what he ranked as the number one pile of junk in the U.S. fighter arsenal, the Bell P-39Q Airacobra, no longer suitable for interception or dogfighting because the more maneuverable enemy fighters outclassed it. The P-39's heavy arsenal of two .50 cal. machine-guns mounted in its underwing pods and two more .50 cal. guns plus a 37mm cannon in the nose created too much weight for its short wing span. Many of the Airacobras went to the USSR as part of the lend-lease program. The Soviets liked the P-39 in spite of its flaws and used it for ground attack.

After Hank made some classic swoops over ground targets, he flew the Airacobra through some acrobatics. Coming out of a vertical bank, Hank spotted a P-38 Lightning stalking ten thousand feet above and staying behind at the five-to-six o'clock position. Wondering who intended to make a cheap bounce at the expense of the less maneuverable P-39, he wanted to know what he could do with the inferior fighter and accepted the challenge.

As Hank anticipated, the P-38 came out from the sun and dove from above and behind in a classic pursuit curve. He flew a straight course until the P-38 closed to about fifteen hundred feet away. Hank pulled up and snap-rolled to the right. The abrupt slowing of the P-39 caused the Lightning to overshoot its target. The P-38's pilot tipped its wings in a challenge to a dogfight.

They turned back to the attack, passed each other head-on, and zoomed again for altitude. When the P-38 completed a pure Immelmann, Hank's slower fighter managed at best a piss-poor chandelle. After another head-on pass and climb, Hank realized he faced no greenie but a skilled throttle jockey and felt a frustration common to fighter pilots all over the world when flying an inferior plane against a talented foe.

Hank applied every tactic and maneuver he knew. He added wile and guile, all useless against a gifted pilot in a superior fighter. After he found himself less than two hundred feet in front of the P-38's gun sights, he conceded defeat and broke off the combat.

Hank straightened the P-39 and allowed the Lightning to draw beside him. He waved a half-salute, which his opponent returned with more animation and glee than he thought appropriate.

The P-38 landed a few minutes after Hank, who waited for the pilot on the tarmac. A short, slight fellow climbed from the cockpit, and Hank went to congratulate the victor's aerial combat skill.

The Lightning pilot looked at Hank, overcome by an uncontrollable fit of laughter. Hank despised gloaters.

Off came his adversary's helmet and goggles, and Hank received one of the greatest surprises of his life. He had been bested in aerial combat by a young woman with close-cropped curly blonde hair.

***

That evening in a cozy banquette at a restaurant near the base, Hank had not yet recovered from encountering Winty McCabe after close to four years. She had blossomed into a fresh, no-frills beauty not in the least diminished by the gray-green slacks and light gray shirt of the WAFS, the Women's Auxiliary Ferrying Squadron. Hank figured she must now be around twenty-one.

No wonder the feisty little blonde won the dogfight. Before Hank reported to Randolph as a cadet, Winty had already soloed. She also took aerial combat instruction from World War I ace Leo Kilrain. Winty's tactics had been pure Kilrain, which caused Hank to rethink the prejudices he held about the unsuitability of women flying aerial combat.

In the middle of their meal, Winty was still exhilarated from their mock combat. "It's so unfair, Hank. You saw it. I can dogfight better than most men."

"Don't rub it in."

"You know I didn't mean it that way. I've heard that women are flying combat for the USSR. And doing a good job, too! Lidia Litvak, the White Rose of Stalingrad, may have reached 15 victories, and another girl has 11."

The waiter interrupted them and brought their steaks. They were dining by dim candlelight, and Hank speculated for a moment it might be horsemeat, a common enough experience those days for civilians who never knew what they bought with their ration stamps. It wouldn't matter tonight. Those cocktails before dinner had anesthetized their taste buds; and the restaurant had added its infamous secret sauce.

Winty's commitment to flying reminded Hank they'd had much in common from the start. But why had she run from him so often? He intended to ask Winty about it, and was prepared to hold the little blonde by the arm if she made a sudden move away from the table.

"Hank, I want to know everything that's happened to you since Kelly."

"I got assigned to bombers."

"I'd heard. It must have been awful for someone with your dreams and temperament."

"It was."

After Hank summarized his experiences with TWA, ferrying bombers to England, and testing planes at Wright,

Winty said, "Aren't we a fine pair of grounded eagles? You can't seem to get yourself overseas into combat, and I'm not allowed to fly for my country because of my gender."

Hank took note of Winty's WAFS uniform. "Is that why you didn't enlist in the Army Air Force?"

"Oh, Hank, I'd have died being a typist or some desk officer's girl-Friday coffee brewer while men with less talent than I've got amassed hours in the air. So I did the next best thing."

Winty described how the previous September, she had been one of twenty-eight experienced women pilots who signed with the WAFS, organized by Nancy Harkness Love. It didn't hurt that Uncle Roy was elected to Congress.

Winty had lived a Gypsy's life at first. She was stationed at New Castle Army Air Base, Delaware, and ferried light aircraft all over the USA and Canada in the Ferry Division of Air Transport Command. Then in November, the WAFs were taken into Jackie Cochran's WASPS, the Women's Air Force Service Pilots, and Winty flew multi-engine planes to bases all over North America.

"You must have ferried plenty of fighters too. You did great in your Lightning today, Winty."

"I've sneaked in extra hours to fly aircraft of all types. And I'll confess... I went out of my way to deliver that P-38J to Wright for you to test."

"I'd say it's already been tested, and damn well at that."

"I know you'd have had me in any other fighter. The P-39 is a real piece of junk, isn't it?"

"The worst." Sunuvagun, it was how he'd evaluated the Airacobra. He had never met a brighter young woman than Winty. She knew aircraft as well as any male pilot.

"I hate to think of our boys being forced to fly P-39s against the enemy."

"I think we'll end up giving most of them to the Soviets. Last week, I checked out some Russian pilots in the Airacobra."

"Why did they pick you?"

"Can't say. Someone must have read the part of my résumé, which lists my knowledge of foreign languages, including some Russian I'd learned from an émigré professor."

"What is it like dealing with them?"

"Comical. I was rusty in their language, and they had their own ideas about cockpit procedures and aerial discipline. After one confusing session, I looked out over the airfield and counted four Airacobras either standing on their noses or lying flat on their bellies on the runways and grass. Those Russkies tore up the P-39s faster than the new aircraft arrived. They'll probably lose an airplane every five hundred miles or so from here to Siberia."

Winty shared Hank's laughter at that image, then became serious. "Are you stuck here for the duration?"

"No, I leave for CCTS in two days."

"I'm so happy for you, Hank. Any idea where you'll be going after that?"

"I don't care as long as I get into the thick of things." Hank acknowledged a wave from another officer at Wright who had entered the restaurant with a voluptuous blonde. "Say, what ever happened to your sister?"

"Nancy? She married a wealthy rancher and has two children. She's put on plenty of weight too. Take my advice. If you ever settle down, never marry a woman with a short neck."

For a girl not much taller than five feet, Winty had a long neck, trim proportions too.

"You've disappointed me, Hank."

"In what way?"

"Where's the scarf I gave you at Kelly Field?"

"I lost it off the coast of England when I had to bail out of a bomber I'd been ferrying." He didn't want to go into the details of getting hit by a Me-109.

"Then I'll have to get you another."

"Won't one of your boyfriends get jealous?" Hank fished.

"I have no jealous boyfriends. No boyfriends at all. You men, why do you all have to be so nervous if a woman can fly, or do anything as well as you? If you're all like that, I'll never marry."

Hank became aware of the slow, romantic music coming from the jukebox. "Dance, Winty?"

"Sure, and I'll let you lead."

Winty followed light as a feather and smelled wonderful, not perfume-syrupy, but rainwater fresh. The half-light inside the restaurant added a touch of mystery to Winty's features. They danced cheek-to-cheek. When Winty's fingers touched the back of his neck, Hank felt a loss of control. He looked to see if she was offended. Winty's eyes were closed, expression dreamy.

Until tonight, Hank had been unable to understand why girls across the United States went crazy over that skinny crooner whose voice came from the jukebox. From now on, he would remember Winty whenever he heard "All Or Nothing At All".

After dinner and dancing, Hank got into the driver's seat of his blue 1941 Plymouth Coupe and kissed Winty. She responded as he'd hoped. Back at Randolph, if anyone had suggested one day he would be attracted to the tomboy, he'd have laughed in the fool's face. Right now, Hank wanted the little blonde more than he had desired any other woman.

"Winty, there's a motel ...."

"Oh, no, not you too, Hank." Winty moved against the passenger door. "You want me only for tonight."

"It's all we have. You're leaving tomorrow morning. I'm off to CCTS the day after, and then overseas. No one knows how long the war will last. We may not see each other for another four or five years."

"That's an unoriginal line, Hank."

"No line, Winty. It's the truth."

"I can't do it. Please understand, Hank. I'm not being coy. Years ago, I told you my husband would be the first, the only one. I meant it then. I still do. That's the way I am. If I do want you now, what about tomorrow, next year, forever?"

Hank didn't know if he wanted Winty forever. The war caused emotions to intensify and romance to be magnified out of brief encounters and prolonged separations over great distances. Too many lonely officers and men weakened and made poor marriages on the spur of the moment. He thought about the aerial combat ahead with opportunities to become an ace, or go down in flames. He didn't need to be encumbered by falling in love and making a nice girl like Winty an early widow.

She had enough of Hank's silence. "Please, drive me to my quarters."

They said good night without kissing and did not see each other in the morning.

The week after Hank reported to CCTS, he received a white silk scarf in the mail and a note from Winty: "Watch out always for strange birds bursting out of the sun."

# Chapter 17

## "A hero could end matters ...."

On the day of Karl's release from the hospital at the end of August 1943, he had to use a cane. Swollen toes caused pain and lack of balance. Face gaunt, uniform loose, Karl had lost several kilos. He needed to eat well and exercise to regain muscle tone, strength, and stamina for the demanding days ahead.

Because Karl's feet had been unable to withstand pressure, he had performed most of the exercise therapy regimen with arms, shoulders, and abdomen. Karl worried he would never see combat again after a severe infection set in the area of his toes at the end of 1942 and he had to spend more frustrating months seldom out of hospitals as the most cantankerous, ill-tempered patient in the Luftwaffe.

Those long days and nights of healing throughout the first half of 1943 might have been more bearable if the Schwarze Engel who haunted his dreams had appeared. Karl became obsessed with the brunette specter. Each footstep in the corridor sparked the expectation she had at last come, until the appearance of yet another nurse plunged Karl into a deep gloom.

Visitors only intensified Karl's depression. On separate occasions, Gerd and Bruno related how Der Führer's fabled intuition no longer existed. Hitler's meddling in the day-to-day conduct of strategy led to severe military defeats in the USSR, North Africa, and in the skies over German cities.

Gerd lamented the anti-Nazis had waited too long. During their meeting at Casablanca in January 1943, Roosevelt and Churchill agreed to accept nothing less than unconditional surrender from the Axis, which killed any possibility of a separate peace with the West. Gerd and Bruno worried Germany would be partitioned, with the Soviets sharing in the spoils of war. If the anti-Nazis did remove Hitler and all the Nazi thugs, the Americans and British still seemed bent on creating a power vacuum on the Continent, which could have but one result: all of Eastern Europe and much of Germany would become part of the Soviet empire. They believed their opponents in the West lacked an elementary understanding of geopolitics.

But what was he, a solitary fighter pilot, supposed to do about it? What could he do?

***

Mariya-Xenia awaited Karl at Eppelborn with Elsa, and they exchanged polite greetings. He went into the study, placed his cap, belt and holstered Luger on a side table and sat in a soft armchair by the fireplace, then took off his boots and rested his sore feet on an ottoman like a gouty English lord. He completed the image by savoring a cigar and caressing a large snifter of cognac.

Karl stroked Elsa and watched Mariya-Xenia chain smoke and arrange documents on the desk. She wore a cheerful white and blue cotton print dress after an extended bath. A desire to be clean had become a fetish, as if she could never wash away the filth from living in Berlin.

Dark shadows ringed Mariya-Xenia's blue eyes. Lines Karl had not noticed before formed parentheses around his wife's mouth. Everyone in the Reich suffered exceptional strain. The war had come home with a vengeance because of the relentless bombing raids that created shortages of food and water, increased political and puritanical repression, and lengthening casualty lists.

How long had they been married? He had to think. Almost eighteen months. Karl speculated how enjoyable it would be to make amends in the bedroom, to show Mariya-Xenia once and for all that he was not a beast and could indeed make tender love.

What was he thinking? Karl did not want to face what might happen if he were unable to perform. Better to make small talk.

"Mariya-Xenia, I cannot tell you how delighted I am that you've moved here."

She continued to work at the desk. "I couldn't take the bombing anymore."

Karl did not want to hear Mariya-Xenia recite the horrors of the RAF night raids that killed her mother in Berlin during the devastating bomber attack on 2 March. "What did you do when you weren't working?"

"When I wasn't cowering in a bomb shelter?"

Karl had no choice but to listen to Mariya-Xenia's description of the Allied bomber raids on Berlin and other cities and towns, similar to what the Germans had done to all of Europe and England, except on a larger scale. Buildings collapsed and buried people alive. Those not killed or maimed suffered from the death of loved ones and loss of property. They slept little and walked around like zombies; yet, as with the British, the bombing did not create a mood of defeatism. It had the opposite effect, one of defiance, proof to the enemy they could cope.

"Karl, people can be petty under such stress, but generous and heroic too, with odd eccentricities. For example, I have become an expert on sounds. The first hum of bombers. Differences between American and RAF bombs. The eerie warbling sound of spent cartridge shells falling from the sky. You can prepare yourself for death, but once the bombing raids begin, primal fears of maiming, entombment, and blindness return."

"Yes, we all want a quick death. Some of our pilots assume they're already dead so they can get through each sortie. I don't think they believe it, though."

Mariya-Xenia lit another cigarette. "I read, or I listened to the news. Either way, I seemed to be involved with fiction. I remember when Göring boasted that if one enemy bomb fell on Germany we could call him Meier. Now we can call Göring Israel."

Karl did not miss Mariya-Xenia's biting Berlin tone. She had become an independent, mature, thinking woman. Or had she never been the person he thought she was? "Yes, it's best, safer to be away from the center of trouble in Berlin." He switched to English, "But did you have difficulty leaving the Abwehr?"

Mariya-Xenia looked toward the door. No one outside could hear or understand if they continued to speak in English. "Bruno encouraged me to leave because of the SD. The Sicherheitdienst, the security service of the SS, has absorbed the Abwehr. The Nazis doubt the loyalty of the aristos and their cohorts to the Hitler regime. SS personnel have already begun to infiltrate key positions. Unpleasant beasts. They suspect all Russians to be Bolsheviks."

Karl believed Mariya-Xenia still worked for the Abwehr and the anti-Nazis. He didn't ask. He didn't want to know. "The SS types do seem to have limited intelligence."

Mariya-Xenia ignored Karl's pun. "There are exceptions, such as your uncle."

"Yes, Poldi has always believed that the Abwehr is a haven for anti-Nazis."

"I had to see your uncle in order to obtain the information you requested relating to your property, bank accounts, and vineyards. I am preparing papers for you to sign."

Karl understood the percentages of surviving the war as a fighter pilot and did not want Poldi to inherit anything. That was why he'd arranged for Mariya-Xenia to be the administrator of the Pfalz-Teuffelreich estate with power to make decisions and be sole inheritor should he die in combat.

"The Bürgomeister and the Chief of Police are coming tonight to witness our signatures."

"I suppose Poldi is sleeker than ever."

"No, he is thinner, haggard. He has an air of defeatism, yet he continues to mouth Goebbels' most obnoxious propaganda slogans."

"I have always wondered what he wanted. Poldi is as rapacious a collector as Göring, but he has handled my estate honestly. Women don't interest him. Nor is he obsessive about pretty boys."

"Perhaps he is a hedonist, or a cynic who sees no meaning in life."

Karl poured more cognac. "My father said Poldi never recovered from our defeat in the last war. Then his bride died in the Great Influenza. I think he is a classic Berserker. Poldi's hands are drenched in blood, and he cannot stop."

"I disagree. Bruno told me the Abwehr file on your uncle has turned up two interesting facts. Poldi has squirreled away a considerable amount of gold in Switzerland, which is typical behavior of our fearless leaders who urge the populace to suicidal extremes. More revealing, he has begun to learn Spanish and visits often the Argentine Embassy."

"You suspect he'd rather play the rat if our ship sinks and not go down to glory in a Gotterdammerung."

"Yes, I think he'll end up somewhere in South America." Mariya-Xenia left the desk and sat on the arm of Karl's chair. "Enough of your uncle and other unpleasant matters. Estate business and a respite from the bombing are not the only reasons why I came here. I want to spend extensive time with you."

Karl tensed. Was she going to make demands he might not be able to meet?

"I must confess, Karl, I behaved badly on our wedding night."

"You had good reason."

"Not good enough. I have not fulfilled my conjugal duties. Of course our separations haven't helped, but now that you and I will be together under the same roof for the first time in a year and a half, we can begin to ...."

"I am sorry, Mariya-Xenia. Tomorrow, I leave to receive my overdue awards and then to my next assignment."

Mariya-Xenia stood and lit another cigarette. "But you're not fully healed. You've done more than your share. It isn't fair."

"Nothing is fair during war. The situation is desperate. Some of the pilots are flying without fingers, others with legs amputated."

"You prefer to go. I can no longer have illusions that you wish to be with me."

"Be strong, Mariya-Xenia. The war will be over soon."

"Of course. The enemy is collapsing everywhere so rapidly that they are frightened into getting rid of all their bombs. On us. In Berlin, I saw bombers all above the city and not a single Luftwaffe fighter went up to challenge them. Who is responsible for the idiotic strategy of not letting you fighter pilots defend their homeland?"

"Those I shall see in Berchtesgaden."

"Why must you go to Berchtesgaden?"

"The Victory Credits Board has confirmed my 100th and 101st Luftsiegen I got my last day in Russia. I shall be picking up my Pilot's Badge in Diamonds."

"Can't they send it to you? Some aide will hand it over with no ceremony, the same as they did last year."

"Not this time. The Almighty Himself is giving it to me."

"So, you are going to meet our Liebschen."

It was the second time Karl had heard the anti-Nazi faction's ironic name for Hitler, the ironic Darling. He had a clinical curiosity about this dynamic man who restored Germany to a preeminent position, made the world dance to his tune and yet could become the great destroyer of his own creation, the Third Reich.

"A pity. I wish I had known sooner."

"What difference would that make?"

Mariya-Xenia stared at the side table where Karl had placed the Luger. "Those to be invested with awards are not permitted to carry their handguns in the presence of our Liebschen. If the guards overlooked it just once, a real hero might end the Nazi madness."

***

Karl stood with his back to the railing at the Overlook outside Hitler's Tea House three klicks to the east and about four hundred meters above the Berchtesgaden valley below. He posed with three other pilots who were to receive awards from Der Führer at the same investiture.

If the abstemious Hitler knew about the pilots' condition, he would have gone into one of his patented rages. On the train to Salzberg, the aces had drunk cognac through the night and compared combat experiences. Among the four of them, they had accounted for over five hundred Luftsiegen.

The photographer shot them in a group, then individually. Hitler's Luftwaffe aide, Major Nicolaus von Below, told them Der Führer took afternoon walks from the main residence, the Berghof, to the Teehaus where he liked to relax with trusted underlings, nap, and decide upon domestic policies and military strategy and tactics.

Von Below next escorted the pilots into the Teehaus. The coffee had not yet cleared Karl's head when they stood at shaky, swaying attention in front of Der Führer and an entourage of aides and guards. Hitler's ordinary appearance and average size disappointed Karl, who thought his Pfalz-Teuffelreich chauffeurs and liveried attendants had worn their uniforms with more style and elegance.

Mein Gott, how had this common Austrian peasant, who mangled German style and grammar, dominated better men? Was it by sheer will?

Karl glanced at his comrades to see how they were reacting. The poor bastards were trying so hard to appear sober they did not look at their Führer.

Hitler seemed too preoccupied with more pressing matters to notice their inebriated condition. He shook hand, gave each man a medal, and posed with the pilots for a group photo and then singly. After the photo session, he led the flyers into an adjoining room for tea. Before they sat, Hitler stood face-to-face with Karl.

"I am impressed you have been so successful flying. Which fighter do you think is more productive for our war effort?"

Karl had not expected to be addressed by Der Führer. More disconcerting was the effect of Hitler's cold, porcelain-blue eyes boring into his. He now experienced the elemental force and concentration of will emanating from a man who defied ordinary criteria of evaluation. Karl preferred to believe that reaction had been caused by over-imbibing cognac, not by the Austrian corporal.

"My Führer, I know only the Me-109."

Hitler continued to fix Karl with an unwavering stare. "And what do you think of the Stuka as a night fighter?"

"It is better than nothing, but...."

Karl hesitated when he saw Göring enter and stand near the doorway. The Reichsmarschall, said to weigh more than one hundred-and-thirty kilos, had on a baby blue uniform weighted with medals and orders, and he wore a ring on each finger.

Hitler mumbled a thank-you to Karl and shook hands again with the pilots. Der Führer, so electric moments earlier, shrank to resemble a worried, harassed old man before he shuffled out of the room.

Göring sauntered to the four pilots, congratulated each man, and addressed von Below. "Did he get angry and harp on fighting to the last man again?"

"No, sir. He appeared preoccupied, lost in his private thoughts today."

"Good, I want to see our Führer now. Gentlemen, please go to my Landhaus where I shall join you presently."

***

Göring's typical Bavarian mountain lodge, with rocks on its shingle roof for added insulation, had a spectacular view. The interior contained oversized rustic furniture, animal heads, and paintings on the walls confirming the Reichsmarschall's passion for the hunt.

The other pilots stared about the room in awe. Karl went over to a coat-of-arms prominent on one of the walls. *How egocentric and parvenu.* Göring had created the design for himself, a mailed fist grasping a bludgeon. The Reichsmarschall liked to be thought of as Der Eiserne, the Man of Iron.

Göring entered, smoking a long cigar, and spoke with the assurance of one who knew he would not be interrupted. "As you know, RAF night bombers came over the night of 16/17 May, and you did not prevent them from hitting the dams at Eder and Möhne. Now, because the American day bombers have become a nuisance, we have been forced to disperse our manufacturing facilities. The submarine pens along the coast are bombed almost daily. The Americans are poor marksmen, but they are sometimes lucky. Also, our reconnaissance shows that they now have hundreds of B-17 Flying Fortresses in England, with many more to come."

Göring paused, then vented at each pilot, "Now, I do not see what is so difficult about bringing down those bombers day or night. During the last war, I could shoot down anything that flew in front of my guns and always came home with ammunition to spare. We must make every bullet count. Get in close to your target before firing. Fifty meters. Closer." He caught his breath, and screamed, "It is your fault, the fault of all you fighter pilots! You want the glory we earned in the last war without working for it. Your conduct is disgraceful."

Göring next lectured the pilots about fighter tactics, lessons not relevant to the modern era of oxygen masks, radar, and mass fighter-escorted bomber formations. Instead, he rehashed the techniques and glories of 1917 and 1918. The fighter ace of a more primitive Luftwaffe gesticuated to illustrate his concept of proper air-to-air combat tactics.

Göring's forceful manner and eyeball-to-eyeball contact caused Karl to see in the Reichsmarschall the 22 victory ace of the First World War who had taken over the famous Flying Circus after von Richthofen was killed. But it was now 1943, not 1918. Göring's ranting confirmed everything Karl had been told by Mariya-Xenia and Bruno. The Reichsmarschall was blind to all opinions but his own. After Von Richthofen's successor died in an accident, the twenty-five-year-old Göring was brought in from another squadron to lead the Flying Circus. To the veterans, he praised the Red Baron as a combat pilot, criticized the great ace as a leader, and told them the individualism of the old days was to be replaced by absolute obedience to his authority.

Karl believed when von Richthofen was shot down in April of 1918 it may well have signaled the Luftwaffe's doom in the next war. Göring and other members of the Nazi hierarchy made plans for a limited rather than protracted war, with no concept of modern warfare in the skies.

Karl's companions gave no indication of their feelings. As good soldiers, they would stifle dissent and obey the most distasteful command. His own situation was different. He was the Fürst zu Pfalz von Teuffelreich, entitled to lead by heredity and ability. Where had things gone wrong? If the royals and aristos had asserted their traditional rights in the first place, Germany would not be fighting a war at an ideological and military disadvantage.

He caught the Reichsmarschall's eye and gestured for permission to speak. Göring paused in mid-sentence and nodded for Karl to go ahead.

"Sir, with all due respect toward your great record and experience, the dimensions of aerial warfare have changed drastically. The enemy's technology enables them to fly day and night in bad weather and at high altitudes. We need superior navigational devices and new methods to counter their armament and tactics."

"Absolutely not. More important than equipment, what you need is to make a better effort. When you attack an enemy plane, you must bring him down, Bring him down at all costs. Yes, as our Führer has so often demanded, what we require from you fighter pilots is the ultimate effort."

Karl had difficulty digesting what he had just heard. He protested Göring's orders for German suicide attacks and attempted to make a cogent case for the fighter pilots.

The Reichsmarschall waved his cigar to silence the young officer, amused rather than angry, as if reprimanding a mischievous child. "Leutnant, don't be an Arschloch. Shut up and learn something about combat for a change."

Karl found it intolerable to be treated with such vulgar lèse majesté and open condescension, yet he had to take it unless he wished to be court-martialed and liquidated. He complied with the order, and Göring resumed his pathetic reminiscences of obsolete combat tactics.

Karl listened to the Reichsmarschall distressed, that Göring was incapable of understanding modern aerial warfare. The Luftwaffe had become irrevocably linked to the Reichsmarschall's personal inadequacies, and its Fighter

Arm doomed to be the ready-made scapegoat for every Yank and RAF success.

An aide entered with a message for the Göring, who read it and turned beet red. "Send these messages immediately.

"To the Fighter Leader, Sicily. During the defensive action against the bombing attack on the Straits of Messina the fighter element failed in its task. One pilot from each of the fighter wings taking part will be tried by court-martial for cowardice in the face of the enemy.

"To the Second Air Force. Together with the fighter pilots in France, Norway, and Russia. I can only regard you with contempt. I want immediate improvement in fighting spirit. If this improvement is not forthcoming, flying personnel from the commander on down must expect to be remanded from the ranks and transferred to the Eastern Front to serve on the ground.

"Göring, Reichsmarschall."

He turned to Karl. "As of this moment, you are promoted to Hauptmann. You will take two weeks leave and report to JG-26. Congratulations. I wish we had a hundred more like you."

The mercurial Reichsmarschall took Karl by surprise. More astonishing, von Below had been so worried about the pilots' sobriety, he failed to remove their side arms.

Karl recalled Mariya-Xenia's wish that a hero might end the Nazi madness in an identical situation. His wife, Bruno, and Gerd would vent their frustration were he to describe his failure to assassinate Hitler and Göring.

# Chapter 18
## No Longer Knights of the Skies

Hank and Seth met for the first time when they reported to the 375th Fighter Group as replacement pilots along with several other greenies. The 375th operated out of Thetford, seventy-five air miles due north of London between Cambridge and Norwich. Although Hank was a captain and Seth a first lieutenant, the briefing officer assigned the replacements as wingmen.

In the European Theater of Operations, second lieutenants were wingmen, first lieutenants element leaders, captains commanded flights made up of two elements, and a major lead a squadron of three to four flights. With few exceptions, a pilot could not receive a promotion until he performed the appropriate duty, and he could not perform the duty unless promoted.

The officer next described how they awarded medals in the ETO, the last thing Hank and Seth had on their minds. They were eager to mount their fighters and see action. A pilot, the officer intoned, got the European African Middle Eastern campaign medal for being there. The Air Medal was awarded for every five sorties flown, but instead of receiving the medal each time, they were awarded a small bronze oak leaf called a cluster. A silver oak leaf cluster represented ten air medals. The Distinguished Flying Cross was more difficult to earn. It required surviving twenty-five missions or accomplishing some special feat in combat.

The briefing officer assigned Hank to the Group's 135th Squadron and Seth to the 136th. After more orientations and briefings, NCOs escorted the new pilots to their squadrons' hangars to meet their crews and receive their fighters. Flying combat against the Germans more than compensated for their disappointment they would be flying the Lockheed P-38 Lightning, a fighter inferior to the Luftwaffe's Me-109s and FW-190s.

Before they separated, Hank turned to Seth. "Want to wager who gets the first victory?"

"A bottle of Scotch says it'll be me."

Hank shook Seth's hand. "We'll see about that, friend-o."

***

At the 136th Squadron's hangar, Seth learned his leader would be 1st Lt. Homer "Zeke" Zachary, who was on the verge of acedom with four victories, due to return later in the evening from R&R in London. Seth's P-38 had identifying numbers and code letters for its fuselage and tail, CG X, the X identifying the airplane, and on the vertical tails forward of the rudders a large white triangle. Many flyers named their birds after wives or girlfriends. Some preferred hometowns or states. Zeke had a representation of Apollo on his Lightning that he'd named THE GOLDEN GREEK.

A hard hitting tackler from his first football game in high school, Seth acquired the nickname Bruiser, but he asked the squadron artist to paint on the fuselage of his P-38 a copy from one of the photos of Miriam placing her atop a piano in a slink satin dress. He named his bird MY GERSHWIN LADY.

By chance, the Mac Herlihy Band had a twelve week appearance at the St. Francis Hotel in San Francisco when Seth received his commission, and Miriam made the trip to Mather so she could pin his wings and bars and he could give her an engagement ring. His parents opened their home to Miriam and fed some of the band members, who appreciated home cooking.

***

On the 135^th's hardstand, Hank met 1st Lieutenant Phil Jordan, an urbane Manhattanite whose element had been grounded for the day's mission because of mechanical problems. They agreed the Lightning was a great cross-country plane and a fair fighter, but, as Jordan explained, it had some serious flaws during combat

The Lightning's twin engines created blind spots during combat, which required teamwork to an "nth" degree. Its electrically controlled propellers, battery, and generator had to be in good operating order or else the props would run away. A flyer had to yank the control wheel into his lap in order to check the voltmeter and ammeter every few minutes because both instrument dials were located behind the yoke in level flight. A pilot could get into serious trouble over hostile territory when he searched for enemy planes and gambled on the battery and generator continuing to work.

"Milroy, few checks are made in a combat zone, and as a result, many of our boys who find themselves with runaway props in enemy air space become easy prey for the Luftwaffe. Are you a good shot?"

"Guess I won't know for sure until I get into combat."

"Well, if you have an innate ability to pull off deflection shots of 30 degrees at several hundred yards from the enemy, you'll do well. If not, when you get close, get closer, as if you're sticking your fighter's nose up a 109's butt before you fire a burst. What will you name your bird?"

Same as Seth, Hank appreciated the output from the group's artists, some of whom had worked for the Disney and Lantz studios and created pugnacious Donald Ducks, Dumbos, and Woody Woodpeckers. More realistic and revealing of what was on the minds of many pilots were the luscious pin-ups on their fighters created with as much precision and fantasy as any Varga or Petty Girl. Jordan had painted on his Lightning a long-legged dancer and the name MY SWEET ROCKETTE.

Hank thought of the most prized possession he'd brought to the ETO. "I'll call my fighter STETSON."

***

At pre-dawn forty-four P-38s of the 375th Fighter Group stirred up the dust and took-off in flights of four. The 135th Squadron had its full complement of sixteen Lightnings. Its Leader, Major Rollins, was Red One or Red Leader for the mission and Jordan Red 15. Because last place in the formation was always reserved for the greenhorn, the most recent arrival, Hank became Red 16, the last pilot in the last element of the last flight, the tail-end Charlie of the entire formation, the plane easiest for the enemy to spot and attempt to knock out of the sky.

What did the Germans see and think when they encountered the great bomber armada the 375th Group escorted? Each B-17 was 74 feet long with a wingspan of 103 feet. Its cruising speed was 193 mph and about 287 mph its maximum. The Flying Fortress carried a crew of ten, which included gunners on the nose, sides, top, tail, and belly, with a payload of up to eight thousand pounds of bombs. Eighteen to fifty-four Fortresses flew in flights of six at 24,000 to 27,000 feet in interlocking box-formations 1170 feet wide, 800 feet long, 1050 feet high, and one-and-a-half miles apart.

Effective for mutual defense against Luftwaffe fighters, that tactic made the boxes vulnerable to flak. The German Fliegerabwehrkanonen, antiaircraft batteries, had Würzburg or Mannheim radar, searchlights, a cannon control computer, an optional range finder, and four 88mm to 108mm guns that fired flak shells timed to explode near the bombers.

No direct hit was necessary to cause damage. An 88mm shell exploding within sixteen feet of a B-17 was enough to knock it out of the sky. Each Fortress shot down meant ten USAAF officers and men were killed, captured or missing. B-17 losses could be horrendous. After the Regensburg-Schweinfurt raids on August 17, sixty bombers did not return.

The Lightning fighter escorts, with less fuel and flying time available, took-off after the B-17s headed east and rendezvoused with the bombers as they coasted-in over the Continent. The German tactic was to fly in the same direction as the American formations and radio enemy speed and altitude to the flak guns. Often, they flew close enough to the fighter escort to lure them into a chase. When some of the Allied pilots went after them, other Luftwaffe fighters swooped down from their out-of-sight hiding places and attacked the bombers with devastating effect.

Hank and Jordan operated as a fluid tandem, their element flying as one. Much of the time neither used the R/T for instructions. The leadership qualities and can-do attitude of the 375th's officers and men impressed Hank. Despite long held romantic impulses, he agreed with the unchivalrous tactic of a surprise hit-and-run bounce on the weakest flyers in a formation. Any enemy plane shot down was one less for them to send up tomorrow. Each novice pilot killed meant one less potential enemy ace. Terror and revenge bombing of civilian centers by both sides added a new ugliness to air warfare. Why should the fighter arm to be untouched?

Adieu Falcons of France.

Farewell, Knights of the Air.

***

Like Hank, Seth meshed with his leader in combat and at play. A wiry extrovert from Boston, Zachary's accent never failed to amuse and confuse, like the first time Zeke asked if he knew how to play "hats", known in the real world as hearts.

On Seth's eighth escort mission, a gaggle of FW-190s attacked some B-17 boxes heading back to England, and Zachary's element received permission to engage the enemy. Still a couple of miles away from the 190s, Seth saw two Me-109s coming out of the sun. Hank suspected they were the Abbeville Boys of JG-26, the crack, yellow-nosed Luftwaffe fighter squadron reputed to be brave and deadly foes. He called out the enemy, and Zachary broke into their attack at the right moment. The two 109s sped past them, one breaking right and zooming to altitude and the other breaking left and downward.

Zachary went after the climbing 109, and Seth chased the low man at full power. The P-38 could not equal the Messerschmitt's speed. The German pulled away, broke into a hammerhead stall, and came back at Seth. Staring into the barrels of its 20mm cannon and despite his fear, he chopped one throttle, kicked full left rudder, and made an uncoordinated turn-in behind the 109, which sped out of firing range. The German passed, then pulled into another climb that positioned the 109 about two hundred yards behind Zachary, who was chasing after the other Yellow Nose.

Seth cut across the circle to save Zeke. Sighting on the 109 as the range closed, he added another ten degrees of lead. Seth pressed the trigger and saw tracers fly ahead of the 109's nose. Before he corrected his aim, the 109 moved into the bullets. White flashes appeared on its cowling as . 50 cal. slugs tore into the plane.

The German pilot applied rudder and slipped out of sight below Seth's left engine cowl. Seth pulled up for altitude and banked for a look below. A trail of white vapor streamed behind the Messerschmitt as it went into a whipstall and spun toward the ground.

Forgetting the air was filled with hostiles, Seth watched the 109 fall earthward and its pilot bail-out. His first aerial victory came with an element of luck. It was like eating peanuts. He wanted more.

***

Zachary called for silence at the jammed 375th's Officers' Club bar inside an oversized Quonset at Thetford. "And now, let's give three cheers for the best goddam wingman in the ETO who lost his friggin' cherry today!"

Seth accepted a flagon of stout from Zeke. He absorbed good-natured slaps on the back of his leather flight jacket and punches to the arm, and shook hands until he was weary. He was reminded of the sweet old days of high school and college when he celebrated with his teammates in the locker room after a Lowell Indian or Cal Golden Bear victory. Flying combat had at least one advantage over college sports. He could drink during the season of war.

Zachary stood on a chair so everyone could see and hear him. He raised his own flagon of stout. "Bruiser, you sweet bastard, you did it all. You protected my ass like a good wingman should and set me free to become an ace today. Now I'm going to catch and pass those Eagles, Blakeslee and Goodson, and all the other top guns. But hot damn on a pogo stick, if my buddy here didn't bag his own Me-109 too, a kraut who could have split my bung wide open." He reached out to muss Seth's hair. "Bruiser, you're my guardian angel."

Upon a signal from Zachary and to the accompaniment of cheers and hurrahs from other flyers in the club, Seth chug-a-lugged the stout. He lit a cigar and bought a round of drinks for the entire squadron.

Seth loved the raunchy collection of characters like Milroy who made the 375th the best fighter group in the ETO. They were the real starting lineup of the USAAF, and the most fantastic, motley assortment of individuals in the entire ETO.

They came from all parts of the United States and different backgrounds, and Seth related to each one of them. Filled with self-confidence, every flyer thought he was the world's top fighter pilot, invincible too. Every man in the squadron believed he could score with any lady, drink the most booze without showing effect, and require the least amount of sleep.

The fighter pilots' choices of headwear reflected their diverse personalities. Like Zeke and Hank, Seth wore his fifty-mission hat without the grommet, its stiffener, so the radio headset earphones could be placed over his ears. Others preferred flying helmets and goggles on a combat mission. The fighter pilots seemed to wear their fifty-mission hats everywhere else, including, as rumor had it, in bed on base or elsewhere with a de-icer. Further underscoring their nonchalance and individuality, other pilots wore the slash cap, the little go-to-hell hat that could be removed and tucked under the belt for safekeeping or in the event a quick getaway was necessary.

The fighter pilots' distinct spirit also manifested itself in their uniforms. Sometimes they sported a fur-collared flight jacket or a light leather summer jacket. A few wore neckties; most did not. Many flyers could be found indoors and out with no headgear at all, and it was not unusual to see several in a well-worn flight or jump suit.

When the new round of drinks arrived, Seth led the cheers for Zachary, who had it all to become the top ace in the European Theater of Operations. With no running-in time necessary and in less than a month, Zeke had shot down five Germans. There were more cheers and drinks for the pilots from other squadrons of the 375th who had scored today.

Hank came over, slapped Seth on the back, and handed him a bottle of Scotch.

Twenty-year-old Ballantine. Milroy was no el cheepo. "We'll open it together when you bust your cherry."

"You're okay, Braham."

After the toasting ran its long course, Zachary tugged at Seth s arm. "The bus to London is outside. We're not flying tomorrow, and the Savoy will be jumping."

Seth thought about it for a moment. "I'll pass."

"Your first kill bothering you?"

"No, it's the opposite. I'm too pumped up. I need to be alone tonight and sort out my thoughts. Good hunting, Zeke."

"I'd do better with those lovely roses if my wingman came along. It always helps to be with a friend who's uglier and richer."

"In your dreams."

***

Seth had been tempted to join Zeke for a night's carousing with the girls. When not killing time or making their marginal quarters livable, the men of the 375th chased after eligible and ineligible young women in the neighboring villages. The English roses were fetching and charming, with long, show-girl legs and fantastic bodies, and all that delicious cake iced with soft, refined accents. They seemed pleased to be fussed over and kissed by the Americans, who were so unlike their more reserved and shy countrymen, The faster nurses and WAC officers approached one-night-stands with the same zest and lack of sentimentality as their male partners.

Sometimes Seth envied the married men in the 375th and others who were engaged or had understandings. They received photos, packages, and loving letters from their wives and fiancées, which they shared with the less fortunate. During those moments, the bachelor pilots recalled all the girls they dated, and those not asked out. Faulty memories clouded original judgment, played tricks, and they idealized them all. Each became prettier, nicer, and more compatible, which made them regret not pushing matters with this one or that. True memory returned and reality set in whenever a buddy received a Dear John letter. Some had complaints about female hygiene, which reminded Seth of a ditty composed by the dissolute Earl of Rochester in the seventeenth century:

Fair nasty nymph, be clean and kind
And all my joys restore
By using paper still behind
And sponges for before.

Each night to calm himself, Seth reviewed the letters he received from Miriam through his parents. He wrote his fiancée every other day and sent the mail to his home address so they'd reach her whenever she contacted his parents. Seth received mail from his brother Alan, DeLuca and his daughter Carla. He planned to write the Coach and describe in detail his first victory.

One letter made Seth feel proud of his brother. After eighteen-year-old Alan graduated from Lowell High School in June, he enlisted in the Marines. At six-three and one-ninety-five, Alan would be a terror in combat, in barroom brawls, and with the girls. Seth looked forward to exchanging stories with his brother after the war.

Seth tossed the last dart, missed the center of the target, and left for the hangar. The Group artist had had already painted a swastika and type of plane Seth had shot down printed above it. It looked lonely on the fuselage and needed company.

# Chapter 19
## Elfi

Karl chose not to stay at the Hotel Florida by the Tergensee reserved for fatigued pilots. He decided instead to enjoy offerings of the Riviera as a conqueror. Sitting on a blanket, he observed the flow of foot traffic from cabanas along the beach. The sky was clear, the water translucent, and the women and men sun-bronzed. Because many were soft and corpulent, he suspected they were civilians from among Germany's allies and the neutral countries, perhaps war profiteers too. A few would be combat veterans like himself taking a necessary rest.

When Karl saw a slight tanned brunette in a grass green blouse and white shorts emerge from a cabana, he blinked several times to make sure he was not the victim of sunstroke, or dreaming in a hospital bed. Electric currents coursed along his spine at the shock of recognition. This beautiful young woman could be none other than the Schwarze Engel.

Karl's heartbeat quickened when she spread a blanket on the sand about six meters ahead and stretched out on her stomach to read a book. The brunette's shorts rode high and exposed the enticing curve of a rounded compact derriere.

The moment her legs spread apart, Karl experienced his first non-combat erection since the regrettable day he brutalized Mariya-Xenia. He lay prone to conceal the inopportune tumescence and concentrate on the azure sea to soften it before he could go over to her.

Karl believed he could make love with the little brunette. He rested his chin on crossed forearms and studied the young woman through his dark glasses. Karl figured she was about one and-a-half meters tall, around 45 kilograms of weight, tiny by any standard, but with delicious curves in all the right places.

When she turned to lie on her back, Karl decided this young woman was the loveliest creature he had ever seen. A long neck suggested modeling or ballet. Dark brown ringlets of hair framed an oval face, the color of her eyes still a mystery because she wore sunglasses.

Karl approached the young woman. She removed her glasses and squinted.

That smile—Mein Gott, dimples too. Karl's pulse raced with the same excitement he experienced in combat. He felt a similar surge of adrenaline and stared into the mysterious depths of the young woman's enormous brown eyes.

Karl hesitated before speaking. What language ought he to use? The brunette did not look German. She was too fine-featured and small-boned to be Italian, too clean to be French. Perhaps she was the daughter of a Party functionary, a neutral businessman or diplomat, perhaps Swiss or Spanish. Regardless, Karl decided to address the young woman in formal German.

"Good afternoon, Fraülein. Please forgive my boldness. I saw that you were alone. And, as I am also...."

"Yes, of course." She made room for Karl on the blanket. "Please, sit here."

"Thank you." Delighted the young woman spoke fluent German, he thought it prudent to withhold his title and rank. "My name is Karl, Karl Sebastian." Not a lie but an incomplete name.

"And I am Elfriede Köppe."

"Then you are German."

"Yes, from Frankfurt."

"We are almost neighbors. I come from the Pfalzland."

"Really? You speak like a Berliner."

"I spent a good deal of time there before the war. I didn't know our country produced such tiny, slender brunettes." Elfriede tensed and became guarded. Had he said something wrong? Karl could not imagine what. "I meant it is a compliment."

Her good humor returned "Alas, my type is not politically correct. Were I tall, fleshy, and blonde ...."

"You put them all to shame." *Including Mariya-Xenia.*

They made small talk about the Riviera and the weather. When Elfriede touched a scar running along Karl's arm, he trembled. She recognized Karl's emotional state and withdrew her hand.

"Not the dueling scar on your cheek, but these, all over your body, they tell me you have seen much of the war."

"Are you an expert on scars?"

"I am a nurse."

"You have served on the Western Front?"

"All fronts, and inside Germany too. We go where we are needed most. Are you in the Wehrmacht?"

"Luftwaffe. Are you alone?"

"Very much so. My husband was killed last December when his Panzer unit was annihilated at Stalingrad, and I lost my parents and younger brother three months ago in a bombing raid."

"I suppose you've come here to get away from the war."

"One cannot escape the war."

Karl reached out and covered her slender hand. She did not draw away. "Elfi, will you dine with me this evening?"

"Elfi? No one has called me that since I was a small child."

"You are still tiny, like a little elf. Now then, about this evening?"

"Yes, Karl, I would like that."

"Where are you staying?"

Elfriede pointed at a building along the strand. "At that pensione."

"I shall come for you at nineteen hours."

"And I shall be ready on time."

Karl saw himself behaving like a schoolboy having his first crush. It was imperative Elfi find him attractive before he revealed his title.

***

Carrying a bouquet of roses Karl arrived at Elfi's door at seven. The brunette's sun-browned body was wrapped in a shimmering sea-green and black print dress, and she made Karl feel more welcome than he'd felt at any other moment of his life. In the dining room, the obsequious maitre d'hôtel greeted Karl with exaggerated deference in spite of an earlier admonition never to address him as Fürst.

"Karl, why is he groveling? Hauptmann is not an exalted rank. Have you bribed him, or does everyone behave as if you were royalty?"

Karl waited until they were seated. "I promise to answer all your questions if first you will tell me everything about yourself."

"Fair enough, Karl. Or do you prefer that I call you Hauptmann?"

Elfi's imitation of the groveling maitre d'hôtel amused Karl. "You are absolutely stunning."

"Thank you, but I fear you've been in combat for so long your sense of appreciation is warped. My eyes are still red from my troubles of the past year, and my clothes are out of fashion, a condition that will last, I am sure, until the end of the war. Are those two Luftwaffe officers over there in your Gruppe?"

Karl started for a moment, afraid he might be recognized, then thanked St. Horridus they were strangers from a different unit. "No."

The sommelier served glasses of champagne. Karl wanted to embrace Elfi, kiss her, but instead, he clicked his heels when they touched glasses.

During their first dance between courses, Karl exerted self-control. Elfi pleased him more than he could express, and desire for the slight brunette replaced flying the Me-109 in aerial combat as the acme of existence.

Karl crushed Elfi to his chest. It was all he could do to keep from making an utter ass of himself, from committing some boyish faux pas. His heritage, upbringing, and training should have prepared him to meet such challenges without revealing how he felt.

"Elfi ...."

"I do not know what has come over me since we met this afternoon, and you have no more self-control than I."

"A walk on the beach might do us more good than dinner."

"No, Karl, not the beach."

***

When they entered Karl's room, Elfi saw his medals on top of the dresser. "I ought to have known. You are a hero."

"Oh, those baubles? They award medals merely for surviving. Every pilot has at least one. It is something like the Great Inflation of the 1920s."

She held Karl's Pilot's Badge in Diamonds. "Tell me how you earned this one, Hauptmann."

Instead of reciting combat experiences, Karl described his long periods in the hospitals. He named each one and the dates he was a patient. Elfi confirmed that she had been at the same hospital the first time he was wounded.

"And you thought I was a hallucination?"

"I cannot tell you how delighted I am that you are flesh and blood, and that I found you at last." He moved to kiss her.

Elfi kept Karl at arm's length. "Tell me the truth. Are you married?"

*Women and their inexplicable intuition.* "We are estranged. Because of the war, we have delayed our inevitable divorce."

"Or reconciliation?"

"Never."

"I wonder."

The memory of what he had done to Mariya-Xenia haunted Karl. He gave Elfi light kisses and tried to remove her necklace. Karl's hands shook, and he was unable to undo the clasp.

"Karl, you are too nervous. So am I. Here, let me do it. You take care of yourself. And please, be gentle. It has been almost a year for me, and my husband was my first and only."

They did not sleep the entire night and discovered every millimeter of each other. Heated moments gave way to periods when they lay side-by-side looking at one another in awe.

When the morning sun cut across Karl and Elfi through slits in the shutters, she went to close them. He stretched and yawned, smug and satisfied. His impotence had been banished, and he was in love.

Elfi returned to the bed and fell into Karl's arms. They did not go out any of the remaining days and nights of Karl's leave.

***

During an extended calm interlude, Karl satisfied Elfi's curiosity and described how he met and married Mariya-Xenia. When he asked about Elfi's background and life before the war, she was reluctant to go into detail. He pressed for answers. "What was your family name before you married?"

"Wohlmann."

"Go on. Tell me about your parents, your entire family."

"My background is petit bourgeois. My father was a Professor of Engineering at...." She began to sob. "Vati, Vati ...."

Karl held Elfi while she cried.

***

The morning of Karl's last day of leave, Elfi watched him shave. "I feel guilty. Because of me, you have no tan. When will you be able to lie in the sun again?"

"Of more importance, when shall we be together again?"

"Whenever you wish. Whenever you can."

Before Elfi, Karl had looked forward to more combat and Luftsiegen in a day-to-day existence. Now, for the first time in years, he thought of a future that did not include flying.

"Elfi, I love you. I love you with all my heart, as I have loved no one else. I swear it. Will you be mine?"

"Yes."

# Chapter 20

## Gains and Losses

Hank took off for yet another escort mission flying top cover for the B-17s. During the climb, the 375th had to penetrate a cumulus cloudbank lying athwart their course so thick nothing except Jordan's P-38 flying off wing was visible.

Over-water flying was dangerous when the sky was the same color as the Channel and North Sea with no defined horizon. On those grey days, each leader had to watch the dials while his wingman searched for enemy planes. It was almost impossible to see before too late the Messerschmitts and Focke-Wulfs making sudden appearances through the gloom. One comforting thought, the Luftwaffe pilots had the same problems, and Hank imagined them jumping out of their hides whenever they found themselves head-to-head with a P-38. More often than not, neither friend nor foe had time to gain a shooting position before the target disappeared.

At 17,000 feet, the sky took on a lighter hue. The first danger point would come when they broke out on top of the clouds. Enemy fighters might be lurking nearby for an ambush.

When Hank's P-38 nosed above the smooth and flat cloud tops into bright sunshine, the other fighters of the 375th were visible. At the extreme right position of the formation, he dropped right wing, looked over his shoulder, and spotted two FW-190s and an Me-110 two hundred yards away flying a parallel course. Hank touched the radio transmitter tit.

"Bandits. Three o'clock level."

Hank broke to the right and bore toward the enemy. He lined his sight on the closest FW-190 and touched the trigger. The first tracers were on target, and he continued to press the firing tit until the FW-190 exploded. Chunks of metal and pieces of the pilot flew out of the fireball and down toward the undercast.

The second 190 and the Me-110 pushed over and turned under Hank's nose to prevent him from firing a shot. Excited by his first aerial victory, Hank almost asked over the R/T if anyone had seen it happen but had enough self-control to maintain silence. He searched for the fighters of the 375th. Jordan alone was visible three hundred feet behind in perfect position.

Two decoy 109s appeared nearby to lure the group into a trap, but Hank called into the R/T, "Red 13, bandits at two o'clock low position."

"Roger, Red 14. You take him. We'll follow you."

Hank flew over the decoys as if he had not seen them, rolled the P-38 on its back, and dove for the pair of bait aircraft. As if welded in position, Jordan flew at Hank's right rear ready to attack the 109 on the right.

The German pilots were smart tacticians and knew when to end the game. One broke left, the other to the right. The sacrificial lambs became predators and executed a sandwich ploy, a tight 360-degree turn in opposite directions to bring the P-38s across the sights of their guns.

Hank's best option was to make a tighter turn to head them off, which was what the Luftwaffe pilots wanted. The Germans knew the Lightnings would lose speed in a tactical turn and place them in the sights of the opposite Me-109s.

Hank reduced twice the amount of speed the Germans anticipated. When a Me-109 overshot him, he crossed the controls and went into a snap-roll. The German fighter wallowed in front of Hank, who pressed the trigger but missed. Another Messerschmitt burst from the undercast. It went into a vertical climb and zoomed past Hank into a hammerhead stall in an attempt to latch on to his tail.

Hank turned the P-38 upward to meet his opponent head-on, and they passed within a few feet of each other unable to get clear shots. He chopped throttle and kicked bottom rudder, expecting the Me-109 to come again. The Lightning slewed left, and as Hank turned to stay beneath the 109, he spotted another pair of P-38s on the perch. The German saw them too and started to break into the two Lightnings.

Hank anticipated the German's reaction and pulled 7Gs in a turn to the right calculated to put his Lightning behind the 109 when he rolled out. The 109 pilot fishtailed to slow the fighter but overran Hank's P-38 and slid sideways ahead. Hank fired a burst and shattered the entire side panel of the 109's engine cowl. Along with other debris, the cockpit canopy flew off. The pilot looked at Hank and waved him away.

Surprised by the personal communication from an enemy in the middle of battle, Hank slowed and slid to the left. The German burst out of the cockpit and passed fifty feet off Hank's right wing as he glanced back at the flaming

109. It began its final plunge to disappear into the heavy overcast five hundred feet below. Hank searched for the pilot who had fallen into the clouds. Had his chute opened or not?

"Red 14, great shooting. Turn right and join up. The Jerry got a good chute."

That put a broad grin across Hank's face. He still held the Great War romantic notion he shot down planes, never the pilots.

Back on the ground, Jordan and Hank's gun camera confirmed the two victories, and Seth opened the bottle of scotch to celebrate. Afterward, Hank's excitement at losing his cherry gave way to mixed feelings. He would never forget the German pilot blazing toward him in a hellish ball of fire.

Hank wrote a letter to his parents:

... and so, it happened at last. I shot down two German fighters. It wasn't the fun I always dreamed it would be. Today I also killed a man ....

***

After that same mission, the CO upgraded Seth to element leader because the 136th Squadron had lost a flight leader and Zeke replaced the lost officer. Each day Seth learned something new about flying and conduct of war. At morning briefings, the pilots received estimates on the latest order of battle. Intelligence believed the Luftwaffe was reorganizing its Western Front air defense because of increasing Allied bomber strength in England and now had more than fifteen hundred Me-109s and FW-190s. Still, the order held firm not to chase enemy fighters during bomber escort.

Zeke complained that directive interfered with his scoring more victories. All pilots felt like sitting ducks waiting for the Luftwaffe to deliver the first blow.

A subsequent mission confirmed their concerns. Over the Zuider Zee, more than forty Me-109s and FW-190s came out of a frontal cloud bank in a dive and pounced on the escorting P-38s of the 375th. One moment Zeke was visible off Seth's right, an instant later an FW-190 blasted his buddy out of the sky.

The Germans continued straight into the bombers. Two 109s went down in flames, and their comrades completed the dive through the massed B-17 formation. The enemy knocked down seven of the big birds and out-ran the American fighters who could not have caught them if they tried through Christmas.

That evening after the debriefing, the somber pilots of the 375th gathered at the Officers' Club bar. The Group CO called for quiet and offered toasts to Zachary and all the other good men they lost. Hank commiserated with Seth. After the pilots drank to their fallen comrades, they began their usual animated conversations with characteristic gestures to simulate aerial combat.

Seth would write a letter to Zeke's family in a day or two when he felt up to it. He ordered another drink. And another. Other pilots from the squadron had been shot down or killed in accidents, but this was Seth's first loss of a close friend in combat. If he had ever tied one on before, those bouts were amateurish compared to the binge he planned to go on for good old Zeke. He vowed never again to become attached to any other fighter pilot for the duration of the war.

Seth had his darkest thought yet. That pilot he had shot down during an earlier mission had gotten a good chute. What if he flew the 190 that blasted Zeke out of the sky? Seth would never know for sure, and that possibility haunted him. He might not be ready to shoot down parachuting Germans, but from now on he intended to make sure they never got a chance to escape from their planes and return to combat.

# Chapter 21

## Gallant Gesture

Hank's element leader Phil Jordan completed his 50th mission and was rotated home to be a pilot instructor. Upgraded to take Jordan's place with a wingman, Hank had a better chance to score aerial victories, provided they'd be allowed hot pursuit.

On subsequent missions, Hank scored two more kills that had to be confirmed by the Victory Credits Board, whoever they were back in the USA. In combat zones, the tendency at group and squadron levels was to give a pilot credit on the spot for each victory, but after the gun-camera film and paper reports were assembled in Washington D.C. where the Almighty Board sat, the picture often changed and credits were denied.

It happened to Hank after a melee over Belgium when he shot down a pair of FW-190s with no eye witnesses. He saw both planes plummet into the undercast, one flaming, the other smoking. After Hank returned to Thetford, the gun-camera film showed nothing. If the gun-camera was set for light exposure and the pilot fired his guns down-light, he got a perfect record of the action. If he fired toward the sun, all the pilot brought home was film filled with sunbursts.

Every pilot had the same frustrating problem. Having company for his misery failed to compensate Hank for being denied acedom.

On his next mission Hank's fighter took a series of hits after he ran out of ammo. The Lightning was still flyable, but he prepared to bail if the German made another pass for the kill. Instead, the 109 moved parallel to Hank's P-38 until their wings almost touched. Its pilot escorted Hank out of the combat zone. The German further astonished Hank with a salute before he broke to the east.

Hank returned the salute even if 109 pilot never saw it. From now on, he would search the skies for Me-109 number 23 with a wine bottle and the word SPRITZ on its fuselage. He had to learn that German's identity and the reason for his gallant gesture.

***

Karl created a stir when he returned to JG-26. Everyone was astounded to see the prince smiling and less aloof. Before dinner on the evening of his arrival, he offered to give sabre lessons to some of the younger pilots.

Whenever Karl thought about Elfi, he could not resist a broad grin. He had never been so at ease with anyone outside his caste, nor had he ever imagined himself loving a commoner.

Karl took command of a Schwarm and wounded a P-38 that had fired out its guns. Instead of preparing for the kill, he remembered something his father described. Karl interfered with other pilots of his Schwarm who wanted to poach for an easy Luftsieg and escorted the Amerikaner out of the combat zone. Foolish? Perhaps. He hoped the Staffelkapitän would understand.

Still in too benign a frame of mind for combat, Karl tried not to think of Elfi when he led his quartet of Me-109s through a P-38 escort and a wall of .50 cal. bullets into an attack against a box of B-17s. He positioned his 109 behind the lead bomber and aimed so its crew might be able to bail out. The Yank pilot reefed the Fortress in an evasive maneuver. Karl's first shots hit and exploded the bomber. He uttered a brief prayer to St. Horridus for the Americans.

When Karl maneuvered into a 4G pull-out, he heard the distinctive sound of bullets tearing into metal. A powerful blow to the left shoulder jolted Karl. He never saw who hit his Me-109.

Karl went into a vertical climb and near the stalling point saw blood specks on the windshield, his blood. He fought intense pain and struggled to stay conscious. Karl's holed Me-109 came out of the rhubarb still in one piece and flyable. The other three fighters of his Schwarm also survived the attack against the B-17s and flew escort. Somehow, Karl nursed his Me-109 to home base and, after a successful landing, passed out.

He came to in a hospital bed, his left shoulder, back, and upper arm bandaged. An attending nurse attempted a reassuring smile. "Fürst, I can guarantee that in time you will be all right and fly combat again. But not before Christmas."

Karl had to let Elfi know where he was. She should be the one nursing him, not strangers.

*** 

To keep their pecker up, as the British called morale, 8th Air Force rotated its fighter pilots on schedule for a few days R&R in London. During his first three-day pass as an element leader, Hank awakened shaking in the room at the Savoy he shared with Seth and another officer. Braham also was having a nightmare and strangling a pillow.

From the day they arrived in the 375th, Hank felt an affinity with Braham. They spent much of the time telling tales of football and other sports they played. They were in the same boat when it came to women. Braham was engaged and loyal to some band singer, and despite his own desire to roam, he couldn't stop thinking about Winty. Before Hank fell asleep again, he thought it would be great if he and Braham ended up in the same squadron.

***

After a gallon of coffee, steam bath, shave, and shower Seth was still hung over. His eyes were red with dark satchels underneath. As Jack Benny once said of radio rival Fred Allen, "Even his bags have bags."

Seth lit a cigar and turned from the mirror to say goodbye, but Milroy was stacking zees on top of the blanket where he'd passed out in the wee hours of the morning. The crapped-out cowboy lay there bare-assed naked except for a white silk scarf around his neck and a Stetson.

Friendly acquaintances from the day of their arrival at the 375th, yesterday they had bonded and tied on a good one. Seth had relished Milroy's tales of growing up in Wyoming, encounters with women, and cadet days in Texas. They had also compared their athletic and combat experiences and successful sorties on the fair sex.

Each time they got on the subject of women they'd known, Milroy had compared every girl to some little lady named Winty. The poor guy loved her and didn't know it. Seth was not about to tell him that. Milroy would have to find out for himself.

Seth left a Havana on Milroy's nightstand. Too bad they weren't in the same squadron. That was some tale Milroy told about Me-109 number 23 with a wine bottle logo and the word SPRITZ. It reminded Seth of other tales of gallantry from the First World War. Maybe he'd encounter Number 23 too.

# Chapter 22

## Good Chute

Promoted to Captain and upgraded to flight leader responsible for two elements of four aircraft, Seth had three confirmed victories. On a cold late December morning, he stood outside the operations shack in his winter flying suit. The sun would not rise above the horizon for another hour, and he listened to the B-17s throbbing overhead as they joined up from bases all over the United Kingdom. The bombers flew lights-on to lessen the chance of mid-air collisions in the moisture laden air.

It was still dark that far north when the Flying Fortresses took off at 0800 hours. They circled at their assigned altitudes until all planes assembled, a task that consumed an hour. Then, at a coordinated time, the mission got underway and the formations flew toward the Continent.

P-38 engines in one of the nearby hardstands roared into life and returned Seth's thoughts to his part in the mission. The bombers were to hit Saarbrucken in the heart of the Pfalzland, with Ludwigshafen as an alternate target. Intelligence briefed the pilots that Luftwaffe would contest them. The Germans had been seen occupying additional airfields during the past few days reinforced by veteran fighter units from the Mediterranean or Soviet Fronts.

Visibility dropped in the light fog to one mile. When bombers took off under those cold damp atmospheric conditions, their propellers created vapor trails so thick they often caused the planes scheduled to take-off behind them to cancel their participation in the mission.

This morning, the mist being formed by the twirling props was not persistent enough to set up an all-encompassing fog. Nevertheless, the day would be gray all the way to the target and back. The weather prophets had prognosticated no horizon visible at any altitude. Forward visibility would be one mile at ground level, three miles at all altitudes up to twenty thousand feet, and ten miles above that.

*** 

The P-38s of the 136th took off in pairs. The squadron CO climbed straight out, leveled at fifteen hundred feet, and began a big circle over the field to allow the fighters taking off behind him to join up. When Seth's flight of eight assembled, he led them to a designated position on the CO's right wing. The entire group now formed in one circle and minutes later climbed to altitude on course for the Continent.

They approached the French coast at first light. Seth saw the B-17s trundling along in their massive formation about three miles south. When the bomber armada coasted-in over Calais, the 375th's CO led the group on a slight swing away from Fortresses to an estimated ten-mile separation to the north of the German air defense systems.

Seth thought it idiotic to plot a course straight through a known hazardous flak zone like Calais. The seaport had the heaviest concentrations of anti-aircraft guns on the entire coast, but Bomber Command had no respect for ground fire.

As Seth anticipated, over Calais the sky around the bomber stream erupted when German flak batteries opened fire. He saw three B-17s explode and a damaged half-dozen lose altitude and turn back to England. How many more had been hit? Seth saw only a small portion of the Fortress formation because visibility was no more than seven to ten miles at that altitude.

The B-17s tightened their boxes and continued to fly through the flak. They took their chances because the overall loss rate was tolerable. Seth had heard bomber crews chide fighter pilots for abandoning their formations and flying around the heavy flak zones as if they were yellow. The fighter boys countered it was better to be a prudent and live pilot than a stupid and dead one, but whenever the 109s and 190s appeared in the vicinity, the fighters would fly with the bombers through the murderous flak.

No enemy rose to challenge them. Ten miles southeast of Calais, the little friends moved nearer to their big friends, but no closer than a mile. Fighter pilots suspected the majority of bomber gunners, in order to avoid being foot soldiers, had bullshitted their way through the eye-test portion of Air Force physicals. Too many tail, side, and belly gunners thought every airplane in the sky, other than their own four-engine mammoths, was the enemy.

On every run, some jerk blasted away at the escort with . 50 cal. guns, which spooked everyone in his bomber and the other B-17s nearby. Then some panicked bomber pilot would yell Bandits! on the radio and cause all hell to break loose. At that point, the safest place for the escort fighters was to be far out of range of those lethal .50s.

From the first mission flying bomber escort, Seth gnashed his teeth in frustration at the tragic accidents caused by jumpy gunners. Too many good men had been killed by their own comrades in this war.

The Initial Point of the bombing run was Pirmasen, a town located in the middle of a triangle formed by Saarbrucken, Ludwigshafen, and Karlsruhe. That IP had been selected to make the Germans believe the target would be either Ludwigshafen or Karlsruhe.

When the lead B-17s were over Pirmasen, they turned and headed for Saarbrucken to begin their bombing run over the Primary Target. The rest of the bomber stream followed as the fighter escort wove a back-and-forth course alongside the Fortresses and waited for the Luftwaffe to appear.

Twenty-three kilometers west of Pirmasen over the village of Zweibrucken, a horde of 109s and 190s burst out of the undefined sky. They made a head-on pass at the bombers and ripped through the formation all the way to Pirmasen. Several B-17s exploded, and Seth saw men, bombs, and pieces of metal flying off the hit bombers. Other flaming Fortresses fell earthward. Few men got good chutes.

The Germans then zoomed east into the same gray soup with designated flights of P-38s in hot pursuit. Seth's squadron continued to shepherd the big friends. He led his flight on a turn to the right and passed over Homburg at 18,000 feet. When he reversed and headed left toward Saarbrucken, four FW-190s materialized out of the haze head-on.

Seth sighted on the second from the left. The closing rate between the two fighters must have been over 650 mph, but he did get off a one and-a-half second burst. Seth saw tracers go toward the target and then flashes where bullets hit the nose of the oncoming FW-190.

"That's for Zeke, you Nazi bastard."

"You got him, Lead'. He's on fire."

Too busy to react to his fourth kill, Seth scanned the sky for more enemy fighters and spotted a Schwarm. Moments later, he saw two Me-109s ahead and a thousand feet below streaking toward the bomber boxes. Seth banked left and led the way across the top of the bombers, wary of the enemy planes and trigger-happy B-17 gunners. Sure enough, the German fighters zoomed above and ahead as they attacked the Fortresses.

Seth slid behind a 109 and fired from five hundred feet. The German fighter blew white coolant smoke as bullets hit home, and the plane began a series of slow rolls that developed into a tailspin. The canopy fell away, and the pilot tumbled out of the cockpit.

The other 109 broke away, and Seth looked back at the parachuting German. "You lucky s.o.b."

"Good shooting, Lead'." Then a scream: "Watch it. Break ...."

Too late. Seth heard bullets tearing through his Lightning. The canopy shattered. Dirt flew. The fire warning light from the right engine glared. Yawing sideways, the P-38 snapped into a spin. Seth pulled the throttles to idle and after three turns recovered, but he could not keep the plane from entering a spin in the opposite direction.

"You're on fire! Get out."

Seth released what was left of the canopy, unfastened harness and seatbelt, and stood in the cockpit. Centrifugal forces threw Seth clear of the crossbar between the tail booms. He yanked the ripcord of the chute and watched his P-38 spin toward its inevitable crash.

***

Seth's chute snagged on the branches of a tall tree in a forested hillside. He hit the quick release button on the harness and fell to the ground with the silk floating down beside him. He gathered in the chute and scanned the silent deserted forest, worried someone might have seen him parachute even though visibility was less than a mile.

What had happened during the past few minutes hit Seth full force. He had scored two kills, which, if confirmed, would bring the total to five; but instead of celebrating acedom with his buddies back at the base, he faced an indefinite period of time as a fugitive in a hostile country.

A crackling sound in the distance broke the silence of the forest. Did the P-38 crash in the woods and set some trees afire? He could not see or smell any smoke.

The sharp morning chill caused Seth to shiver. No snow had fallen recently, so he would not be leaving obvious tracks. He had to move out. A silver mist swirled over the ground and offered cover until darkness. Seth had no idea how far he drifted in the chute. He figured he landed somewhere in the Saar. Near what town was still a mystery.

He recalled USAAF instructions about escape and evasion and took inventory of the escape kit and other supplies: Six small photos for a fake passport, compass, map, several hundred Deutschmarks, three packs of cigarettes, candy bars, a few cigars, hunting knife, and a .45 pistol

Seth studied his flight map and compass before heading west toward the French, Belgian, or Dutch borders, beyond which he hoped to link with one of those underground groups that helped downed pilots get back to England. He didn't want to think of the alternative, spending the rest of the war as a POW at the mercy of Nazis.

Seth verified his .45 was loaded, short knife in a convenient place for a quick draw, and buried the chute and straps in the deep recesses of the forest. For six hours, he jogged and walked a zigzag course. He often checked the compass and paused to make sure he was not followed. By the time pitch-black night fell over the Saar, Seth had not yet figured his precise location. Flight maps were great in the air; for ground calculations, they left much to be desired.

Seth froze when he heard harsh voices growling in one of the local German dialects. He listened carefully, heard footsteps, and saw two soldiers staggering in-trail about four yards apart along a path covered with soggy leaves. They floundered in a drunken stupor, bombed-out-of-their-minds.

One of the men stumbled and fell. Cursing loudly, he struggled to get up and slipped again. The other soldier mumbled something but did not slow or stop. Soon he was out of sight in the dark and mist.

Their presence indicated a Wehrmacht base was not too far away. Something to avoid. Seth drew his short knife and moved cat-like behind the prone drunken soldier. He did not relish killing a defenseless drunk in cold blood, but if necessary, he would.

The German cursed loudly on all fours and tried to stand. From behind, Seth kicked the soldier hard in the groin. The man collapsed unconscious on the icy leaves. Seth searched through the private's pockets. No money. The kraut must have blown it all on beer.

Seth found cigarettes and a matchbook from Das Schwartze Walfisch, a Gästhaus in Eppelborn. That meant he was a few dozen miles from the French border.

Seth decided against putting on the German's clothes. If captured out of uniform, the Nazis would condemn him as a spy with certain execution after long bouts of torture. He had no plan, no specific idea what to do when he reached Eppelborn. With some luck, he might be able to steal a car, or better yet, a plane.

***

At misty pre-dawn, Seth approached Eppelborn and saw something odd before he reached the town. An enormous English style manor stood at the edge of the forest isolated in the middle of several acres of cleared land. Seth thought he could get to it before daylight without being seen. He hoped no ferocious barking Doberman or German Shepherd would be there to greet him.

The first window Seth tried had been left unlocked. He drew the .45, climbed through, and stepped into a kitchen. Seth waited for his eyes to adapt to the quarter-light until he could move about without bumping into walls and furniture. Ravenous and tempted to forage for food, he first had to see if the house was occupied.

Seth inspected the downstairs rooms and noted the high quality of the furniture, heavy silver tea service, and priceless paintings and tapestries on the walls. He swallowed hard when he saw a picture of a young pilot shaking hands with Hitler and another of the same officer standing beside Göring. Bad luck, he'd broken into the home of a family with serious Nazi connections. Seth found no evidence of accumulated dust in the ground level rooms. Not yet daybreak, its occupants would be sleeping upstairs.

Seth climbed the steps to the upper floor. Doors had been left open to the right and left, both bedrooms unoccupied. He listened for snoring or heavy breathing from the other rooms. No sounds, but a black and white kitten appeared at the far end of the hallway. It stretched, yawned, and bounded along the hall. The kitten rubbed against Seth's leg and purred, its motor so loud he was certain everyone would awaken convinced a bomber formation flew overhead. With the kitten at his heels, he moved toward the room from where it had come.

Who would be sleeping there? Fat burgher, middle-aged couple, scrawny spinster, or armed Nazi?

Seth opened the door to body width. He almost cried out in surprise at an unbelievable sight. A pale blonde lay asleep in a canopied bed. In spite of the morning chill, a down cover and sheet reached no higher than the young woman's waist, and one strap of her pink nightgown had fallen off shoulder to reveal a breast shaped like the dome of the Taj Mahal. So perfect of form and face she could have been sculpted out of marble. He moved closer.

Aware of a presence in the room, she opened her eyes, and Seth placed a hand over the blonde's mouth to muffle any cry. What now? Seth had two choices. Kill or release the woman. And how the hell could he shoot or knife a defenseless female? Of course if she were a vicious Hitler loving Nazi ....

"I am an American. Amerikaner. Verstehen Sie?"

The blonde blinked that she understood.

"Sprechen Sie English?"

She did not respond. Seth had received A's in German at Cal, but they had been more for reading and translating than conversation. He continued auf Deutsch, "Do not cry out. If you do, then I must kill you." He took his hand away. "Are you alone?"

The young woman covered her exposed breast. "My husband is at the front. I have no servants. Yes, I am alone. You say you are an American, but you speak German like a Rhinelander."

Seth started at a sudden sound and movement. The kitten had jumped onto the quilt to lie besides its mistress.

"What do you want?"

"To get out of here. You must help me escape."

She glanced at Seth's .45. "And if I refuse?"

"I will feel regrets, but I will kill you." Seth doubted he could and hoped she wouldn't call his bluff.

"And our propaganda describes you Americans as being soft and sentimental."

"Then you are fluent in English." Seth had been trying so hard to make himself understood in German, he now realized she had been speaking flawless English.

"I learn languages easily."

At the sound of a motor, Seth went to the window and looked out into the gray morning mist. A farmer's aged truck wobbled down a road in the distance. No sign of any search party. "I need a car. Do you have one?"

"Yes, but you will not get far alone."

"Then I will take you with me."

"Indeed?" She reached for a blue robe, which had fallen to the floor, and left the bed to put it on.

Her height surprised Seth. "It would be unwise to resist me."

She stepped into fur-lined slippers. "I shall not resist."

Seth peered out the window again. He saw more activity on the road, some of it military. "I'll wait until dark and chance driving with you." She moved toward the door. "Where are you going?"

"To my morning toilette. Do you intend to accompany me?"

# Chapter 23
## Valuable Information

She wore a drab, gray wool dress that fell to mid-shin above riding boots and a bulky blue sweater. Seth thought the blonde to be more beautiful than first impression despite those dark shadows ringing her eyes. How might she look under normal conditions, or dressed for an evening on the town? They descended to the first floor and moved through treasure-filled rooms toward the kitchen with the kitten following.

"Very impressive. I suppose you confiscated all this from Jews and the conquered countries."

"No, they are my husband's inherited possession. We brought them here from our other estates and homes because we thought this would the safest place to protect them from the bombing. Now then, as we shall be having breakfast together, I think it proper for us to introduce ourselves. My husband is the Fürst zu Pfalz von Teuffelreich."

"I thought royal Germans disappeared with the Kaiser's court after the last war. Where is your entourage?"

"Entourage? There is a war on, you know. Our former servants work in positions more vital to the war effort. I have a woman who cleans twice a week. She comes tomorrow. Otherwise, I am quite alone."

"What do I call you? Fürsten is too awkward."

"Mariya-Xenia will do. And you are called?"

Time to learn how committed a Nazi she was. "Captain Seth A. Braham, United States Army Air Force."

"Braham, a typical English name."

"It was originally Abraham."

Mariya-Xenia studied Seth's features. "You are a Jew?"

"Absolutely."

"Mein Gott, you do not look the least bit Jewish. Forgive me for laughing, but it is so absurd. I look at you, and it is all so incredible."

"What is?"

"It is too much for me to digest on an empty stomach."

The sausage and eggs prepared by Mariya-Xenia were agreeable, the ersatz coffee undrinkable. Seth petted the purring kitten, which had settled in his lap. He ought to be regarding the princess as an enemy, a patriot who would betray him to the Gestapo without hesitation. Most disconcerting, Seth liked Mariya-Xenia, felt comfortable with her... hold everything. What was he thinking? Mariya-Xenia's husband posed with the top monsters of the Third Reich. To fantasize was more than lunacy. It was suicidal. How far could he trust her, if at all?

Mariya-Xenia finished the small piece of Hershey's chocolate Seth had given her and accepted a second American cigarette. "So, Captain Braham, what are you? A spy?"

"No, I'm a pilot, and please call me Seth."

Her eyes narrowed. "Not bombers."

"No way, I fly fighters. One of your boys got lucky and caught me from behind. All I want is to make it back home to have another chance to even the score."

"So, you are a fighter pilot. Are you good?"

"I thought I was, until yesterday."

"The best are shot down many times. I believe it is all a matter of luck."

"I'd like to think you're right."

"How many victories have you?"

Seth saw no harm telling the truth. "Five."

"Only five? You must be new to combat."

"I suppose you're going to tell me about those inflated totals your propaganda machines claim for your pilots."

"You may wish to believe they are absurd, but I know what they have accomplished. Our men fly hundreds of sorties. Some have reached a thousand."

"Unbelievable."

"You have five victories in how many sorties?"

"Thirty."

"So few?"

"When I get back to England, I hope to do better, but until yesterday, we hadn't seen too many of your fighters in the air."

"Yes, that has been our complaint every time your bombers devastate our cities. We're outnumbered. On the Eastern Front, the odds against us are sometimes twenty-to-one. Scores rise quickly when so many targets are available."

Seth tried to imagine himself immersed in a sea of enemy aircraft at those extreme odds. Then he chided himself for talking too much. If he'd been captured by the military or Gestapo, he'd have given his name, rank, and serial number, nothing else.

Seth had a perverse image. Mariya-Xenia might be the ideal person for the Luftwaffe to use as an interrogator, and he'd had the odd piece of bad luck to drop right into her lap. She was gorgeous, charming, and intelligent. She spoke fluent English with a delightful British accent and handled a discussion about aerial combat as well as any pilot.

"How do you happen to know so much about flying?"

"My husband is also a fighter pilot. Come with me, I wish to show you something."

She took Seth into the living room and picked up the photo he had seen earlier. Prince Karl did look like a Hollywood image of a German prince, an almost pretty young man, with a dueling scar on his cheek. Bedding Mariya-Xenia might be a pleasurable act of revenge against the Germans, but it would not, however, decide who was the better fighter pilot in the skies.

"Is your husband a Nazi too?"

"No, he despises them. Those photos were taken at an awards investiture. He is apolitical. We display them to impress the right people. Here is another photo of Karl when he was in Russia."

Seth marveled at how well groomed the prince looked in front of an Me-109. Perhaps they would meet in the skies after he escaped. "Does your husband always fly number 23?"

"Yes, it was his first assigned number. He feels comfortable with it. Pilot superstition, I suppose."

Was it this prince who had escorted Hank out of the combat zone? Seth wanted more identification. "Has your husband named his fighter for you?"

"I have not been so privileged. He names his fighters SPRITZ with a wine bottle for its logo."

Bingo. He was the pilot who saved Hank. Seth stared at the familiar contours of the Me-109 and decided to obtain more information from Mariya-Xenia. USAAF intelligence might find some of it useful. "How many victories does your husband have?"

"I can't say for certain. I believe he now has more than 150 Luftsiegen."

"150 kills? But isn't it true that your pilots count victories by the engine, four for a big bomber."

"No, that has to do with awards. It is one plane, one victory. How many does your top ace have?"

Seth chose not to answer. "Your husband must be the greatest fighter pilot of all time."

"How Karl would like to believe that. Other Luftwaffe aces have higher totals. Rall, Nowotny, Graf, and Barkhorn have passed 200."

"Good God, they must be fantastic shots!"

"Of course they fly many missions. It took Karl about three hundred-and fifty sorties to get 149."

"That's batting over four hundred."

Mariya-Xenia did not understand Seth's use of baseball terminology. "Karl has been lucky after a fashion. In three and-a-half years flying combat, he has spent almost two years in hospitals and at home recovering from wounds. Imagine if he had been healthy all that time."

"So many missions… that explains why your Luftwaffe fighter pilots have accumulated such high totals."

"They seldom have more than ten Luftsiegen by their hundredth sortie. Karl says one does not get to be a good shot before then."

Based on what Mariya-Xenia told him, the 8th Air Force top guns who were getting double digit victories in less than fifty missions had to be super fighter aces.

***

"It's almost dark. I must leave."

"Will you believe me if I tell you a full division of our Wehrmacht is in the middle of winter maneuvers nearby for another day or two? After things are back to normal, I will do everything I can to ensure your escape is successful."

Seth tried to read Mariya-Xenia's expression for signs of lying. What the hell. He either had to accept everything she said or put a bullet through her head. Seth's gut told him to trust the princess.

"Why are you doing all this for me?"

Without going into great detail, Mariya-Xenia told Seth about the activities of the anti-Nazis. They had set up a network of safe houses to hide their countrymen wanted by the Gestapo, including several Jews, whom they helped escape to neutral countries, and downed American and RAF pilots.

Mariya-Xenia chain-lit another cigarette. "Do you believe in God?"

"Not enough. I'm not observant."

"I believe. I believe God sent you to us."

***

New Year's Day, 1944, Seth drank alone sequestered in his hiding place while Mariya-Xenia hosted the Bürgomeister, civil and Nazi officials of Eppelborn, and ranking Wehrmacht officers stationed nearby. Later that evening she brought a visitor to Seth's sanctuary and introduced the tall, sleek young man as Bruno von Strachwitz from the Abwehr, a guest for the next two days.

When Seth reached for his .45, Mariya-Xenia stood between them. "You can trust Bruno. He is part of the anti-Nazi faction in the Abwehr."

"Thank you, Zizi." Bruno faced Seth. "I am one of Karl's best friends and his cousin. Zizi tells me that I am to assist you in your escape to England." He gave Seth a roll of film. "You will not be able to read it, of course. It has been coded and is to be destroyed if you are captured."

Seth put the film in his pocket. "And if I am not captured?"

"You will deliver it to the proper authorities in England. I shall give you their names. If successful, you may help shorten the war."

"What exactly am I carrying?"

"The less you know the better, in the event you do get caught."

"Perhaps you can answer another question. Why haven't you anti-Nazis assassinated Hitler?"

"There have been attempts. One of my cousins, a major on the Eastern Front, planted a bomb in Hitler's plane when our Darling visited Russia last winter. Unfortunately, it flew too high and too rapidly. The mechanism froze."

"Surely you Germans, who are known for your organizational abilities, could pull off a successful plot."

Mariya-Xenia chain-lit another cigarette. "All plots have failed. Hitler is lucky and a cunning devil too. He comes and goes with no set schedule, or he does not appear at all, and he has several doubles. If you can deliver the film, we may yet surprise the world."

***

The following day a regiment of infantry passed through Eppelborn and headed west. Mariya-Xenia turned from the window. "They are reinforcing units at the Atlantic Wall. That was the last of them."

Mariya-Xenia led Seth to one of the other bedrooms. She opened a wardrobe and took out the uniform of an SS Oberst. "Bruno brought it and these Dutch civilian clothes for you."

"How did he know my size?"

"I have a short wave radio on a special Abwehr frequency. I am in contact with the resistance whenever there is someone we can help. If these clothes do not fit, I can make alterations. You must shed your Nazi uniform before you contact the underground in Holland who will help you escape."

*And be shot as a spy if captured or betrayed.*

"When do I leave?"

"Tonight."

He donned the SS uniform. "What do you think?"

"You look intimidating. This uniform frightens people. No one will dare question you."

Seth stared at his reflection in the full-length mirror. The black uniform, so vivid a symbol of organized terror, fit Seth as if he had been born to wear it.

Mariya-Xenia opened a map in the study, her voice crisp and authoritative. "Here is the route Bruno suggested we take by auto. I will leave you there at the border. After that, you must change clothes and travel at night. never by day. If you think you will be captured, destroy everything Bruno gave you, or my friends and I, we shall all be lost."

Mariya-Xenia gave Seth a capsule.

"Cyanide?"

"Only a rare few have withstood the Gestapo's tortures, and afterward they are never the same."

Anybody who doesn't have fear is an idiot. It's just that you must make the fear work for you. Hell, when somebody shot at me, it made me madder than hell, and all I wanted to do was shoot back.
- *Brigadier General Robin Olds, USAF.*

# PART THREE

# The Year the War Should Have Ended 1944

My greatest enemies are the Vons who call themselves aristocrats.—*Hitler to Mussolini*

# Chapter 24
## Revelations

Karl returned to combat in the west with JG-26 operating out of Lille after qualifying in an improved FW-190. By the middle of May 1944, he accumulated 18 Luftsiegen for the year, bringing his total to 175. Other fighter pilots lucked into multiple kill situations. Karl caught infrequent singles. At this rate, he would never overtake the top aces.

The loss of two gifted pilots troubled Karl. 21 January, a distant cousin, Major Heinrich Prinz zu Sayn-Wittgenstein, was shot down after scoring his 83rd night victory. 3 March, Major Egmont Prinz zur Lippe-Weissenfeld, with 51 night Luftsiegen, died in a crash during a daytime flight. Had the hereditary princes fallen under a curse, with the Fürst zu Pfalz von Teuffelreich fated to be next?

The Gruppenkommandeur ordered Karl to take a few days leave of absence. The timing was perfect for a meeting with Elfi. They had not seen each other in almost nine months. Karl left Elsa with his crew chief and took off in a Fiesler Storch, a high wing liaison and observation plane. For the flight to the Italian Riviera, he donned a uniform he had not worn in almost half a year. It brought home to Karl that he had lost more than five kilos. All the pilots in the Geschwader were gaunt and hollow-cheeked despite a proper diet. The impossible number of missions they flew under intense pressure was the least of their problems. RAF and USAAF bombing raids caused the heaviest emotional burden and consumed officers and men with worry for their loved ones when their cities or villages were hit hard. In many cases, a pilot's capabilities and efficiency deteriorated over concern for his family. Some went berserk in an insane desire to wreak revenge and committed fatal errors.

Karl was prepared to accept any loss with the exception of Elfi and the precious Moselle and Rhine vineyards planted by the Romans. Over the centuries, the vines of Schloss Teuffelreich had survived war, plague, blight, and politics. They must make it through the current troubles as well. For that, he relied on Mariya-Xenia, who was as fine a woman as Elfi. Karl regretted he could not feel the same love for her. His wife deserved the best too. Perhaps Mariya-Xenia had met someone else. He wished her well in that case.

***

Elfi was not at the pensione when Karl arrived in San Remo. He hurried to the deserted beach. The sky was cloudy, the weather cool. Covered by a heavy gray overcoat, Elfi sat on a bench along the walk absorbed in a book. Karl kissed the back of her neck.

Elfi turned to slap whoever presumed to be so familiar, then stopped. "Karl, it is you! Are you all right? You are not wounded, thank God. How did you get here? How long do you have? What's happened to you? You're so thin."

Karl put a finger to Elfi's lips. "One question at a time."

They kissed until she pulled back out of breath. "I must stop this spectacle and take you to my pensione before we disgrace ourselves on the beach."

Karl was so fatigued he collapsed on the bed and slept around the clock. Elfi watched over him until she too fell asleep. Afterwards, as Karl could do with no other except Elfi, he unburdened himself. She had an uncanny ability to help him purge unpleasant thoughts and feelings. The longer Karl spoke, the more he relaxed. That slight pain in his stomach, a forewarning of the most prevalent pilot problem in the Luftwaffe, an ulcer, disappeared thanks to Elfi's soothing company. Was this what happened in the office of a psychiatrist? No matter, he had to talk, and he had a loving woman who listened. Karl addressed every topic that came to mind until she knew everything about his life, thoughts, and aspirations.

Elfi snuggled against Karl as the morning sky took on deep purple to bright yellow hues and heralded the birth of a glorious new day. Karl saw those same colors as the perfect metaphor for the range of his feelings, from deep passion to tender romantic enchantment and respect.

"Elfi, I doubt if I could have the stomach to deal with all those mangled bodies. How do you manage?"

"At first, I was in a state of perpetual nausea. Then an experienced nurse advised me how best to deal with it. I forced myself to concentrate on the details. A splinter of a broken bone. A square centimeter of torn flesh. It worked during operations, but making the rounds in the wards is still difficult because I must always be cheerful and reassuring to those who have lost limbs or will die. There are so many of them, so many wounded and dying. And they are so young."

"So are my pilots."

"And there's the nonsensical bureaucratic decrees, like the order that forbids nurses to wear makeup and lipstick. Because I have thick and long dark eyelashes, the senior staff members have me under perpetual surveillance. They are convinced I'm using forbidden Hollywood Allüren, mascara. All makeup is Verboten now."

"Idiots."

Karl toyed with the metal tag around Elfi's neck identical to the one he wore with his full name. Their names had been stamped twice on the metal. If either or both were killed, half would be broken off and sent to the nearest kin or loved one. That must never happen.

"Elfi, I have withheld some personal information."

"That you are the Fürst zu Pfalz von Teuffelreich?"

"How did you learn ....?"

"I read your name on the tag while you slept."

"Are you angry I did not tell you?"

"No, I am sure you had your reasons. I somehow suspected you were of the aristocracy. Karl, tell me the truth. We are losing the war, losing badly."

"The worst part is we did not have to come to such a pass. If the right decisions had been made, if... well, in any case, we must persevere and do our best. Whatever happens, you must never fall into the hands of the Soviets. Seek asylum in Switzerland and remain there until the war is over."

"Karl, I prefer to go anywhere with you. I could be your nurse. I am also good with tools. I have helped put bodies together. I could do the same with planes, be your mechanic."

Karl smiled at the absurd image of Elfi crewing his fighter and held her small, delicate hands. "These were not meant for metal and grease. I insist again. Go to Switzerland. The SS and Gestapo have committed beastly crimes that have enraged our enemies. If we lose, all Germans will be made to pay."

Elfi tensed, pushed away from Karl, and got out of bed. She put on a robe and paced back and forth like a restless nocturnal jungle cat. "Remember when we met last year, you did not want to tell me you were a prince? I also have a secret, one I have kept from you, from everyone. That day we first met, I was trying to sort out some important matters and come to a decision. In truth, I was considering going to Switzerland and sitting out the war."

"I understand. You had lost your husband, your family."

"It is more than that. I have hesitated crossing the border because I have heard many stories about the Swiss, how they prevent refugees from seeking asylum if they have no relatives or influential friends in their country. Also, it is well known that the Swiss often return Jews to the Nazis and certain death."

Karl stared anew at Elfi. True, she was slight and dark, definitely not an Aryan propaganda poster girl. But Elfi's features and mannerisms? No. Impossible. Nothing Jewy about her. "How much Jewish blood have you? How have you survived without detection?"

"I did not know anything about it until my parents were killed. When I went through some old family papers, I discovered something about my paternal grandfather, who died when my father was four years old. He was Jewish by birth, but his family converted to Christianity."

"Then, you're a one-quarter Jew." Hölle, she could have been a full-blooded Jewess, and he would still love Elfi no less.

"Karl, for your own preservation you must cast me aside before the Reichskommissar für die Festigung Deutschen Volkstums discovers my blood trace."

He left the bed and cupped Elfi's face in his hands. "My darling, even though you are a Jewess according to Nazi doctrine, it makes no difference to me. In fact, my father used to infuriate my mother's family by asserting we also could claim Jewish ancestry."

"How is that possible?"

"As the story goes, sometime during the sixteenth-century, the daughter of a Spanish grandee prominent at the court of Holy Roman Emperor Charles V married one of our Teuffelreich forebears. My father said her family had converted to Christianity a century earlier. Why, we might be related."

"As Jews we still would be divided by caste. You have grandees among your Jewish ancestors. Mine may have been peddlers."

"Regardless, my father would have adored you as much as I do now." Karl described the stunning Jewish actress who had been Prince Friedrich's mistress.

"Mistress, but not wife."

"That is unfair. He was already married with children. Divorce was impossible."

"Karl, I believe I have the right to ask you this. Have you also made plans for your wife to flee Germany?"

"Mariya-Xenia does not have a role to play in our future."

"There must be a day of reckoning. It may be cruel for me to say this. You cannot be passive and wait for the war to resolve your marriage, either by her death or yours, God forbid. Karl, you are a man of honor. Your conscience would not allow you to leave Mariya-Xenia helpless, defenseless."

He kissed Elfi's hands and fingers. "You are a precious, rare jewel, Elfi, and I give you my word that I will see to Mariya-Xenia's safety and wellbeing." Karl sat at the small desk, opened a drawer, and took out paper and pen. "I will give you the names and addresses of relations and close family friends in Switzerland, with letters of introduction and instructions for my bank. You must go there, Elfi, or else my worrying for you may cloud my mind in combat."

# Chapter 25

## Mustangs

The first months of 1944, the 375th suffered heavy losses despite orders not to mix with German fighters. Hank accepted most combat casualties as part of the fortunes of war, but he never became used to those caused by pilot error or flat-out stupidity. A good twenty-five percent of fighter losses occurred at home airfields as a result of take-off and landing miscues and in the air when the call was Break Left and a pilot Broke Right into a leader or wingman. Hank believed no one at home should ever know a son or husband had been killed by a comrade in arms.

The P-38s could not to hold their own in daylight against the late model Me-109s and FW-190s appearing on the scene. On several occasions, he had seen those German fighters pass up opportunities to strike at Spitfires, Jugs, and Mustangs if P-38s were in the combat area.

Worst of all, 8th Air Force limited the Lightnings to flying in bad weather, and a new tactic hated by the fighter pilots the same as strafing called drop-snoot bombing raids. Each P-38 carried two five hundred-pound bombs. One modified Lightning was designated as the leader with a radar bombing sight. It navigated to a designated position over the assigned target and released its bombs through the clouds. At that same point, the other P-38s dropped their loads. Drop-snooting was nothing more than blind bombing, and Hank found it to be boring work.

The 375th also was ordered to fly low at treetop level when necessary and strafe at will parked aircraft, hangars, trains, automobiles, river barges, flak towers, ground troops, and depots to weaken the Channel defenses and interfere with the enemy's supply network in advance of the long awaited Allied liberation of Europe.

On each sortie the Group lost at least one plane to ground fire. Most fighters came home with some damage, and many of the pilots lost their nerve or zest for the strafing missions when they saw visual evidence of how close they came to being shot down.

During one sortie, Hank ran out of ammunition. When he looked up and saw four FW-190s coming out of the sun, he called them out on the radio. His P-38 staggered as bullets ripped into it and tore up the turbo superchargers located in the top side of the long tail booms. The Lightning's hydraulic system had been holed, engine power limited, and red warning lights flashed all over the cockpit.

The 190s zipped past Hank with a gaggle of Lightnings queuing behind them. Because his fighter was too damaged to maneuver away from trouble if the enemy made another pass, he headed for England confident he could make it to the nearest air base at Manston, and with luck to his home base at Thetford as well.

The radio noise filled with sightings of enemy planes and yelps for assistance when the 375th pilots tangled with the 190s. Hank climbed to two thousand feet and called his wingman, who was doing S-turns behind. When he received no reply, he concluded the transmitter was damaged.

Hank would have jumped out of his skin cartoon-like were it possible when a pair of Me-109s came out of the sun and latched behind. His wingman saw them too and broke into their curve. One headed straight for Hank's P-38, and at five hundred feet away, the German opened fire.

Chunks of metal flew off Hank's right wing. The controls became so heavy he couldn't turn fast enough to break away.

*Was this how it all ended?*

Incredibly, the faster Me-109 sped beneath and rose in front of his Lightning. On reflex, Hank pressed the trigger, and he cursed his bad luck to be out of ammo. The German pilot had slowed the 109 to avoid the overshoot; and at reduced speed backed into the left propeller of Hank's P-38. The noise was deafening as parts banged against Hank's fuselage. The 109 reared high over the top of Hank's Lightning and spun before disappearing from view.

Hank's fighter vibrated, and he was unable to hold it level. After he hit the left prop feathering switch, the propeller slowed and came to a standstill. At least one engine functioned despite a foot of steel having been ripped from one blade and the others grooved.

Thirty-five long minutes later, Hank bellied-in at Manston. He hit a jeep parked on a perimeter road, totaled the Lightning, but escaped with minor lacerations. After release from the hospital, Hank reported to his CO, Colonel Cy Wilson, a West Pointer without the superior attitude.

"Congratulations, Milroy, you've received credit for downing that 109 without ammo. That confirmed kill makes you an ace."

Hank accepted a cigar. "Thank you, sir. Not the ideal way to achieve acedom, but I won't complain."

"You're also up for another DFC and Air Medal."

More fruit salad for the chest, which was what all the services called those ribbons. Hank believed he didn't deserve yet another Purple Heart for light wounds, when others received the award for losses of limb, eyesight, and worse. Hank valued acedom more than any award. Any flyer who survived could earn a batch of Air Medals and DFCs, but only a small percent of the fighter pilots achieved acedom.

"Now then, Milroy, because of our high P-38 combat losses, General Jimmy Doolittle, Commander of 8th Air Force, went to General Arnold, Chief of the USAAF, and described the Lightning as a second-rate fighter compared to the 109s and 190s. Therefore, an order has been issued to withdraw all P-38s from ETO combat, except those in reconnaissance squadrons. Our 375th will be switching over to P-51s, and you'll be the first in our group to become proficient in the Mustang."

***

Mustangs.

At last the 375th had a plane that could hold its own against the vaunted Me-109s and FW-190s. Hank had tested the P-51B Mustang during his stint at Wright Field and thought it the best then. He loved this new bird more. The D model was about 50 mph faster than the FW-190 from the ground up to 28,000 feet, and 70 mph at higher altitudes. Against the Me-109, it was 30 mph faster up to sixteen thousand feet and more than 50 mph at thirty thousand.

The P-51 could out-dive the FW-190 at any altitude and was better in a dive than the 109. It could out-turn the 109 at any time and match against the 190. In rate of roll, the 190 continued to have no peer while the 109 and the Mustang were even-up.

The 375th pilots were told to exploit their superior speed against the FW-190 and turn capability against the Me-109. Combat tactics were reduced to a basic formula: Hit-and-run against the FW-190. Turn-and-fight the Me-109.

Hank said prayerful thanks to Tommy Hitchcock, the World War I ace and ten-goal polo playing great, for insisting that the Mustang was *the* fighter the USAAF must have. Morale in the 375th rose to new heights when word came that the Group no longer had to stay close to the bombers whenever the Luftwaffe made an appearance.

Hank named the sleek fighter WINTY. Presumptuous or not, he had been clobbered by a late thunderbolt thrown not by Zeus but by Cupid. He had written his parents, Roy McCabe, and buddies stationed stateside to get Winty's address so he could write and propose marriage.

Now a major, Hank took charge of the 135th squadron. The men felt secure flying under the command of a genuine ace, and Hank's can-do leadership inspired them to make greater efforts than they had dreamed possible. With permission to engage in hot pursuit of the enemy, Hank realized his full potential as a fighter pilot in the Mustang.

The P-51 turned around statistics for the entire 375th, which lost one plane for every six Germans downed. He added two Ju-88s, a Me-110, two Me-109s, and two FW-190s to the first five for a respectable 12 victories during that run. Hank considered the possibility he might become top ace in the ETO. He always said a prayer for his victims to get a good chute and dreaded seeing another human fireball bursting like his first kill over the Channel. That episode continued to give Hank nightmares.

The group's aircraft-in-commission rate became the highest in 8th Air Force and their abort rate the lowest. The 375th flew more combat hours and its aggressive gung-ho pilots scored faster than any unit in the ETO. Yet, grueling five to seven hour missions in the long range P-51Ds caused some of the men to crack and become flak-happy after they escorted the bombers out and beat up airfields, railroads, and highways along the way home.

Every major population center and hundreds of other towns felt the muscle of the American and British Air Forces: Schweinfurt, Wiener Neustadt, München, Augsburg, Frankfurt, Cologne, Hamburg, Berlin, and Bremen.

Many jokes about the youthful, high-ranking pilots made the rounds in the ETO. All fliers liked best one of Bill Mauldin's cartoons published in *Stars and Stripes*: A baby-face bird colonel embracing a battle weary older enlisted man with the caption: "Uncle Willie!"

A twenty-six year old Major, much younger than the Infantry and Tank equals in rank, Hank felt a generation apart from the pilots flying in the 136th. All but three were under twenty-two. The worst aspect of leading such young men into combat was the heartbreaking and difficult letters he had to write whenever one of his kids failed to return. Hank now took as much pride in bringing all the boys back from a mission as accumulating more victories, but he was always on the alert for Number 23.

# Chapter 26
## The Plot

Poor weather grounded the Luftwaffe but not the American and RAF bombers. They increased the frequency and intensity of their raids along the Atlantic Coast. The reasons for the Allies' bad-weather heavy bombing runs became obvious on 6 June at Normandy when the U.S., British, and Canadians made successful landings and established beachheads.

Karl's Staffel retreated to a base less likely to be hit by an enemy air raid. By 10 June, the Americans were operating out of their first airfield in Normandy. That same night of 10/11 June, Karl slalomed through an American formation to blast out of the sky three fortresses and two P-38 fighter escorts, all in less than twenty minutes, to increase his overall Luftsiegen to 180, the first good sortie of the year.

Karl pushed the ground crew to new standards of excellence. He complained about the declining quality of mechanics responsible for maintenance. On each mission, the equipment gave too many problems, and he often lost sleep trying to figure out what went wrong. He concluded that the older, more experienced mechanics, so dedicated and precise, were a scarce commodity, whereas the younger men did not often have their hearts in their work. They slighted some tasks, became belligerent, and lied that things were all right when they were not. He could trust no more than ten percent of them. Consequently, Karl found himself becoming finicky with the crewmen to the point of becoming obsessive and maledictive.

After each communiqué, Karl studied a large map of Europe and noted the Wehrmacht's receding tide. Rome fell to the Americans 4 June. The Red Army swept through Rumania toward Minsk and beyond. The anticipated conquest of Eastern Europe had begun.

The Normandy beachhead spread like a giant malignant amoeba. The Wehrmacht gave the Americans stiff resistance outside Cherbourg and bravely contested the British and Canadians in bitter fighting around Caen, but he had no doubts about the ultimate outcome.

Karl was aware those unfortunate soldiers on the bloody battleground below looked up at the sky and asked the same nagging question: "Wo ist Die Luftwaffe?" The soldiers did not know that the Americans and RAF had won air superiority the previous February; since then over a thousand fighter pilots had been killed, captured, or too maimed to fly.

Another stroke of genius by Göring. Aware an invasion had been imminent somewhere along the Atlantic Wall, the Reichsmarschall withdrew several fighter units from the western bases and moved them to Hungary. They were to intercept RAF aircraft flying out of Italy to drop supplies to Partisans sabotaging German military efforts along the Eastern Front. Another Luftwaffe mission was to intercept enemy bombers going after targets around Vienna, Bucharest, and Budapest. Now in the west, the Luftwaffe faced odds of eight to one.

Karl stabbed the map with a knife, and each cut fell where more American and RAF airfields were likely to be built. He damned all those ass-lickers surrounding Hitler. Before the sixth of June, Rommel wanted to prevent the enemy from establishing a successful beachhead in Normandy, but the Field Marshall's superior, von Rundstedt, decided to let the Allies land and crush them in a pincer movement. Von Rundstedt's plan, inferior to Rommel's in Karl's opinion, was never put into effect, even though the Wehrmacht had two elite Panzer divisions waiting for a landing at Calais thirty-two kilometers across the Channel from England.

Worst of all, each strategic and tactical decision had to be approved by the Great Austrian Amateur. Hitler continued to dictate strategy and tactics from Berchtesgaden and refused to turn loose the Panzers on the Normandy Front. After that faux intuitive decision, Darling took sleeping pills and napped, during which time the Allies secured the beachheads. If they knew better, the toadying senior staff officers lacked the innards to contradict Hitler.

The enemy advanced everywhere, and he, one of the great killing instruments of the Luftwaffe, sat on his ass in Lille getting betrunken on bottles of wine. Karl read the label on a 1938 vintage Moselwein sent by Mariya-Xenia. The once elegant, fragile wine had passed its prime, as had the Third Reich.

***

Karl had not slept in over twenty-four hours and was poring over a map of the Western Front when he sensed a presence at the entry to his tent. It was the new orderly, a skinny Bavarian peasant who still stank of manure.

"Well?"

"Sir. You have a visitor."

"Who is it?"

The orderly stepped aside for a Panzer officer who wore dark glasses over a face without form, whose features had been melted and left to harden without being reshaped. Karl concealed his horror at the Brigadegeneral's grotesque appearance. He stood and saluted the dust-caked officer.

"In the name of God, Karl, please relax. I know what I look like."

Karl forced himself to study the misshapen face, and he embraced the General. "Albert."

They sat at the map covered table and shared a bottle of wine. "Prosit, my dear friend. To better days."

"I regret to say afraid they are days that were, not those ahead." Albert stroked Elsa, who lay at his boots. "We come from another world, Karl, a world buried in the rubble of false hopes and evil dreams. You and Gerd were so close then."

"We still are the best of friends."

"Then you have not heard."

A stab of pain pierced Karl's innards. "Heard what?"

"Two weeks ago, Gerd got caught in a daylight raid. My brother was blown to pieces."

Karl wanted to cry out, to blast from the skies the American bomber that had killed his best friend and to exterminate the leaders who left Germany defenseless against air raids.

"I drink to Gerd. He was the best." Karl wanted to change the topic of conversation, anything to remove the knife from his gut. "How are things with Rommel?"

Albert placed a finger on the map. "We are withdrawing to a more viable line of defense. The situation is impossible, and I can assure you, Karl, within twenty-four hours, your Staffel will be leaving this base for one farther back. As you know, the Americans have begun to build airfields in Normandy."

"So, the war is lost."

"Militarily, as Rommel predicted if we allowed the enemy to secure a beachhead. But it must not end in a Götterdammerung for Germany. We need to arrange a separate peace with the Americans and English before we are overwhelmed by the Slavic barbarians."

"Is it possible?"

"Not while our Liebschen lives. Come, let us walk so no one can overhear us."

"Yes, Elsa can use the exercise."

They strolled along the perimeter of the base throwing sticks for Elsa to fetch.

"Do not ask how it was accomplished, Karl. I have your orders for a month's leave beginning next week. You will go to Berlin and await further instructions. It is time for the aristocracy and the professional officer corps to do what we have abandoned for so long, our duty to preserve the Fatherland."

A nerve-jarring chill enveloped Karl. So, the moment had at last come for a coup against Der Führer. He remembered the oath of personal allegiance sworn by all the officers and men in every branch of service. It was terrifying to imagine a German officer would go against a sworn oath no matter how great the provocation. The precedents would reverberate for generations. Karl experienced another severe stabbing pain in the gut. If anything could cause his ulcer to flare, it would be participation in a plot against Hitler.

"Albert, is this more talk and no action?"

"We can no longer afford to talk. In 1938, we contacted the English and promised to remove Hitler and his gang if they supported the Czechs at Munich. Those fools feared the Soviets more than the Nazis. Last year, after the Big Three demanded our unconditional surrender, we asked them to give us some inkling of their plans for Germany if we eliminated Hitler before the war ended. They told us nothing, and we failed to act. Now, many officers despair it is too late. Karl, it must never be too late for us to restore our lost honor."

"Then there is a definite plan."

"We are still divided. Rommel prefers not to assassinate Der Führer. He wants a Panzer unit to capture and try Hitler before an open Peoples Court. Others believe our Darling must be shot on sight because of the hold he still has over the people in spite of the bombing, his seclusion, and recent reverses. At any rate, the plan is to proceed as follows. Rommel will head a Provisional Government during the crisis. Whether Hitler is to be killed or captured, the National Socialist rule over Germany will end. Next, Rommel will appoint a Council of Generals who will go to Eisenhower and negotiate an armistice on the Western Front. Of course, we shall request they stop bombing our Fatherland.

"Do you think the Americans and British will agree?"

"They would be foolish not to. We must keep the Slavs and Mongols out of Germany. We have to convince the West the Soviets will place every square meter of land they occupy under communist domination. Surely wise men in the United States and British governments will do anything to prevent bolshevism from spreading westward."

Karl had trouble assimilating the enormity of removing Hitler and the Nazis, fighting a war against the Russians, and negotiating with the Americans and British. Was it naiveté or desperation that led Albert and the conspirators to believe the western Allies would abandon the Soviets and agree to their requests? That so many were involved in the coup increased the chances of failure or being discovered.

"And what role am I to play?"

"Our man, who he is I am not at liberty to say, will take care of our Darling. In Berlin, the center of national communications, we need all the trustworthy officers we can find. You will learn your task there. You might be the man who deals with Göring if he is in Berlin. It is possible all the surviving hereditary rulers may play a part in the new government as constitutional monarchs in a new Federated Germany."

Karl had no doubt he could assassinate the Reichsmarschall should it become necessary. "Tell me, if you can, Albert, has my wife been involved with the coup, and Bruno von Strachwitz too? They are Abwehr."

"The less any of us knows the better."

That was answer enough for Karl, and he led Albert back toward the tent. His Staffel was on standby alert, and the moment they returned, the klaxon blared. Karl gathered his helmet and goggles and shook hands with Albert.

"The Sergeant Major will give you a bed for the night. We shall talk further when I return. I need to know my part."

"Sorry, Karl, I must go elsewhere. I might catch up with you at your new base sometime during the next few days. If not, perhaps in Berlin."

"Until then."

***

Karl attacked a B-17 box, and the rear bomber dropped in front fifty meters dead ahead at the bottom of its corkscrew. He centered his sighting dot on the windscreen of the tail gunner's compartment and pressed the firing tit. Bullets struck its vitals, and chunks of metal flew away. The explosions shook Karl's fighter. He recovered and set ablaze another B-17, gratified this time its crew was able to bail out.

By now Karl flew in the middle of the German flak zone. He needed to climb at least another five hundred meters to be safe. As he called out the last kill, brilliant flashes exploded below and behind, and shrapnel hit the 109. Karl felt the concussion push and shove the fighter with sudden acceleration. G-forces he could not identify confused his seat-of-the pants feel.

The tail gone, Karl pulled the emergency canopy release cord and throttled the engine back to idle. The violent gyrations smoothed out, but the altimeter showed 2300 meters and dropping. He hit the shut-off switch, unfastened the radio cord to his helmet, seat and shoulder straps. Catapulted out of the cockpit, Karl pulled hard on the ripcord handle of the parachute and heard the muffled, welcome kerwhump of its opening. Karl's body jerked hard at the arrest of his falling speed.

Bomber engines and flak bursts shattered the serenity of the summer day. Karl also heard the higher pitched noise of a plane in a power dive close by and twisted toward the sound. As the plane passed, vortices from its wing tip or prop wash tugged at the chute and disrupted Karl's concentration. Too late, he bent his legs in anticipation of contact with terra firma. Karl's knees and chin met hard, and he was knocked unconscious.

Karl came to. The world spun, and he saw a dark sky filled with stars sparkling, dying, and flashing again. He counted seven moons too, which meant he must be dead and on the way to pilot Valhalla. Karl moved into a more comfortable position after a severe pain in his left leg shocked him to full consciousness. The stars no longer spun. He saw the sun.

*Not again. Yes, again.*

Karl tried but could not stand on both feet. At minimum he had a broken ankle. He tugged at the chute and pulled it loose from a small brush ledge. He wrapped it around the ankle and cursed.

German soldiers on patrol found and carried Karl to the nearest medical facility. A doctor set the ankle and told him he must wear a cast for at least four weeks.

They moved Karl to a hospital outside Berlin. Closer to the nexus of the impending coup against Hitler, of what use could he be to Albert now? Karl may have agreed to help his brother aristos and fellow officers remove Hitler and the Nazis, but they had yet to give him the details of the time, place and part he was supposed to play.

# Chapter 27

## Messenger and Interrogator

Mariya-Xenia kept her promise to deliver Seth to the Netherlands and the Nazi-hating Dutch underground, who moved him from hiding place to hiding place until June. A submarine rendezvous was arranged to bring Seth and several other downed Allied airmen to England.

Back in Jolly O, Intelligence debriefed Seth. A rare few believed his accounts of Luftwaffe aces with 200 victories and a thousand missions. All were skeptical about the existence of good Germans who wanted to remove Hitler and end the war.

Several unsympathetic officers treated Seth as if he were a dupe of the Nazis. He aroused their suspicions because he was vague and evasive about the time he spent with Mariya-Xenia in Eppelborn. Not surprising, no one revealed the contents of the film he delivered.

Worst of all, Seth encountered disbelief or lack of interest whenever he raised the controversial issue of Nazi extermination camps. Most regarded Seth as a typical over-sensitive Jew making more out of a regrettable situation than necessary. One sympathetic but realistic interrogator conceded the Germans were indeed behaving badly; but if the land of Bach, Goethe, Lederhosen, and Cuckoo Clocks was committing vile atrocities, the top priority of the Allies was to win the war as the quickest way to end the Nazi tyranny.

After sending his parents a telegram letting them know he was alive and to contact Miriam wherever she was, Seth wrote a long letter to reassure the family he had not been wounded or caught some foul and loathsome social disease.

A pile of mail awaited Seth on his return. His parents were well. His older brother, Dave, was an Army Captain quartermastering at Fort Ord. Leah had married a physician and was expecting her first child. Alan was with the Marines somewhere in the Pacific. Seth dashed off a letter to his younger brother wishing him good luck. He also replied to Coach DeLuca and Carla, who continued to flirt through the mail.

Seth saved for last several letters and a box from Miriam forwarded by his parents. She was now the Mac Herlihy Band's female soloist under the name of Mimi Kay. One oversized envelope contained an eight-by-ten glossy of Miriam in a satin dress atop a piano signed "To the Man I Love from his Gershwin Lady." The box contained a dozen recordings of Miriam singing hit tunes with the band. She wished the band was touring in the ETO instead of the Pacific Theater.

Seth wrote a long reply to Miriam in care of his parents describing how he'd been shot down and hidden by anti-Nazis and the Dutch underground. Then he invited Hank to his quarters, and told his best friend in the ETO how Mariya-Xenia had facilitated his escape.

"Her husband had around a hundred-and-fifty victories back in December when I was there, and I saw photos of his fighter. He flies Me-109 Number 23."

"23? Did you see a wine bottle with the word Spritz on the fuselage?"

"No, but his wife said that was his logo. Here's one of the photos I liberated. Let me introduce you to Karl, Fürst zu Pfalz von Teuffelreich, the pilot of 23 Spritz."

Hank gazed at the handsome Luftwaffe officer whose eyes were those of a hunter. "May I keep it?"

"Sure."

"Karl, Fürst zu Pfalz von Teuffelreich? By golly, that's some mouthful. I'll ask the Intelligence boys if they have more information on the prince."

***

USAAF policy held firm for Seth. No pilot shot down over enemy territory was allowed to fly combat again. He avoided being Z.I.ed, sent back to the States (the Zone of the Interior) to be an instructor, because his fluency in German was useful for interrogating captured pilots. Most of the USAAF translators were refugees from Germany: artists, writers, musicians, and teachers without the technical expertise to handle the arcane details of flying.

Most nights, Seth had vivid nightmares of flying combat, or of Miriam tortured by the Gestapo, raped by the Red army or blown apart by bombs. He awakened in a sweat from a dream in which he strangled a Nazi brute. Seth's powerful hands had twisted the pillow into an hourglass shape.

***

Hank did not like his assignment, which made it seem he was betraying a good friend when his superiors ordered him to observe Braham's interrogations of POW Luftwaffe airmen. Several Germans had accused Seth of violating the Geneva Conventions for treatment of prisoners.

In an adjacent room in the interrogation Quonset hut through a one way glass, Hank watched Braham prepare to question an arrogant FW-190 fighter pilot who had parachuted near Thetford. The questioning was going "According to Hoyle," and Hank lit a cigar, pleased he would have nothing detrimental to report about his buddy.

***

Seth offered the German a second cigarette and continued asking relevant questions in a polite, matter-of-fact tone. Some the POW answered, others he declined, as was his right. After half an hour, Seth terminated the interrogation and put his pen on the legal notepad. He rose and prepared to escort the pilot out of the room when the German blew smoke in his face.

"I cannot understand you Americans. You are absolute idiots to fight for the International Zionist Communist Conspiracy and your Jew-President Rosenfeld."

Seth slapped the cigarette from the POW's mouth and gripped the man's throat with the same hand. Oblivious to his surroundings, he did not see the man he was choking. The unfortunate pilot's contorted face became that of all cruel Nazis Seth had seen in newsreels and photos.

Hank burst into the room, followed by two MPs. "Braham. Let him go. You'll ruin your career."

Seth came to his senses and flung the POW against the wall. The pilot thrashed on the floor and gasped for air. Seth stood over the POW and said with all the contempt he could muster in German, "Master race? Übermensch? Never forget that with one hand, this Jew could have snuffed out your worthless Nazi bastard's life."

Hank gripped Seth's arm. "I'll verify as a witness that he assaulted you."

"Witness?"

"Our superiors have received complaints that you flaunt the Geneva Accords for...."

"That shouldn't apply to these bastards."

"But they do. So live with it." Hank confronted the MPs. "This German POW assaulted Captain Braham. That is how I'll write it in my report. Any questions?"

The MPs had none.

Their skeptical CO chose to believe Hank over the German. He gave Seth a three day pass to get whatever was eating him out of his system or face dire consequences.

***

At the Savoy bar in London, Seth saw a covey of top brass sauntering toward the dining room. One of the generals looked familiar. Seth paid the tab for three double scotches and followed the party into the dining room. Consumed by target fixation, he zeroed-in on a short two-star with the features of a not-so-benign bulldog smoking a cigar.

"General Kilrain. Sir, I apologize for the intrusion, but I was hoping you'd remember we met back in 1928, Armistice Day. You took me up for my first flight in a Trusty at Chrissy Field."

Kilrain squinted at Seth. "Goddam, I do remember. You were that little daredevil who was with my old friend Andy DeLuca."

"That's right, sir."

Kilrain turned to his party and described that long-ago day at the Presidio. "How is Andy?"

"Great, sir, a grandfather many times over."

"Send Andy my best."

"Will do, sir. You inspired me to become a fighter pilot that day at Chrissy. And I'm an ace too, five confirmed kills."

"Glad to hear it, Captain."

"I know this is not the time or place, but I have an important favor to ask of you. I've another day of R&R, so we can talk any time between now and then."

Kilrain searched Seth 's face. "I can give you a minute or two. Be at my office tomorrow at 07:30."

# Chapter 28
## Failure

Karl sat alone in a wicker chair wearing pajamas and robe, his injured leg in a cast and propped on an ottoman. Other patients in the hospital recreation room read, played cards, or cogitated over chessboards. He had not heard from Albert or anyone else involved in the plot who could inform him about his role and the date.

At 18:30 hours, they heard an announcement on the radio. An attempt to assassinate Der Führer had failed and all Germans must stay tuned to their radios for more details. Patriotic music followed. Karl listened in a state of shock as more patients and hospital staff hurried into the recreation room.

"Unbelievable."

"Awful."

"Who would dare to do such a horrible thing?"

"They must pay for this."

A nurse misread Karl's concern. "Do not worry, Hauptmann. Our Führer is indestructible."

The speaker promised Der Führer would address the German people. He repeated the announcement often during hours of relentless patriotic marches until 0100 hour when Hitler spoke for the first time.

"Men and women of Germany. If I speak to you today it is first in order to hear my voice and that you should know I am unhurt and well ....

"... and secondly, that you should know a vicious crime unparalleled in German history has failed ....

"... but I survived the vicious bombing plot hatched by traitors ....

"... a sign from Providence that I am meant to carry out my tasks. The traitorous gang of criminal elements will be destroyed without mercy ....

"....we shall settle accounts with them in the manner to which we National Socialists are accustomed."

Poldi entered, wearing an SS General's uniform, accompanied by a Gestapo officer carrying a physician's satchel. He ordered everyone to leave the recreation room and handed Karl a paper. "You will leave now and report to your new unit on the Eastern Front."

Karl read his orders. Poldi was sending him to the Jagdgeschwader with the highest attrition rate in the East. "This is absurd."

"You almost brought ruin upon both of us."

"What are you babbling about?"

"Wittelsberg was taken alive."

Karl masked his concern for Albert. "You must be confused. My friend Gerd died in a bombing ...."

"Do not dissemble with me. Although Wittelsberg has not yet confessed, I believe he mentioned the coup to you."

"Your belief is not proof of anything."

"The fact you were in contact with each other in June may be enough for the authorities to arrest, interrogate, and try you for treason."

"We are uncle and nephew, to both our regrets. Were I to be arrested, you fear I might name you as a conspirator. That is why you hope I will die in Russia before the purges begin."

"They have begun. With so many of our caste involved in the conspiracy, being a von can be proof enough of treason. Your wife, your friends Wittelsberg and Strachwitz, the entire Abwehr, all are suspect."

"Nonsense"

"Heiser."

The Gestapo physician took a small hammer from his satchel, dropped to one knee and broke the plaster on Karl's leg but left the bandages now leaking blood. "As you have so ordered, Herr General, I have certified him fit to fly in the East. Heil Hitler."

"Heil Hitler."

"The hospital doctors said I would need the cast for another two weeks."

Poldi pulled Karl to his feet and thrust a pair of crutches at him. "Dress now. A car is waiting to take you to the airport. I must return to headquarters. Wittelsberg ought to have regained consciousness by now."

"Albert is a valiant Panzer officer, a loyal German. He does not deserve—"

"No, he is a traitor who broke the Führereid, his oath to Hitler. He shall die."

***

Karl read more into Der Führer's hysterical pronouncements than mere words. He believed Hitler now hated the German people, as he must have always hated mankind, and blamed them for all defeats. Der Führer might decide to take everyone with him in a national Götterdammerung if he believed the war was lost.

Each day at Lemburg, Karl heard distressing news of the aftermath. The failed attempt on Hitler's life gave Der Führer and his minions an excuse to exterminate large numbers of the princely and Junker castes he hated.

Officers returning from Berlin reported that every aristo had become suspect. Karl accepted all stories of revenge as truth. The Nazi berserkers had indeed been turned loose. Accounts of humiliations and tortures suffered by those accused of participating in the coup sickened Karl. Hitler ordered the executions filmed and gorged on chocolate cakes while he watched convicted conspirators hanging naked from meat hooks and strangling by piano wire.

The prominent victims included Dr. Gördeler, Mayor of Leipzig; Dr. Strolin, the Lord Mayor of Stuttgart; General von Beck, former Chief of the General Staff; Alexander von Falkenhausen, Military Governor of Northern France and Belgium; and General Karl Heinrich von Stulpnagel, Military Governor of France. The von der Schulenberg brothers, one the Mayor of Berlin and the other a former ambassador to the USSR in 1941, had also been arrested.

Karl suspected avarice, even more than fear or desire for revenge, as a motive behind many arrests. The Nazis were imprisoning entire families and confiscating the estates and personal wealth of the accused aristos. Over fifteen thousand Germans had been implicated in the plot and marked for execution. Many committed suicide by poison.

Before Field Marshal von Kluge took cyanide, he wrote a letter chastising Hitler:

If your new wonder weapons have no particular effect in the air, you must end this war ... the German people have suffered so unspeakably that it is high time to make an end of this horror.

****

Karl needed several more weeks of healing before he could fly aerial combat. He convinced a sympathetic flight surgeon to transfer him to JG-52, now based at Lemburg. Karl believed he could handle a Me-109 without too much pain and become combat proficient again in his favorite single-seat fighter. He was eager to return to action. German positions on the Eastern Front were deteriorating faster than anyone foresaw.

The Red Army steamrolled through Estonia, Latvia, and Lithuania, approached Königsburg in East Prussia and the great port city of Danzig. Advance units reached the outskirts of Warsaw and captured Lwow and Ploesti, depriving the Reich of oil. Continuing to dictate strategy, Hitler ordered the Wehrmacht in the East to defend untenable positions to the last man.

****

The entire Intelligence service had been compromised as disloyal to their Darling and accused of being the nexus of the failed 20 July plot. Declared the greatest traitor, The

Abwehr's chief Admiral Canaris was arrested, tortured, and strangled. Anyone in the hands of the Gestapo might denounce Mariya-Xenia and Bruno, even if they were innocent. Karl's worries for Elfi became unbearable. The Gestapo intercepted and read all mail. It would be impossible to contact the little brunette until the bloodbath ended.

*Would it end?*

Karl sought comfort in the skies. His first breaking-in sortie as wingman came in mid-August. On each subsequent flight, he worked his way to leading a Rotte, a Schwarm, and a Staffel. Karl flew as if he had never been away from the Me-109. During his first two weeks as a Staffelkapitän, Karl shot down 14 Soviet planes, but those Luftsiegen seemed to have no effect against the Soviets. Each day, he saw more than a thousand enemy planes in the air.

He had been picking off the easy ones and avoiding dogfights. Karl hit his targets at high speeds and ran. Those safer tactics required precise shooting. He tried to forget about being in a race with others for top honors. That would lead to taking unnecessary chances to score a victory. Besides, the top aces were uncatchable. A week earlier on 24 August 1944, young Erich Hartmann, a true aerial combat prodigy who had not seen action until October 1942, shot down 11 Soviet aircraft for an astonishing 301 Luftsiegen; wonderful for an individual Luftwaffe ace, ominous for Germany, as it indicated how many enemy were arrayed against them.

Karl continued to fly in perfect rhythm similar to a slalom run on skis. He weaved in and out and around the enemy bombers as if he and the 109 were one, a perfect fusion of man and machine, and reached 226 Luftsiegen by mid-September.

Upon landing after the final sortie of the day, Karl reported to the CO. Inside the operations shack, a celebration was launched by the Staffelkapitänen.

One of the pilots hung a wreath of vines, leaves, and berries around Karl's neck. Another gave him a glass of champagne. The Gruppenkommandeur called for silence.

"Fürst, Reichsminister Hermann Göring has sent you this award, the Schwerten, Swords with Oak Leaves, promoted you to Major, and sent you new orders. You will report to Lechfeld 3 October for transition to the new Me-262 jet fighter. We regret losing you, and we have gathered to celebrate your good fortune. Gentlemen, let us drink again to our comrade, Fürst Karl."

The men cheered, hoisted their glasses, and drank. Karl tried to make his responses to each man seem natural and not so damn formal. The *cabbage knives and forks,* as the pilots called the Schwerten, and promotion to major mattered much less than to be one of the few selected to fly the Me-262.

# Chapter 29

### Return to Combat

Mid-September, Seth stood at ease with Hank in front of Colonel Wilson at 375th Group HQ. "Received permission to fly combat again, sir."

Wilson read Seth's orders. "From General Kilrain himself? How did you pull it off?"

Seth told Wilson the story of his first flight at Chrissy Field when he was eight. Hank stepped forward. "Colonel, we do need veterans to help stabilize things here. We've got too many novices, and Captain Braham is a proven leader and an ace."

"But not yet qualified in a P-51."

"I've already checked out Braham in the Mustang. In my opinion, he's ready to lead an element or a flight in my squadron."

"I won't disappoint you, sir."

"You'd better not, Braham. Okay, he's all yours Milroy."

"Thank you, sir." Seth saluted and made a quick exit. Outside the office, he shook Hank's hand. "Thanks, I owe you."

"You can pay me back by helping our kids survive."

Seth had the Group's best artist paint on his new P-51 five swastikas, MY GERSHWIN LADY, and the illustration he'd had on his P-38. He scored no victories during the next few weeks. Seldom did the Luftwaffe challenge the Fortress armadas, and the number of flying days decreased as the weather worsened. Seth performed so well as a leader that Hank put him in charge of his squadron whenever he took over the group for Colonel Wilson.

Seth was leading the 135th Squadron on the return leg of a routine escort mission and passing near Stuttgart when a pilot called out over the R/T, "Green Leader, bandits at one o'clock high."

Seth acknowledged Lt. Mercutio's call, led the 135th after a rare Schwarm of FW-190s, and took on a tenacious kraut. He was not about to out-hero this top gun, whoever he was. Seth directed his wingman into maneuvers for a series of hit-and-run shots. Mercutio was good, and they both scored hits on the FW-190 for a shared victory. The German abandoned his fighter and chuted downward.

The other 190s fled the scene, and Seth received permission to beat up ground targets at Echterdingen Airfield near Stuttgart. He spotted a gaggle of small primary trainers in the traffic pattern practicing a series of circuits and bumps. Those sitting ducks were harmless students but Luftwaffe embryos, who would soon be killing American pilots and crews and strafing GIs. Within minutes, the 135th shot down 17 trainers, 3 confirmed for Seth, and 2 for Mercutio.

***

That evening at the Officers' Club bar, Seth celebrated with Hank and the men of the 135th. He ordered the first round of drinks and bought swarthy Lt. Dominic Mercutio, his aggressive wingman, a bottle of Scotch. "For losing your cherry today after ten missions. You're a goddam prodigy. Two-point-five victories. You're halfway to acedom."

Mercutio accepted Seth's offer of a Havana. "I'll catch the next round, Paisan. And may you improve on your 8.5 kills."

Seth had vowed after Zeke's death to make no close friends during his second tour in the ETO, but he could not resist the good-natured charm of Mercutio, a five-foot six-inch, bandy-legged weightlifter with the torso of a six-footer.

"Level with me, Paisan, do you think I'll get a reply?"

"Sure you will."

Carla DeLuca had sent Seth two snapshots, one a full face portrait, the other revealing the girl's luscious full figure in a skimpy bathing suit. When he showed them to Mercutio, the young pilot expressed interest in the girl. Seth then encouraged Mercutio to write Carla.

"You're sure my schnozzola won't put her off?"

"Hell, you'll remind Carla of her father. When you do meet, I hope she'll be able to tolerate the smell of that Lucky Tiger slop you splash on your hair."

# Chapter 30
## Decisions

Karl perspired during the flight to Berlin in a small light transport, a classic fighter pilot reaction. He disliked being a passenger in planes or automobiles. If an enemy fighter should bounce them, he would be defenseless.

Upon landing, Karl hitched a ride with a staff officer who was driving in the direction of the Pfalz-Teuffelreich home. Bomb-ravaged Berlin shocked Karl. The beautiful city had become a moonscape of craters, rubble, and blackened ruins. Every standing structure they passed had some damage from the bombs that leveled half the city. Detours had to be made because many streets and avenues were impassable. The general populace, mostly women, children, and the elderly, scurried like rats in a garbage pit searching for belongings, worked with the military to clear rubble, or waited in long lines for food and water. More soldiers than civilians roamed the streets.

The Luftwaffe's successes in the East had made no difference. Of what value was it to shoot down so many Soviet planes when Americans by day and the RAF by night bombed Germany at will? Because they had destroyed the family villa, Karl decided that he had no reason to stay in Berlin. All his friends were dead; either from combat, bombing, or the aftermath of the coup. On the plus side, Bruno may have escaped the purges, and Mariya-Xenia still resided in Eppelborn.

Karl resolved to have another meeting with his wife, whose cooperation and assistance were essential before bombs destroyed the Schloss Teuffelreich vineyards and before Yank and British ground troops drank the cellars dry. Back on 14 September, they had taken Aachen, the first great German city to fall, and their armies were poised to assault the Siegfried Line. With those dangers in mind, Karl developed a master plan to hide the wines of Pfalz-Teuffelreich. After the war, when money was certain to be unstable, those noble vintages would hold up better than any currency.

Karl left Berlin and visited his estates and vineyards in the Rhine and Moselle regions to make preliminary arrangements with loyal and trustworthy family retainers. He delayed going to Eppelborn until the last possible moment.

***

Smoking a cigarette, Mariya-Xenia gave Karl a formal greeting. Elsa, who had been sent to the manor after his last injury in the West, barked, jumped on him, and licked his face.

Karl made himself comfortable in the study with a cigar and favorite cognac. Mariya-Xenia was thinner, close to emaciation, her pallor almost matching the gray wool dress she lived in. The causes of his wife's physical deterioration were obvious: too many responsibilities in a nation losing a war, poor diet, tension from the aftermath of the failed coup, fear of arrest, and bombing raids coming closer and closer to Eppelborn.

Those were the externals. Mariya-Xenia had developed into a mature individual with walls of thought and experiences he would never be able to penetrate.

She lit another cigarette. "You are indestructible, it seems, in spite of what Poldi tried to do to you."

"Did he at least leave you alone?"

"Poldi placed me under house arrest for the entire day of 21 July. Except for the secret rooms, every square centimeter of this manor, each orifice of my body, everything was searched by those Gestapo swine who interrogated me about you and our associates."

"And Poldi permitted your temporary arrest, the body search?"

"Do not be naive, Karl. He ordered it. Poldi is convinced you would have participated in the plot if you had been healthy. He believes you knew enough to be implicated anyway."

"The swine. I shall deal with my uncle when I see him next."

"And at the time, I was hiding Albert's wife, Lotte, and her three children. I thank God the youngest never cried."

"They are safe now?"

"Yes."

"Then the von Wittelsberg bloodline shall continue. And Bruno?"

"In Switzerland, or Sweden."

He stroked Elsa to calm her. She could not get enough attention from him. "You have kept busy?"

"Yes, as a nursing assistant. I help where I can at the children's ward in town. The poor things are brought in from Zweibrucken, Pirmasens, all the cities and towns being hit by the bombers."

Karl winced. He did not want to be reminded of Luftwaffe failures to protect the Reich.

"I have a request, Karl. All the cities along the Rhine have been devastated. There are tens of thousands of wounded, many of them children. Have I your permission to turn the Schloss at Bad Dürkheim into a children's hospital, which I shall administer?"

"Noblesse oblige and all that? Of course." How ironic Mariya-Xenia was now a nurse the same as Elfi. Princess and commoner.

Mariya-Xenia opened a desk drawer and took out a package of cigarettes. "Forgive me. I ought to have offered you one."

Karl lit the cigarette and sipped cognac. Elsa relaxed and lay contented nearby. The first inhale caused Karl to cough. "So strong. It cannot be German."

Mariya-Xenia showed Karl the package of *Lucky Strikes*. "I have a few left."

"Is the enemy dropping these with the bombs to seduce us into surrendering?"

"No, an American pilot was shot down near Eppelborn, and he gave them to me. I helped him escape. These cigarettes almost gave me away to Poldi, but I lied convincingly. I said you had taken them from a Yank POW."

Karl was amazed he did not feel anger, resentment, or any desire to restore his honor when Mariya-Xenia described how she saved an American fighter pilot from capture. Did they have an affair? Karl often speculated how and when Mariya-Xenia might deal with his neglect of conjugal duties and would not be surprised if she had taken with another man.

Karl did not inquire if his wife and the American shared the same bed. A wise man never asked questions that may have answers he preferred not to know. Karl interrupted twice to insist Mariya-Xenia not describe the American or mention his name. The more anonymous the Yank pilot remained, the easier Karl could pretend he never existed. It was a matter of pride, not jealousy, until they divorced.

"Mariya-Xenia, I love another."

"Indeed? I cannot imagine you feeling love for another person. In any case, we shall divorce after the war if we defy the percentages and both of us survive. In the meantime, I hope your woman brings you happiness."

Because Mariya-Xenia was of like mind, she agreed to help Karl hide the wines and to preserve choice cuttings from the vineyards. She insisted papers be drawn making her an equal partner in the wine business, to continue after their divorce. He saw no reason to refuse. Mariya-Xenia had managed well all his financial matters to date.

After the preliminary papers of partnership had been prepared and each of them signed, Karl terminated the visit. "I bid you farewell. I will take Elsa."

"As you wish."

Karl clicked his heels. "Until then."

"Yes, until then."

# Chapter 31

## Convergence of Aces

Hank led the 135<sup>th</sup> squadron across the Zuider Zee to sweep Luftwaffe airfields before the bombers roared in for a big raid. Seth commanded a flight, and Mercutio an element. Near the end of the mission, Hank spotted a tiny contrail and took three fighters south toward Pforzheim to investigate. They came across a Dornier twin-engine DO-17 Flying Pencil. Its escort, a pair of FW-190s, veered to mix with the Mustangs.

Hank swerved away from the fighters and closed toward the bomber. With less than a hundred rounds for his six 50 cal. guns, he sent the Dornier crashing to earth in a hellish gasoline explosion.

"Cowboy Leader, bandit on your tail."

The warning gave Hank time to execute a snap-roll that placed him behind an overshooting FW-190. He pressed the trigger and shot away its canopy. The German pilot abandoned the plane and parachuted. Hank looked for the other FW-190 and saw, sick at heart, the German shoot down the greenest Mustang pilot in his element and speed away.

*No chute. Another painful letter to write.*

Still a good hour out from Thetford, Hank experienced one of the great discomforts flying the P-51 on long, six to seven hour sorties: lack of normal bathroom facilities aboard the slim single-seater. The pilot had available for use a funnel shaped hard rubber cone about six inches long and a few inches wide at the top attached to a tube that vented beneath the Mustang, but Hank first had to deal with a new G-suit. It resembled cowboy chaps except it was high-waisted with bladders that inflated to prevent the pilot from graying or blacking out when a force of 2-Gs or more was applied on the airplane.

The agonizing pressure of Hank's own bladder became so severe he could no longer put it off. He slid the fighter away from his wingman, and flying with his knees, he reached under the seat, detached the relief cone from its bracket, and placed it between his legs.

Hank's G-suit was equipped with a two-way zipper that opened it from the bottom or the top. He pulled at the bottom zipper and fumbled with his shorts. Damn, he'd forgotten to unfasten the seatbelt. Hank hoped the Germans would not choose this moment to make another appearance as he tried to locate that appendage, so big when admired but now so small when he needed to find it. Dammit-to-hell, now, he had to unfasten the parachute leg straps to pull out his flange.

Hank's Mustang wandered all over the sky at close to 300 mph suggesting a drunk was at the controls. He lifted himself off the seat so he could stretch his personal extension cord toward the cone of the relief tube. After more desperate groping, he placed it in the cone and began to pee.

The first indication of disaster came when the cone failed to drain. The relief tube was frozen at the bottom, and his urine overflowed at the top of the cone. Hank cursed into the oxygen mask and took stock of the situation. He held his penis in the right hand, the relief tube with the left, and controlled the Mustang with his knees. Piss or fly, he could not do both.

Hank dumped the relief tube on the floor of the cockpit, and prayed he could last until he reached Thetford. He never considered the alternative of relieving himself in the flight suit.

At home plate, the alerted ground crew removed Hank from the P-51. Aware of his predicament, they rushed him to the nearest water closet and out of his G-suit. Seth followed to make sure he was okay. Hank proved to himself he had an iron bladder and survived the ordeal with no harm to certain vital working parts. He must have been delirious though.

A familiar face grinned at him in the bathroom mirror.

"Howdy, good buddy."

Hank turned, stared in disbelief at the newcomer, and they exchanged bear hugs. "Brax, Braxton Mobley. What a surprise. By golly, it's great to see you. What are you doing here at Thetford? Last I heard, you were in the ZI and banging the hell out of movie stars."

"Hot damn, Milroy, am I ever-lovin' glad to lay eyes on you. I hoped you'd still be here and not fenced-in over the Channel in Kreegie-land."

"I came close a couple of times, Brax, but how were you able to make it here to Jolly O?"

Brax patted his basket. "Pure brain-power."

"Goddam, it's great to see your gorgeous, dissipated face. We can use your help too. You were always a great air-to-air gunner, and I'm leading a pack of green, mediocre shots. I lost one of them today. Any objections to flying in my squadron?"

"Try keeping me out."

"By the way, this is my good friend and one of the best flyers in the Group, Seth Braham. Seth, Brax was my roommate at Randolph when we were cadets."

"Heard a lot about you, Brax."

"Y'all will hear a lot more about me once I get back into combat."

"Well, I'll leave you two to catch up with each other."

Outside the latrine, Seth went to his room **a**nd Hank walked with Brax to the ops shack, delighted to see his old roomie. As the United States came closer to certain victory, many pilots had become obsessed with not being one of the last unnecessary casualties to flak, accidents, or an enemy fighter. They were eager to complete fifty missions so they could go home permanently. Others concocted clever reasons to get themselves scratched from certain sorties. Brax thrived on combat.

"I may run the 135th, but we'd better clear it with the Old Man. If I'd known you were coming, I could have had everything all greased up for you."

"No sweat." Brax lit a cheroot and gave one to Hank. "I stopped off to look for you at your quarters first. I didn't find any booze. What's this, the Sahara?"

"I limit my drinking to the club. There's too much temptation to kill off a bottle in the evening. Now, tell me, what happened back in the States?"

"You know how hot I am to become the top fighter ace of all time."

"You and everyone else. I've 16 now, friend-o."

Brax's eyes flashed competitive fire. "Just you wait 'til I get up there again. Anyway, for me the ZI was one great bedroom, but I had to get back into combat. So I did the only intelligent thing. Some Yankee Senator got the hots for one of the starlets I was plowing, and I made a deal to set him up if he'd get me back to the ETO. I didn't intend to get city-slickered, so I made sure my orders were cut, and I got out of there before the shit hit the fan."

"What?"

Brax guffawed. "Hank-buddy, after spending a week with me, do you think she'd take a roll in the sheets with some blank-firing old fart, even if he is a Senator?"

"You're lucky he didn't shaft you to Alaska or Greenland."

"Shut yo' mouth, boy. The walls have ears." Brax opened the door to the ops room. "Who the hell is your boss anyway, and how soon before you're running the entire group, good-buddy?"

Colonel Wilson expressed regret at the loss of Number 14, congratulated Hank for his two victories, and welcomed Brax. He was all for having another ace in the group. "Even though we're ten percent over-strength on pilots, I want Mobley active in your squadron immediately."

"Yes, sir, and you'll have it." Outside the CO's office, Hank sobered. In spite of the excitement of flying combat with Brax for the first time and having two more confirmed kills, he'd have to write the parents of the unlucky, green pilot the FW-190 had blasted out of the sky.

"Am I going up with you tomorrow?"

"One thing at a time, Brax. First you'll have to qualify to my satisfaction in the Mustang."

"No sweat."

Hank looked at darkening sky. There would be no mission tomorrow. "After that, weather permitting, for the first combat sortie or two, you'll fly wing for me and work your way back up to a leadership position. Just last week I broke in a new element commander and a new flight leader. I hate to bounce them so quickly. Bad for morale. Unfortunately, not everyone is talented or lucky. There are days when we lose more men to accidents and pilot error than in combat. We can expect attrition to speed your rise to flight leader."

"Are the broads plentiful?"

"More than you can handle."

Brax slapped Hank's back. "That'll be the day, good-buddy."

# Chapter 32

## Kommando Nowotny

Karl brought Elsa with him when he reported to his new unit at Lechfeld, situated near the Messerschmitt factory at Augsburg, and the German Shepherd was made welcome by all the men. He was honored to be one of the elite selected by thirty-two year old General Adolf Galland, Inspector of Day Fighters, who had been appointed General of the Fighter Arm at twenty-nine. The cream of the Luftwaffe had been chosen to form JG-7, the Luftwaffe's first Me-262 jet fighter unit, also called Kommando Nowotny for its talented CO. Major Walter Nowotny, who at twenty-four, the same age as Karl, was a natural leader and a gifted shot. He had become the first ace to reach 250 Luftsiegen in less than 450 sorties.

Karl had to contend with an unpleasant surprise at Lechfeld. A critical shortage of jet planes existed with no justifiable excuse. Only strategic and tactical military stupidity explained why they had not been produced in large quantities. Inexcusably, only three two-seater Me-262B-1a aircraft were available to familiarize the pilots with new procedures and performance, yet the technology and capacity to produce unlimited quantities had existed for years. The long range four-engine Ural Bomber capable of destroying Soviet factories east of the great mountain range, V-1 and V-2 missiles, and the folding-fin air-to-air rockets also should have been given top priority before 1940. Now, Germany was paying a high price for Hitler's and Göring's lack of foresight.

Karl reflected on what might have been, ought to have been. On 18 July 1941, a Me-262 V2 powered by two Jumo 004 engines had already soared toward the sun for the first time; two years later, an improved model was tested by Adolf Galland, who said he felt as if angels were pushing the jet plane when he flew it.

In 1943, Hitler believed the conflict in Europe would last another six months to a year at the most, with a German victory of course. He insisted the war be fought with equipment in existence rather than developing new weapons.

Everyone agreed the Me-262 was a fighter pilot's ultimate dream, with two fond nicknames depending on one's point of view: Stürmvogel, the Storm Bird, and Schwalbe, the Swallow. With an astonishing top speed of 840 kph and the heavy firepower of four 30mm cannon supplemented by twenty-four 50mm rockets, it could handle any enemy fighter and blast B-17s from the skies with ease.

Pilots had to adjust to new tactics required by its high speed. Rhubarbs were out. Any Allied fighter could turn inside the 262's large curving radius. With higher speed came slower deceleration, engine failure, compressor stalls, and burned-out turbines.

Less maneuverable than piston-powered fighters, with poor downward visibility and short endurance, the jet's advantages were its high speed and no requirement for top cover. For those and other tactical reasons, a three plane Kette replaced the four fighter Schwarm.

The tactics were classic. With occasional support from the new rocket-powered Me-163, the Me-262s climbed to high altitudes and dove at near-sonic speeds to attack massive day bomber formations; they passed through the fighter escort and on down to the Flying Fortresses in an ultimate application of hit-and-run. After inflicting severe damage on the bombers, the 262s out-climbed and out-ran the P-51s and P-47s.

Occasionally, a jet pilot was able to bag a fighter on his way down to the B-17s, get the big bird, and then either continue a high-speed dive to safety or zoom to high altitude for another attack. The American fighters could do little except watch them pass by.

Unfortunately, those individual successes of the Me-262 were minuscule when weighed against the massed armadas of eight hundred bombers escorted by seven hundred fighters that appeared day and night over the Reich. Seldom could the Luftwaffe scramble up to twenty jets. More often, two or three rose to take on the awesome numbers.

The Fighter Arm also awaited the Arado 234 jet, with a top speed of around 725 kph and armed with two 20mm cannon, but no more than ten would be available to supplement the 262s by the end of the year.

Karl figured if one included all Me-109s and FW-190s among the active rolls, under the best of conditions the Luftwaffe would have seventy-five top line fighters to battle against the enemy bomber armadas, which could number as high as fifteen hundred planes plus hundreds of fighter escorts. One could not be exposed to such odds without eventually losing through attrition the best qualified fighter pilots. The American fighter pilots' skills had improved with more combat exposure and battle-tested instructors. At the same time, attrition wore thin the ranks of the Luftwaffe's best flyers, and their inexperienced replacements were easy meat for the Americans and British.

Nowotny's luck ran out on 8 November. He had brought down 258 aircraft, including two in the Me-262, before plunging to earth at 800 kph to die in a fiery crash and explosion.

Karl added discouragement to inertia, and doldrums. After more than a month with JG-7, he had yet to go up for the first time in a Me-262 and had too much time to worry about personal matters. Aftershocks of the 20 July continued to reverberate throughout the Reich. Back on 14 October, the Nazis forced Rommel to commit suicide, then announced he died in a car crash. 10 November, they executed Ambassador Friedrich Werner Graf von der Schulenberg. The Gestapo had found his name on a conspirator's list as the designated Minister of Interior or State Secretary of a post-Nazi cabinet. No matter he had not been asked. He was a von. He had to be guilty. More trials and executions had been scheduled by the People's Court to last well into 1945.

Karl assumed his name might appear on a list he knew nothing about or escape the lips of some poor soul under severe torture. Nothing he could do about it. *A waste of time and energy to worry.* At least he managed to wrap up business affairs with Mariya-Xenia, who moved to the Schloss and converted it to a children's hospital.

A loner, Karl preferred Elsa's company to the other pilots and crew. Then a week after Nowotny's death, his turn came to fly the Me-262. He sustained an insouciant attitude in front of the other pilots despite his excitement as he walked toward the jet fighter with Elsa at his side. He strained his eyes and ears in anticipation of yet another enemy raid.

Karl's CO had briefed his pilots and crew about new tactics applied by the Americans to counter the effectiveness of the jets. Throughout October and into November, their high-speed reconnaissance planes flew over Lechfeld. The Me-262s were able to bring down most of them, but the survivors escaped with important photographs of the facilities. The USAAF knew it could not match the jets in the sky. Consequently, 8th Air Force had initiated the tactic of hitting jets at their vulnerable moments, take-off and landing phases of flight, with waves of fighters sent thirty minutes ahead of their B-17 formations. That placed the P-51s in the right slot when the Me-262s scrambled. Twenty-six Me-262s had been lost in combat or from malfunctions and accidents. Today was no different. The Americans raided Lechfeld before Karl could mount the Stormbird. He zigzagged with Elsa between sprays of bullets tearing up the airfield and dove into a shelter. His loyal Shepherd lay bleeding, dead on the tarmac.

The Mustangs destroyed fourteen Me-262s parked on the tarmac and damaged several more during strafing runs, including the jet Karl had been scheduled to fly. He doubted he would fly a Stormbird at Lechfeld. Karl grieved alone after he buried Elsa.

The pilots resumed training in the few operational planes left. Checking out in the jet required yet another tedious wait, and bad weather grounded the pilots most of the time. Karl learned that more 262s would not be available until January, and the Luftwaffe could not mount a full scale jet attack before February, too late to alter the course of the war.

Karl's two months at Lechfeld had been a turning point that had failed to turn. His CO said he would have to wait for an assignment to another jet fighter unit yet to be formed. Karl asked for an assignment to an active combat Gruppe. He did not care where, east or west. He would fly any fighter. More delay could be fatal. Karl had not seen extensive action since September, and he needed to maintain flying and shooting proficiency. Hours later, Karl's CO handed him new orders with a cryptic comment.

"Fürst, if you hurry and report to your new Geschwader, you will be pleasantly surprised."

# Chapter 33

## Top Tandem

By the middle of December 1944, SHAEF, Supreme Headquarters Allied Expeditionary Force, operating out of the Trianon Palace Hotel at Versailles, believed the Germans could not mount a large scale attack, and the war in Europe would soon end. The Wehrmacht retreated on all fronts. In the West, Allied troops poised to crack the Siegfried Line. Metz fell to Patton. Americans broke through the Hürtgen Forest, and the Canadians crossed the Dutch border into the Reich.

Despite intelligence reports that Marshal von Rundstedt ordered over a thousand trainloads of equipment and supplies into assembly areas near Cologne and Bitburg, on December 15, Field Marshal Montgomery, Commander of all British and Canadian forces on the Continent, issued a statement:

> The enemy is at present fighting a defensive campaign on all fronts; his situation is such that he cannot stage major offensive operations ....

Lulled into the same overconfidence to which Hitler had fallen victim earlier in the war, the Allies relaxed, and that was how von Rundstedt's Wehrmacht caught them in the Ardennes Forest the following day. The German offensive coincided with terrible weather that grounded Allied aircraft. No one in the 375th was more frustrated than Brax, who had yet to score a victory since returning to the ETO and qualifying in the P-51.

In one week, the Wehrmacht forged a fifty mile long and fifty mile wide penetration into Allied lines. The Americans surrounded at Bastogne were called upon to surrender.

Seth cursed the Nazi fanatics for prolonging the war for perhaps up to a year, enough time to kill every poor soul in the death camps. At their table in the Officers' Club after yet another day of no flying, Mercutio blew smoke from a cigar and hoisted a glass of whiskey.

"Looks like we won't be home for Christmas after all."

"Or July 4th," Seth mumbled into a glass of Scotch.

They heard Brax making crude, bigoted remarks about assorted minorities at the bar.

"Ahhh, my Paisan, Bilbo's dildo is in top form tonight."

Seth caught Mercutio's reference to a notorious segregationist and all-around bigot, Mississippi Senator Theodore G. Bilbo, who each year introduced a bill in Congress to deport all Negroes to Africa. Seth and Mercutio often discussed the nature of prejudice. As a runty Italian Catholic growing up in Protestant northern European-dominated Kenosha, Wisconsin, Mercutio had suffered social ostracism, verbal abuse, and physical assaults. That explained his obsession with bodybuilding and why a prominent beaked nose slanted to one side.

No lessons would be learned from the war, despite the Nazi atrocities becoming exposed to full light of day. Still suffering under the Nazis and the Soviets, Polish partisan units were claiming chunks of Lithuania for their homeland and persisted in slaughtering Jews. Lithuanians and Latvians were doing the same.

Before the last of their ruthless German occupiers retreated, the Greeks began a bloody civil war. Yugoslavia was a madhouse: South Slavs fought against their German and Italian occupiers, patriots against Croatian Catholic and Bosnian Moslem fascist collaborators, communists against monarchists and anti-communists, and assorted nationalist groups were taking revenge against centuries-old enemies.

At Eppelborn, Bruno von Strachwitz had described how the Soviets prepared communist puppets to take over each country they liberated and stay in power as a fait accompli with the aid of the Red Army. How could anyone expect an American-style Bill of Rights and multi-party democracy to exist anywhere in Eastern Europe after the war?

In spite of all that, Seth knew this was a good war. Nazism, Fascism, and Jap totalitarianism had to be destroyed. He'd worry about dealing with the bigots after the war.

A familiar sound from the club jukebox turned Seth's thoughts to Miriam. She was singing her latest hit, not a Gershwin tune, "I'll Walk Alone." He raised a glass to his fiancée in a silent toast. At the band's live performances, Miriam always dedicated her last song to "My College Boy, wherever you are," but not on any of her recordings.

***

December 22 dawned bright and clear for the first time in two weeks. American dive-bomber units of the 9th Tactical Air Command flew support for the surrounded ground troops at Bastogne with 8th Air Force fighters providing top-cover for the dive-bombers.

Seth missed the sortie. He was assigned to 8th Air Force HQ at High Wycombe Abbey about thirty miles northwest of London for the next few days to help interrogate a POW high-scoring fighter ace; rumors had intensified about the Luftwaffe planning something big.

Hank sat next to Brax in the mess hall at breakfast. "Briefing will be at 0600, and we'll be airborne before dawn. Because you've been out of combat for a year, do you want to drop out of the first mission so you can make a daylight take-off on the second sortie?"

"Hell no. You know better than that. I can do the blindfold check with no sweat. Hank, good-buddy, I am ready to go."

"Then you'll fly wing for me. Because of your skill and experience, I'll give you full latitude. You take the lead on all breaks in your direction."

"I lead and you follow. Just like we used to talk about back at Kelly."

Hank saw no point to correcting Brax.

***

Over snow-covered western Europe, the sun rose above the horizon and the Mustangs of the 135th pressed eastward into its glare at twenty-five thousand feet. Hank reminded his boys to be alert for Germans coming at them from out of the sun. He was the first to spot an intermittent vapor trail above and fine as silk thread. It came from a jet or rocket propelled plane climbing high above the 135th. Hank dipped his wings, alerting the squadron to move into combat formation and be ready for anything.

They headed northeast over the Meuse River when Hank sighted four Me-109s in a long dive. Were they going after C-47 transports carrying supplies to the beleaguered Allied troops or heading toward the 9th TAC dive-bombers assaulting Wehrmacht positions? More enemy had to be nearby. He led the 135th in a turn to the south and heard Brax cry out:

"Blue Leader, two bandits at eleven o'clock high."

Hank saw them and guessed they were after someone else. He led the break into their dive, placing Brax nearest the two Me-163 rocket planes. Hank applied full war-emergency power. Brax broke away as if running from the rocket planes but instead cut across their circle to close the distance and get sufficient lead to make a good shot.

The speedy Luftwaffe fighters were a thousand yards away when Hank saw flashes of hits strike the trailing fighter, which exploded in a fireball. "Beautiful shot, Blue Two."

"Hot damn, Blue Leader, I'm proficient again. Wait 'til I really warm up."

Hank broke left, and Brax followed suit. In perfect crossover formation, the Texan dropped behind Hank and gave the less experienced men in the 135th a lesson in accurate timing and professional teamwork.

Two FW-190s materialized and closed on the other P-51s. The Germans failed to see Hank's flight and broke into him. He took a split-second shot without time to aim and missed. Brax, got off a full burst at the trailing FW-190, which exploded into lava-rock bright fragments.

"Another beaut', Blue Two."

"Thanks for the confirmation, and your set-up, good-buddy."

Hank stabilized his flight at 15,000 feet. Off in the distance, he saw several flights of P-47 Jugs strafing a wooded area and dive-bombers working over the Panzers. Tank and other vehicle tracks were outlined in the deep snows between smoldering metallic pyres. He signaled the squadron to return home.

Back at Thetford the airplanes of the 135th refueled and rearmed, and the pilots were debriefed, then briefed for the next sortie. In the ops shack, Hank quieted his men to announce the results of their first mission of the day. The 135th scored five kills and two probables. They lost one Mustang seen bellying into a new airfield being constructed on Allied-held territory. Everyone hoped that good old Blue 12 escaped uninjured. At any rate, five-to-one was damn good odds.

Hank congratulated Brax for the two kills, all the more amazing because of the Texan's long layoff. "I thought they were moving too fast for your gun-sight to track them."

"I had to estimate the point where I'd be closest to the 163s. I cranked an extra inch of lead on the pipper sight, and when the rockets moved into an imaginary point far in the distance, I pulled the trigger. I'd been aiming for the number one plane and, shee-yit, if I didn't catch number two instead. Those Me-163s must have been moving a hell of a lot faster than I'd estimated. Next time, I'll add another half inch of lead to my aim and for certain hit the target I want."

Their dream of being a super tandem was aborted because one of Hank's flight leaders succumbed to the malaise common to the most confident and aggressive pilots. Blue 5 froze in the seat of the fighter after landing, then shook uncontrollably. He'd almost bought it on the first sortie and believed his luck had run out, another iron-man who realized he was a mere mortal after all. Hank modified the briefing instructions and appointed Brax element leader in Blue 5's place.

Over the Continent on their second sortie of the day, Hank took one flight of the 135th to 29,000 feet to act as top-cover for the rest of the squadron racing toward the German border. Brax led the other three flights at 21,000.

Between Liege and Aachen, someone called out a sighting at ten o'clock, and the entire squadron went into ready alert. As another pilot called out a bandit at one o'clock high, a Me-262 jet flashed through the squadron without firing at the Mustangs and continued its dive to shoot down a twin-engine bomber several thousand feet below.

Hank cursed. It was impossible to catch the Me-262, which had to be steaming at over 600 mph. Besides, a Schwarm of FW-190s was headed full bore toward the 135th. He latched his top-cover flight onto their tails less than a mile behind. The FW-190s raced at maximum speed, and the P-51s were not fast enough to catch them. The sky filled with tracers and bullets. Neither side scored hits.

The German fighters were bent on returning to their base, and Hank's P-51s were down to minimum fuel with a long flight back to England. He deemed it inadvisable to initiate another full-throttle chase. Instead, he led the 135th in a turn toward home.

***

The following morning when the 135th pilots hurried toward their fighters, a C-47 transport landed on the runway, taxied to the ops building, and disgorged a single passenger. They cheered when they recognized Blue 12, shot down during the first sortie yesterday, and they charged into their mission at peak morale.

The 135th was airborne before sunrise to help escort bombers to Merzhausen near Frankfurt in the biggest air raid yet in the war, 609 Liberators, 1322 Fortresses, 502 RAF heavy bombers, and 1100 Allied fighters all taking part.

After the lead flotilla passed Brussels, the first German fighters appeared. Brax scored an amazing accurate seventy-degree deflection shot, shattering a Me-109. Hank then led the 135th into a slow turn toward the bomber stream and saw a FW-190 slewing through a sloppy vertical bank ahead at only fifty yards. Hank's finger tightened on the trigger, and the 190 went down for victory number 17.

The 135th flew ahead to meet on schedule the bombers they had been assigned to protect for the return to England. After Hank settled the 135th into escort position, the pilots relaxed on the assumption they'd seen their last enemy fighters of the day.

The Germans had other ideas. Two Me-109s attacked the 135th as if the odds were just right at sixteen-to-two. Hank suspected their real intention was to lure the squadron into a big chase so the other Luftwaffe fighters could attack the exposed part of the bomber stream.

Instead of ordering the entire squadron into hot pursuit, Hank dispatched his last flight after the 109s. Then, after scanning to the south and catching a glint from a canopy several miles to the left, he turned the other Mustangs toward that direction and placed them on the perch for a classic pursuit curve attack against two Schwarmen of FW-190s racing toward the bombers.

"Ten o'clock low. Follow me."

The Mustangs turned with all sights tracking to intercept the 190s. The Luftwaffe fighters ignored the P-51s and pressed toward the bombers. The pilots of the 135th flew within fifteen hundred feet of the 190s and fired their first rounds, Their inexperienced foes made every possible wrong move. Hank sighted on a fighter in the center of the line and saw bullets flash when they hit the 190. The stricken plane nosed up sharply, then stalled when a wing broke away.

Brax scored on a 190, aimed at the end man, and registered hits on the second FW as well. One of the Germans yanked his aircraft into a vertical left turn and collided with Brax's first target. Locked together, the two 190s broke into flames and spun together in a death-waltz to the ground. Other pilots also scored, and in less than ten seconds, the 135th knocked seven FW-190s out of the sky.

The German leader in the eighth plane was something else. He might be outnumbered, but he intended to make it a costly fight for the Americans if they were so inclined. He used every trick of the flying trade and invented others. The Americans reciprocated. Each time one of the P-51s got in position for a shot, the pilot had to break away to avoid colliding with a friendly fighter or running into the 190.

Except Brax. Hank read his mind. The Texan thought he could get off a ninety-degree deflection burst and reduce it to fifty-degrees before overshooting the target or breaking his lock-on. Sure enough, Brax maneuvered into position and fired. The 190 flamed. Hank whistled at yet another of Brax's impossible shots. When the German pilot bailed out and chuted between two speeding Mustangs, the American pilots waved at him.

Hank radioed Brax. "Hot damn, friend-o, you now got six ETO , which makes you a two Theater of War ace."

"Just warming up good-buddy."

Donald Michael Platt

292

When we see a silver plane, it is American. A black plane, it is British. When we see no plane, it is German.
—*Wehrmacht joke*

# PART FOUR

In Lonely Lands
1945

# Chapter 34
## New Year's Eve, 1944/1945

The afternoon of New Year's Eve, Hank lounged comfortable in pilot fatigues over long johns and went through the mail. So far, no one had been able to locate Winty. He tipped back his Stetson and read a letter from Bob Chilton, erstwhile Cadet Captain and Eagle Squadron fighter pilot. Chilton wrote about the successes and tragedies of classmates they had known back in Texas and included a morale-deflating rumor about Wayne Miller. The fool who confounded all in 39B by not washing-out was now a lieutenant colonel with seniority in rank far beyond that of proven combat leaders. Worse, Miller requested and received an assignment to head a group in the ETO so he could obtain credit as a combat leader for his resume. Hank prayed it would never be the 375th.

Brax entered ready in pinks for the festivities at the Officers' Club. He planted himself in front of a mirror and admired his reflection.

"If any girl is unlucky enough to fall for you, she'll become the loser in a romantic triangle."

"Hank, good-buddy, you-all just don't want to understand. It isn't that I'm in love with my face. Goddam it, man. Don't you realize if I get to be top ace, why I'll be sure fire to have a great movie career from the start."

"Sonny Tufts, watch out."

"Sure, I know you're razzing me. Even if I make crappy B-movies and can't act, the loot is great, and the broads all gorgeous and available. But dammit-to-hell, Gabreski has 28 ETO kills, so I've got plenty of catching up to do."

"Be patient. With your super shooting eye, it won't take too many more missions."

Brax jerked a thumb toward the window. "At the rate these skies remain empty, I might have to change my opinion, and pump up my score by including all those crates on the ground I strafed into junk."

"Not while I'm boss of the 135th, friend-o."

Hank never let on how much he hated those low level runs. It might negatively affect his kids' morale. Skill and experience counted for nothing. One lucky shot from the ground and the pilot would never have a chance to eject.

"Good-buddy, I sorely need aerial combat. Why do I have the bad luck to fly in a war during the worst European winter in twenty years? And where's the enemy? We haven't seen any the past few days. I can't believe the krauts ain't got no more fighters."

"Neither do I."

"Hank, where do you-all think the krauts are?"

"I don't know. It worries me too. I think something big is being planned. Maybe another surprise offensive, this time in the air."

Brax adjusted his fifty-mission cap at a jaunty angle and faced the mirror again. "Well, whatever. We can handle anything they throw up at us. Our Mustangs rule the skies.

I'd sure love to bag a passel of Me-262s. Maybe we ought to be credited with two kills for each one we shoot down. They do have two engines."

"Dream on."

***

Hank decided to meet Brax later at the Officers' Club for a snort, celebrate the New Year with the group, and hit the sack early. First, he stopped at the NCO club to wish the 135th ground crews Happy New Year and buy a round of drinks for the hard-working efficient men who kept the fighters operating, as a thank-you for their efforts. Hank encouraged his pilots to bolster the morale of their mechanics and armorers and made sure they painted the names of their NCOs on the fuselage of each 135th Mustang.

He'd have to speak with Brax again about the outrageous non-essential demands he made upon the crew of his fighter as if they were servants and tell him to stop calling each one *boy*. The NCOs wouldn't shed a tear if Brax failed to make it home from a mission.

Hank pushed inside the festooned Thetford Officers' Club filled with men and women from all the American services and other Allied forces to welcome the Year of Great Deeds and Victory over the Krauts and Nips. No need to tell his pilots to take it easy on the booze. His squadron was not scheduled to fly on New Year's Day.

Hank turned down offers of drinks and joined Brax, who was drinking from a bottle of whiskey and smoking a Havana.

"Happy New Year, friend-o."

"Glad you made it, good-buddy. What say we all make our last ETO New Year's bash worth telling to later generations?"

Before Hank could reply, the randy pilot's eyes bulged in anticipation as a swarm of officer nurses from the big USAAF hospital at Wimpole Park made a noisy entrance. The vivacious gaggle of girls always enjoyed parties at the fighter bases and looked ready for another slam-bang blast tonight.

Hank respected the nurses. Those compassionate women worked long and hard hours to save the lives and limbs of American men. Fighter pilots wounded by German gunfire or injured in crashes all attested to the tender loving care they had received at Wimpole Park. Despite puritanical regulations, relationships often developed between nurse and fighter pilot, which ran the gamut from a one-nighter, through temporary love, to an occasional grand passion.

Brax rated each woman. "Shee-yit, Hank. Nothing but all-American girls here. I can always bang 'em back home. What say we go into London?"

"No, you go ahead." The Texan was more than three sheets to the wind. Hank doubted Brax would have been able to perform at peak efficiency if they had a mission to fly on New Year's Day.

Brax settled for a busty strawberry-blonde nurse lieutenant he sized up as just right. As part of protocol practiced throughout the Air Force, Hank joined the other squadron leaders of the 375th and their CO. Colonel Wilson, who introduced the men to portly Colonel Walter Sanford, reconstructive surgeon at the Wimpole Park Hospital and his lady, a nurse captain, whose dark eyes expressed an effervescent personality.

Captain Patricia Lindsay's bone structure was so delicate Hank wondered if she had the mental and physical stamina it took to be a wartime nurse until he felt her firm grip when they shook hands. Captain Lindsay had to be the most attractive woman at the club. She held Hank's hand longer than necessary while the mob inside the club pressed them together.

"Major Milroy, I've heard a great deal about you and another pilot, Braxton Mobley."

"At the hospital?"

She released Hank's hand and glanced at Colonel Sanford, who continued to chat with Wilson and the other pilot leaders. "I've been on the night staff the past week. There's a young pilot from the 375th who follows me in his wheelchair when I make the rounds. It's against the rules, but he needs someone to talk to." Captain Lindsay's eyes misted. "They're all so young. Do you remember Lt. Quinn?"

"One of my boys, all right. A green kid who got hurt on his third mission two weeks ago."

"Please take me to my table. I'd rather stay with you, but my boss brought me tonight."

"Understood, except why do you want to meet Brax?"

"Lt. Quinn hero-worships both of you and asked me to say hello for him. He told me he wants to be the kind of man you are, and to fly and shoot like Captain Mobley." She squeezed Hank's hand again. "I prefer you as a model for young pilots."

"Thank you, ma'am. A pity this has to end so soon."

"It doesn't have to, Colonel. You can reach me at the hospital. I'm yours whenever you want."

Hank did not respond to the brazen offer, and they wished each other a Happy New Year. He left Captain Lindsay with Colonel Sanford and returned to the bar crowded with dateless pilots, nurses, and WAC officers.

Before Pearl Harbor, a well brought up lady like Patricia Lindsay never would have offered to rendezvous with a man she met a few minutes earlier. In war, however, lifetimes microscoped into short moments, and brief encounters required instant decision and action. Because customs and traditional values had fallen by the wayside, everyone was going to have a difficult time adjusting back to the old ways after the war ended, which would make raising daughters more difficult.

Hank ordered a scotch and watched the lively horseplay of the uninhibited fighter pilots. He tried not to look at the couples dancing cheek-to-cheek. He regretted not behaving better with Winty. Did she still have strong feelings for him? Hank worried he might have written those letters too late and she'd found someone else. Maybe it was for the best. He might be better off never marrying. Hank intended to have an Air Force career after the war. What other woman would understand or tolerate his passion for flying and testing planes?

Hank rejected the attentions of an amorous WAC Lieutenant too drunk to know what she was doing. He considered joining Braham's hot poker game for the next couple of hours and then head for the sack.

Barlowe, Planchek, and Fowler, three of the 135th's greenest kids, bought Hank another whiskey, followed by many toasts and more drinks. Still, he could not get into the full spirit of the celebrations. He had too many responsibilities. There'd be other New Year's Eves.

The next jukebox song started. *Moonlight Cocktail!* Hank's gut wrenched as he suffered an acute attack of nostalgia, reminded of Glenn Miller's recent untimely death. *Of all people to be shot down!*

Hank decided to stay at the bar for one more drink and focused on Brax, who danced glued to a nurse. The Texas Casanova looked like a shoo-in tonight. Yessirree, he had a great shooting eye, through a gun sight or down the length of his pecker. Hank guessed Brax had screwed more women than Hank had met since his first day of puberty. Hank laughed aloud while he observed Brax operating true to form with a hand halfway under the strawberry-blonde's skirt. Then he looked beyond the couple.

*Gloryosky Sandy, am I seeing things or ....*

***

The orchestra segued into another sentimental Glen Miller tune, "At Last", and Hank blinked to make sure what he saw was real. Lord love a duck, his eyesight was perfect. At the entrance of the Officers' Club, WAC Second Lieutenant Winty McCabe waved at Hank. His great vision, which caught many a glint on a Luftwaffe fighter's canopy in the far distance, saw no ring shining on the little blonde's third finger, left hand.

Hank intercepted Winty at the edge of the dance floor. She looked adorable in a heavy overcoat, and when she removed her hat he saw she still wore her hair close cropped and used no makeup.

Winty threw a snappy salute. "Lieutenant McCabe reporting. I've had one hell of a time catching up with you, Major Milroy. Long time, no see."

"Winty, am I ever glad to see you."

This was the time for action not words. Hank kissed Winty's freckled nose, blue eyes, clean cheeks, and delicious mouth. What a prize dolt he'd been, looking for reasons *not* to love her these past years. They had trouble hearing each other amidst the raucous throng in the OC, and it was still a couple of hours before midnight.

"Winty, I'll take you where we can have some privacy without being interrupted. We've got plenty to talk about."

"That's why I'm here, Hank."

"And you won't run away from me again?"

"I promise."

Outside, Hank put an arm around Winty and guided her toward the hangar of his P-51. "When did you get here? Did you receive any of my letters? How long have you been in the ETO?"

"Easy, Hank. Give me a chance to tell you everything."

Back in September, Winty learned the WASPs were to be disbanded. Congress decided General Arnold's plan to make it a similar but distinct military organization from the WACs was duplication, and there were predictions of a surplus of male pilots in the USAAF so there was no need for women flyers. Winty's uncle Roy, now an influential Texas Congressman, got her commissioned as a WAC officer and took his niece to England on a Congressional fact-finding tour. He persuaded their old friend, Major General Leo Kilrain, to place Winty on his staff at 8th Air Force Headquarters at High Wycombe.

"I arrived in London two days ago, and I wheedled a staff car so I could come up from London and see you here at Thetford. Took me over three hours."

They passed Seth's quarters, where a poker game had been going on since early evening.

***

"Come on, Paisan, your turn to deal."

Mercutio's *cri de Coeur* brought Seth back to the poker game from an imaginary world where he was celebrating next New Year's Eve with Miriam at the Top of the Mark in

San Francisco. While Mercutio raked in the large pot, Seth gathered the cards, shuffled, and dealt. He'd given himself a foot instead of a hand and dropped out when the betting began. Seth sat lost in his own private thoughts. He'd had a difficult week interrogating several fighter pilots downed near Thetford. He'd managed to extract enough information to suggest the Luftwaffe was planning something big but with no specifics, which might explain why they hadn't given tactical support to their retreating armies. The Germans in the West appeared to have shot their last ground offensive bolt with the Ardennes Offensive. The Soviets were massing on the Eastern Front. In Italy, the short-changed 5th Army obtained improved weapons for a final push up the spiny peninsula. Everywhere, Allied air forces dominated the skies. It all augured for a quick end to the war that kept him and Miriam apart.

Seth poured another glass from a bottle of wine he'd saved for New Year's Eve. Let the others get shikker on whiskey, beer, champagne, or cognac. He'd used much of his last R&R time to locate the finest vintages available in London and paid a high price for a rare 1927 Lafite Rothschild. Seth regretted he had no quality dinner to go with it, but a wedge of sharp homemade cheese sent by Mercutio's parents and fresh bread from the kitchen created an adequate snack to go with the Lafite.

***

Inside the hangar, Hank turned on the light and showed Winty the logo with her name on his fighter's fuselage. "I suppose it was presumptuous of me."

"Not at all. Oh, Hank, you've made me so proud and happy. Now that I'm stationed in London, we can see each other whenever you get a pass or R&R. Now it's your turn to tell me everything that happened since we saw each other last."

Hank removed Winty's coat, and they sat at the crew chief's desk. He recounted his aerial victories, the friends he'd made and lost, and segued into reminiscing about the time they met. Hank stopped when they heard horns coming from the direction of the Officers' Club. He stood and helped Winty to her feet. "Happy New Year."

They kissed until Hank felt tears on her cheeks. "What's the matter?"

"Hank, I love you. I loved you that first day when we met at my sister's party and you flew Uncle Roy's Waco. Remember?"

"I'll never forget."

"I wanted you to love me and didn't know what to do about it. I've never loved anyone else. I won't ever love anyone but you, Hank." Winty blushed "I guess I've proposed."

"Too late. Leap Year ended a few moments ago. Tonight is impossible, but the next time you can visit, I'd like my squadron to meet the woman I'm going to marry."

"Hank ...."

A Duty officer entered the hangar. "Major Milroy, the 135th Squadron has received orders for take-off before dawn at 0630. You are to proceed to Ath near Chievres in Belgium. The Jerries seem to be cooking up something big to break in the next day or two."

Hank's watch indicated 00:05 hours. "I hope I can round up fifteen sober pilots."

"I made an announcement at the Officers' Club and went to the rooms of those who'd left. But I saw Captain Mobley with one of the nurses at the Motor Pool. I thought it best not to interrupt."

"The redhead?"

The Duty Officer grinned. "No, sir. I believe she was a tall blonde."

Hank worried if Brax would be able to fly today's mission and have enough energy to squeeze the triggers if combat came to the 135th.

Hank glanced at his watch again. He wouldn't be getting much if any sleep either this New Year's morning. "Very well, Captain. Have all the men awakened no later than 0500 and breakfast ready at 0530. Crews all notified?"

"Yes, sir."

Winty put on her overcoat. "I should leave now. You'll also need to stack some zees."

Hank turned off the hangar light and walked Winty to her car. "Can't predict when I can see you next. It appears I'm going to be spending some extended time on the Continent."

"At least you'll know where I am. Be careful tomorrow, Hank. Now that I found you, I don't want to lose you."

"You'll be facing more danger in London from the Germans' V-1 doodlebugs and the V-2 rocket bombs. I'll be safer in a Mustang."

Hank helped Winty into the car and waited until it disappeared into the darkness.

At the Motor Pool Hank found Brax with a woman backed against the front fender of a lorry, and the noise told him it was the worst possible time to interrupt. She was not a tall blonde, nor the redhead he'd seen earlier. Brax was banging away at Captain Patricia Lindsay. Colonel Sanford would have his ass if he found out.

***

Seth led the toasts and exchange of good wishes for the New Year, with a special one for Mercutio. "May you and Carla hit it off."

"Paisan, I thank you. Now deal, goddammit."

Seth remembered the previous New Year with Mariya-Xenia and looked ahead to others with Miriam. He was fortunate to have survived being shot down over Germany and achieving acedom. The year also had its negatives: so many young men killed, never to realize their potential. Success had a sweet smell, aerial combat deaths the aroma of skunks. What the hell, he'd suffered through lonelier New Year's Eves. This damn well had better be the last one without Miriam. The goddam war had gone on for too long and should have ended by now.

"Come on, Paisan, shit or get off the pot."

Seth alone stayed in for Mercutio's raise. He was tempted to re-raise but wasn't out for blood. He called, and Mercutio showed Aces over Jacks.

"Bet you kept a kicker and got a lousy pair."

"Wrong, it's six tits." Seth laid out three Queens and saw Hank. "Join us?"

"Didn't the Duty Officer advise you dudes to be up at 0500?"

Mercutio collected the cards. "Last hand, sir. Can you tell us where the hell is Ath? Sounds like a hole."

"It's a Belgian town close to Chievres and not far from Leuze. Get what sleep you can. Tomorrow we'll be up to our ears in alligators. Good night, men."

Holding a middling two pair, Seth dropped out of the pot when the raising became hot and furious. He closed his eyes to concentrate on the last glass of Lafite. The longer the wine breathed, the better it became.

Seth often equated wines with women. Each offered great promises to be met, exceeded expectations, or brought disappointment. Miriam reminded him of a full bodied, luscious Grandes Echezeaux. Girls like Carla were like raw, earthy Chiantis. Seth compared Mariya-Xenia to a quality Moselle Spätlese Riesling, cool, elegant, refined, with subtle spritz and....

Spritz.

*Will Hank or I see Prinz Karl in the morning sky over Belgium?*

# Chapter 35

## Der Grosse Schlage

0430 hours on New Year's Day, Karl sat with a hundred pilots in the JG-3 operations room at Gladbach drinking ersatz coffee and waiting for their briefing to begin. Take-off for Operation Bodenplatte had been scheduled for 0840 or as soon as the weather cleared. Forty fighters were to hit Eindhoven, and forty more were to proceed on to Brussels and destroy all enemy aircraft at the bases in a surprise attack.

Karl's new Me-109 carried his good luck number, 23 and personal logo, SPRITZ. Karl did not care what position he flew. He wanted to get back into action and enjoy the heady feeling of being on the offensive again. Karl volunteered to fly last position in the formation, an excellent joke to play on their opponents. Wouldn't the RAF and Yank pilots be surprised to encounter a skilled fighter ace instead of a green, panic-stricken novice?

Back in October 1944, Adolf Galland had conceived the largest and most decisive Luftwaffe air battle plan of the war with several objectives. At least two thousand fighters of the First Fighter Corps in eleven combat formations were to go into action against the approaching bombers. Then, during the enemy fly-ins over German targets, another hundred-and-fifty fighters of Luftwaffe Command West would be sent up against them, followed by a reserve of five hundred more fighters. About one hundred night fighters were to screen the borders between Sweden and Switzerland to intercept damaged or straggling bombers.

The goal was to shoot down up to five hundred four-engine bombers and inflict unacceptable losses on the enemy, which would force them to halt the big raids over Germany. The Luftwaffe estimated a loss of four hundred aircraft and no more than one hundred-and-fifty pilots.

Since 12 November, eighteen Geschwadern with thirty-seven hundred aircraft and their pilots, the entire fighter arm of the Luftwaffe, had been ready for action. Unpredictable and unfavorable weather forced Göring to postpone the operation several times.

Throughout the past forty-nine days, waiting and false alarms frayed the pilots' nerves. So did reports of massive bombing raids going unchallenged over their hometowns.

With nothing to do except wait and think, Karl's own nerves had been peeled to the last strand with worry for Elfi after a pilot who served in Italy said most of the hospital personnel there had been transferred to the East.

*God help Elfi, Mariya-Xenia too, and my vineyards with the Americans poised to push into Eppelborn and beyond to the Pfalzland.*

When briefing commenced in the ready room, Karl learned that the objectives and scope of Der Grosse Schlage, the Big Blow, had been changed without Galland's consent and ought to have been renamed Der Kleine Schlage. Operation Bodenplatte reduced the number of fighters committed from more than three thousand to around a thousand. Worse yet, too many pilots were reserves and novices; their experience had been in defensive flying against bomber formations at best. Today they were about to be tossed into combat without training in strafing and dive-bombing. Karl anticipated many would lose their lives during the course of the day's action because the Luftwaffe intended to strike at more than twenty enemy airfields in Holland, Belgium, and France.

After briefing, the airfield at Gladbach exploded into action. Fw-190s and Me-109s warmed up in the murky darkness of a snowy morning. While Daimler-Benz engines idled, propellers cut little circles of vapor trails from their tips like wispy corkscrews.

Despite the seriousness of the situation, Karl found it comical to watch a hundred pilots easing their fighters down the taxi ramp, with at least two-thirds of them not sure of what they were supposed to be doing. Some of the more inexperienced boys had trouble getting into their proper Rotten or Schwarmen. They were callow, untried, green cannon fodder for their experienced opponents and anti-aircraft units, but no one could question their enthusiasm and courage.

*Amend that last thought. One person did question their courage.*

The tension between Göring and every pilot in the fighter arm had reached crisis proportions. The Reichsminister and other Nazi leaders allowed a pernicious rumor to spread unabated: the fighter pilots lacked courage to stop the relentless bombing raids.

Göring and Hitler were blind to the fighter pilots' spirit and pride in their battles against much heavier odds. After this war ended, the German people would hear the terrible truth about their leaders. But would they believe it?

# Chapter 36

## Chaos in the Skies

After a fifty-minute flight, the sixteen Mustangs of the 135th flew over Chievres, home of the 487th Squadron, and landed at Ath before a fog patch obscured the field. It was still dark, and some of the pilots were nervous about their first night-flying in several months.

Hank led his men to the ops shack for briefing while ground crews set about refueling their P-51s. Ath was a typical advanced combat area airfield, with primitive sanitary and showering conditions, pieces of pierced-steel planking for a runway, and mud oozing between every plank when it was not frozen. A bleak countryside surrounded the snow-turned-to-slush-covered olive drab tents, and frost and fog depressed the pilots used to the lush greens of England.

Luftwaffe fighter bases were much closer, and the 135<sup>th</sup> would have little more than a split second to line-up and study the target on their K-14 gun sights before touching their trigger tits. This meant the risk of friendly fire would be higher higher than usual. Under normal circumstances the Jug resembled the FW-190 at a cursory glance; likewise, the Mustang and Me-109 could be mistaken for each other. Worse and more terrifying than being targeted by an enemy were those moments when some other American had a countryman in his sights, ready to blaze away with all guns and cannon. Those errors were not discovered until the gun camera film was developed, and the screen displayed positive evidence that the unlucky pilot shot down a yet more unfortunate American instead of an enemy.

In short, the rules of engagement were simple: don't get in front of anyone's guns unless you're damn sure he knows you're on the same team.

Briefing at Ath was short and to the point, which those 135th pilots who suffered most from hangovers and lack of sleep appreciated. The reconnaissance flights came home with plenty of photos showing hundreds of Luftwaffe fighters assembled at forward airfields. Intelligence guessed the Germans would attack around noon, but experienced fighter commanders did not believe the Luftwaffe would wait that long. The 135th had orders to take-off as soon as the alarm sounded.

The impending combat snapped the pilots out of their hangovers and lassitude. Many looked forward to their first opportunity to achieve acedom against large numbers of Luftwaffe fighters for a shoot-out at the O.K. Corral.

Hank liked what he had seen of Braham and Mercutio during earlier missions. He set up a flight with himself and Brax as interchangeable leader and wingman, and Seth to lead Mercutio in the second element. Hank tried not thinking too much about Winty. He needed a clear head for combat.

After daybreak, Hank and the 135th waited in their idling fighters. In the distance, slag heaps now visible suggested pyramids. Then a high-pitched, agitated voice shattered radio silence.

"All fighters take-off immediately. Enemy aircraft coming in low from the east. Use extreme caution."

Other voices broke in: "Red Flight, crank 'er up."

"Bandits! Bandits!"

"Enemy coming in from the north. Range five miles."

Hank noted it was 09:33 hours, New Year's Day, and from that moment, events no longer had a linear progression. Time became an exhilarating, dangerous all-at-once. Puffs of clouds burst from anti-aircraft guns at the far end of the field, and low on the horizon more than a dozen FW-190s headed straight for the 135th. Until they were airborne, they'd be sitting ducks.

Hank taxied into the take-off so eager to get the 135th airborne he forgot to run-up the engine and check the magnetos. He gunned the fighter into position and started the take-off roll. He looked in the rear view mirror and was gratified to see his men beginning their rolls. Airborne, he retracted the landing gear and eyed the sky, anticipating potential mid-air collisions.

Luftwaffe fighters circled the field. One gaggle strafed the base at treetop level protected by another Staffel arcing below the overcast at five thousand feet. Hank glanced back at the runway and saw three plumes of black, oily smoke rising from burning aircraft. He could not identify if they were enemy or 135th.

Bursts of friendly flak exploded close to Hank's fighter, and he led his flight of four fighters into a steep turn behind three FW-190s maneuvering to make a strafing run. The other 135th Mustangs pressed attacks on the nearest German fighters, many of whom appeared to be confused. Hank guessed most of the 109s and 190s were flown by greenies, raw meat, a definite indication the Germans were short of talented manpower with little time to train reserves. Brax ought to be salivating over all those easy targets.

Planes zipped past, dropped, and zoomed in all directions around the clock, their guns blazing, while flak bursts clouded the angry sky. Hank found it impossible to keep track of the number of German fighters crashing to the ground. He needed to sustain complete situational awareness and be alert to intruders while he closed on the trio of 190 across Belgium.

Over Aarschot, Hank fired a short burst at a FW-190 but saw no hits. When he broke right to avoid three Me-109s coming at three o'clock, he saw Brax clobber a Messerschmitt.

***

Mercutio called out eight German fighters barreling in at nine o'clock low. Seth broke toward the FW-190s, then back into a vertical right turn, which caused the Germans to pass below and behind. He reversed his position with a 7-G turn to settle behind a Focke-Wulfs.

The distance between the fighters expanded because of the high speed of the German attack. Seth accelerated and sprayed lead at all eight Luftwaffe fighters. He saw the flash of a hit on the engine of a 190, which slowed and fell out of formation.

Seth's closure rate increased, and he had the wounded fighter bore-sighted. Five hundred feet away, he fired a short burst and set it ablaze.

Mercutio called out yet another Schwarm of FW-190s at five o'clock low. Seth broke left to look for the new arrivals and heard "Bingo" when Mercutio called in a kill.

"Nice shooting, Blue Four."

Seth spotted two FW-190s turning half a mile away. He aimed a forty-five-degree deflection shot at the leader and tugged at the trigger for a two-second burst. Instead, Seth shellacked the second fighter, which snap-rolled out of control. The pilot bailed out less than a thousand feet above ground. The Rottenführer sped away.

Dodging P-47s, Mustangs and enemy FW-190s and Me-109s, Seth and Mercutio caught up with Hank and Brax as they zipped past Geel. Or was it Mol? No matter.

***

Four Messerschmitts broke left in front of Hank and into the 190s he was chasing. A 109 cut off the tail of a Focke-Wulf. Both enemy fighters crashed in a cloud of metal and dust. Hank saw no chutes. What percentage of combat casualties were self-inflicted?

"The South has risen."

He heard Brax's call and spun around in time to see the Texan knock the left wing off a FW-190 with a seventy-degree deflection snap-shot. Hank saw another Mustang shoot down two 109s. He couldn't get close enough to identify if it was a 135th boy. A mile away to the right, two fighters flamed. Mustang and Thunderbolt.

The aerial battle moved closer to Eindhoven and Brax called out, "Blue Leader, bandits coming in level at two o'clock."

A great formation of at least sixty enemy fighters covered the entire horizon ahead. Hank led his flight to the perch for a bounce on the approaching armada where he encountered a Schwarm of 109s. At the same time, the Luftwaffe fighters below began a shallow dive toward the airfield at Eindhoven.

***

Karl's Geschwader arrived at Eindhoven in time to catch an American bomber group lined for take-off at the far end of the runway. Their first pass set half the B-25s afire. Many of the bomb-laden Mitchells exploded and took nearby aircraft with them.

From the tail-end of his Staffel, Karl saw eight Mustangs below. Called Indianern by the Luftwaffe, those P-51s could make plenty of trouble if left alone. Off to the left, a FW-190 burst into flames, A P-51 sped away under the stricken Focke-Wulf.

Karl turned his attention back to the airfield and concentrated on a Spitfire breaking ground. At 520 kph, he swung behind the Englander's fighter doing less than 240 kph. The RAF pilot made a snap-shot at a 190 off to the left. Karl saw hits followed by flames on the FW but did not let it interfere with his concentration. He centered the pipper on the Spitfire and fired a short burst at its wing root. Dust and coolant vapor flew from the Spitfire. It nosed down, crashed to the ground, ricocheted high into the air, and disintegrated, scattering millions of particles of man and airplane into the air.

Karl wanted to utter a short prayer for St. Horridus to save the soul of the gallant Spit pilot. But too many Mustangs and Spitfires filled the sky. When an RAF fighter flew into his path, he fired a burst while maneuvering to avoid a mid-air. He zoomed and overshot the flaming opponent by mere centimeters. That maneuver brought a near miss with a Mustang.

*Gott im Himmel.* Today Fraülein Kismet would determine who survived. He had to get out. Too many planes were in the arena. After calling out his 228th Luftsieg, Karl took one last look at Eindhoven Airfield, now a holocaust of flaming oil and gasoline. He could not begin to count the individual pyres and estimated a hundred enemy planes had been destroyed. If the attacks had gone as well at the other bases, the Luftwaffe indeed would have struck its biggest blow of the war on the Western Front.

Karl's suit was soaked with perspiration, his hands trembling, the physical effects of his first combat in months exhausting. Karl made the turn toward home and scanned the formation ahead. Twenty-four fighters of JG-3 survived to make the swing back to the east.

***

Over Eindhoven, Mercutio called out a kill. Seth confirmed it, and set up the Paisan for another so the young pilot could become an ace. Then they broke away from combat and headed home.

***

With Brax flying wing, Hank flew behind a Me-109 and sent it crashing to the ground on a pass over burning Eindhoven. Fighters and B-25s struggling to get off the ground had to taxi around countless bonfire-infernos. Hank watched one Spitfire take off, and the moment it was airborne, the RAF pilot pulled into a chandelle and came up to shoot down a FW-190, unaware a 109 was on his tail.

*Yikes, number 23.*

Unable to intercept it, Hank called out, "Spitfire. Break right."

Because the Englishman was not monitoring the American frequency, the Me-109 scored hits on the RAF fighter, which exploded into numberless particles of metal and flesh. Hank avenged the death of the unknown Brit pilot by bringing down a nearby FW-190. With Brax on the wing, they attacked the German fighters still beating up Eindhoven.

Most of the krauts flew as if they were confused novices in their first combat, fixed on targets with absolute tunnel vision. Hank bagged three of them as they prepared for another strafing run.

*A goddam turkey-shoot.*

But their Rottenführers were not greenhorns. Hank saw one Me-109 leader shoot down three Spitfires and a Mustang in less than thirty seconds. The same German fighter then broke downwards, strafed two more Spitfires rolling to take-off on the Eindhoven strip, set both aflame, and continued at treetop level back to the east.

Brax also saw the feat and broke away in pursuit of the hotshot 109. Hank swung into position as his wingman, and the chase was on. Over Roermond the two P-51s closed on the Me-109, when they were bounced from above by four FW-190s. The attack forced the Americans to swerve into their new adversaries, who broke in all directions.

One German turned so he was in perfect position for Hank to fall in behind. An instant later the 190 flamed and spun toward the ground. Hank's guns went dead as Brax called out two more kills, which Hank was unable to confirm visually.

"Blue Two, I'm out of ammo. Let's go home and load up."

"Roger, Blue Lead'. I'll ride shotgun. I've got a few rounds left."

***

Hank circled Chievres and Asche, which had been hit hard but appeared to be better off than Eindhoven. He saw at least eighteen smoldering wrecks lying on or near the airfield. From the air, he could not identify which were German or American.

Given the green light, Hank landed first, taxied to the hardstand, and shut down. He counted the Mustangs following him. All the young men of the 135th made it back.

Hank had had his greatest day as a fighter pilot, five victories in one sortie, 23 overall. He removed helmet and goggles and held up five fingers to the approaching crew. They congratulated Hank, helped him dismount, and prepared the Mustang for its next sortie.

Brax hurried to Hank exhilarated, blue eyes bulging, face flushed. "Zingo-zowie, good-buddy, I got four more! That gives me ten ETO kills." He shook Hank's arm. "Did you see me get them?"

"I can confirm two kills for you, Brax. You were behind me most of the time, so I couldn't see if you got any more."

"But don't you remember when we turned into that last Schwarm of 190s?" Brax gestured to show how he had taken a high-angle deflection shot at the lead Focke-Wulf, scored hits on fuselage and engine, and sent it diving straight into the ground. "Then another FW-190 turned right in front of my sights, and I dispatched it with a short burst."

"I told you, I couldn't see what you were doing."

Brax patted the film cartridge. "No sweat. This sweetheart ought to confirm the rest. How did you do, Hank? I think I saw you get three yourself."

"Five, Brax. I got five today. If it's all on film, that's nine between us. I can't wait to hear how the rest of my squadron did today. The best news is everyone made it back." Hank counted his pilots, some dismounting, others approaching. "And all in one piece too."

"Mercutio got three and I bagged two."

Hank turned to Seth and Mercutio, who joined them and shook their hands. "That's a total of fourteen for our flight."

Seth slapped Mercutio's back. "I can visually confirm all three, which makes you an ace."

"Thanks to your generosity, Paisan, but I'm still behind my future father-in-law."

Brax kicked the turf. "Goddammit, Where's our transport? I want to get over to ops, make a quick report, and get up again. I'm hot, good-buddy, and if I catch me some more today, I'll be on my way to be numero uno in the ETO, and pass those guys in the Pacific too."

Seth tugged at the flight-suit. He was soaked through with sweat, had pissed in his pants, and each muscle ached. Incredibly, Brax looked as if he had on a fresh suit, never perspired, and had enough energy to do it all over again.

Other pilots came over as their transport appeared in the distance. All were so exhilarated from the recent combat they chattered among themselves until they entered debriefing at Operations. Besides Hank's Blue Flight, the other 135th pilots claimed eleven German planes. Because the combat gun camera film still had to be developed, positive confirmation of all victories would have to wait.

After debriefing, the pilots rushed to their aircraft in anticipation of another German follow-up attack. One Intelligence report stated a raid would come within minutes. Another rumor had it that the Luftwaffe would not mount another attack and their squadron was to return to Thetford today for an escort mission.

Two of the 135th's flights stood airborne alert; the rest dispersed around the field, with pilots in the cockpit at the ready. As the day wore on, it became evident the Luftwaffe was staying home to lick its wounds. Hank used much of the time to digest the morning's combat. Unlike Brax, who hungered to be top ace, he was content to rank himself alongside his heroes of the Great War. 23 victories tied him for second with S.C. Rosevear behind legendary Eddie Rickenbacker's 26.

Hank hoped one day to learn firsthand how Marine pilot Joe Foss shot down 22 Jap planes, including 16 Zero fighters, during a mere six weeks out of Guadalcanal, and the number of minutes it took Navy ace David McCampbell to score nine kills and two damaged on a single mission in the Pacific.

***

Karl landed at Gladbach amidst chaos. Damaged planes flown home by courageous pilots littered the airfield with more coming in behind. Karl eased his fighter along the tarmac between Me-109s and FW-190s on their bellies or tails up. Crews scurried in all directions searching for their pilots. Ambulance sirens added to the din.

Karl parked at a hardstand and dismounted. Soaked through with sweat, muscles aching, he maintained military bearing on his way to the Ops shack and passed a 109 that lay upside down. A crew struggled to free the burned pilot from the cockpit and shouted at a pair of approaching medics to hurry.

Near the parking area, a propeller curled back over the engine cowling of a FW-190 with no landing gear. Elsewhere, a Focke-Wulf had climbed onto the tail of a parked DO-17 bomber to create an absurd metaphor of two airplanes mating.

A 109 ahead had a gaping hole in the cowling and a larger lacuna two centimeters square in its kaput engine casing. The young pilot who'd flown the fighter home sat inside shaking.

Karl walked around an FW-190 with its canopy gone, bullet holes in the fuselage, and blood dripping from the cockpit. Yet its wounded pilot had held up long enough to land before dying.

*Admirable. So many brought damaged planes home instead of bailing.*

More planes came in for landings, some crashing, others plowing into debris. An ambulance arrived with nurses who reminded Karl of Elfi. He tried not to think of his little brunette. Worrying was a distraction and served no useful purpose. Elfi's fate was out of his hands.

Karl entered the hut that served as both operations and briefing room for the Geschwader. Most pilots seated inside had ashen faces. Some inquired about the fate of missing comrades. Others were too unhinged to speak. Most sat in silence with eyes closed and hoped their nightmarish visions would soon go away. A few described their combats, and compared times and locales of their Luftsiegen.

One officer approached Karl and distracted him from his post-combat tensions with rapid fire discourse. "Fürst, I congratulate you for making it back. I thought you were finished after you shot down a Spitfire. You avoided a mid-air by a centimeter, and when you turned away, my own Kaczmarek also missed you by a few hairs. It was so crowded up there."

At the debriefing desk, Karl described his Luftsiegen and listened to more pilots tell their tales of the day's combat. He regarded with condescension and sadness the trainees and novices who survived their first combat. Filled with suicidal bravado, they swaggered, confident of their immortality. Such spirit might have been useful at the start of the war, not in 1945.

Enough reports came in for Karl to estimate what had happened. The Luftwaffe claimed close to four hundred Yank and RAF planes destroyed, but incurred devastating losses: three hundred aircraft, too many irreplaceable leaders, skilled veteran aces, and a much larger number of new pilots who should not have been flying at all. Each Staffel had been reduced by more than half, whereas the Americans seemed to have an unlimited reserve of well-trained replacement pilots and improved planes.

Karl brooded over those distressing results. The Luftwaffe paid a price for Operation Bodenplatte it could not afford.

*And now, what?*

***

After standing their turn at alert, Hank and Brax returned to Ops to learn how badly the enemy had been hurt, what damage had been done to Allied airfields, and for confirmation of their victories. Reports trickled in. The anti-aircraft batteries claimed three hundred German planes shot down

Brax whistled. "Three hundred? Shee-yit, good-buddy, I'll bet half were ours."

Hank had heard that typical fighter pilot reaction many times. The flak boys had their own views. They often accused the throttle-jockeys of spotting the crash of a plane shot down by anti-aircraft guns, making a strafing run on the downed aircraft, and taking gun camera pictures in order to claim a cheap victory.

New results filtered to the front line units. No matter how one looked at it, 1945 had not begun well for the Western Allies. According to preliminary reports, the Luftwaffe destroyed 127 Allied aircraft on the ground and damaged 133. Those totals would climb as the investigation progressed because they did not yet include Allied aircraft shot down or missing in aerial combat.

Twenty-seven Allied bases had been attacked by more than 650 Luftwaffe planes, and all but a few had been taken by surprise. On their radio broadcasts, the Germans announced that more than four hundred enemy aircraft had been destroyed, which seemed valid and logical to Hank, considering the extensive American and British losses seen by the 135th pilots during the day's combat.

On the other side of the ledger, Allied fighter pilots claimed 160 Luftwaffe planes shot down in aerial combat. 300 more alleged by the ack-ack units created a total of 460 German aircraft destroyed.

Hank made his own calculations. All Luftwaffe planes brought down by the flak units should have fallen in Allied-held territory, as well as ninety percent of those shot down in aerial combat. So far, the count was 91 Luftwaffe fighters found along with 33 bodies of German pilots. Another 63 captured after parachuting added up to 96 men.

***

That evening, Hank settled with a cigar and cognac in his tent and chatted with Seth about cabbages and kings. Mercutio interrupted with more news. The Germans admitted 100 of their planes had been shot down and almost 200 damaged. In spite of those heavy Luftwaffe losses, the pilots agreed the enemy was many months away from being defeated.

The three flyers heard a commotion and stepped outside the tent into the freezing night air. Brax staggered toward them, disheveled and roaring drunk. Seth and Mercutio steadied the Texan.

Hank glared at Brax. "Dammit, you know better than to get blotto."

Brax shook off Seth and Mercutio. "How many of my kills will you confirm?"

"Two, I already told you."

"But I got four."

"And I saw two."

The impeccable ace's one-eighty-degree change surprised Seth. Brax always came out of the grueling, bloody combat without a single bead of perspiration as if his Mums deodorant never failed. Tonight, he was unraveled by booze and self-pity. All those gals who'd flocked to Mobley would not find him attractive now.

Brax threw the film cartridge to the ground. "It's blank. Those goddam pricks have taken away another two kills from me. If I had better film, I'd be tops in the ETO right now."

"It's rough, Brax, but we've all had bad luck," Seth commiserated. "Go back to your tent. Get some sleep, and things will look better when you're sober in the morning."

"And you'll still be a Jew-kike in the morning."

Seth decked Brax with a right to the jaw and in a red rage fell on the bigot to strike another blow. Mercutio pulled Seth to his feet, and Hank stood over Brax.

"That comment wasn't called for. You got what was coming to you."

Brax sprayed blood and spittle in all directions and checked his teeth to make sure all were still attached. "The Jew-boy is in on the conspiracy too."

Mercutio held on to Seth. "Let the asshole be, Paisan. He's drunk. He doesn't know what he's saying."

"Conveniently, Dom, they never do."

Brax struggled to his feet. "Come on, Hank old-buddy, give your pal a break. Write up all four."

"I can't do it, Brax. Like Braham said, it happens to all of us."

"Sure, I know. You're like all the rest. Y'all want to be numero uno yourselves, so you're screwing me out of my legitimate kills."

Hank watched Brax weave like a skid row drunk toward the tents. He wasn't sure if the real Brax had insulted Seth or if it had been the booze that spoke. He wanted to believe it was the latter.

# Chapter 37

## Firestorms

February 14, 1945, Valentine's Day, Hank arrived first in the morning darkness and turned on the lights inside the briefing room. He warmed his hands with a mug of hot coffee and stared at a large wall map of Western Europe. Dresden, the day's target, was about one hundred miles south of Berlin and eight miles north of Prague.

The RAF hit Dresden hard all night, and the Americans were scheduled to come in for a follow-up daylight raid. Hank could not recall any previous mention of significant military targets in and around Dresden and doubted a giant German communications center appeared overnight smack-dab in the Florence of the North, which was the reason given by Allied Air Staff to justify the massive bombing raids. To the west of Dresden lay Meissen, another familiar name. The two cities conjured images of elegant china and porcelain dolls.

Seth joined Hank at the map. "Dresden?"

"It makes no sense. To the best of my knowledge, Dresden is no industrial center and has no military targets. It's also too far from the Western Front for an attack to interfere with transport of men and supplies against our ground troops."

"But close to the Russians." Seth ran a finger down the map southward from the Baltic Sea. "According to my contacts with the Intelligence boys, they're getting reports that Marshals Zhukov and Konev have massed enormous armies on the other side of the Oder for a big drive on Berlin."

"What's next, Seth? Orders to give air support to the Soviets?"

"Not yet, but God knows what goodies we promised them a couple of days ago at Yalta."

Other pilots of the 375th Group entered and took their favorite seats. Hank believed his 135th squadron had the finest starting lineup of flight leaders in the ETO. He liked how Seth set up kills for the greenies so they could gain confidence, and how he helped Mercutio blossom into a top fighter pilot and leader with eight and a half victories in forty-one missions. Hank had recommended Mercutio for promotion to captain and gave him command of the tail-end flight. Mercutio was bright-eyed and bushy-tailed for another reason. He let everyone know he'd received signed photos and encouraging mail two days in a row from some girl in San Francisco.

Hank figured Brax to amble in last and hung over as usual, bragging about his latest conquest and complaining about lack of combat against the Luftwaffe.

***

Seth sat next to Mercutio, who re-read a long letter from Carla and stared at one of her signed wallet-size photos "Tell me, Paisan, who will be my biggest competition?"

"When I last saw Carla, she was footloose and fancy free."

"You never messed with her?"

"No, I always saw Carla as a kid sister."

"Paisan, the moment I hit the States, I'm heading for Frisco."

"Call it San Francisco or the City if you value your life."

"Okay, San Francisco. First, I'll woo and win Carla. Then I'll go back to college and finish getting my degree."

"In what?"

Mercutio thought for several moments. "I can't say. Madon', I really don't know."

"The war is almost over. Don't stay here beyond your fifty missions, Dom."

"That's what I've been thinking, Paisan, now that I've maybe got a girl to come home to. I've proven I'm as good a fighter ace as Carla's father was. Nine missions to go. Hope I don't screw up now."

"I'll make sure you don't."

***

When the Boeing Fortresses and their Mustang escort arrived over Dresden, the city was still ablaze with uncontrolled fires from the RAF night incendiary bombing. No German fighters appeared on the scene, and the B-17s took their time to line up assigned targets and bomb the undamaged parts of Dresden.

Convinced the Fortresses were not in any danger, Hank circled the city away from the B-17s and took the 135th down to beat-up military targets on the ground, if they could find any. He was appalled by the devastation of the once beautiful and irreplaceable Renaissance buildings and horrified by the sweeping indiscriminate destruction of human life below. Thousands of refugees clogged roads leading out of the city as the Fortresses delivered a second round of death and terror to the doomed population center.

The packed highways reminded Hank of newsreels he had seen a few short years before of Poles, Dutch, Belgians, and French fleeing Stuka dive bombers. No newsreel, he was participant in a current appalling reality.

Hank saw another Mustang squadron strafing burned-out hulks of aircraft at an airfield on the outskirts of Dresden. At the same time, a third P-51 outfit raked a main road choked with fleeing civilians, including women and children. When he demanded to know why they were shooting at defenseless civilians, someone answered over the R/T that the Germans had rifles and fired at the fighters first. After a low flying Mustang crashed into a beer truck, he radioed his boys to avoid strafing civilians at all costs.

Hank led the 135th around Dresden's perimeter at less than five hundred feet and saw piles of bodies stacked high and wide like cordwood in the open spaces by survivors of the RAF raids. Flying a wider circle around the devastated city, he saw more stacks of corpses and countless abandoned wagons loaded with the dead scattered along streets and in the fields. The Americans had caught survivors of the night bombing cleaning up their city and interrupted the transport of more bodies. The Germans panicked, and many ran into still burning buildings instead of away from danger.

The carnage was beyond all imagination. Overcome with nausea, Hank almost vomited into his oxygen mask. He stifled the urge, unsnapped the mask, and swung it away from his nose and mouth. Instead of the familiar clean cockpit aromas of leather, metal, cordite, and fuel, Hank inhaled a pungent odor, reminiscent of the enticing, mouth-watering smell of barbecued steak.

Not steak, it was human.

Hank struggled against the unwelcome knowledge that cooked human flesh smelled like a T-bone prepared the way his dad used to do it back home, just right, medium rare. He barfed into a paper sack with no time to remove the ham and cheese sandwich he'd brought along to still the hunger he always experienced on these six to seven hour missions. It didn't matter. He'd have no appetite for food for a long time.

Hank continued to fight nausea while he led the 135th in a right hand circle around the edge of Dresden. Five-hundred-pound bombs dropped by B-17s created geysers of dust, rubble, and flame when they tore into the city. One box-formation of Fortresses unloaded their cargo when making their turn, and most of the bombs fell a half mile outside the city. The explosions came close to the front of the 135th, and he led a break away to the left.

Hank's Mustangs circled Dresden four times without having a shot fired at them, nor did they see anything resembling a military target in the skies. He took one last look back and down at Dresden before he led the squadron in a climb to altitude above the bombers. Hank hooked the mask across his face and turned it to one hundred-percent oxygen to blot out the smell of cooked human flesh.

He moved the 135th into an escort station behind the last B-17s in the long stream heading home. The memory of the carnage and the mass of dead bodies cooking in the fires brought on another wave of nausea. Nothing was left in Hank's stomach except bile. He broke into a heavy sweat in the low temperature of the cockpit, and a severe chill made him shiver. He couldn't hold the Mustang straight and level and camouflaged his sloppy flying by weaving back and forth.

Brax was not fooled. "Blue Leader, you're weaving side to side. All okay?"

"Nauseated, but okay."

***

Like Hank, Seth struggled to stifle nausea and a sense of betrayal. The same as Hank, he recalled his indignation reading newspapers and watching newsreels document the unnecessary air raids perpetrated by the Luftwaffe on civilian population centers: Guernica during the Spanish Civil War, blitzing England, leveling the Open City of Rotterdam, and strafing roads clogged with pathetic refugees carrying and carting the remnants of their belongings.

Hitler had told the Allies if they wanted to defeat him, in the end they would have to resort to the same ruthless methods he used. Like it or not, Seth had to face the fact he participated in the fulfillment of Der Führer's dismal prediction. What a lousy war. The blood of non-combatant civilians had at last splattered all over the fighter pilots.

***

"Gawd-a-mighty, did you see those cremation stacks?"

"I damn near barfed in my oxygen mask."

"Me too."

"Come off it, you guys. Every one of those dead bodies had a lathe tool or screwdriver."

"He's right. We're destroying German industry."

"What about the women and children?"

"Serves 'em right. They're all Nazis."

"Yeah. they started it."

"At least we weren't the ones dropping the bombs."

"It's the same thing. We rode shotgun for the bombers."

"We're just as bad."

"What's the rationale for slaughtering their civilians anyway?"

"The British wanted revenge for the Blitz, and we went along with it."

Hank walked with Brax to the ops shack. "A sorry mission, wasn't it, Brax?"

"You know it, good-buddy. Shee-yit, again I didn't get to bag me any Heinies."

Hank wasn't sure he'd heard right. But Brax was unshaken by what they had all gone through over Dresden, and he repeated to everyone within earshot his worn litany of lost opportunities to score kills and all the times the gun camera failed.

"I've been shafted up the gi-gi. I've been wired at 8 ETO and 13 overall since New Year's Day. And I've shot down at least seven more, maybe twelve if you count my damaged too. Kee-ryst, we'd be better off using Agfa film."

"You goddam egomaniac. How the hell can you think about your victory totals after today? Don't you feel anything for the civilians? Were you immune to the stench and suffering down there?"

Brax cursed at Hank, and when several men stepped between them, he headed toward the Officers' Club.

Inside the briefing room, Seth smoked a cigar to kill the stench in his nostrils. "After I make my report, I'm heading to the club to tie on a big one. I can't face my own thoughts or be alone."

While Mercutio and the other pilots echoed the same disgust, Hank took Seth aside. "Brax will be at the club too. I thought he was my best buddy in the Air Force despite his flaws. After today, I don't know."

"Any of my business?"

"Brax didn't give a hoot for those civilians down there. He was immune to the stench and suffering. All he could do was complain that he hadn't bagged a Jerry today. In his mind, the war exists so he can achieve personal glory."

Seth exhaled smoke from his cigar. "Brax is one hundred-percent gland. Dammit, I still need a drink to wash that smell from my nostrils."

"Stick around, will you, until debriefing is over. Make your report and come over to my quarters. We'll kill a bottle in private. What about you, Mercutio?"

"Sir, if you don't mind, I need to write a letter to Carla."

***

Hank stretched out on his bed in fatigues, white silk scarf, and Stetson, drinking whiskey neat and puffing on a Havana. "Seth, you'd have thought Bomber Command would have learned from the Blitz. It stiffened the British spirit of resistance. Why do they think the Germans are made of lesser stuff than the English and will cave in and surrender after our massive bombing raids?"

Seth poured himself a whiskey and straddled a chair. "Maybe it's cold-blooded revenge. I wonder, what the hell kind of world are we making?"

"A better one than if we were to lose." Hank balanced the whiskey glass on his chest. "I'm almost sorry I took this second hundred-mission tour. I could have been instructing and testing planes, and I'd still have my moral cherry. I lost my virginity over Dresden, raped by USAAF policy."

"So did we all. The refugee women and children slaughtered down there at Dresden are the wrong targets. Our bombers should be seeking out and killing the Nazi architects of the war and the death camps. They're still alive and secure in their bunkers prolonging the fighting and misery."

"Until it's over, we can't afford to look at this war from the other guy's point of view. It might inhibit us. It's preferable to make mistakes from strength and apologize, if necessary, after victory, rather than err through weakness and beg for mercy after defeat." Hank refilled their glasses. "If it wasn't a planning error or our going along with a British desire for revenge, is there any logic for demolishing Dresden and slaughtering the civilians?"

"I don't know for sure. Intelligence thinks it has something to do with the Big Three meeting at Yalta. I'm convinced of one thing. It's retaliation bombing on the part of the British. The Germans are still doing the same thing to London with their indiscriminate Vengeance V-1 and V-2 attacks."

"I guess some of our people believe bombing targets like Dresden will fill roads with innocent civilian refugees and cause other logistical problems to interfere with German conduct of the war."

Seth disapproved of the term innocent civilians. In total war, no one was *innocent*. Excepting infants, he could not view any German non-combatant as guiltless. In England and back in the States, it was the same. Their entire populations supported the war effort against the Axis. Women worked in war plants and joined the services to free more men for combat. They nursed and mended broken bodies to be sent back to the front.

Before shipping overseas, Seth had seen small boys in San Francisco play soldier and defend Golden Gate Park against an imagined Jap invasion. They'd have carried weapons into combat if they could, and would too if the war lasted long enough. Children of both genders and all ages contributed to the war effort collecting tinfoil, rubber, aluminum, and newspapers. All were committed to defeating the enemy. In modern warfare no one was innocent anymore, only defenseless.

"Hank, when you were a boy, did you read books like *Falcons Over France* and listen to veterans of the First World War refer to fighter pilots as Knights of the Skies?"

"Sure did, Seth. We all idealized the romance and glory of aerial combat, even the gallant way each side honored their fallen opponents and as captors welcomed their prisoners with cognac or champagne."

"Like in that film *The Grand Illusion*."

"Yeah, but we never imagined the horror of a firestorm when we were kids."

Hank and Seth discussed how fires from incendiary bombs heated the air above. As the hot air rose, more air rushed in to fill the vacuum. The inrushing air fanned the flames and turned small fires into larger conflagrations more heated and rising higher. At the same time, those powerful convection currents caused hurricane-force winds of up to 150 mph. The firestorm repeated, multiplied, and expanded itself, and the flames blazed to temperatures exceeding one thousand-degrees centigrade. They grew to cover up to ten square miles of a populated area and incinerated everyone and everything in its wake. That is what had happened to Dresden. That was what Allied bombers had been doing to cities all over the Reich. And still, Germany did not sue for peace.

"Those horrors below at Dresden are something no gallant Falcon or Knight of the Skies ever saw over France in the Great War. I'll never forget them, or the stench of cooked human beings.

Hank wanted to change the subject away from Dresden "Where the hell was the Luftwaffe today?"

# Chapter 38
## Squadron of Experts

*My own jet fighter.*

At Brandenburg base west of Berlin and Potsdam, Karl stroked the sleek fuselage and walked around his Me-262, pleased to see how well the Staffel artist had painted his logo SPRITZ and 23 on the fighter. The twin-engine Me-262 Stormbird was the most advanced fighter in the world, and flying it produced feelings like no other he had ever experienced. The past weeks of inactivity had been well worth the wait for the perfect instrument to smash the enormous enemy bomber formations. Karl wished the 262 had been given priority among armaments. At least a recent blunder had worked to his advantage.

After Operation Bodenplatte, Göring dismissed Generalleutnant Adolf Galland as Inspekteur of Day Fighters because the gifted commander and ace dared criticize the Reichminister's half-hearted response to the New Year's Day raids. Göring and Gestapo Chief Himmler threatened him and other like-minded fighter commanders with arrest and execution. In March, Hitler intervened and Göring told Galland to form an elite Staffel to prove his theories about using jets as fighters instead of bombers. The Nazi leaders hoped the maverick commander would be the first to buy the farm in combat against enemy planes roaming at will over the skies of Germany.

With the help of Oberst Johannes Steinhoff, Galland recruited the best pilots from all the Jagdgeschwaders and hospitals and created Jagdverband-44, "the Squadron of Experts." The organization table of JV-44 was top-heavy, staffed by one general, two colonels, one lieutenant colonel, three majors, two captains, and eight lieutenants, with an equal number of NCOs.

Karl felt honored to fly in the most elite air unit in history, greater than the ill-fated Kommando Nowotny, as if he had become part of the Luftwaffe's fighter pilot Olympic team. With so many great guns in JV-44, the Ritterkreuz might have qualified as the Staffel badge. Galland, Steinhoff, Heinz Bär, and Gerd Barkhorn together had almost nine hundred Luftsiegen. Other aces were well into the hundreds and two hundreds.

At the same time, the aces endured intense stress in JV-44. Enemy bombers continued to devastate Germany. Mail and phone communication had been so disrupted no one knew if family and loved ones escaped the latest raids or where they were.

Karl, despite his iron will, was not immune to anxieties. Was Elfi among hundreds of thousands of troops, support personnel, and civilians retreating from the onslaught of the barbaric Slavic and Mongol hordes of the USSR? Had she been caught in the horrible destruction of a major population center teeming with refugees, such as Dresden, where relentless bombing continued throughout another night and day?

Karl had met with Mariya-Xenia the previous month at the Schloss Teuffelreich, which had become a children's hospital. Self-composed, with a mysterious aura, she seemed to glide rather than walk. She repeated two conflicting rumors about Poldi, who had disappeared from their lives: Either he was part of an SS team trying to negotiate a separate peace with the Western Allies in Sweden, or he had been seen going into the Argentine embassy in Switzerland and was already on his way to Buenos Aires. Karl believed of all the people he knew, Poldi would come out of the war in healthy financial, physical, and perhaps cleansed political condition.

***

Karl's crew chief signaled the Me-262 was ready to go. At least up there above the clouds, he would not have time to worry about big unsolvable problems and could concentrate on the microcosmic bliss of aerial combat. Satisfied the other two jets in his three-fighter Kette had been readied for take-off, he mounted the cockpit.

Karl checked his straps, parachute, and all instruments before he started the engine and rolled to the take-off point. Overhead a flock of Me-109s and FW-190s circled the base to cover the vulnerable Me-262 take-offs, as they would also do during return landings.

Karl received clearance and advanced his throttle to 8000 rpms. The 262 built speed slowly, which made a long and vulnerable take-off roll necessary. With a slight amount of nose-heavy trim, the Stormbird flew off the ground at around 160 kph. Karl released the throttle and moved the gear-up switch. His fighter surged forward as the gear retracted flush to the wings. Airspeed increased when Karl pointed the nose upward at more than 45-degrees above an overcast horizon and began a steep climb above the scud into a sunlit blue sky.

Captain Otto Blumenau, a 122 victory ace, settled at Karl's right about three hundred meters away. The third pilot in the Kette, Leutnant Heinrich Gabel, an outstanding twenty-two year old pilot with 146 Luftsiegen, flew behind at eight o'clock position.

The radar controller broke in: "Faaken-Ein, I have you on my scope. Climb to 11,500 meters on a heading of two-eight-zero. Bombers at 8,000 meters and fifty kilometers away at your twelve o'clock position. Hals und Beinbruch."

At 7,000 meters, Karl adjusted the oxygen mask, which pinched his face, and checked the instruments and gun switches. The three-jet Kette emitted long, persistent telltale vapor trails from its engines. They would be visible for miles and alert the Americans.

Karl climbed through the vapor trail atmosphere and passed 10,000 meters altitude. The jets moved through the clear blue sky above the overcast. Karl heard a slight whine from the turbine engines and wind whistling over the Me-262's streamlined canopy. At this moment the jet was more Schwalbe than Stürmvogel. If he felt so beatific floating along like this in his jet fighter, could pilot's Valhalla be any sweeter?

At 11,500 meters altitude, the vapor trails were almost invisible when Karl saw huge gaggles of B-17s approaching. He lifted the fighter to 12,000, where the trails disappeared altogether, and turned his Kette around to pass over and ahead of the Fortress boxes. He planned to go into a split-ess and attack head-on fifteen meters under the bombers and continue the full length of the formations with guns blazing.

Karl's high speed and rapid rate of closure would make it impossible for the bomber gunners to shoot without endangering their own comrades. At best, their lead and tail end aircraft would get poor shots. Many times Luftwaffe pilots had witnessed gunners from one B-17 shoot down another Fortress in their eagerness to track enemy fighters.

Before Karl swooped into the attack, he spotted a Staffel of sixteen Mustang opponents climbing to about 2,000 meters below. The P-51s could present a serious problem after the jets pulled away from their attack on the B-17s. But because the vapor streamers were no longer visible, the Indianern would not see his Kette until the bombers called out the attack.

Below at 8,000 meters, the bombers emitted their own persistent vapor trails, and Karl led his Kette into the attack. Moments later he called out: "Horrido."

# Chapter 39
## The Gland

Dresden still burned from two consecutive night bombing runs by the RAF that set thousands of fires, and the American day raid of February 14. This second 8th Air Force day assault on the leveled city was supposed to be a mopping-up affair with the Fortresses unloading tons of bombs on everything and everyone still standing or living down there. At the morning briefing, Hank heard RAF estimates that upward of fifty thousand perished in the firestorms and explosions. Because Dresden had been swelled by countless refugees who fled from other cities and towns to avoid falling into the rapacious hands of the Red Army, Hank believed true figures would never be known because the fires consumed so many bodies.

Hank faced the 135th's second run over Dresden with distaste. He was not alone. Most of the pilots had no appetite and took only coffee. They worried about having another barf session over Dresden. Not Brax. He filled his tray with a mound of scrambled eggs, sausages, and toast.

*Unbelievable. Does Brax ever have a thought in his head?*

***

Brax did have thoughts as he scanned the sky after take-off.

*Damn it all to hell, when will those chicken-shit kraut bastards make an appearance? I ain't registered a single verified kill since New Year's day, while in the Pacific, Bong has reached 38 and McGuire 36. And what's bugging Hank? His bowels sure are in an uproar. Kee-ryst, if we didn't nearly come to blows. Why give any thought to those Heinies cooking down at Dresden? They asked for it. But the war is almost over. Gotta' score a brace of kills pronto. That's far more important than riding shotgun. Besides, those Fortresses can take care of themselves.*

*Yessirree, Hank is getting soft in the head, a changed man, no longer the carefree shoot-'em-up hotshot pilot I knew in flying school. He's become too serious, takes on responsibility where it's not required. Well, tough shit. I ain't about to listen to more whining about Dresden. Who does Milroy think is doing all that Heil-Hitlering anyway? Besides, according to Braham and the other Jew-boys, the Nazis are doing far worse.*

Brax cursed the skies empty of enemy fighters. Like the day before, no challenge came from the Luftwaffe.

***

The bomber armada dropped its payload over Dresden and swung around toward home. Forty miles west of Bohlen, a Me-262 burst into the bomber boxes ahead of the 375th Group's fighters and shot down two of the B-17s. No one saw the jet or called it out before the surprise attack.

Brax's flight was closest to the Me-262 as it pulled around for another pass. Two miles behind it was another jet. Blind-hungry for more aerial victories, he went into a curving dive to cut across the circle and catch them at the bottom of their next pass at the bombers.

The lead Me-262 broke away from the Mustangs. Brax followed and led his flight into the path of four fighters from the 136th Squadron. Brax's wingman collided with the prop of a 136th bird.

Unaware of the mid-air diaster, Brax continued diving in pursuit of the jets. Again he cut across the circle and shortened the distance. Aware they were chased, the 262s abandoned their priority targets and turned to deal with the Mustangs.

Doing well over 500 mph, the German leader pulled his Kette into a wide loop. The Mustangs tried to follow, and Brax's bird indicated 375 mph at the bottom of the pull-out. In a desperate attempt to follow the Me-262, he almost stalled at five thousand feet below them.

Brax nosed down to gain speed, and two jets turned in behind. He pulled into a split-ess, but the Me-262s gained. Brax tucked under with negative Gs believing he could pull out of a dive closer to the ground than the jets with their extra 150 mph advantage and force them to crash if they followed all the way.

Brax dove toward earth, then pushed the fighter to 6-Gs. Not enough. To clear some trees looming in front of him, he went into 7.5 Gs to avoided crashing. On the zoom to altitude, Brax's gray-out cleared, and he found himself climbing vertically with a Me-262 crossing his path 2,000 feet ahead. He centered his pipper on the jet, doubled the normal lead, and pulled the trigger. Brax's six .50 caliber guns answered the electrical signal and sprayed bullets toward the Me-262. Flashes off the right wing and right engine of the jet fighter were followed by trailing black smoke. The 262 yawed from lack of power on one side, started a right turn, and pulled up. Its canopy flew away, and the pilot ejected from the stricken plane. Another Mustang came onto the scene from another direction and fired at the still airborne 262, causing it to explode.

Brax screamed into the R/T, "Get the hell out of here, you goddam sponger!" He looked back for the men in his flight.

"Blue Seven, don't waste ammo on a bird already clobbered."

"Blue 5, this is Blue 8. We lost Fowler in the trees on your low pull-out. Someone else shot at the 262. I don't think it was a 375th bird."

Brax saw four Mustangs circling low over the edge of a small forest patch where a column of black oily smoke marked the final resting place of Fowler.

***

Hank led his flight around the site of the crash and searched in vain for Lt. Fowler. He must have blacked out from pulling too many Gs following Brax. "Blue 5, do you read?"

"Roger. This is Blue 5."

"Blue Lead' speaking. Blue 8... Lt. Planchek ... you take the lead, and Blue 5, you fly wing until we get home. Understand?"

Brax steamed, furious with Hank's orders. He'd settle their differences when they landed. He didn't care all that much about leading anyway. The combat was over, and he'd caught a rare Me-262 jet witnessed by Blue 8, and maybe Hank too.

*I'm back on the confirmed scoring trail. Bong and all the others watch out. Hollywood, get those ever lovin' bedrooms ready.*

***

Seth felt acute physical discomfort from one of the fighter pilots' major nuisances. At high altitude, his stomach expanded and he needed to fart. The tightening straps restrained him. Seth dreaded doing it during a combat mission, but he loosened them anyway to rip off a long and satisfying machine gun fusillade.

***

Hank agonized all the way to home base. He had recommended Brax for additional command and responsibility; yet the Texan lost all sense of proportion and had squandered the lives of others in the quest for aerial victories.

Brax was the last to park and fill out the flight form. He approached Planchek, oblivious to the lieutenant's frame of mind. "Stan-buddy, did you see me clobber that Me-262?"

"No, I didn't. I told you that over the R/T. Some other Mustang came in and blasted it out of the sky."

"What? Didn't you see me hit it before that P-51 came in shooting?"

"I blacked out in that crazy suicide dive you took us through, and when I came to, I looked back and saw the flames where Fowler piled into those trees. That's when you were busy shooting, I guess."

Brax spat out a stream of obscenities. "You blind asshole greenie."

"What's your worry, Captain Mobley? Your film will show it."

"No, it won't. The goddam film sprocket tore through the leader, and I don't have an inch of film. This is the umpteenth time it's happened to me, and I just tore a strip off the photo boys about it too."

"Listen to me, sir. Don't you ever lead me into a suicide dive like that one again. If you do, I'll leave you on your own."

Planchek sauntered toward the ops shack. Brax's head ached, and he craved a drink. He'd take care of the little puke later. He followed Planchek to operations, surprised by hostile looks from the other pilots.

Hank did not look at Brax. "My administrative chores are compounded by letters I must write to families and loved ones of the deceased."

"That is one job I never want, good-buddy."

Hank continued to write so he would not lose his temper in front of the men. He'd begun a somber reappraisal of his classmate. Up to now, he'd liked Brax in spite of certain obvious flaws of character. These two missions over Dresden changed everything. Brax came off as a callous sunuvabitch. True, he was a great natural flyer and a great shooter, perhaps the penultimate ace. All the best fighter pilots took chances, broke rules, and shattered precedent. Each had the special fire, aggression, and cockiness necessary to be the best. Brax did things with a fighter no thinking man would attempt, but the positive qualities of a fighter pilot were exaggerated in the Texan. That was the trouble. Braham's evaluation had been on target. Brax was all gland, whether hunting an enemy fighter in the air or a woman on the ground.

Hank remembered Brax's reaction to Monahan's death at Kelly and cruel treatment of Wilma Lee. He came to the regrettable conclusion Brax cared not the slightest for any other human being.

Brax coughed to get Hank's attention. "My camera sprocket has gremlins again. But I did get a kill. A Me-262 at last. Can you confirm it?"

Hank still did not look at Brax. The miserable bastard had no idea he might be responsible for the death of two pilots. If Hank could have proved it for certain, he'd have ordered an immediate court-martial inquiry. He deserved one himself for being blind enough to put Brax in charge of a flight.

Brax placed his fists on the desk and leaned forward. "Well?"

Hank told the other men to leave and waited until they cleared the room. He took a thorough look at Brax for the first time since the Texan had landed. Brax sweated like a horse after a race, pupils dilated, face flushed. The bastard had taken amphetamines against their CO's orders.

"Which kills would you like me to confirm, Mobley? The jet, or Fowler and Barlowe? I saw you get all three."

"What? You're blaming me for their greenhorn mistakes?"

"Of course I can't prove it, but my judgment tells me you are responsible. You were their flight leader, Brax. You might be the best fighter pilot in the ETO, but because of your selfishness and lack of concern for the men under you, the ground crews too, you're a danger to the entire group. I'm tempted to ground you, but that's up to the CO. In the meantime, I'm warning you. You will fly the straight and narrow, stop taking amphetamines, or else I will have your ass."

Brax snapped to exaggerated attention. "Yes, suh."

Hank stood and stared at Brax eyeball-to-eyeball. "Don't go into that schoolboy routine with me. Can't you see you've become a greater menace to our pilots than the Luftwaffe and flak combined?"

"Suh, I request an immediate transfer out of this chicken-shit outfit."

Hank handed Brax the forms. "Granted."

"You used to be a great buddy and damn good fighter pilot yourself. Now all you care about is regulations and maintaining your goddam precious formations. Rank and screwing around with a Congressman's niece have gone to your head, Major Milroy, suh."

"Diss-missed, Mobley."

After Brax stormed out of the ops shack, Hank tried to finish the letter to Fowler's parents. The right words would not come, and he couldn't stop his hands from shaking. He felt lousy, sick at heart, and tired of a war that ought to have ended months ago if Germany had sane leadership.

Maybe USAAF policy had wisdom behind it after all, that flying fighters in combat should be left to callow, non-introspective boys under twenty-four years of age and that after fifty to one hundred missions a fighter pilot became stale or depressed, with the exception of thick-skinned, obsessive bastards like Brax. Revenge for the bombing of their cities or a refusal to see they were losing the war must be keeping those Luftwaffe pilots going while they accumulated hundreds, some more than a thousand missions.

Hank still loved flying a single-seat fighter in combat. Nothing was more exhilarating than soaring above the clouds in the clear blue sky alone and in command of one's destiny. Leading a squadron through the clouds had its most transcendent moments when four, eight, sixteen fighters floated as one, wingtip to wingtip, as if they were not moving at all.

Command had its negative side too. It was gut-wrenching to write letters to parents and other loved ones of the kids he led. An ache in the solar plexus concerned Hank. Was he getting an ulcer? He needed the soothing balm of Winty's presence.

***

Winty must have read Hank's mind. She met him at a pub in Thetford that evening and found him drawn and out of sorts, still shaken from the raids over Dresden and Brax's insensitivity.

"Hank, why are you staring at me that way?"

"I was imagining how you'd look in a cocktail dress."

"I prefer coveralls or a flight suit. I've never gotten the hang of walking in high heels. I might embarrass you as a service wife and cause you to get passed over in rank."

"No way. Look how you've charmed General Kilrain and all the other brass. He's looking forward to giving you away at our wedding."

"And when will that be? We're not even engaged."

"After I finish my second ETO tour, so we can have a honeymoon too. Leaping Lena, I haven't had time to shop for an engagement ring."

"No rush." Winty reached for Hank's hand. "I've never seen you so gloomy. Those missions over Dresden must have been awful."

"You've got great radar, Winty."

Hank described everything he had seen and smelled over Dresden after the fire storms. He also expressed his disagreement with USAAF policy regarding those missions.

Winty told Hank the same arguments were going on at 8th Air Force. Some bomber experts wanted more Dresden-style raids in the belief they would interfere with German conduct of the war and for revenge. Others preferred to hit synthetic oil refineries, transportation and communication networks, and industry. The rest wanted to do both. Regardless and like it or not, the fighter pilots would have to fly escort wherever and whenever required.

Winty's grasp of aerial strategy and tactics and her mature reaction to everything he said made Hank love the little blonde more than before. She was going to be one great wife and mother.

Winty listened to Hank's description of Brax's callousness. "From what you tell me, He can't be a faithful husband, a decent father, or a loyal friend. You'll be better off if he transfers out of the 375th and out of your life."

"I guess so. Have I told you lately that I love you, love you one helluva lot?"

"Never enough. And I'm sorry to say I can't stay much longer, darling. I surprised you with a visit tonight because I asked General Kilrain if I could be the one to deliver some good and some bad news. I would have told you sooner, but you were so low when I arrived, I wanted you to get everything off your chest. Colonel Wilson is being Z.I.ed, and Leo recommended you to lead the 375th, but ...."

"8th Air Force selected someone else," Hank finished for Winty.

"Yes, someone you know."

"If he's a good leader...." He read Winty's expression and stopped. "No. Not Wayne Miller?"

"Yes. Miller. He requested assignment to the one group in which his old roommates flew."

"My God, anyone but that dolt."

"General Kilrain says it's to be temporary, for a month or two at most. Everyone thinks it's awful, but Miller's father-in-law is a three-star with plenty of clout."

"So long as he doesn't touch my 135th."

"I'm so sorry, but you're taking it well."

"There's nothing I can do about it anyway, and if we're going to have a military career, this won't be the last snafu, nor the worst. Still up to it as a service wife?"

"Good times and bad. Are you flying tomorrow?"

"Yes, I'm scheduled to lead the 375$^{th}$."

"Then here's the good news. General Kilrain says you'll have the Group after Miller leaves." Winty poured their drinks. "To good times and bad, Hank. Do you think you'll like higher levels of command?"

"Yes, but never as a desk jockey."

***

Seth followed the war news with heightened interest when Patton's 3$^{rd}$ Army rolled through Eppelborn and Bad Dürkheim, the entire Pfalzland and Saar. Did Mariya-Xenia stay at the manor? Did she flee to an untouched part of Germany, to a relation's castle, or to a population center like Dresden? Seth felt obligated to find the princess after the war ended and offer any assistance she might need as a way of thanking her for arranging his escape.

Mercutio went home an ace after fifty missions with a respectable total of 9.5 victories. Seth awaited word from the Paisan or Carla to learn how their meeting went and if true love blossomed. He took solace in Miriam's loving letters that now arrived weekly through his parents. She'd had a run of hit recordings, copies of which arrived about once a month, and sang in two musical films with the Mac

Herlihy band. Of more immediate importance, he read and reread a portion of that last letter dated several weeks earlier to be sure his eyes were not deceiving him. Miriam wrote she might be making a USO tour with the band in the ETO. He would contact the USO and the SHAEF liaison officers in London to learn when and where. Excited by the prospect of Miriam coming to the ETO, that evening and well into the night Seth played her records and imagined scenarios of a reunion with his Gershwin Lady after four long years, each one a Hollywood ending.

***

Bird Colonel Wayne Miller arrived at Thetford. Except for a slight paunch, he hadn't changed physically in the almost seven years since the day Hank rode with him on the bus to Randolph. His former roommate's face was unlined and rosy cheeked in contrast to the gaunt, lined mugs of the veteran flyers and crews.

Miller seemed like an actor playing at instead of being the 375th Group CO. Despite Hank's approval of Brax's request for a transfer, Miller tore up the Texan's papers wrote a recommendation for promotion to major and gave Brax command of the 136th Squadron. He sat at his desk and wrote memos, or he meddled in day-to-day operations to seem important, content to leave Hank in charge of the Group on combat missions at the head of the 135th. Hank selected Seth to lead the 137th without asking Miller.

Miller's demeanor changed whenever he was alone with Hank and Brax. He deferred to his heroes and self-appointed best-buddies with the same puppy dog amiability he'd had that year at Randolph and Kelly, and wheedled them to relate their combat experiences.

One evening after a mission, an NCO from Photo Section approached Hank "Sir, we've got a touchy situation. Captain Mobley's crew chief brought us his camera film because the guns had been fired."

Hank could not imagine what target Brax could have selected. They hadn't seen the Luftwaffe, and no orders came for the squadrons to strafe ground targets.

They went to the photo lab where Hank viewed Brax's film. It had been triggered when he fired his guns at low altitude to strafe some farm animals, but he also killed four children who were tossing grenades into a lake to catch fish. Had Brax fired at the explosions or deliberately at the kids?

Hank took possession of the film. "Sergeant, not a word about this to anyone."

"Yes, sir."

Hank couldn't show the film to Miller. The dolt hero-worshipped Brax and might destroy it, and he wouldn't be able to take the film to Kilrain until after tomorrow's mission.

***

The inevitable moment Hank dreaded came in the morning, but it was not any confrontation with Brax. Basking in the reflective glory of 375th's previous and current deeds, accumulating Theater of War time and more fruit salad for his chest was not enough for Miller. He needed to add at least some bomber escort missions to his résumé.

At the pre-mission briefing Miller announced he would lead the 375th as head of the 137th Squadron and delegated Seth to be in charge of the base until he returned. Hank wasn't sure how well Miller had qualified in the P-51 or if he'd ever led a squadron in practice formation.

Over Germany, Hank led the 135th along the entire length of the formidable box formations of about thirteen hundred B-17 Fortresses and B-25 Liberators winging eastward. Then he saw something he didn't like. Hank warned Miller over the R/T he was leading the 137th too close to the B-17s and might panic their gunners, who had trouble distinguishing friend from foe in the middle of combat.

Brax interrupted the transmission with a rebel yell when he saw vapor trails from the perch at the head of the 136th and called the sighting to Hank.

"Blue Leader. Two jet contrails fifteen miles ahead."

"Roger, Green Leader."

Hank took the 135th to the left in the same direction where the vapor trails began to disappear. The jets stalking the bomber stream could not be seen. Hank tensed, ready for anything to happen. In an instant the 262s might be zipping in fast and hard.

After five minutes, Brax broke radio silence. "Looks like the chicken-shit bastards took a powder when they saw the size of our armada."

Cocky-wrong again.

The lead B-17 of the armada exploded and folded off the wings of the two nearest bombers, causing them to spin like falling leaves into the undercast. Hank saw a bomber in the second box rear up like a wounded animal, stall, and fall into a tailspin. Farther back in the formation, another Fortress was on fire.

The B-17 gunners fired in all directions, bringing down several fighters of the 137th Squadron. At the same instant, a pair of Me-262s fired rockets at their targets and two Fortresses disintegrated.

Hank barked orders into the R/T for Seth's flight to break right and intercept the jets. If the enemy pulled away from Braham's attack, it would place them in perfect position for Brax to get off some shots. As Hank anticipated, the two leading jets broke toward the 136th Squadron. Brax shot at the closest 262. Another patented, accurate sixty-degree deflection burst, and smoke poured from its right engine. The wounded 262 zoomed, lost speed, and its pilot bailed out.

"Good work, Green Lead'."

"Thank—" As Brax acknowledged Hank's visual confirmation, 30mm cannon shells slammed into his P-51's empennage and left wing.

The other 262 flashed by, fired at another 136th Mustang and exploded it into flaming confetti.

From his perch above, Hank admired the skill of the Me-262 pilot who knocked down three Fortresses and one Mustang in less than ten seconds before outdistancing his pursuers and disappearing into the clouds

"Blue Leader, my plane's hit."

Hank turned his attention to Brax, whose Mustang, minus left aileron and flap, trailed a white fog of vaporizing gasoline from its left wing fuel tanks. He ordered two 136th pilots to guide him home.

# Chapter 40

## Stormbird

Karl had accumulated four Luftsiegen in the Me-262 since joining JV-44. Today he hoped to become a member of the elite of elite fighter pilots, a jet ace. Confident Gabel or Blumenau covered him he sighted on the leader of the American bomber formation.

Scheisse!

A small intervening cloud caused Karl to lose sight of the B-17s for a moment. The bombers came into view again, and he closed on the lead bomber at a speed of over 1200 kph. At the five hundred meter separation, Karl pressed the trigger for a short, one-second burst. The B-17 exploded as its own bombs detonated, and he was astonished to see the force of the blast blow away the nearest wings of the Fortresses on each side of it. Neither bomber exploded. They snap-rolled and fell in tailspins spewing parts and crew.

Karl continued to hold his 262 close to the bombers. He passed over remnants of the box he had attacked and fired into the next formation. This time Karl did not see hits. Instead, he spotted a gaggle of Indianern coming from the left and broke in their direction and up to face another batch of onrushing P-51s coming from above to join the rhubarb.

"Gabel, watch yourself."

Karl's warning came too late. One of the Mustang pilots made a superb deflection shot, and pieces flew off Gabel's plane. The P-51 veered to its left. Good, the Amerikaner had turned the wrong way. Now he had him. Before Karl's closing speed caused an overshoot, he fired a short burst, saw hits, but had to break to the left unable to see what damage had been done.

In front was another Mustang. Karl had time to get off another one-second burst and see flashes on its wing. As he dove for safety into the undercast, he worried about Gabel's fate. Karl had seen at least seven parachutes falling into the clouds but could not ascertain which were German.

Karl landed at Brandenburg, alert for a possible uncontested strafing sweep by enemy P-51s and P-47s when he was most vulnerable. His crew chief helped unfasten the straps. When Karl stood in the cockpit, he saw a group of pilots and more crew hurrying toward him, yelling words he could not hear because his ears were still clogged from the rapid changes in altitude he had gone through.

What on earth was going on? Why was this pack of madmen so excited and happy?

Several pilots held bottles of champagne and popped them open as they neared. The first arrivals prevented Karl from dismounting off the wing. They hoisted him onto their shoulders and paraded around the ramp to resounding cheers. Someone handed Karl a bottle of champagne.

He drank with gusto and passed the bottle to the nearest man. 'What is happening?"

"Fürst, don't you know? You scored 4 Luftsiegen today."

Another pilot took the bottle and emptied it. "You are now a jet ace with 8 kills, 236 over all."

After they set Karl on the ground, he whipped off his helmet and goggles. "But I am not the first jet ace, nor am I tops. I still do not understand the reason for this celebration."

One of the officers shouted, "Do we need a reason?"

More flyers and crew arrived to congratulate Karl, and he drank to the noisy accompaniment of: "Prost, Trink auf, Zum Wohl, Husasasahusasa."

***

Hank fumed all the way to Thetford. The Group had been chewed up by Me-262s, flak and most frustrating of all, by some would-be Annie Oakley gunners in the Fortresses, all caused by Miller's incompetence. The weenie had lost half the 137th Squadron and was too shaken to be of any use. As Deputy CO, Hank landed first and sat in the cockpit with radio on to monitor the conversations of the returning pilots. The two 136th pilots escorting Brax to home plate reported Green Leader was in trouble.

***

Brax could make no more than 125 mph top speed. The R/T was out, and the main gear half retracted. Fuel streamed from the wing tanks, and hydraulic fluid covered the bottom of the aircraft. Rudder locked or frozen about ten-degrees to the right, Brax had a difficult time making the P-51 fly straight. Trim tab and right aileron was the best way to bring in the crippled bird. To top it all off, the guns shorted and fired out. Brax bled altitude down to five hundred feet after crossing the channel, and with so little power available, he suspected four cylinders of the engine were damaged. No way could he climb to a safe bail out altitude. Parachutes worked if a pilot bailed above a thousand feet.

Brax had seen two hundred chutes drop-tested from C-47s. Of fifty kicked out at five hundred feet altitude, one opened before hitting the ground. At seven hundred feet, five out of fifty opened in time. At one thousand feet, about eighty-percent had opened. In spite of official claims of three hundred feet being safe enough, no one had ever made it. No thanks. He'd take his chances with the P-51 before he'd trust the silks below a thousand feet.

***

Seth joined Hank, who counted the airplanes as they landed, many hit and damaged. Four Mustangs were missing. Hank had seen two go down in flames, which left the others missing. As soon as Brax was on deck, he'd start the debriefing and try to learn what had happened to them.

By the time Brax entered final approach, Hank commandeered a jeep, and Seth got in alongside him. Hank sped to where Brax should be bellying-in, then braked. A thin wisp of vapor trailed behind the P-51; Brax was in serious trouble. No longer a wisp, that trailing vapor became solid and black.

***

Brax dropped to an altitude of fifty feet when the engine began to quit. He closed the mixture control and turned off the fuel valves when the propeller touched ground and made a twangy-thumping sound. Brax yanked the stick into his gut to force down the tail. No response, and an unbearable rise of temperature inside the cockpit seared Brax's face and hands.

*On fire. Shee-yit. Why did I unfasten my oxygen mask and take off my gloves? Asshole. How much more stupid can I get?*

Being trapped inside a fighter on fire was the death pilots dreaded the most, and Brax was no exception. The tail settled down, and his P-51 slid along the ground, its air scoop under the belly gouging great chunks of earth.

The Mustang came to a stop less than five hundred feet after touch-down. Brax struggled to unfasten the safety belt and chute harness in the searing heat. Eyes closed, he went over the side of the cockpit, aware of stinging blisters forming on his face and hands. Brax rolled off the wing's trailing edge and fell into a pool of burning, high octane gasoline. Engulfed in flames, Brax rose and burst screaming from the conflagration.

***

Hank sped down the rest of the runway toward Brax's stricken Mustang. He swerved left and right to avoid fighters rolling to their hardstands. Beyond the tarmac, he saw a human torch running in blind panic. He braked and sprang from the jeep.

With Seth close behind, Hank tackled Brax head-on. They beat at his body with their jackets and rolled him over in the mud and wet grass until they snuffed the flames.

Seth looked away ready to vomit, and Hank stood transfixed with horror over the faceless fighter ace. Eyelids burned away. Flesh and skin hanging in shreds from face, neck, and hands. Hank remembered Brax's request after

Monahan bought it back at Randolph, and touched the handle of his .45.

Seth had heard of pilots giving a merciful coup d'grace to their dying buddies and held Hank's arm. "Don't do it. He's unconscious now, and help is on the way."

A firefighting unit arrived and went to work on Brax's burning Mustang. The wail of an ambulance siren wound down when the transport stopped a few feet away.

Hank waved for the medics to hurry. "Do your best. He's my buddy."

# Chapter 41

## Hog Wallow

At Parchim, a green flare rose from Operations into the cloudy morning sky and arced to the top of its course, signaling Karl to take-off and intercept boxes of Fortresses and Liberators winging toward Leipzig. The third highest scoring jet ace with 10 Luftsiegen, he watched the tailpipe gauges to make sure he didn't overtemp the singing Jumo 004 engines. The Stormbird rolled more than five hundred meters before Karl felt the rudders taking effect. After the airspeed indicator passed through 110 kph, Karl eased back the control stick. He felt the jet's nose rise and its weight lighten for a typical Me-262 take-off until the left main landing gear vibrated like a G-string plucked on a mandolin.

His fighter slewed sharply, and its left wingtip dragged on the ground. The 262 swerved thirty-degrees to the left before Karl could arrest the turn. The nose dropped, and its landing gear hit dirt. Full right stick raised the left wing again, and he steered across rough grass terrain until the nose gear struck a hard object. The Stormbird reared high in the air, and its tail assembly hit the ground. Karl retarded the throttle to cut-off position and braked when the main gear touched earth again.

Moving at 120 kph, Karl skidded into a small dip and up the other side. Momentum lifted his Me-262 into the air before it dug back into the earth. Nose and left landing gear wrenched away as the twin-engine fighter slewed left, spun counter-clockwise, and came to a splashing stop in a wallow of mud and home of several dozen squealing porkers.

Karl abandoned the cockpit, leaped off the wing, and landed in the deepest mire of the hog-wallow where he lost his footing, slipped, and fell face down. To avoid drowning or asphyxiating in pungent swine excrement mixed with generous portions of mud, compost, urine, and rainwater, Karl rolled over and sat up coughing and vomiting.

His crew and several pilots ran over to the site of the crash and first encountered two dead pigs killed by Karl's sliding jet. The horrified officers and men assumed the bloody carcasses were the Prince's remains until they saw a blob of mud moving at the far end of the wallow.

Karl wiped nature's gunk from his face surrounded by three curly-tailed hogs also recovering from the shock of the crash. Their obstreperous squeals broke the tension. Officers and men added their uncontrollable laughter to the noise, and they doubled over at the sight of the erstwhile immaculate prince immersed in mud and surrounded by a retinue of swine courtiers.

Karl suffered no injuries except to his ego, but the hog-wallow where he had wiped-out the 262 was a pungent location. Every pig in the area used it as a spa and latrine. Karl smelled so vile he was not allowed into Operations and pilots' quarters until he divested himself of clothing and submitted to a further loss of dignity. Karl would have preferred one of Mariya-Xenia's warm baths. Instead, he had to stand naked outside in the freezing weather while his crew poured buckets of lukewarm soapy water over him until, as one wag put it, he stopped smelling like a Russian.

The 262 had been ruined beyond repair, and Karl would not receive another. The jets had become scarcer than before in the fighter units because Hitler ordered most of them sent to the fighter-bomber Gruppen. Parchim had few functioning Me-262s and a wasteful surplus of high-scoring fighter aces. Those with the most time in jets could stay with JV-44; the rest had their choice of front line Geschwadern until more 262s became available, which, Karl assumed, would be a wintry day in hell—or a warm one in the USSR.

The war could end any day. The Soviets had entered Königsberg in East Prussia and occupied Vienna. The Americans and British approached the Elbe, ready to link up with the Red Army and cut Germany in half.

Karl was desperate for news from East and West. Was Elfi safe? What happened to Mariya-Xenia and the Pfalz-Teuffelreich vineyards now that the Western Allies occupied the Saar and the Pfalzland?

Karl was one of the top jet aces, but he fell in with the low-timers. Despite warnings that he would be executed as an aristo if captured by the Reds, Karl selected JG-52 because he wanted to do everything possible to slow the Soviet steamroller. His most compelling reason for returning to the East was to defy all odds and search for Elfi, who might be with a hospital unit somewhere along the Russian Front, if she were still alive.

# Chapter 42

## Drenched in Sweat

Hank jinked and reefed his Mustang to avoid those blood-red fireballs rushing toward him. He had Me-109, number 23, in the sights. Spritz. Prinz Karl. He made a fine adjustment in the sight and touched the firing tit. Silence. Overpowering silence. Hanks left hand moved on reflex to the arming switches. Nothing wrong there. They were on. He touched the triggers again. Still no firing.

It could be fatal for a pilot to look from an enemy plane to the switches, but in this instance Hank had no choice. The electrical panel confirmed everything was A-Okay. Hank checked six o'clock. Sure enough, two other Me-109s were queuing behind. Hank's pucker factor shifted to full-force. He snap-rolled the fighter in an evasive maneuver. At the end of one-and-a-half rolls, he popped the stick full forward and jammed the throttle to the firewall. Hank's panic intensified when he failed to hear the engine surge in response.

Hank cried out in pain and shouted a stream of epithets when his left elbow was struck a painful blow. The sounds cut through the still of the night. Awakened by a throbbing ache, Hank turned on the nightstand lamp, safe on top of the bed. Electric shocks still shot through the crazy bone. He must have hit it on the edge of the nightstand.

Another bad dream. Hank rolled into a sitting position on the edge of the bed, his sheets soaked from sweat. Hank's muscles ached from flying combat in the vivid nightmare, and he was no less exhausted and high strung then in those real aerial battles he'd lived through. Was it a premonition of terrible things to come, or a composite of past experiences?

To erase the apocalyptic vision, Hank focused on a brown Morocco leather photo album on his desk. He left the bed, lit a cigar, and thumbed through the pictorial autobiography he'd been working on before going to sleep. It contained photos dating back to cadet days at Randolph and Kelly, all the way to the more recent, cluttered panoramic shot of the 375th Fighter Group taken March 20, the day he replaced Wayne Miller as its CO. After he lost half the 137th Squadron, Miller exited from Thetford within minutes of landing, while Hank and Seth rescued Brax. He received an instant posting back to the ZI to resume his relentless climb to supreme General of the USAAF and JCS.

Monahan was in one of the early snapshots. How many planes would he have shot down had he survived? Hank smiled at photos of aircraft he'd tested and flown in combat and almost cried when he saw so many eager youthful faces of now dead pilots.

Hank lingered over a photo in which he stood arms-linked with Brax in a best-friends-forever pose. The Texan had been one handsome sunuvagun, and Hank cringed whenever he recalled the flesh melting away from Brax's face.

*The poor bastard. The poor, poor bastard.*

Hank chided himself for getting upset over a mere dream, when Brax was certain to face years of painful surgery with no guarantees he'd ever have normal features again. Maybe that had caused the nightmare.

Yesterday afternoon Hank had visited the Wimpole Park Hospital. Brax was sleeping off the effects of another operation, so he hadn't been required to make false cheerful small talk and pretend everything was all right. The Texan resembled something Hank had reacted to with horror many years ago when he was a kid. What the hell was the name of that picture? A gangster film. *Public Enemy.* The last scene. James Cagney at the front door wrapped in bloody bandages. More monstrous than any Mummy in a cheap horror film.

That's all Brax had become, a mummy. How could he be certain it had been Brax anyway? It. The bandaged-swathed body in the bed had become depersonalized, a thing, not quite human. A doctor told Hank that Brax's face required major reconstruction. The eyes were okay, but the lids had been burned; he needed a grafting operation developed by the British, involving circumcision. The foreskin of a penis most closely matched the skin of eyelids.

Hank recalled the old saw that in time of danger a young man reaches to protect his balls, an older man his eyes. He suspected Brax's genitals were un-singed.

*Which will I reach for first if it ever comes to that?*

They had scheduled Brax for immediate evacuation to Fitzsimmons Hospital in Denver, and Hank wrote his parents to locate Wilma Lee and tell her about her ex-husband's bad luck. Would she find it in her heart to visit the man who wronged her? It was a remote chance. Wilma Lee might still love Brax enough to visit and cheer him.

After all the bandages were removed, the vain flyer was going to have special need for someone who cared.

Brax would never fulfill his ambition to become the top United States fighter ace of the ETO. Much worse, unless there existed a miracle-working plastic surgeon, he also could kiss goodbye the romantic swashbuckling movie career he wanted so badly, unless he was willing to play villains, or try horror films.

Hank never showed Brax's film to Kilrain or anyone else. The Texan had paid a heavy enough price for all his sins.

# Chapter 43
### Beating the Odds

Karl reported to JG-52 in a new Me-109, assigned to the 9th Staffel of III Gruppe. Oberstleutnant Hermann Graf, the Geschwaderkommodore, assigned him a tent amidst primitive facilities. Almost daily, JG-52 retreated before dusk, which created monumental problems in supplying and maintenance. Too often, they had to abandon aircraft when the fighters needed minor repairs. If a spare part was unavailable or could not be salvaged from another more damaged fighter, the airplane was cannibalized before being burned.

JG-52's mechanics worked around the clock and slept when they could. The brutal pace led to shoddy maintenance. Fatigued crewmen often put off corrections of defects in instruments and controls until after the next flight, and those delays resulted in more fighters being unable to fly.

When replacement 109s arrived, the pilots had no time to make an acceptance shakedown inspection, test flight, and to zero-in and harmonize the guns. Flyers and crew chiefs had to assume all that had been done before the aircraft was dispatched to the front. More often than not, their assumptions were erroneous.

Yet, JG-52 retreated with relative impunity. The Soviets would not fly more than seven to eight kilometers into German-held territory unless they had absolute air superiority and could mount a massed attack using several hundred dive bombers.

***

In the spring twilight of his first day with JG-52, Karl watched astonished an unusual aspect of the operation, entirely unlike anything he'd experienced in the West or earlier with the Geschwader. Wives, children, and other family members were arriving at the bases in large numbers. They fled their homes to escape the advancing Soviets and to be near their men in the fighter units. The women reasoned it was better to face the end beside their husbands, to die with them, rather than submit to barbarous conquerors.

The civilians complicated each retreat to the next airfield, but they gave essential assistance to the Geschwader. At first they had been employed in the kitchens, but soon many helped service the aircraft. They handed tools and parts to mechanics like nurses assisting doctors in surgery. They cleared windshields of the Me-109s, wiped oil from engines and cleaned cockpits between sorties.

By the time Karl arrived at JG-52, many of the women had been there long enough to become excellent mechanics in their own right, and in some instances improved the level of aircraft maintenance. The men liked having their wives and girlfriends with them. It freed their minds from worry that a loved one had been incinerated or crushed under rubble from the latest bombing raids.

After four Luftsiegen in one sortie, Karl dismounted from the Me-109 and examined some small caliber bullet holes in the vertical stabilizer and rudder. He heard his crewman cry out a warning and looked up. Another Me-109 coming in for a landing ground-looped into the parking area fifty meters away and crashed into a FW-190. Parts of the plane scattered into the air, but there was no fire. The unhurt Messerschmitt pilot scrambled off the cockpit and ran from the wreckage.

Karl saw a mechanic trapped inside the 190's cockpit. The prop of the Me-109 had struck the Flight Sergeant across the lower forehead and bridge of his nose. Karl and three mechanics worked twenty minutes to free the wounded man from the tangled wreckage. When they placed the wounded Feldwebel on the ground, he lapsed into semi-delirium and called out a name. "Elfi. Elfi."

Shaken, Karl asked a tearful young woman standing next to him, "Who is his Elfi?"

"His wife. He's been expecting her to arrive any day now. Ach, maybe she's one of them."

The woman pointed at a truck coming to a stop near the runway. It disgorged several dozen ragged women and children.

One of the crew waved to the new arrivals. "Anyone named Elfi among you?"

A small figure wearing a fatigue cap too large for her head ran toward the Feldwebel and was intercepted by one of the women. "You are Elfi?"

"That is my name."

"Feldwebel Hoffmann's wife?"

"No."

When the Feldwebel repeated his wife's name, Elfi understood the situation, moved past the woman, and sat on the ground by the dying young mechanic. "Your Elfi is here. Your Elfi is here, so now you must relax. We will take you to a hospital. Do not worry. You will be all right because your Elfi is here. I will not leave your side."

The mechanic smiled before he died. Karl witnessed the ordeal in an emotional turmoil and helped Elfi stand. "Gott Sie Dank, thank God it is you."

Elfi cried out Karl's name and fainted in his arms.

# Chapter 44
## A Challenge

Hank scanned around the clock at the head of the 375th with every plane in the Group soaring close to the sun in formation as one. Sun flashed off a cockpit in the distance, and Hank alerted the Group to the presence of bandits stalking the bombers. Soon he saw a formation of four German fighters paralleling their course two miles away to the right.

The April sky had the sort of haze common during Indian Summers along the Atlantic Seaboard. Linear visibility at 16,000 feet was around five to seven miles. As always, a grayish white mixture of fog and smoke hung over the area, and those cunning bandits were moving closer and setting themselves up on the perch preparatory to the classic bounce.

Hank called out the potential attack by the Germans, and a sharp-eyed flight leader at Number 9 position complicated matters with another sighting.

"Eight bandits at three o'clock. Holy shit, they're Russian Yaks, and it looks like those bastards are planning a run at us. Watch out for 'em, Chief."

"Roger. On my command, Flights One and Two break into them. Blue 9, you lead Flights Three and Four. Watch out for the Me-109s at eleven o'clock high. If they turn back after us, you guys take 'em on."

Hank pointed his fighter toward the oncoming Yaks. By the time the war moved from March into April, Mustang pilots were finding the Soviet Migs and Yaks to be a serious problem caused by consistent misidentification. Me-109s, P-51s, and Yak-9s looked alike, and the Russian Lavochkin-5s and 7s with their air-cooled engines were confused with P-47s and FW-190s. Consequently, as the Western and Eastern Fronts advanced to squeeze Germany into a tight corset, a pilot had to approach each bounce with caution until close enough to make positive identification if friend or foe shared the sky.

The Yaks continued their menacing dive toward Hank's squadron, and he was able to distinguish the two separate coolant radiators of the Yak-9 series fighter, one under the nose, the other under the belly. No doubting it, they were not about to abort their attack dive and pursuit against the 375th.

Unable break into the Russian frequencies and tell the Reds his Group was American, he ordered the first two flights to break right into a head-on approach toward the Yaks. The first flight of Soviet fighters also broke to the right and away from the challenge. The second flight of four must not have gotten the message. The Yaks wheeled around in a sharp turn onto the tail of the last flight of P-51s.

One of the Russians fired a burst at the Mustangs and hit Number 5 in the formation. The Yanks accepted the challenge, hungry to test the ability of Soviet airmen and quality of their planes. P-51 against Yak-9. Mustang versus Ostronosyi.

Hank thought the Yak-9 to be the best fighter in Europe when flying below 15,000 feet. He figured the Soviet pilots had never mixed it up before with Americans and knew little if anything about the capabilities of the Mustang. He led the formation to higher altitude, secure in his knowledge the P-51 performed better as altitude increased and the Yak-9's abilities deteriorated.

After the first turns at higher altitudes, two Yaks were on fire and spinning toward the ground. One had been hit by Hank's 50 cal. bullets, the other by Lt. Stan Planchek, Number 3 in the flight. The other pair of Yaks broke away from the battle and sped eastward.

"Goddammit, come back here, you Muzhik bastards!"

That aggressive reaction came from Planchek, the Russophobic Pole in the flight, who wanted to get them all. Satisfied Number 5 Mustang had only a few holes in the fuselage and would have no trouble making it back to base, Hank gathered his chicks, headed west again, and called the other two flights of the 135th. They never made contact with the Germans and expressed disappointment at being kept away from the shoot-out with the Russkies.

Back at Thetford, Hank approached the ops shack with mixed feelings. If he was going to get grief from the brass because they clobbered two Soviets, he intended to justify it at any court-martial. Up there, it had been either the Reds or Hank's men, and he had one damaged bird to prove it. From what he knew about the Soviet attitude and behavior toward the Western Alliance, there wasn't going to be any buddy-buddy relationship with them after the war anyway.

# Chapter 45

## Grounded

Hank left his Deputy CO Seth in charge of the 375th and arrived mid-morning at High Wycombe Abbey. He reported to the one man he trusted to give him a sympathetic hearing.

General Kilrain listened without comment until Hank finished, and he locked the combat film in a drawer.

"Milroy, as you have a few more missions to go before making it another hundred, have you thought about what it would be like to get experience outside a combat unit?"

Blood rushed to Hank's face. The brass had decided to punish him after all. "But those commies attacked us."

"I believe you, and I wish you'd gotten them all. Now, forget it. I'll keep your film and enjoy watching it when I am alone. The Reds will never acknowledge we got the better of them, so they won't make an issue of it. I have something else in mind." Kilrain took Hank to a map of Europe covering one wall. "The Germans are through. Those fanatic followers of Hitler just don't know it yet."

"Sure, but we still have to deal with the Japs in the Pacific."

"Good God, man, haven't you had enough? You've flown almost two hundred missions. That's challenging the law of averages."

"The German fighter pilots fly five times that number."

"And most are dead or maimed as a result."

"So, because we nailed some bolshies in self-defense, you're punishing me with a non-combat assignment."

"That's not the reason. Your orders were cut yesterday, and I was going to summon you anyway. Milroy, you want to make a career in the Air Force, and I want you to go all the way. That entails more than flying. Other types of commands. Staff assignments, more schooling, and some desk jockeying at the Pentagon. We're going to need men like you after we finish the Japs, because we'll be confronting an even greater threat than the Axis powers."

"The Soviets."

"Damn right. Those Yalta Agreements will allow the Reds to occupy all of Eastern Europe, and half of Germany and Austria after the war in Europe ends. We can be certain that Stalin will force Soviet style dictatorships wherever the Red Army is stationed to enforce his will. Everywhere else, communists, fellow travelers, and useful idiots will do Moscow's bidding and plot to overthrow or weaken the democracies."

Hank recalled his History lessons and how some things never changed. "Sir, Russia was an autocratic imperialist menace long before communism. After Waterloo until the decade before World War I, the British Empire alone limited Tzarist expansion. Through bribery, they created Afghanistan as a buffer state against a potential Russian invasion of India. From 1853 to 1856, they allied with France, Sardinia, and the Ottoman Turks in a war to ensure the Russian Navy stayed bottled in the Black Sea. In 1902

England signed a naval alliance with Japan to thwart Russian penetration into Asia and the Pacific. A greater threat to the British colonial empire by German Kaiser Wilhelm II caused a policy reverse, the Anglo-Russian agreement of 1907 that partitioned Persia into *spheres of interest* and led to an alliance in the Great War."

"Well said, Milroy, which is one of many reasons why I've thought of you as my protégé and as the son I never had from the time you were a cadet at Randolph and Kelly."

Hank wanted to say he regarded Kilrain as his second father, but the General continued. "You see the big picture, or, as the British statesmen referred to the containment of Russia, The Great Game. Any alliance we make with Russia or the USSR is an anomaly in the sphere of geopolitics."

Kilrain invited Hank to sit and offered him a cigar.

"After victory in Europe and Asia, only the United States will have the strength and resources to replace an exhausted England as the one nation capable of stopping the spread of traditional Russian imperialism under its new guise of Soviet international communism."

"Sir, as you know, authors like Sun Tzu and B. H. Liddell Hart have influenced my thinking on military and grand strategy. So have our discussions and those books written by Homer Lea you let me borrow back at Randolph."

Hank and Kilrain spoke of the little hunchback eccentric genius who had two prophetic books published before he died at age thirty-six in 1912. *The Valor of Ignorance*, 1908, alerted the United States it faced eventual war against Japan; *The Day of the Saxon*, 1912, advised England to prepare for another inevitable conflict resulting from German naval and colonial ambitions. If both the United States and England defeated Japan and Germany, Lea foresaw they would then face the most dangerous adversary of all, Russia, in a final global struggle. Lea planned to title his third book *The Swarming of the Slav.*

"Sir, I never forgot these words Homer Lea wrote before The Great War and Bolshevik Revolution. *Today, the Russian Empire draws to a close. It approaches the Empire of the World.*"

"Homer Lea was not the only prophet to write about the Russian threat, Milroy." Kilrain swiveled in his chair, removed a worn volume from a bookshelf behind the desk, and opened it to a dog-eared page. "Farther back in the 1850s, prescient Commodore Matthew C. Perry predicted a great conflict between the United States and Russia, or as he phrased it, the Saxon and the Cossack, and this is what he wrote:

> *"The antagonistic exponents of freedom and absolutism must then meet at last, and then will be fought that mighty battle on which the world will look with breathless interest. On its issues will depend the freedom or the slavery of the world— despotism or rational liberty must be the fate of civilized man."*

"Perry was on target, sir."

Kilrain closed the book. "Now, back to you. Milroy, you are going to have a most interesting and challenging mission. Forget about flying aerial combat in the ETO. It won't exist anyway by May. According to SHAEF, the war can't last beyond another four weeks. Our Army units are capturing hundreds of German pilots daily who prefer to surrender to us because they fear Soviet retribution. The ground pounders need someone knowledgeable about airplanes to interrogate them at the point of capture and seize their log books. Some have experience in jets and rocket planes. Because you've tested and flown just about every fighter ever made and already have some experience as an interrogator, you fit the requirements perfectly. Follow me?"

"Yes, sir."

Hank remembered Seth wanted to thank the princess who aided his escape. "Can I take Major Braham with me? He's better in the lingo than I am."

"No problem. He's probably worn out the same as you. I'll cut Braham's orders before you return to Thetford." Kilrain grinned as if he had given lessons to the Cheshire Cat. "You will report to General Patton's headquarters."

Hank almost choked on smoke from his cigar. "Patton?"

"His exec said he asked for you by name. You must have treated Old Blood and Guts to a real show that time you flew him through the Grand Canyon."

"Truthfully, I'd rather fly combat. But what the hell, sir. If the war ends in a few weeks, it won't matter."

"And don't worry about your group. We recalled Cy Wilson from the ZI to take over again." Kilrain handed Hank a small box. "Winty will want to pin these on. Your promotion to full colonel has come through. We've expedited a quick promotion for you because the Germans are hyper rank-conscious. Do you hear me? You're a bird colonel now, and Patton will probably want to make you a general when he hears you've knocked down a Soviet fighter."

Kilrain reached out to shake hands. "Congratulations, Colonel Milroy, and good luck. Now, take the afternoon and night off and spend some time with Lt. McCabe. She knows nothing about your promotion and new assignment."

***

Walking from the flight line to the Ops shack, Seth felt like an old man in his G-suit. Every muscle ached. He was soaked through with sweat and continued to shake from his second escort mission as head of the 375th while Hank was at 8th Air Force HQ.

Seth hoped the brass hadn't lowered the boom on Milroy when he saw Cy Wilson inside Operations going over papers at the desk and Milroy, who had returned, seated opposite the colonel.

Hank answered Seth's unspoken question. "Kilrain grounded me this morning. Cy is taking over the 375th again."

Seth shook hands with Wilson. "Glad to have you back, sir, but don't misunderstand me. I think it's chicken-shit to punish Hank for shooting down the Reds in self-defense."

Seth did not see Colonel Wilson wink at Hank before the CO barked, "You're grounded too, Braham."

"What for? Guilt by association?"

"If that's the case, we'd have been hanged a long time ago."

"What's going on? Hank, you're sporting eagles."

"My promotion to bird colonel came through, and General Kilrain gave me a new assignment. I'll be interrogating captured German pilots as we pick them up on the Continent."

"The Continent? Wait a minute. Than grin of yours. Am I going too?"

Hank gave Seth his orders and a small open box containing silver oak leaves. "Yes, you're accompanying me on this unusual sortie, and promoted too. Kilrain said the

Germans are rank-conscious, and he wanted to give you more of an edge."

Seth looked at the orders in one hand and silver oak leaves in the other. "I don't know what to say."

"Save it for later. Come to my quarters after you freshen up. I've got some personal matters to discuss with you."

Seth's head spun with possibilities and matters to which he must attend. He sent off a letter to let his parents and Miriam know he'd been taken out of combat and signed it *Lt. Colonel Braham.* That ought to cheer them.

*****

Over cigars and fine cognac, Seth touched snifters with Hank. "Thanks, beaucoup thanks. This assignment you've gotten me has saved my life. I didn't think I'd make it back from today's mission. I've been in bad shape ever since Dresden."

"We all have."

"Now I can see the sense of taking men out of combat after 50 missions. Hank, after the war, I assume you're going to be a career officer."

"As long as I can fly. And what about you?"

"My main focus will be to wed Miriam as soon as possible. Anyway, what did you want to see me about?"

Hank poured more cognac. "To be my best man. Winty and I have set a date to marry. Will you stand up for me?"

Seth touched glasses with Hank. "Of course I will. Winty is the perfect woman for you. When does it take place?"

"In June, I hope. As my Deputy CO and designated Best Man, there's a more pressing matter for you to take care of. I'm expecting you to arrange our farewell party from the Group for tomorrow before we join Patton's 3rd Army."

"Colonel Milroy, I promise you a bash never to be forgotten."

***

Seth procured the best food, unlimited booze, and an ample supply of WACs and nurses. He invited all officers and noncoms of the 375th to the Thetford Officers Mess, which had been decorated with poster messages and bedecked with colorful ribbons and favors to soften the stark interior of the Quonset hut. By 1900 hours the party was well underway.

Hank began the dancing with Winty. *Sunuvagun!* Every tune he had mentioned liking to Braham was being played on the Victrola, from "All or Nothing At All" and "At Last" to "Sentimental Journey". That he was not yet twenty-seven and already a full colonel with 23 victories, excluding the Yaks and the unverified, boggled Hank's mind. He considered himself beyond fortunate that high-ranking officers and immediate superiors like Kilrain and Cy Wilson recognized his abilities. They pushed him forward instead of feeling threatened and limiting deserved advancement, as so often happened in the military.

Between dances, several of the veteran 375th pilots kidded Hank and Seth because they were going to, of all things, a tank outfit, but serving under Patton would make it bearable. Then the toasts began. They were so numerous Hank decided to take charge of the festivities before he and Winty became too smashed to function. It was the first time he'd seen her drink more than a glass of wine or polite highball.

When the band blastd away with a spirited rendition of "The Boogie Woogie Bugle Boy of Company B" for the hepcats, Hank took Winty to one side. "Having fun?"

"Yes, except I don't like it that you're going to be farther away from me."

"Don't worry. Seth will be my chaperone."

"Maybe I'll steal a fighter and fly over to see you. Did you know that I haven't flown a plane since I came to the ETO? Life with you had better be worth all this sacrifice."

"I'll make up for it."

"And you know I'm a better fighter pilot than anyone here. I beat you in a dogfight, remember?"

"A most humbling experience I'll never forget."

Hank stopped the music, stood on a table, and called for silence. "Ladies and gents, you know we've gathered, to celebrate my farewell to the 375th, and Colonel Braham's too. Hold the cheering and applause. As you all know, there's my promotion to bird colonel and to celebrate, most important of all, my formal engagement P-39s to and intention to marry in June ... with approval of the USAAF and the Congress of the United States ... the greatest lady flyer in the world. WAC Lieutenant Winty McCabe."

Amidst more cheering, one last paper banner was unfurled with best wishes for Hank and Winty in large bold red print. Seth lifted Winty onto the table so she could be close to Hank and receive congratulations from the entire Group. Then he recited a brief farewell speech, which received heavy applause and shouts from several pilots who had become aces thanks to Seth's generosity setting them up.

Hank followed with one last toast. "To my buddy, Braxton Mobley. May he be restored to full, handsome lady-killing health."

"Oh, please, yes!" That loud plea by one of the nurses sparked good-natured cheers and rowdy laughter.

Seth played the engaged couple's favorite recording, "At Last", another time. Hank took Winty to the middle of the floor.

Leaping Lizards, she was so adorable and cuddly, he wished they could marry now. At least they'd have three days together.

Seth cut in and circled the floor with Winty to "Paper Doll". "My congratulations."

"Thanks, Seth. I'm glad Hank picked you to be best man. And good luck with your singer."

"Hank told you?"

"Yes, Mimi Kay is my favorite band singer, and I hope to dance at your wedding too."

"That would be swell, Winty."

Colonel Wilson cut in, and Seth went to drink with Hank and several of the veteran leaders at the bar. When they toasted the 375th, Hank asked Seth, "What's so amusing?"

Seth raised his glass. "To the 375th, to the Regiment. All that's missing are Sir C. Aubrey Smith, Errol Flynn, and the exchange of our khaki and olive drab for scarlet tunics."

"By golly, Braham, you're right. The Group is our regiment." Hank felt proprietary toward every man, plane, and piece of equipment. He might have other assignments, lead other units, but the 375th would always be his.

A grim Duty Officer entered the mess hall and handed Hank a message. He read it, stopped the music, and needed extra moments to find his voice.

"Everyone. Quiet. Please. I have some extremely bad news. I regret I must tell you the President of the United States, Franklin Delano Roosevelt, passed away less than an hour ago at Warm Springs, Georgia."

He continued over gasps and cries. "Cause of death was a massive cerebral hemorrhage." Hank asked for a fresh drink. "I propose a toast to our departed President. Ladies. Gentlemen."

All present bottomed-up their glasses, and the farewell-engagement party turned into a wake. At first there was oppressive silence. Then all present began to express their reactions to FDR's death. Someone brought in a radio so they could hear the latest reports.

Many wept. Roosevelt had been in the White House forever, it seemed. Seth knew that regardless who and how many would follow FDR in his lifetime, for him, "Hail to the Chief" would always conjure images of Roosevelt's jutting jaw, cigarette holder between clenched teeth, and flowing cape. For many, peripatetic Eleanor, and Fala, their Scotty, had long ago become honorary members of their families.

Hank listened to the radio, astonished to be so affected. The British must have felt something similar when Queen Victoria died after reigning sixty-four years. It was the end of an era, and FDR's death could not have come at a more critical time. The United States would win the war, but there was no guarantee it would win the peace.

Hank held Winty, who cried until exhausted, and toasted the new President, about whom he knew nothing. "Good luck, Mr. Truman. You'll need plenty of it now."

Now I understood what there was in all those mutilated, torn, strange bodies. It was a red laugh. It was in the sky, it was in the sun, and soon it was going to overspread the whole earth ... that red laugh.
—*Leonid Andreyev, The Red Laugh*

# PART FIVE

## MADNESS IN MAY
## 1945

# Chapter 46

## Advance to the West

Karl and Elfi stood in front of the Operations shack, part of a semi-circle of pilots, mechanics, and their women. They listened to a Party functionary detailing the death of America's Jew-President *Rosenfeld*. Karl did not share the Nazi's belief that the miracle to turn the war around had arrived. Despite the success of the American and British landings at Normandy, 6 June, 1944, the failure of the Ardennes Offensive, the collapse of the Eastern Front, and lack of adequate air defense, many fanatics still believed Hitler could pull off a victory. Yet rational anti-Nazi Germans like Karl himself also continued to fight.

Karl resolved to ponder the true meaning of courage another time. At the moment, his one goal was survival. Despite of the imminent defeat of the twelve-year-old Tausend Jahren Reich, Karl found pleasure in these chaotic times because he had found Elfi.

She had postponed writing Karl until she made a final decision whether or not to wait out the war in Switzerland. Then events took control of Elfi's life. When news broke about the 20 July Plot, Elfi thought it unwise to contact

Karl. Before she could act further, the entire hospital staff was transferred to the Eastern Front, and she served wherever needed. Elfi's medical unit had fled a Soviet advance patrol the day she appeared at the base.

Karl thought Elfi looked beautiful despite being exhausted, undernourished, and filthy. They seldom washed, and then under the most primitive conditions. He tried to build Elfi's stamina and health by sharing rations and foraging for extra food.

Elfi never left Karl's side except when he was in the air making final lone wolf hit-and-run bounces against the Red Air Force. After each sortie, she wiped the windshield, cleaned the cockpit, and refueled the tanks of Karl's Me-109. She applied her recently acquired mechanical and electrical knowledge to tighten the correct bolts and repair damaged wires. Elfi's wish to become Karl's mechanic, made long ago, had come true.

Despite massive Soviet dive-bombing raids, JG-52 and other Luftwaffe units continued their daily moves westward to new bases away from the swarming Slav and Mongol hordes of the Red Army. During their brief respites from combat, retreating from the Soviets, and readying the fighters, Karl and Elfi made intense love. Each time might be the last.

***

1 May, word came to JG-52 that Adolf Hitler and Eva Braun, Josef Goebbels and his entire family had committed suicide in their respective Berlin Bunkers. Fanatic party members and idealistic young pilots chose to believe their Führer was still alive and well. Karl reacted to Hitler's death with indifference. The damage had already been done. 1945 was not 1815. As in 1919, Germany had no diplomatic genius to divide and conquer the enemy. The Fatherland had no

Talleyrand to convince the victors it was Hitler's fault and the German people were not to blame. The defeated would not be allowed to sit at a bargaining table as equals with the victors.

More so than after the previous European war, every German man, woman, and child would pay for the policies of the Nazis. If Hitler could have been taken alive, perhaps all hatred and desire for revenge would focus on Der Führer alone. Instead, it would be dispersed among all Germans, innocent and guilty alike.

***

The war dragged on for another week, and JG-52 operated out of improvised airstrips at Deutsch Brod in Czechoslovakia. The situation had so deteriorated that further retreat would result in advancing toward one of their Western opponents. Word arrived that after Göring learned of Hitler's decision to commit suicide, he sent a telegram to Der Führer asking to assume control of the Reich. Hitler viewed that request as treason. He fired Göring from all positions, expelled him from the party, and ordered his arrest. A rumor circulated that Göring had surrendered to the Americans.

***

Top ace Major Erich Hartmann returned from a brief reconnaissance sortie to learn where the nearest Red Army spearhead might be. He encountered a Soviet pilot in a Yak-11 performing acrobatics over Brüun and scored his 352nd Luftsieg, which may have been the last Luftwaffe kill on the Eastern Front.

After Hartmann reported, Graf asked him, Karl, and other top aces to stay. "Air Fleet Commander General

Seidmann has sent orders for us to fly to Dortmund and capitulate to the British. All other JG-52 personnel must surrender to Soviet forces at Deutsch Brod."

Hartmann, the top ace fighter ace of all fronts and all wars with 352 Luftsiegen, had done all his damage on the Eastern Front, and the Soviets were poor sports in victory. Karl had been included because he was a royal with 244 Luftsiegen, many of them Soviet aircraft, and as such he could expect summary execution if he fell into the hands of the vengeful Russians.

The officers discussed alternatives to Seidmann's order. They would never abandon their responsibilities toward all three thousand men, women, and children now comprising their extended family. Graf suggested they surrender to the Americans who had been seen a short fifteen kilometers to the west, and repeated his proposal before all ranking officers and NCOs. Karl knew the unanimous response before it was voiced. Of course, they must go westward to Pisek and link up with the Yanks before the Soviets caught them from the East. Everyone believed the Americans would behave humanely toward their women and children.

Graf ordered all Me-109s destroyed, including the ten still able to fly. After pilots and crew complied, he commanded everyone to move out, alert not only to Soviet troops and Czech partisans but also zealous SS units who had orders to kill any and all who attempted to surrender. Black smoke from burning fuel helped the Soviets zero in their artillery, and a shell landed on a loaded truck near the runway, killing twelve men.

They trudged along a country road through dark spruce woods and verdant fragrant meadows of the Bohemian Forest toward Pisek. No other enemy rounds fell near the column of more than three thousand pilots, crew, and civilians. Some rode in trucks and staff cars. Most walked.

Karl touched the holster holding his loaded Luger. If they did not reach the Americans first, the Red Army must never take him and Elfi alive.

Everyone in the Gruppe had heard about Soviet political commissars' screeds and propaganda sheets that encouraged the Red Army to wreak merciless revenge against all Nazis, aristos, capitalists, and their officer corps. They also punished German women with rape and murder for being mothers and daughters of fascists, and inflicted similar harsh treatment on Polish, Czechoslovak, and Soviet females for fraternizing with the occupying Wehrmacht troops.

German soldiers and pilots who surrendered to Czech partisans fared no better. After handing over their arms, they were executed on the spot.

Karl was well aware of what the Red Army would do to Elfi. Despite all adversities, she looked so damn lovely he allowed himself the luxury of imagining the little brunette presiding over the Pfalz-Teuffelreich estates. No, he must not dwell on such unproductive sentimental fantasies that might prevent him pulling the trigger before it was too late.

Karl believed there was a last best-moment of death for each person, a final moment of choice, after which others decided when and how one would die. Albert von Wittelsberg's last chance to have a decent death was to commit suicide before the Nazis arrested him for his part in the 20 July plot. He waited too long. Albert's final hours and death became the property of the SS.

Everyone assumed the Americans honored the Geneva Conventions for treatment of prisoners of war and civilians, but there were no guarantees they would reach the Yanks before the Soviets fell upon them. Karl needed the discipline to command what was left of his and Elfi's destinies. He must never surrender that choice to the Soviets.

# Chapter 47

## Cornucopia of Aces

Hank read the mileage gauge and studied a map on the passenger side of his jeep. He was part of a column of eight tanks, several support vehicles, and a dozen trucks filled with combat-ready infantrymen moving along the main road from Pilsen to Pisek through the verdant Bohemian Forest, a natural barrier between Czechoslovakia and Bavaria. They had traveled more than forty-four miles from Pilsen, liberated May 6th by U.S. troops, and where he'd celebrated the cessation of hostilities the following day. Now they were less than six miles from Pisek, between Pilsen and Budweis/Budejovice near the Stava River.

High above the trees, an occasional roar of a Mustang or RAF Mosquito on reconnaissance intensified Hank's yearning to be airborne again. Rooted to a ground unit, he felt imprisoned, claustrophobic, and ravenous for the release and freedom he could achieve at the controls of a single-seat fighter soaring close to the sun.

Hank looked up through the network of dense spruce branches and leaves and searched in vain for the Mustang. The lucky bastard was off and away into the high blue toward the late afternoon sun. And here he was, still attached as an interrogator with the 90th Division of Patton's Third Army.

A review of his significant flying achievements cheered Hank somewhat. During the past seven years, he'd accomplished several long-held goals to become one among a talented few. Back in 1938-1939, a small number qualified to become Army Air Corps cadets, and fewer made it through to Pursuit. Of the more than five thousand fighter pilots in 8th Air Force, a mere five-percent became fighter aces, about two hundred-and-fifty men during a three-and-a-half year war. 23 victories placed him somewhere in the top fifteen of the entire ETO.

Yesterday, VE Day, had been an Historic Great Moment, and Hank regretted not having shared Victory in Europe with Winty. It would have been great to celebrate back at Thetford with the kids he'd led, visiting the wounded at Wimpole Park, and toasting the wonderful guys who failed to make it to the end.

Hank chose to remember only the good times he shared with Brax and hoped someone had contacted Wilma Lee. He'd left a long letter at the hospital for the nurses to read aloud when Brax was off medications and lucid.

Hank thought of Braham, more tormented than ever by what he saw in the death camps. How could they have known their interrogation assignment would carry them through concentration camps liberated by the 3rd Army? Things were worse and more incomprehensible than the most extreme reports they'd heard, more sickening than any newsreel, photograph, or reporter's description.

General Eisenhower was so appalled by the death camps, he cabled Washington and London to send journalists and members of their governments to view and record in detail all evidence of Nazi inhumanity. Patton was said to have vomited at his initial exposure to the camps.

No one must ever doubt such unthinkable acts had indeed taken place. Hank and Braham saw warehouses filled with neatly arranged bins containing spectacles, dentures, clothing, bales of women's hair, and more depraved horrors: stacks of starved, unburied corpses; gruesome remains of sadistic medical experiments; bodies boiled for soap; evidence of tattooed skins used for lamp shades; and the tortured, emaciated survivors unable to move, staring with hollow eyes into hell. One bin stuffed with thousands of pairs of baby shoes intensified the GIs' cold hatred toward the Nazis.

After their walk through the camps, Braham was no longer fit to deal with any German and had to be restrained from tearing apart the first SS man he saw. Hank told Seth to seek the princess and then report to Kilrain in London.

Hank lit a cigar and turned to his driver, Private Will Johnson, a leathery, tobacco-chomping combat veteran from Oklahoma whose lighter patches on his sleeves informed the observer he had been busted in rank more than a few times. "It won't be long before we reach Pisek."

"Piss-ek. With a name like that, it's got to be a hole, sir."

The quality of life in a sleepy Bohemian town was of no concern to Hank, who worried about potential ramifications of this 3rd Army incursion into Czech territory. The USSR had been chosen as the official liberator of the central European nation, another questionable decision on the part of the Allies at Yalta, and he suspected this foray by Patton's forces was intentional.

Hank was well informed about Patton's views regarding the USSR. Was the anti-communist general trying to provoke an incident that could lead to a war between the USA and the Soviet Union?

"Sir, will you look at that?"

Johnson swerved off the road when the tanks and vehicles ahead of them halted. Hank ordered him to drive the jeep parallel with the U.S. column until they reached Stevenson's command car.

Hank sat alert. The two point tanks of their convoy faced a long procession of several thousand German soldiers and civilians, some of whom raised white flags in a gesture of surrender. Interspersed among them were staff cars and military jeep-type vehicles. The second U.S. tank and Stevenson's staff car wheeled to the left onto a two-acre field of yellow mustard alongside the road to a position giving the colonel a clearer view of the Germans.

Other tanks chugged and whirred to the edges of the clearing much like the covered wagons of pioneer days taking up defensive positions. Officers shouted for all Germans to leave their vehicles, to drop their personal belongings along the road, and to move out into the field. Small groups of Czech civilians who dogged the column looted and ran off with the Germans' possessions under the benign gaze of the Americans.

Hank was surprised to see so many women and children. He left the jeep and moved ahead through the GIs toward the throng of Germans, who were grimy and dusty from their long journey. Some, however, appeared neat and military in blue uniforms or fur-collared leather jackets. A few wore leather overcoats. Hot damn on a pogo stick, the men in uniform were Luftwaffe personnel. He'd have plenty of work over the next few days.

Hank joined Lt. Colonel Hiram Stevenson, the stocky task force commander in charge of the foray into

Czechoslovakia. Stevenson was typical of Patton's officers, ramrod stiff and immaculate in tanker uniform. Three Luftwaffe officers approached with white flags. Hank heard one of them identify their unit as JG-52.

If the stories of that Jagdgeschwader's fantastic records were true, his interrogations would provide a treasure trove of data. According to some of the more talkative German POWs he'd encountered during the past two and a half weeks, JG-52 had brought down over 10,000 Soviet aircraft. At least two of their aces had surpassed 300 victories, and one of their pilots had shot down eight RAF Lancasters in seventeen minutes while serving on the Western Front in night fighters. Gloryosky, Sandy, and they were all here for him to interrogate.

The Luftwaffe Lt. Colonel, a hatchet-faced little man with a Roman nose and straight black hair, introduced himself as Oberstleutnant Hermann Graf, Kommodore of JG-52. Graf was one of the Luftwaffe's most decorated aces and the first man in history to score 200 aerial victories. The boyish blond Major to Graf's right, Erich Hartmann, had led I Gruppe and was one of the two fighter aces reputed to have more than 300 kills. *Son-of-a-B, Graf and Hartmann both here.* The third officer, Major Hartmann Grasser, Kommodore of JG-210, had over 100 kills.

Graf said the Gruppe had destroyed their remaining aircraft and all military materiel and supplies before moving out to surrender to the Americans. He concluded with a request that their women and children be treated with respect and kindness. Several American officers, who remembered the concentration camps they liberated, commented among themselves about the degree to which the Germans had massacred, tortured, and brutalized populations of conquered countries throughout Europe during the past six years.

Many of the ground troops who'd seen the death camps had become downright murderous toward all Germans. During the past weeks, many received reprimands for breaking rules of military conduct. The United States had not been bombed, or conquered by the enemy, nor had it suffered reprisals and atrocities committed against prisoners, non-combatant civilians, women and children on its soil, as had happened to all of Europe.

That brought home to Hank one more time how remote and impersonal the air war had been for the fighter pilots. He might have retained many more illusions if he hadn't served a second tour in the ETO and seen firsthand the concentration camps, casualties from heavy fighting on the ground, and targets leveled by bombers and ripped apart by fighter strafing runs.

Stevenson scanned the large number of non-combatants. "Why are so many women and children with you?"

Graf struggled to explain that the civilians had fled ahead of the Red Army. Another Luftwaffe officer, whose English was better, stepped forward. "Sir, the women have come to us for protection, and they have been cooking for us. They are not combatants. We beg you to treat them as civilians."

It was obvious to Hank that Stevenson wished he could find a page in the good old U.S. Army Manual to tell him how to handle this unusual situation. Hank noticed the reactions of GIs to the more attractive German women and girls. Stevenson also saw their ogling and ordered all tank officers to instruct the men no one was to touch or fraternize with any female. Rape and pillage might be normal Soviet tactics after battle, but such breaches of civilized behavior were not tolerated in the 3rd Army under Patton's command.

Groups of GIs went to the Luftwaffe vehicles and personnel to "liberate" souvenirs: medals, compasses, and wristwatches. Hank collected their logbooks. He believed they would tolerate anything if their women and children were not abused.

Hank focused on a major standing apart from the rest with a petite grease-smeared young woman in an oversized leather overcoat. The blond officer in Luftwaffe blue was slight of build with handsome features marked by a dueling scar. Hank recognized the officer from the photo Braham gave him.

*Me*-109 *number 23. Spritz. Prinz Karl.*

In an ironic twist of fate, they were to meet face-to-face at last, not in fighters one more time as equals in combat, but on the ground as victor and vanquished.

***

A JG-52 pilot took the major away from his woman and introduced him to Stevenson and the other American officers. Hank and Major Karl Fürst zu Pfalz von Teuffelreich stared at each other eyeball-to-eyeball. Neither blinked. That was the way it had been in combat too.

Somewhat relieved and relaxed after introductions in the tranquil clearing on a redolent, fresh May afternoon, the Luftwaffe officers closest to Hank expressed their surprise to find a flyer with the American Panzers. Hank listened to their conversations but watched the Prinz return to the young, appealing gamin. They stared back at him, almost as if in recognition.

*Sunuvagun! Maybe the prince knows his wife rescued an American and wonders if I'm the one.*

Hank heard a Luftwaffe officer nearby say, "I wonder what this pilot did to be punished with serving in the infantry?" He walked over to answer.

"I am an interpreter-interrogator. We shall be having many conversations over the next few days."

"It is obvious why you were selected, Herr Oberst. Your German is excellent."

Another peered at Hank's chest full of ribbons and said to a comrade, "This American must be good. He is undoubtedly a fighter pilot."

Hank told the German he was correct and offered him and his comrades a pack of cigarettes. Their manner toward Hank became guard-down, but each time one of the tank officers approached, they tensed and broke off conversation in mid-sentence.

Stevenson walked over to Hank. "Milroy, you're attracting these guys like flies. They seem to be wary of us ground-pounders, so you stick close and herd them along. Okay?"

"My pleasure, sir."

Stevenson informed Graf the Luftwaffe officers could retain their side arms and be responsible for maintaining order. In response to an oft-asked question, the colonel promised under no circumstances would he hand over any of them to the Soviets, which reduced much of the tension. He then gestured to the west. "Colonel Graf, we need to put some distance between ourselves and the Red Army."

The Germans returned to their vehicles and what was left of their belongings. Several tanks formed the rear guard, two more went ahead to the point, and the mile-long procession moved out. Hank watched the prisoners for any display of Nazi overtones in their behavior. The Luftwaffe men and officers did not use a raised Heil Hitler salute.

Instead, they touched their right eyebrow with the right hand, similar to a casual USAAF salute.

Then Hank chided himself for being naive. Hitler was dead. They had lost the war. Surely, out of practical necessity they would have eliminated anything suggesting Nazism. Still, he could not resist asking the nearest Luftwaffe officer, "Was your air force exempt from the Hitler salute?"

"Not always. The men at the front reserved such crap for visits from Party dignitaries. In a combat area, who has time for such foolishness?"

Hank sat two senior JG-52 officers in the back of his jeep. Colonel Stevenson and his staff settled in a command car. Karl refused a ride. He took Elfi's arm and joined the ranks of those trudging behind.

By the time they had driven less than a mile, the Germans and Hank chatted as fellow professionals. After he told them he had 23 victories, they demonstrated an easier camaraderie and trust. They were surprised most American pilots were removed from combat after flying fifty missions. Many of the Germans flew over a thousand. Erich Hartmann had scored 352 kills during 1,405 sorties, which included 850 combat encounters.

The pilots went on to compare the capabilities and quality of fighters they had flown, their hairy combat experiences, and some amusing ones too. Hank and the Germans shared a mutual revulsion at having to strafe defenseless targets. Should he believe them? Why not? He also found their precise choice of words interesting. The Luftwaffe pilots referred to the Americans and British as opponents and the Soviets as enemies.

The conversation turned to the sad situation of a fine flyer like Hank being cemented to a tank unit. One officer persisted in getting at the truth. "Tell us, Herr Oberst. What did you really do? Land in the garden of some general's wife?"

Hank had a hunch he could level the last walls of distrust if he assumed the role of a randy rogue, a vital element of the international fighter ace mystique. He embellished one of Brax's affairs with a CO's wife as if it had been his own, which was what the Germans expected to hear. He went on to describe the encounter with the Soviet Yaks as the final straw in his fictional demise. The Germans appreciated the irony of allies mixing it up in the air.

When the column stopped for a piss-break, Hank heard Colonel Stevenson laughing aloud in the command car. "Just look at them. If you tied the arms of a fighter pilot to his side, he'd be unable to speak."

Hank couldn't argue with Stevenson's assessment. When he compared air combat stories with the Germans, all flailed their arms and hands to illustrate each tactic.

Stevenson could not resist another jibe. "If you fly boys would talk all at once with your hands waving in the air, I'd bet the goddam jeep would take-off."

# Chapter 48

## Impatient Patient

Brax awakened with a start to bandaged darkness in the hospital ward and reached for his crotch to make sure no vital parts had been removed while he slept. Two balls and a pecker attached where they'd always been. He counted them twice to be sure. But all was not the same. That bandage around Brax's flange reminded him he'd been circumcised.

Kee-ryst, he'd become a cuffy, a clipped-dick, just like a Jew-baby. Why the hell had *that* operation been necessary? He hadn't been injured down there. Brax had overheard some of the staff joke about the pilot's new look in the South, but the physicians had promised he'd enjoy women the same as before. It might be true, but Brax hadn't felt his loins stir from the moment he regained consciousness after the first surgery. Not that it mattered. To judge the age of the nurses from their voices, Wimpole Park had to be hosting an old biddy convention. Where had all those beauties gone, the ones he'd pranged last New Year's Eve?

Brax felt as if he had been mummified for eternity. Hospitalized March 19th and kept in darkness throughout the month of April and into May, Brax was aware the bandages covered more than the severe burns he'd suffered. Parts of his body had been sacrificed for necessary skin grafting.

Any day now, the unveiling was to take place, but what if he'd been blinded for life? Lying still with too much time to think, Brax struggled to keep from feeling sorry for himself. He had a modest victory total frozen forever at 15 overall, well below Bong in the Pacific and Gabreski and Johnson in the ETO. Less than Hank, too.

Brax broke into a sweat whenever he imagined what he must look like under these bandages. He'd been told not to expect miracles overnight. First the burns and grafting needed to heal. Then after his recovery progressed, he could have reconstructive surgery. Brax kissed goodbye any chance at a career in films.

Forced to be introspective for the first time in his life, with reflection came some regrets. Had he been loyal to Wilma Lee, she'd be here at his side during the coming difficult days, along with pretty little M'liss to give solace.

Whenever Brax's bleak moods evaporated, he fantasized about the future with his streamlined joystick and hoped some of the younger nurses might appear and be available for a test run. Hell's bells, he couldn't even cadge a drink out of the puritanical staff, and right now he wanted booze more than a woman.

The arrival of several doctors and nurses interrupted Brax's reveries. His personal D-Day had arrived. He sat on the edge of the bed and recognized the smug voice belonging to Dr. Walter Sanford, chief reconstructive surgeon at Wimpole Park Hospital. Sanford had begun the repairs on Brax's face, and he reviewed for physicians and nurses the pilot's condition when he first arrived at the hospital and the grafting techniques he'd applied since.

Sanford patted Brax's shoulder. "They tell me you were panic stricken that we'd turned you into a soprano. I know you've been anxious and curious. Can't say I blame you. Your face was badly burned, melted would be a better word. But you were fortunate. We saved your eyesight, but you lost most of your eyelids. Not to worry, the English made a novel discovery. Who would have thought the foreskin of a penis makes the best grafting material for lost or damaged eyelids? So, you didn't lose your foreskin. We just put it somewhere else. Do not be surprised if from now on your eyes bulge during moments of sexual excitement."

Brax heard snickers and fumed. Sanford cut tape and unwound gauze from Brax's head and face. "You may open your eyes now."

Brax squinted at the bright light, his eyelids tight. Everything was blurred at first. Brax focused and relaxed. He could see perfectly out of both eyes! He surveyed the small gathering. The surgeon, who looked familiar, accepted congratulations from colleagues and nurses.

"No, Mobley, do not touch your face. We have a mirror. Mobley, I worked wonders on you, if I say so myself. You'll see the before-photos later. We took them between operations, so you'll be able to appreciate how far we've come. If you were to call me a Michelangelo, it would not be too much flattery."

Brax couldn't be certain of anything until he saw his reflection. "Give me that mirror."

The surgeon held a photo of Brax taken before the accident. he glanced at it, then spoke softly. "You were a handsome devil. Bet you had all the women you wanted. Like my lady last New Year's Eve, Captain Patricia Lindsay. Remember? Unfortunately, you won't resemble your old self. While we do deal in miracles, we cannot accomplish the impossible."

Brax snatched the mirror from the nurse standing next to him. he stared. He didn't recognize the grotesque monster in the glass. But it was his face. Each tentative probe by Brax's fingers confirmed it. He felt like vomiting at the sight of that torn mouth, lack of nose cartilage, discolored swollen eyes, deep scars, the stitches, the gaps, the bald spots.

"We can understand your disappointment, Mobley. Perhaps my enthusiasm raised your hopes. But think, man. You are alive, physically whole, and you can see. Yes, from a professional point of view, you've had a damn fine piece of patching."

"What happens to me next?"

"Plastic surgery after your face has healed."

"But you're not sending me out there looking like this?"

"Surely, you do want to get out of here."

"Damn right I do, but can't y'all make me look normal first and not like some Frankenstein patchwork monster?"

The surgeon removed his spectacles and wiped them. "Mobley, you do not seem to appreciate what we do here. Our job is saving lives, repairing bodies. We do not perform Park Avenue paint jobs."

Hit full-force with the horrifying reality his good looks were gone forever, Brax panicked. No beautiful girls flocking to him anymore. No longer handsome, he would be forever hideous, a monster to be shunned.

*Better to have died in that fiery crash.*

A primal roar, and Brax unloaded a haymaker to Sanford's face.

# Chapter 49

## Out of the Darkness

A typical Bohemian town on the Otava River dominated by church spires with medieval and nineteenth century edifices, Pisek was a major railroad nexus with an estimated population of fifteen thousand, according to one of the officers walking with Karl and Elfi. U.S. and local Czech authorities herded the several thousand men, women, and children of JG-52 into a large pasture outside Pisek near the farm village of Schüttenhofen. The field was surrounded by trees and enclosed by chicken wire. The new arrivals joined thousands more civilian refugees and soldiers from other disbanded units who'd arrived ahead of them.

Stevenson's tanks and armored vehicles took positions around the perimeter to maintain order and to prevent prisoners from escaping. Graf told his officers that more than thirty thousand people had been packed into an eight-acre field.

Karl scanned the entire enclosure. An impossible situation. Dazed and haggard, officers and men no longer stood stiff and proud in their uniforms, Karl included. He could no longer sustain an aloof dapper façade. Karl lacked energy and suffered from diarrhea. Caste no longer mattered, but with rank came the authority to maintain order.

Despite the grim conditions, everyone in JG-52 agreed the Americans were certain to be more humane than the Soviets. Many officers and NCOs wanted to believe some of the soldiers guarding them might be of German descent and would feel a tribal affinity.

Karl suspected the main reason for American kindness was the failure of the Luftwaffe to develop an Amerika bomber to fly across the Atlantic and devastate their cities and infrastructure. How chivalrous would these Yanks be if their country had been blitzed like England, or ravaged by the SS and Gestapo?

Karl saw a small stream winding through the pasture. A serious sanitation problem loomed if so many people continued to inhabit the area. They were fortunate the war had not ended in the middle of winter.

With Elfi at his side, Karl toured the section of pasture allotted for JG-52 and looked for a secure, comfortable place where they could settle. Those who arrived earlier occupied the best sites, the same as at a public beach on a hot summer day.

Several POWs claimed to have heard the Yanks encourage elderly civilians, women, and children to walk to the west. No one would stop them if they left in small groups and not too openly.

At first skeptical, Karl soon noticed women and children straggle out of the compound and head toward the German border eighty kilometers away to the west. Some of the Yanks assisted the escapees with maps and meager handouts of chocolate and GI rations. Being responsible for thousands of civilians was an impossible assignment for combat-trained men to carry out well. The guards figured the refugees would be better off foraging for themselves and finding their way home than facing malnourishment at Pisek where food was scarce.

Karl urged Elfi to walk away. "My little elf, we are not yet out of danger. The Russians are too close, and we officers must face an interrogation from that American pilot. We shall be separated eventually because I am likely to be sent to a prisoner of war camp."

"Then I shall stay with you until the last moment."

Karl saw a family moving out from a thick mound of grass near the stream, and he claimed the choice location. He made sure Elfi was warm in his leather overcoat. He worried she had lost too much weight and might be vulnerable to illness.

The roar of P-51s zooming above the trees in the twilight interrupted Karl's thoughts. Those Indianern had been tough opponents and played havoc with the jets. He wished them well and envied all lucky pilots still free to fly close to the sun or soar among the stars.

A JG-52 officer approached Karl. "Fürst, come join us. Some American guards who are tired of their processed meat ... Spam they call it ... have given us six tins of the stuff, some coffee, also a few bars of chocolate. One of them handed over a complete package of food he received from home, food like we have not seen in months."

Karl wanted a share of that treasure for Elfi and joined the other officers. A small fire browned the Spam. The aroma of cooked food wafted downwind, and all in its wake stared at their leaders who had been favored by the Americans.

Without speaking a word, the officers beckoned other individuals from JG-52 to join them and apportioned a small amount of food, chocolate, and coffee to each. Karl was surprised at how far the rations went. He returned to Elfi with some cooked Spam, a bite-size section of a Hershey bar, and genuine coffee, which they appreciated most of all.

Karl could not recall the last time a German could purchase anything except ersatz coffee. Elfi did not smoke, and he enjoyed by himself half an American cigarette from a pack divided by the officers.

After Elfi fell asleep, Karl unsnapped the holster guard on his pistol scabbard and removed the Luger. The Americans might yet betray them and hand everyone over to the Soviets. After all, they had the word of only a colonel. If the generals and politicians were of a different mind, now was a last best-moment to choose a proper death.

Karl looked at Elfi, so beautiful in the moonlight. No. Impossible. He returned his pistol to the holster and snapped it shut. Overwhelmed with love, he crushed Elfi to his chest.

That night Karl and Elfi clung to each other in the damp pasture. They heard others stealing away from the enclosure to begin the long, uncertain trek back to Germany. Those who knew the Czech language or had the instinct to forage for themselves would have no difficulty and could treat it like another hiking trip in the country. Most were certain to reach sanctuary and never spend another day in a prison camp.

Elfi refused to leave without Karl, and like the other JG-52 officers he could never disguise himself as a civilian and desert his comrades.

***

That same night, Hank was billeted at a comfortable inn that served as Stevenson's headquarters. He drank from a liter bottle of delicious Czech beer. Hank would have sold his soul for a moment with Winty. He thought of Karl in the pasture with the appealing little brunette who adored him. He envied the prince's good fortune in adversity.

Hank raised the bottle. "To your health, Prinz Karl, and to you, Seth Braham. May you find the princess alive and well and soon be with your singer." He drank again and wished Brax a speedy recovery at Fitzsimmons.

***

A plane flew above Fitzsimmons Hospital in Denver, and Brax identified it as a P-51, an ever-lovin' Mustang like the one he'd flown in the ETO. Suddenly, he was seized with an irresistible longing to jump back into the cockpit and soar above the clouds again. Brax conceded he'd taken flying for granted ever since he enrolled as a cadet back at Randolph. It had been a means to several ends: to escape poverty and Wilma Lee, to use his officer's pinks and acedom to get laid, and to rack up high victory totals with plenty of publicity for a movie career.

Brax yearned to be airborne again with a kraut fighter in his gun sight. He vowed to get back in the saddle the day he was discharged from the hospital, but first he'd have to thank Hank and Braham. He didn't remember, but everyone said they'd saved his ass.

Brax started at a noise. Someone opened the door and turned on the light. Brax tensed. Had those goddam hospital authorities let someone visit when they knew he wanted to be left alone? With a face melted beyond recognition, further distorted by patches of skin grafts, new stitches not yet removed, burned forehead, and shaved hairline, Brax didn't want to deal with the disgust that people, including the professional staff, expressed upon seeing him for the first time. Who in the hell was stupid enough visit anyway? The guys he'd flown with would respect his privacy.

"Goddammit. Turn off the light, get the hell out of here, and shut the friggin' door." The intruder switched off the light, and the room returned to secure darkness. "Stay where you are. Don't y'all come near, you hear?"

Brax's heartbeat accelerated when he smelled a woman's perfume. He tried to guess which one she might be. Impossible. He'd burned bridges with each broad he'd bedded. They had been same as aerial victories, like the "Four Fs"—Find 'em, Feed 'em, Fuck 'em, and Forget 'em.

Or had someone come to gloat? Impossible. The staff shrinks would never allow it. "Who are you?"

The answer came to him.

"Wilma Lee?"

"Brax."

"Wilma Lee, what the hell are y'all doing here?"

Her voice trembled. "Hank Milroy's parents found me. They said you were here at Fitzsimmons, that you'd been …."

"Never mind all that. Why did you come? We were finished a long time ago."

"No, Brax. Never finished."

"You told Hank you'd married again."

"No, I've never married anyone but you."

Brax had believed he lost his daughter and Wilma Lee forever. "Where's M'liss now? Did you bring her?"

"No, she's working in Hollywood. She's a successful child actress. We'll have to be careful how we break the news to her you're alive."

"Sure, we don't want to upset M'liss."

Wilma Lee moved closer behind Brax.

"Honey, I can't explain it. I don't know why. I've always loved you, despite all those terrible things you did to me and M'liss. You thought I was a pushover on our first date, but every woman is easy for the man she loves. I want us to be family again, a real family this time. I'm the best possible woman for you. I think you know that. I want to take care of you. You need me. I can't leave you alone now."

"Wilma Lee, my face is destroyed. For good. I've lost the looks you used to admire. I'm a monster. How would we live? I can't support a family. Who'd ever hire someone with my face for any job? Certainly not the Army Air Force."

"Brax, I spoke to your doctors. I've seen your pictures."

"Jesus, no, you ...."

"And they've assured me there's nothing wrong with your mind and body. The doctors also say your nose, ears, and jaw are functioning perfectly, and you can have a military flying career. Everyone wants you to stay in the Air Force. They all say you're one of the best combat flyers ever and a true war hero. And I have the honor and pleasure of being the first to tell you. You've been promoted to Major."

When Wilma Lee touched Brax's shoulders, he didn't protest. She kissed each wound and scar. Brax trembled but managed to hold back tears.

"I love you, Major Mobley, suh, and I will never let you go."

Brax didn't speak for a long time. He reached for Wilma Lee's hand. *Ay, Chihuahua.* He felt a familiar stirring down south for the first time since the fiery crash. Wilma Lee was going to have one big surprise when she got a look at his new cuff.

# Chapter 50

## 23 Spritz at Last

Hank was unable to begin the interrogations because more German soldiers and civilians fleeing the Red Army surrendered to the Americans, and the population of the compound now surpassed fifty thousand. All U.S. officers were needed to organize the newcomers into a functional mass. Not until their third day at Pisek was he able to question the JG-52 pilots by rank and seniority, which delayed his meeting with Karl.

In a tent outside the compound, Hank interrogated aces who had victories in the hundreds, all confirmed by the Gruppe's log books. Sometimes they pled Geneva Convention rules and declined to answer certain questions, otherwise chatting with them was no different than shooting the bull with the boys in the 375th.

Many were so like the guys he'd flown with and led, Hank had to remind himself these same Germans had served Adolf Hitler. He had no delusions he'd established anything but a fragile, unreal affinity that would be shattered if he attempted to press them about their views on the political and racial policies of the Third Reich. That was a job for the Intelligence boys anyway. Most of the pilots had been in the Hitler Youth, and some must have been Nazi fanatics.

Face-to-face at last with number 23 when Karl's turn came, he offered the prince a cigar. What sort of man was he? Hank's history professors called these titled types lounge lizards, a separate breed who'd owned the world for too damn long without contributing anything. He found the prince to be aloof. The pilots in JG-52 had not become close to the prince, but all respected his flying and shooting skills. That much Hank learned from earlier interrogations. JG-52's records gave a clear picture of the aristocrat's impressive career. Karl was one of the best with at least 230, perhaps closer to 250 victories, in over 800 missions.

***

Karl luxuriated in the taste and aroma of rich Cuban tobacco, which made him lightheaded because he was undernourished. He would not, however, allow long-denied sensual pleasures to lower his guard. These Yanks were unpredictable, in many ways like the Soviets, but without their Slavic brutality.

Karl regretted he and the other JG-52 officers had failed to remove all evidence of identity, rank, and awards. There was always a possibility the Americans might go along with the announced Soviet policy of rendering the German officer corps extinct. And what about this Colonel Milroy? Perhaps they had met and passed each other during combat. The skies were so vast. The skies. Karl's heart ached because he was rooted to the ground.

***

Hank began the interrogation, and as he anticipated, Karl answered all technical questions except those regarding the details of jet airplanes. Like most of the other Luftwaffe officers, the prince was no engineer, and his ignorance appeared genuine.

"You also saw combat with JG-26 and JV-44."

"Yes."

"Late 1943, you flew Me-109 number 23." Karl did not respond. "You holed my P-38 and saw I was out of ammo. You waved off the other Luftwaffe fighters and escorted me out of the combat zone."

"So it was you. I cannot explain what came over me."

"I believe I can. You emulated your father. He chose not to shoot down an American pilot who was out of ammo on the last day of the First World War."

"How did you learn that?"

"That pilot was my instructor and is now Major General Leo Kilrain of 8th Air Force. I think I saw you one more time last New Year's Day over Belgium."

"And your intelligence boys identified me and my father for you? Bloody good work on their part."

"Not exactly." Hank noted Karl's British accent. "A friend of mine was shot down over Eppelborn."

"It is a pleasant town."

"He was a guest of your wife, and she helped him escape. He brought back a photo of you and your Me-109 Number 23 with the wine bottle logo."

"I am aware of the incident. I suppose he survived the war."

"Yes, and ...."

"Is there anything else related to my flying you wish to ask? If not, I would prefer to return to the people for whom I am responsible."

Karl's wife must have told him what she had done for Braham, and the prince thought they might have been lovers. Even if they had, why should it matter if Karl loved his little brunette?

***

Seth's driver took him in a jeep through rolling green hills, lush pastures, and dense forests by the Speyer River to Bad Dürkheim, which had been untouched by the war except for the presence of large numbers of occupation troops and vehicles. Undamaged homes and buildings stood in stark contrast with devastated Mannheim and Ludwigshafen on the Rhine River thirty-five klicks to the east. A few kilometers more to the west lay the smaller hamlet of Frankenstein. Was it identical to that village in the Boris Karloff classic?

Seth heard rumors Eisenhower was planning to move SHAEF headquarters from Frankfurt to Bad Dürkheim. Not too shabby a selection, considering its estates, a sparkling wine bottling factory, a restaurant built inside a 1,700,000 liter wine barrel, and a hotel-casino.

Several kilometers past the town, a narrow winding road led to grim, grey Schloss Teuffelreich. If the pristine condition of Bad Dürkheim in the middle of the battle-devastated Pfalzland seemed miraculous, Seth was more astonished at what both German civilians and GIs said when he asked for directions to the Schloss. It had become a children's hospital, and everyone praised its princess for her humanitarian work. There was more.

Throughout the Pfalzland, Germans and Americans praised Mariya-Xenia for convincing a Wehrmacht regiment to surrender instead of fighting to the last man, which spared the local communities destruction. After that, she confronted some U.S. brass and requested they use their trucks to transport more wounded and ill children from the concentration camps. Mariya-Xenia persuaded General Bradley himself to give the hospital medicines, especially the miracle drug penicillin, and to transfer an Army medical unit to the Schloss to help save additional lives. The princess also assisted in operations at the understaffed surgery and functioned as a liaison between Pfalzland Bürgomeisters and the Americans.

If all Seth heard were true, Mariya-Xenia would not need his help. He'd stay for a short while, thank the princess, and hurry to England. Perhaps by now Miriam and her band had arrived in the ETO.

Ambulances and deuce-and-a-half-ton trucks filled with wretched undernourished and wounded children needing medical attention jammed the narrow road. Seth told his driver to park the jeep on a soft shoulder behind them and wait for him. He walked the last kilometer toward the castle's deranged façade, annexes and wings, a mix of German baroque and neo-gothic added to its original medieval tower and walls.

Inside, the Schloss reeked of hospital disinfectant. Nurses and orderlies scurried in all directions and elderly Putzfrauen washed floors and walls. Army medics and hospital personnel wheeled or carried weak and injured children into the hospital. Off to the left of the main entrance a spacious ballroom served as an administrative office staffed with German civilian and GI clerks.

Seth approached a sergeant who called everyone to attention, rose, and saluted. "Can I help you, Colonel?"

"I want to speak with the Fürsten Pfalz-Teuffelreich."

"Yes, sir."

Seth followed the NCO to another wing on the main floor and into a library where Mariya-Xenia in hospital whites smoked, issued commands to nurses and orderlies, and wrote at her desk. A golden Byzantine cross hung from her neck.

After the last of the hospital staff left, Maria-Xenia removed her spectacles. "Seth?"

"I promised I'd seek you after the war ended."

A white German shepherd at Mariya-Xenia's side growled at Seth. She spoke in German to calm it. "Elsa is Prinz Karl's dog. Now she is my protector. Let me take a good look at you. Your eyes, so old and haunted. What have you seen?"

"Hell on Earth. Dresden from above, the death camps on the ground."

"So have we all." Mariya-Xenia led Seth to the window. Outside on a vast expanse of lawn, he saw unsmiling listless bandaged children on crutches or in wheelchairs accompanied by nurses and orderlies. "You will see similar horrors here as well, the unspeakable atrocities those monsters did to these innocents."

"I saw bins of toys and shoes in the camps, and mangled, skeletal bodies."

"At least we can help the survivors. Please, sit."

"Everyone tells me you're responsible for saving many lives."

Mariya-Xenia chain-lit a cigarette. "I do what I can."

"How did you get involved in hospital work?"

"The bombing raids created so many wounded boys and girls, babies too. The Lord spoke to me and said I must turn the Schloss into a children's hospital."

"I came here to thank you for all you did and to offer my help if you were having difficulties, but it seems you do not need it."

"There is one thing you can do for me." Mariya-Xenia shuffled some papers and handed Seth several forms. "Will you swear I helped you to escape?"

"Of course."

"The occupying powers have begun a process called denazification. As you may know, they need qualified Germans to help reconstruct their country, preferably individuals who resisted the Nazis and survived the camps, or protected a Jew here and there. Germans who shall be assuming positions of authority must answer in writing one hundred and thirty-three questions to determine their degree of collaboration with the Nazi regime. The answers place us into one of three color-coded groups: black, grey or white, with intermediate shades for further clarity. I need not tell you what the colors represent."

Seth wrote how Maria-Xenia facilitated his escape, her work with the anti-Nazi element in the Abwehr, and emphasized how she made the Pfalz-Teuffelreich manor in Eppelborn a safe house for Allied airmen and fugitives from the Gestapo. He also described what he knew of von Strachwitz's role as an anti-Nazi.

Mariya-Xenia buzzed her intercom and asked for two witnesses. In front of the sergeant and another NCO, Seth signed his name adding rank, serial number, and unit.

Mariya-Xenia read what he wrote. "Thank you, Seth, this will expedite matters for me. And for von Strachwitz too. It was kind of you to mention Bruno."

"Have you heard from him?"

"Bruno survived and hopes to serve the new Germany, whatever it shall be, as a diplomat."

"What happened to that SS uncle of your husband?"

"He deserted the sinking Nazi ship and most likely fled to South America. Argentina, Paraguay, and Brazil are said to be receptive to such criminals if they bring enough gold."

Seth speculated how satisfying it might be to hunt Nazis after the war. "It's a wicked world."

"We must always try to make our small corner better."

"You already have."

"Not enough. I may be able to help heal some and reunite a fortunate few with their families, but so many are orphans. I wish I knew how best to place them in decent homes."

A German nurse-matron entered. "Your Highness, more trucks filled with children from the camps have arrived. We need you in surgery."

Mariya-Xenia walked with Seth to the corridor. "I have hesitated to ask, but have you heard anything of Prinz Karl?"

"No."

"If Karl is still alive, I hope he is not a prisoner of the Soviets."

***

After a week of confinement in the pasture, the POWs learned they were to march the following day to Regensburg, two hundred and twenty kilometers away. The long journey would be difficult, but the Americans promised vehicles for the sick, the lame, and small children. From Pisek to Regensburg, the captives had to pass through the hostile Czech villages of Strakonice, Klatovy, and Domazliece before they reached the friendly Bavarian towns of Furth and Cham.

Their last night in the enclosed pasture, the Germans busied themselves repairing shoes and garments and packing what little they had left to carry. The children were playful, as if going on vacation or a new adventure. Two armed American enlisted men approached Karl and Elfi with orders to escort them to Colonel Milroy. They did not say why.

Inside Milroy's interrogation tent, Karl shielded Elfi. "Colonel, why have you summoned us?"

"Major, I shall be asking the questions. You will answer them." Hank softened his tone. For your own good, I suggest you rid yourself of that imperious tone and manner. Being a Fürst counts for nothing with me."

Karl did not take umbrage at Milroy's rebuke. The American had spoken the truth.

"Now Major, I wish to speak with your lady." Hank switched to German and beckoned Elfi to approach his desk. "Your name."

She looked at Karl, who nodded for her to answer. "Frau Elfriede Wohlmann."

Hank wrote her name on a form and signed it. "Does she understand English, Major?"

"No."

"Good. Then let us not alarm her." Hank gave Elfi two tins of Spam and a chocolate bar. Karl encouraged her to eat.

Hank stood and took Karl outside the tent. "Major, you ought to know that I am fluent in Russian."

Karl understood Milroy's meaning and winced at a sharp pain. *That damn ulcer.* "But are we not leaving for Regensburg tomorrow?"

"As orders stand, yes, but Frau Wohlmann must leave now. I cannot repay the pilot of Number 23 Spritz in kind for escorting me from the combat zone when I was out of ammo. This is the best I can do for you under the circumstances."

"I must think about it."

"Think? Do you believe you'd be able to protect your lady if the worst happens?"

"No."

"A truck leaves for Regensburg within the half hour. There is room for Frau Wohlmann. If nothing exceptional happens tomorrow, you all shall reach Regensburg as planned. Of course, you will be sent to a POW camp."

They went back inside the tent, and Karl took Elfi's hand. "You will leave tonight."

"With you?"

"No, it cannot be."

"Karl, I will not be separated from you again."

He took hold of Elfi's frail shoulders. "You must do as I say. You will be safer in Germany under the protection of this American Colonel." Karl put a finger on Elfi's lips to stifle any protest. "If you stay here and the worst happens, I will not be able to protect you."

Elfie gazed deep into his eyes. At last she spoke. "Very well. If you insist, then I must go."

Back inside the tent, Karl asked for pen and paper. He sat at Hank's desk, and said as he wrote, "Elfi, if we are still separated after you reach Regensburg, go to Schloss Teuffelreich at Bad Dürkheim. It is being used as a children's hospital. This letter introduces you as a qualified nurse and guarantees instant employment for you. This second letter, which I shall seal, you must deliver to Mariya-Xenia. Colonel Milroy, will you please witness and sign these letters?"

Hank read them. One was a character reference for Elfi as a nurse and said that Karl had hired her. The other contained instructions for the Prinzessen to divorce Karl at the most propitious time.

After Hank signed the documents, Elfi placed them in a pocket of her fatigues. "Karl, I will wait for you in Regensburg and at the Schloss. Forever, if necessary."

Karl and Elfi kissed goodbye before she climbed into the truck. Hank gave Karl a cigar and a light. The night was clear. Karl looked at the stars, lost in his Me-109, reliving aerial combat.

# Chapter 51

## Intolerable Orders

Hank interrupted Karl's musings. "Major, you must return to the POW compound."

Karl saluted, clicked his heels on reflex, and offered his hand. "Colonel Milroy, I thank you for arranging Frau Elfriede's departure."

Hank shook Karl's hand. "Noblesse oblige, Major."

Karl laughed aloud at Hank's reply and wry grin. "Touché."

Hank had trouble sleeping that night. The Reds were too close, and he would not be able to relax until they crossed into U.S. or British held German territory.

At daybreak Hank watched the prisoners form a column in the pasture for their long trek to Regensburg until he heard shouting. He hurried to a cluster of agitated officers.

"Jesus Christ, they'll be massacred!"

"What's the matter with SHAEF anyway?"

"Just too damned far away from the action to know what the hell's coming off."

"It's inhumane."

"If we go ahead with it, we're no better than the Nazis."

"And those chicken shits waited until General Patton was away from command headquarters."

Hank caught the eye of a fuming captain while Colonel Stevenson argued with a superior over the field radio. "What's going on?"

"SHAEF sent an order to General Patton that everyone ... repeat everyone ... Germans, White Russians, all native Eastern Europeans, men, women, children ... everyone who surrendered or came to us ... they must be turned over to the Soviets immediately."

Hank looked toward the teeming weary mass waiting to move out of the enclosed pasture. Sure, punish the Nazi leaders and their henchmen. Hang 'em high by the balls with piano wire. That was okay. Those sadists asked for it and more. But how could the United States be so stupid as to hand over to the Reds these skilled fighter aces, including some of the only experienced combat jet pilots in the world? There was so much to learn from them. Their rocket scientists too. And what about the civilians who fled to the Americans for protection? Who would trust the word of an American after this?

Frustrated and boiling mad, he was unable to get his bosses to change their mind, and Colonel Stevenson shut the field radio. Chewing on a cigar, he glared at the tank commanders and infantry officers. "Goddammit. Shut up. All of you. One does not argue against decisions made by one's superiors. An order is an order, and by God we will carry it out."

Stevenson assigned Hank to be the interpreter when they met the Reds at the exchange point. He next confronted his staff. "Now, you men go out there with the closed minds all military officers are supposed to have and follow your orders. After all, it isn't your asses."

The tank commanders saluted and dispersed to instruct the troops. No more joking and fraternizing with the krauts. Stop flirting with the Fräuleins. Ignore the children. Disarm their officers. All weapons must be at the ready.

They did not inform the Germans of the change in orders and moved them out to the south along a tree shaded road. Shortly out of Pisek, the GIs spotted a lone Soviet tank proceeding parallel with the column about a half mile to the east.

After scouts in the lead vehicles reported, Colonel Stevenson rode ahead, took one look at a threatening situation, and halted the column of American troops and prisoners. Two Soviet officers waited in the middle of a small stone bridge over a shallow stream. Beyond them on the other side lay a good twenty acres of rolling green fields surrounded by dozens of tanks and at least three thousand troops.

Stevenson conferred with his officers. He expressed concerns the Soviets might execute all the German officers and commit atrocities against the rest. Hank suggested they take the women and children to Regensburg anyway. Stevenson agreed to give it a try. He told the men to notify the ranking German officers of the situation and warn them to rid themselves of all evidence of rank and decorations, which encouraged violent reprisals from the Reds. Evidence of coming from a capitalist family also guaranteed a swift execution.

Stevenson took stock of the tactical situation. The Soviets had about one hundred tanks in the big corral across the bridge, the Americans eight Shermans.

Several squads of Red Army troops with automatic weapons at the ready moved on each side of the bridge to support their two officers. Hank heard them shout obscenities at the Germans. Some were roaring drunk.

Hank went with Stevenson to confer with the husky Soviet officers in the middle of the bridge. As instructed, he told the dour Reds that the Americans would hand over their POWs to them here and now but intended to escort all civilians to the Displaced Persons center at Regensburg.

The Soviets demanded that all German captives must be transferred to them. For a half hour, with Hank translating, Stevenson argued with the Soviets. There were moments when the Americans thought a big war might begin here and now on this anonymous bridge. Stevenson broke off the conference. He returned with Hank to his command vehicle and called headquarters on the field radio for clarification of orders.

"Sir, I don't like the look of things at all. There's about three thousand Ivans here, and they all have revenge on their minds. They look like animals, starved and caged animals. Am I to turn over to them all civilians or only the male POWs? Humanity demands we take the women and children with us to the Displaced Persons camp at Regensburg."

Hank heard the answer loud and clear over the field radio. "Stevenson, I have the orders right here in my own hands. They state we are to turn over all, repeat *all* German nationals who surrendered to us in Czechoslovakia to the proper Soviet authorities. The Reds will be in charge of repatriation for everyone concerned. I am informed this order originates with The Big Three themselves, and anyone who disobeys ends his career and jeopardizes Soviet-American relations Remember, we still need the Soviets with us against the Japs."

Stevenson shut off the R/T, cursed, and ordered his men to herd the caravan of German soldiers and civilians across the bridge. Hank tried to shut out their pleas and cries of anguish during what he knew to be a dreadful instance of crass disregard for common sense and human decency.

If it was a Big Three decision, he'd like to have dragged FDR from the grave and Truman from the White House to join Churchill and Stalin at the bridge. Let them witness the results of their decisions. This had to be another one of those rumored concessions cunning Stalin wrung from the dying Roosevelt at Yalta in February.

A Soviet officer shouted a command at the Americans, and Stevenson looked at Hank for a translation.

"They demand we return to Pisek pronto."

Stevenson's face purpled with rage. "Demand? Our goddam orders don't tell us to kiss commie asses. Inform those fuckin' Ivans that we are holding firm and proceeding to Regensburg. Don't play diplomat with them either, Milroy."

Hank enjoyed telling the Soviet officers to take their demands and shove 'em. One important fact he learned from his studies of Russian history, language, and psychology: they respected force and equated compromise with weakness. If you were strong, you took. If you were weak, you negotiated. Right now, the United States had to be looking pathetic and flabby.

Hank also remembered reading what Karl Marx wrote about the Russians almost a hundred years earlier: *The Russian Bear is certainly capable of anything as long as he knows the other animals he has to deal with are capable of nothing.*

Rowdy Soviet soldiers directed the column of dazed, hunger-weakened Germans across the bridge and stream.

Hank watched Karl disappear into the mass of prisoners as the Reds confiscated watches and rings. They separated the men from women and children, and pushed the more desirable females toward a separate ring of tanks.

Hank's driver was among the first to see it. "Jesus, Colonel, they're going to do it here and now."

After all the Germans were on the other side of the stream and the separation of the genders completed, what appeared to be a well-organized plan went into operation. One-third of the Soviet soldiers stood guard manning machine-guns on the tanks and command, and their comrades converged on the women's circle.

Through binoculars, Hank could see these Soviets were a seedy lot, most half-drunk, many of them Asiatics, Turkomen, Tartar, and Mongol, whose regions of the USSR had not been occupied and brutalized by the Nazis. Odds were they had not been fighting for communism or Holy Mother Russia, but for traditional rape and pillage.

A Soviet officer screamed in German, "Our leaders have issued a ukase. Rape all German women. Mothers of fascists. Daughters of fascists. Death to all who resist."

When he repeated it in Russian, the first horde of soldiers rushed into the women's pen. They pawed, tore off clothes, hit and kicked their victims. If a rapist didn't like what he saw after he stripped a woman, he went on to the next. Raging soldiers threw their hysterical victims to the ground, dropped their pants, and fell on their prostrate prey. Some of the women were knocked unconscious or fainted; most screamed while they resisted. The wailing of the German women mingled with feral roars of the Soviet soldiers and anguished cries of outraged fathers and husbands. The Soviets shot all who attempted to rescue their wives and daughters, After each soldier violated a woman, he moved on to another despoiled by his comrades. Several agile young women broke away from the pen and ran toward the stream. Guards caught and tossed them to their pursuers.

Four girls and a mature woman managed to crash through a group of drunken guards and run for their lives across the bridge to one of the American trucks as Colonel Stevenson ordered everyone to move out. The cheering GIs saw them coming, helped the females into a truck, and the driver accelerated full speed toward Regensburg.

The approach to the bridge had been left unguarded. All the Reds were either participating in the mass rape or viewing it as enjoyable spectator sport. Hank saw a small girl running from a soldier. The Russian caught the child at the foot of the bridge, tore away her dress, and threw her to the ground. The child was so young she had no pubic hair. Hank ordered Johnson to head the jeep across the bridge toward the soldier, and before the Russian could penetrate the girl, he jumped out and kicked the would-be rapist in the groin, upending him. Hank grabbed the terrified child and carried her into the jeep.

Johnson accelerated in the best dragster tradition and raced across the bridge. While they sped to catch up with the main column of Americans, Hank cradled the sobbing child and tried to ignore the sounds of the orgy and screams of death.

*What a crappy way for a fighter pilot to end the war.*

One release was available for Hank's anger and frustration. He cursed at his driver. Johnson cursed back.

# Chapter 52

## A Hollywood Ending?

Back in the UK, Seth reported early in the morning to 8th Air Force HQ at High Wycombe Abbey. After he handed Kilrain his notes from the interrogations and described all he saw on the Continent, the general spoke into the intercom. "Now, Lt. McCabe."

Winty entered carrying a folder. "Colonel, you couldn't have returned at a better time. We must leave now. I am driving you and General Kilrain to Wimpole Park Hospital. We should get there in plenty of time for you to link up with a certain lady."

"Miriam's here?"

"She'll be singing with the Mac Herlihy Band at the hospital and in the evening at Thetford."

Seth became so excited he had trouble finding his voice. "Then I'll want to fill out the necessary forms for permission to wed."

Winty handed Seth the folder. "They're all prepared except for a few details I couldn't answer and your signatures."

Seth kissed Winty's cheeks. "One from me and another from Hank."

***

During the two hour drive to Wimpole Park Hospital at Arrington, Seth read the mail accumulated during his time on the Continent. Dated a month earlier, Miriam wrote she would be somewhere in the ETO in May through early June, singing at bases and military hospitals with the Mac Herlihy Band. That letter and three others she wrote were filled with loving words and the hope they could wed.

More good news came in the mail. Seth's younger brother Alan, now twenty, had survived Tawara, Kwajalien, and Iwo Jima, where he received a Battlefield Commission to the rank of 2$^{nd}$ Lt. Seth hoped Alan's luck would continue on Okinawa where he was now leading a platoon with the 2$^{nd}$ Marine Division.

Letters from DeLuca and Mercutio also cheered Seth. The Paisan and Carla planned to marry at the end of August, and Mercutio asked him to be best man.

***

On the lawn in front of the Wimpole Park Hospital, wounded servicemen sat on rows of folding chairs, wheel chairs, and the grass, some lying on gurneys, attended by their nurses and orderlies. As usual, important dignitaries and the top brass had the choice seats. MPs guarded both wings of the improvised stage where the Mac Herlihy Band opened with Charlie Barnett's instrumental "Skyliner". Seth's adrenalin surged the same as in combat when he saw Miriam seated in a red satin dress beside four male background singers in the band's signature beige flannel jackets and dark brown trousers.

Seth and Winty walked toward one side of the stage where two MPs confronted them. "Colonel, Lieutenant, this area is off limits."

"But my fiancée Miriam ... Mimi Kay ... she's singing with the band."

The MP snickered. "That's a good one."

Seth showed them his photos of Miriam. "Read the back."

"Sir, I don't have to. I got eight-by-tens, each signed by Kay Francis, Martha Raye, and Carole Landis, and they ain't my fiancées."

The second MP gestured with his baton for them to back away. "You flyboys had it good and think you're special. You ain't so special now, sir."

Winty intervened. "Major General Kilrain anticipated this." She thrust a note at the MPs. "The general is over there in the front row. If you lunkheads continue to screw things up for the Colonel, and I have to get him involved, you'll be buck privates again on latrine duty for the rest of your time in the Army."

The MPs conferred, apologized, and let Seth and Winty pass through to a wing of the open stage.

"Winty, did Kilrain really write that note?"

"Of course not. I did."

The cheering and applause for "Skyliner" faded, and Mac Herlihy faced the audience. "Now for a change of pace, a romantic tune sung by the mellifluous Mimi Kay and the Harmonizers."

Miriam stood with her backup singers, glanced right, saw Seth, and ran to him. He removed his 50 mission hat, and they kissed to whistles and clapping from the audience.

Miriam led Seth on stage. She whispered to Herlihy, who shook Seth's hand and stepped aside.

Miriam took the microphone. "Many of you know that at each live performance of Mac's band, I always dedicate the last song to *my College Boy wherever he is*. Well, here he is, fighter ace Lt. Colonel Seth Braham." Miriam waited until more applause and cheering ended. "Milt, if you don't mind I want Seth to accompany me for one number."

Seth replaced the pianist, and Miriam sat atop the piano. "The first day we met, Seth said I was a Gershwin Lady. Well, a Gershwin Lady I am, and Seth is the man I love."

Seth took the cue, played a brief introduction, and the band followed.

"Forgive me Mr. Ira Gershwin for changing your lyric. *"Today Seth came along, the man I love, and he's so big and strong ...."*

# Chapter 53
## The Red Laugh

Karl watched Colonel Milroy rescue the child. That noble act confirmed the opinions he shared with other JG-52 pilots. In spite of having fought two wars against the Americans, the Germans felt an affinity with the Yank officers.

*We should have been allies against the Soviets.*

Karl understood why the Soviets felt entitled to take revenge, but their violent drunken assaults on the women were unbearable to watch. Yet Karl could not close his eyes when a young woman raked sharp fingernails across the cheek of a beast about to rape her. The enraged soldier unsheathed a knife and sliced open her belly. As intestines oozed out of the gaping wound, the soldier kicked the young woman's head to a bloody pulp.

A corporal standing nearby shot the berserk rapist in the head. Karl had learned enough of the Russian language during his tours on the Eastern Front and heard the inebriated tank commander demand to know why the NCO shot a fellow soldier. The young man's reply satisfied the officer but astounded Karl.

"The drunken bastard killed the woman I wanted to have."

After he vomited, the hysterical widow of Karl's Feldwebel begged him to protect their terrified twelve-year-old daughter, Christa, whom she disguised in boy's clothes. Karl did not tell the woman the Reds were raping male children too. When he moved deeper into the men's compound with the girl, he heard a woman's screams. Karl did not look back.

A second wave of rapists replaced the first, and then came the men who had been standing guard on the outer perimeter of tanks. There seemed to be more Tartars and Mongols in their group, plenty of dark Georgians and other tribal types from the Caucasus.

Karl thought the slant-eyes from the eastern tribes of the USSR and mongrels from the Caucuses were the most cruel and blood-thirsty. They tortured and killed at the slightest provocation. Too often, the sun glinted on cold steel when they hacked someone to death. Karl believed it was a racial trait of these tribes to be vicious, and they had left their savage imprint on Russia for all time.

He sniffed the air and recognized the aroma of hashish, often found on Soviet troops from those regions whom the Wehrmacht had captured. Karl would be forever in Colonel Milroy's debt for sending Elfi away in time.

The most heartbreaking sight of all was the deflowering of girls young as eight and the buggering of boys. Mothers called out to their children. They pleaded with the Soviets to take them instead and spare their babies. The rapists took both. When the sun began to set, the Reds allowed some of the women to return to their men in the greater enclosure. By the time night fell, those who could walk or crawl had reached the sanctuary of the male compound.

After the Soviets finished their evening meal, they returned to the enclosure armed for another orgy of rape. Christa, the little twelve-year-old Karl protected, never stopped trembling. He was not in much better shape. Weakened by lack of food and diarrhea, he had trouble standing.

***

When the new day dawned bright and clear, a horrible sight greeted the eyes of the living. Hanging from beds of trucks and the few trees in the enclosure were the bodies of over a hundred women who had taken their own lives rather than submit again to the Soviets, Christa's mother among them. During that awful night, upwards of another two hundred-and-fifty women and girls had been strangled by their husbands and fathers to spare them further indignities and brutality.

Their captors were not moved to compassion. By mid-morning, the Soviets made more forays into the enclosure to seek out the younger girls. Some of the women put on men's clothing and scrubbed their faces with mud to make themselves unappealing. When the soldiers saw through a disguise, they dragged the unfortunate woman down to the stream bordering the enclosure, stripped her, and waded out into the shallow water. The river bank became a favorite Red Army fornication site.

The orgy continued on the same scale as the first day. Karl maintained sanity by indulging in philosophic speculation to shut out the cries of tormented women and girls. He had passed the most propitious moment to die unless he defended the women as a way to commit suicide. Well, it did not matter. He was in so extreme a condition of lassitude he lacked the will to take his life.

Lassitude. Yes, that explained why great empires fell. Inadequate nutrition, disease too, made populations supine in the face of conquest. Is that what had happened to Rome, the Persians, and all the other great empires? If true, so much for the myth of military genius ascribed to conquerors.

Karl heard shouting a few meters from him. Two Soviet soldiers caught and threw to the ground a mother and young daughter. Both were naked. The rapists had already shed their trousers.

When the inebriated soldiers saw Karl and Christa for the first time, they waved their bayonets and demanded the girl. He prepared himself for a futile last stand over Christa's virtue and that of two anonymous terrified young women.

*For aristocratic honor and all that bloody rot.*

Other soldiers burst on the scene, shouted for the rapists to stop, and shot their comrades who refused. A sharper Red Army unit had arrived to replace the drunken rabble. New commanders brought order out of chaos and rescinded the rape order. In a display of classic Russian justice, they hanged on the spot anyone who attempted to assault a German woman.

Karl saw several Luftwaffe officers and NCOs cozying to their captors. He suspected they were communists who had gone underground in 1933. A Feldwebel walked with a Red Air Force General and a squad of men with machine guns. He pointed at Karl.

"That one. He flew the Me.262."

The general sent two soldiers to fetch Karl. "Do not harm that man. He is a jet pilot. We need him."

***

Colonel Stevenson halted the column of American tanks, trucks, and jeeps for a piss-stop not far from Cham inside Germany. Hank looked at the sky. Something high above reminded him of his childhood and a more innocent time.

That unmistakable silhouette. Wings long and pointed. Tail tapered at the tip.

The raptor made a graceful banking turn. Its partner flushed quarry from the brush. Bursting out of the sun, the way fighter pilots bounced prey from the perch, wings now taut against its body, the Peregrine began a high velocity dive.

And ended with a kill.

The End

# Author's Note

As in life, an author has many choices to make in a novel, and the reader may also imagine many scenarios of what might have happened to the characters afterward. Here are some realities and possibilities.

The Soviets offered captured Luftwaffe aces a choice: teach the Red Air Force what they knew about the latest aircraft specifically the jets or go to a gulag. Karl would have refused, as did the top fighter ace of all wars, Erich Hartmann, who was reduced in status from POW to common criminal and then to war criminal. Hartmann and other Luftwaffe pilots served more than ten years in Soviet gulags. Upon their release, some helped build the new Luftwaffe or went into business.

Poldi, a typical Nazi opportunist and war criminal, would have escaped to Argentina, Paraguay, or Brazil.

Hank, Seth, and Brax, like the historical fighter aces would have led postwar lives as diverse as their personalities and goals. Many chose a career in the Air Force or flew for commercial airlines. Others returned to civilian life to finish their education or enter the business world. Some tested planes for the Air Force or manufacturers. Veterans would be recalled to active duty during the Korean War like baseball greats and WWII Marine fighter pilots Ted Williams and Jerry Coleman. A few later ran for political office.

The aces married and either stayed wed, or they had multiple marriages. Like Seth, a small number wed celebrities. 13 victory Pacific Theater ace Jim Brooks married big band singer and recording artist "Liltin" Martha Tilton. Triple fighter ace (WWII, Korea, Vietnam) Robin Olds wed film noir actress Ella Raines. Some would eventually be honored and inducted as Eagles for their contributions to flying at the annual Gathering of Eagles at Maxwell Field.

A Russian Princess did work in the Abwehr.

To enjoy the music of the WWII era, one can find original live performances, excerpts from films, and recordings of the Big Bands, their singers and groups on YouTube.

After the war, camaraderie developed between Allied and Axis flyers who met at fighter pilot conventions and entertained each other in their homes. One interesting bond was that between the Jewish RAF hero of the Battle of Britain, Robert Roland Stanford "Lucky" Tuck, credited with 27.66 to 31 victories, and Luftwaffe General of All Fighters Adolf Galland who had 104 Luftsiegen. Each shot down the other's wingman during the Battle of Britain. Galland entertained Tuck after the RAF ace had to bail out over German held territory in 1942, and a friendship began. Tuck later became godfather for Galland's son born in 1966.

Guests at one typical evening in the 1970s included Adolf Galland, Robert Tuck, General Frank Kurz who flew the legendary B-17 the *Swoose Goose* during WWII, the aforementioned Jim Brooks and Martha Tilton, ace Bud Mahuren, 20.75 ETO victories plus 3.5 in Korea, and Johannes Scharff, Chief Luftwaffe interrogator of downed Allied fighter pilots.

Donald Michael Platt

Elapsed time seems to have restored the romanticized fighter ace ideal that began in the Great War: chivalrous Knights of the Skies.

# Principal Fictional Characters.

Hank Milroy

Friedrich Fürst zu Pfalz von Teuffelreich

Karl, Friedrich's son

Seth Braham and family

Leo Kilrain, WWI ace and USAC Officer

Andy DeLuca, WWI ace and Seth's coach and mentor

Wayne Miller, Hank's roommate at Randolph and Kelly Fields

Bob Chilton, cadet officer at Randolph Field

Milt Ashley. upperclassman at Randolph Field

Joe Grant, Upperclassman at Randolph Field

Brax Mobley, Hank's roommate at Randolph and Kelly Fields

Patrick Monahan, Hank's roommate at Randolph Field

Nancy McCabe, Girl Hank meets while a cadet

Winty McCabe, Nancy's younger sister

Leopold (Poldi), Graf von Osterwald, Karl's uncle

Bruno von Strachwitz, Karl's friend

Oberleutnant Albert von Wittelsberg, Karl's friend.

Gerd von Wittelsberg, Karl's friend, Karl's friend

Walti von Frankenthal, Karl's friend

Princess Mariya-Xenia Narishkyn: Karl's wife

Miriam Keramopoulos, Seth's love

Seth's brother Alan and family
Erich Lienau, Luftwaffe fighter ace on the Eastern Front
Phil Jordan, Hank's first leader in the ETO
Homer "Zeke" Zachary, Seth's first leader in the ETO
Colonel Cy Wilson, Hank's and Seth's CO of the 375th Fighter Group
Colonel Walter Sanford, Wimpole Park Hospital surgeon
Captain Patricia Lindsay, Wimpole Park Hospital nurse.
Lt. Dom Mercutio, Fighter pilot in Seth's 136th Squadron
Lt. Planchek, fighter pilot in Hank's 135th Squadron
Lt. Fowler, Fighter pilot in Hank's 135th Squadron
Lt. Barlowe, Fighter pilot in Hank's 135th Squadron
Hauptmann Gabel, Fighter pilot in Karl's Me.262 Kette
Major Blumenau, Third member of Karl's Me.262 Kette
Lt. Colonel Hiram Stevenson, 3rd Army tank commander
Mac Herlihy and his band

# About The Author

# Donald Michael Platt

Author of three other novels, ROCAMORA, HOUSE OF ROCAMORA, and A GATHERING OF VULTURES, Donald Michael Platt was born and raised in San Francisco. He graduated from Lowell High School and received his B.A. in History from the University of California at Berkeley. After two years in the Army, Donald attended graduate school at San Jose State where he won a batch of literary awards in the annual SENATOR PHELAN LITERARY CONTEST.

Donald taught English and Creative Writing at Los Gatos Union High School, then moved to southern California to begin his professional writing career. He sold to the TV series, MR. NOVAK, ghosted for health food guru, Dan Dale Alexander, and wrote for and with diverse producers, among them as Harry Joe Brown, Sig Schlager, Albert J. Cohen, Al Ruddy plus Paul Stader Sr, Hollywood stuntman and stunt/2nd unit director. While in Hollywood, Donald taught Creative Writing and Advanced Placement European History at Fairfax High School where he was Social Studies Department Chairman.

After living in Florianópolis, Brazil, setting of his horror novel A GATHERING OF VULTURES, pub. 2007 & 2011, he moved to Florida where he wrote as a *with*: VITAMIN ENRICHED, pub.1999, for Carl DeSantis, founder of Rexall Sundown Vitamins; and THE COUPLE'S DISEASE, Finding a Cure for Your Lost "Love" Life, pub. 2002, for Lawrence S. Hakim, MD, FACS, Head of Sexual Dysfunction Unit at the Cleveland Clinic.

Currently, Donald resides in Winter Haven, Florida where he is polishing a completed novel set in the 9th century Carolingian Empire about Bodo the Apostate and preparing to write a sequel to CLOSE TO THE SUN.

Photo credit: Michael Potthast,
Potthast Studios
234 W. Central Ave.
Winter Haven, FL 33880
(863) 294-4920

# ROCAMORA

DONALD MICHAEL PLATT

No man is closer to a woman than her confessor, not her father, not her brother, not her husband.

-Spanish saying

Vicente de Rocamora, the epitome of a young renaissance man in 17th century Spain, questions the goals of the Inquisition and the brutal means used by King Philip IV and the Roman Church to achieve them. Spain vows to eliminate the heretical influences attributed to Jews, Moors, and others who would taint the limpieza de sangre, purity of Spanish blood. At the insistence of his family, the handsome and charismatic Vicente enters the Dominican Order and is soon thrust into the scheming political hierarchy that rules Spain. As confessor to the king's sister, the Infanta Doña María, and assistant to Philip's chief minister, Olivares, Vicente ascends through the ranks and before long finds himself poised to attain not only the ambitious dreams of the Rocamora family but also—named Spain's Inquisitor General

PENMORE PRESS
www.penmorepress.com

# HOUSE OF ROCAMORA

DONALD MICHAEL PLATT

A new life and a new name ...

House of Rocamora, a novel of the 17th century, continues the exceptional life of roguish Vicente de Rocamora, a former Dominican friar, confessor to the Infanta of Spain, and almost Inquisitor General.  After Rocamora arrives in Amsterdam at age forty-two, asserts he is a Jew, and takes the name, "Isaac," he revels in the freedom to become whatever he chooses for the first time in his life. Rocamora makes new friends, both Christian and Jew, including scholars, men of power and, typically, the disreputable. He also acquires enemies in the Sephardic community who believe he is a spy for the Inquisition or resent him for having been a Dominican.

Praise for Rocamora, 2012 Finalist International Book Awards:

PENMORE PRESS
www.penmorepress.com

# The Sorceress
## and
## The Skull
by
Donald Michael Platt

San Francisco 1946: A Confrontation of Sorcerers and Seers

For the first time in almost 400 years, Michele born in 1932, a direct descendant of Nostradamus, will have all his gifts of precognition and even greater powers, but they will not be fully manifested until after she enters puberty. More than one secret society has been obsessed with finding and controlling Michele, to learn from her where Nostradamus' unpublished prophecies have been sequestered. Hidden since birth, protected by aliases, an aunt, and a gargoyle, Michele at age 13 has become a fugitive, fleeing across Europe and Canada before finally arriving in San Francisco.

Around Michele deadly forces are closing in, but a new ally, *Le Crâne*, the Skull, has also appeared, coming to the aid of the young seer. Who will hold claim to Michele's powers and at what price to her? And who will succeed in acquiring the hidden secrets of Nostradamus?

A Gothic Horror Novella from Award Winning Author Donald Michael Platt

PENMORE PRESS
www.penmorepress.com

# A Gathering of Vultures

Donald Michael Platt

Murder, mutilation, and carrion.... in paradise?

"There shall the vultures also be gathered, every one with her mate." - ISAIAH 34:15

Professional ballroom dancers Terri and Rick Hamilton aspire to be world champions. Unfortunately, Terri's recurring back and health problems place that goal well out of reach. They travel to Terri's birthplace, Florianópolis, on the scenic island of Santa Catarina off the coast of Brazil to vacation and visit their best friends and mentors.

Along the picturesque beaches, dead penguins and eviscerated bodies wash up on the shores of paradise, and Antarctic blasts play counterpoint to the tropical storms that rock the island. The scenic wonder is home not only to urubús, a unique sub-species of the black vulture, but also to a clique of mysterious women who offer Terri perfect health and the promise of fame—at a terrible price.

PENMORE PRESS
www.penmorepress.com

# HEAVEN
# CRIES
BY
STEPHAN
SILVA

***Heaven Cries*** is a compelling story.

Captain Artemio Battaglia, a young World War II pilot, who when repulsed by the brutality of Mussolini's fascist state, joins a partisan band to fight the Nazi death squads that were terrorizing Italian citizens. Nicolas Gage, author of bestselling *Eleni* praised **Heaven Cries** for reminding *"us of the true spring waters of freedom: hope, kindness, courage, and love. In the dark light of recent events, this history is particularly relevant."*

Now available at Amazon, Barnes&Nobel, iBooks, and Kobo.

PENMORE PRESS
www.penmorepress.com

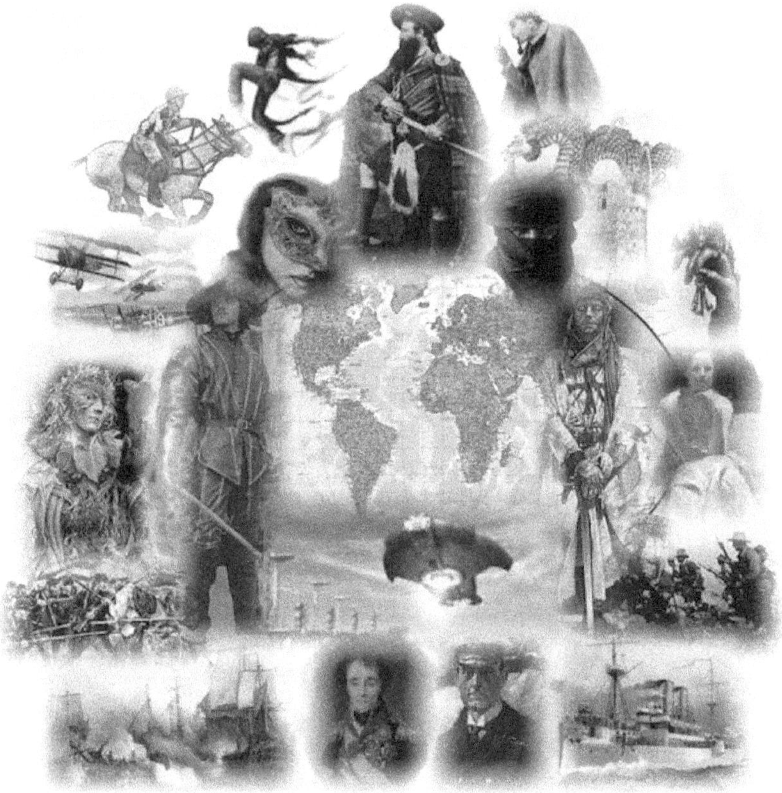

Penmore Press

Challenging, Intriguing, Adventurous, Historical and Imaginative

www.penmorepress.com